Somebody's Baby

"*Somebody's Baby* is a finely honed work of precision writing, the crisp, clear sentences showing how one individual's actions affect an entire family. It is a story of what marriage is all about, and how love and respect are sacrificed in the emotional whirlpool of anger, fear, lust and sexuality, which almost destroy the fragile family unit."

—*Ottawa Citizen*

"The author's portrayal of parental frustration is vivid and maddening. *Somebody's Baby* succeeds beautifully as an evenhanded discussion of the abortion issue. It is the drama of Roe v. Wade played out on a family stage."

—*The New York Times Book Review*

"Sensitively offering pro-choice and pro-life views in her first hardcover novel, Harrison also probes the strengths and weaknesses of love within marriage."

—*Publishers Weekly*

"A down-to-earth story . . . firmly rooted in reality—the reality that comes *after* romance. [Harrison's writing has] warmth and wit."

—*Toronto Globe & Mail*

"The beauty of this novel is the frighteningly brutal honesty with which the author writes. . . . A well-rounded look at a multi-leveled problem . . . This is a daring novel of our times."

—*West Coast Review of Books*

A Mother's Song

CLAIRE HARRISON

POCKET STAR BOOKS

New York   London   Toronto   Sydney   Tokyo   Singapore

"What Is Love" © 1987 by Rebecca Harrison

An *Original* Publication of POCKET BOOKS

A Pocket Star Book published by
POCKET BOOKS, a division of Simon & Schuster Inc.
1230 Avenue of the Americas, New York, NY 10020

ISBN: 0-671-75896-9

First Pocket Books printing May 1994

10 9 8 7 6 5 4 3 2 1

POCKET STAR BOOKS and colophon are registered
trademarks of Simon & Schuster Inc.

Cover art and design by Cathy Saksa

Printed in the U.S.A.

The support of the Regional Municipality
of Ottawa-Carleton is gratefully acknowledged.

Remerciements à la Municipalité régionale
d'Ottawa-Carleton pour son appui.

Part I

FALL 1988

DEAR DIARY,

Friday. Wether—cold and windy. Two zits. There horrible.

Guess what! Something WONDERFUL and SPESHAL! A MIRACEL! Of course I have to keep it a BIG SECRET. Nobody knows and if Mom finds out she will kill me. I mean like DEAD. So Im not telling anyone espeshally not Felicia who is a real big blabber mouth and will tell the hole world. Its so SECRET Diary that Im not even going to rite it down in case you get into the rong hands. The only thing I can say is that I met HER! And it was really NEAT!! And Im going to see HER—

Mom is calling. Have to go.

Bye for now.

MY NEIGHBORHOOD USUALLY BRINGS ME peace. When I turn off Bank Street and drive down Sunnyside Avenue, I enter a different world. I leave behind the cars, the crowded intersections, and the terrain of glass and concrete for quieter streets lined with homes and canopied with trees. I pass familiar faces: children I've known for years, adults I've sat with on school committees and neighborhood programs. The farther I travel from the roar of traffic and the closer I get to my house, the slower I drive. I enjoy the fall colors, the brilliant reds and oranges of the maple that overhangs the corner of Belmont and Brighton. I study a porch that is being reconstructed on Fentiman, approving of its neat white posts. And, as I approach my house, I take pleasure in its sedate air of solidity.

There is nothing whimsical about our house. It has been

standing since the turn of the century. It has a thick stone foundation and a brick facade, high ceilings and dark-stained wood floors. When we renovated, the electrician told me in a grave tone that they don't build houses like ours anymore. By this, I understand that new houses are thin in substance. Their baseboards are narrow, their foundations skimpy. We have the occasional earthquake in Ottawa with tremors our house handles with ease even though our beds shake and we dream of boats and capsizings. The new houses aren't so lucky. Pictures drop from their walls, cracks appear in their basements, and shingles drift down from their roofs like snow falling to the ground.

But today, as I drive down our tree-lined streets, the enjoyment I get from our house is abruptly broken. Someone is standing in our darkened picture window. I brake sharply and pull over to the curb. The afternoon sun is covered by a cloud, and at first I can't tell who the person is. I only see arms outstretched. I feel a frightening sense of violation—*a stranger in our house*—and then the sun breaks through. A ray of light pierces through the window, illuminating the room, and the figure is revealed. It isn't a stranger but my thirteen-year-old daughter, Emma. Her mouth is wide open and her face distorted. Her hair, the color of hot red pepper, tops her head like a flame.

She is singing. She has put an album on the stereo in the living room and is belting out a tune to an unseen audience. For a few minutes I sit in the car and watch her. My sense of violation hasn't completely eased. Without being able to hear the music, I imagine Emma into a figure that is religious, mythical. A Greek *kore*, broken out of her classic and passive stance into someone more aggressive and more sinister. A vengeful Roman nymph, invoking the gods. A young goddess calling down doom on the House of Jane and Philip Wastenay.

Ridiculous, I chide myself and laugh. My husband, Philip, is a professor of classics and I've listened to his stories for too long.

The figure in the window is only Emma.

DEAR DIARY,

Tuesday. Wether—windy and stuff. A gross zit on my chin.

Mrs. Fitch subed again for Mrs. Anderson. As usual she screemed and yelled at all of us speshialy Dana who was passing notes which said Fitch the bitch is also a witch. Dana is such a doorknob. Anyway she got into real big truble as usual and the whole class had to miss recess. It really sucked.

In science I listed all the boys in the class acording to their apeerans and body, rating them out of 10. Of course, Mark comes first then Nick then Peter then Cello the Jello hes cute but not as cute as Mark of course and finaly Jeff. All the rest are geeks assholes or from nerds r us. I passed the list to Lisa who tried to pass it to Felicia. Peter grabed ahold of it but I managed to get it back without his seeing. I mean I dont want Mark to know I think hes gorgeus.

But best of all I got to see Her today. I went to Her Apartmint. Its small and kind of old. I dont think she has much money. But shes got stufed animals all over the place and they all have weerd names like Cabage and Checkout. One is a scuerl named Teenyweeny. She was really nice and made me some hot chocolat with hole milk instead of 2% which tasted really really good. She says the hell with her wasteline.

Bye for now.

WHEN PHILIP IS OUT OF TOWN, I PLAY HOOKY from domestic life. I don't plan organized dinners, and Emma and I eat whatever we want, whenever we want. Sometimes we end up at the dining room table together, but we rarely talk. I've come to believe that these asocial occasions are necessary, providing cooling-off periods for our mother-daughter relationship, which has been under strain. Since Emma turned thirteen, new kinds of behavior threaten our equilibrium. Mouthing off, for example. Low-key irritability shifting to high-key without warning. Disagreements that slip from minor to major with breathtaking rapidity. In one way this is nothing new. Emma has always fought authority and attacked life. She never learned to walk. She ran instead, a headlong rush with such intensity of purpose that she barged into walls and banged into furniture. She wore bruises on her ten-month-old forehead like badges of reckless courage.

What is new is that the battleground has enlarged to fit every corner of our lives and that each square inch is worth a major skirmish. Emma fights over the minutiae of life as if her survival depends on each detail. I try to maintain a distance, but she often exhausts me and I snap back. I love her, of course, but sometimes I wonder about the workings of fate that gave me a daughter so different from what I intended. When we adopted Emma—I'm unable to have children—I had misty visions textured with a pink soft sweetness. The reality is angular, bony, intense, argumentive. When I complain to Philip about her behavior and he takes the time to lift his nose out of his papers, he waves a hand dismissively in the air and tells me it's puberty. Endocrine imbalances, he says, hormones gone wild.

Tonight we sit opposite each other at the far ends of the dining room table. I eat and try to read the *Ottawa Citizen*. Lately I find I can hardly read the news. It's not the subject matter, it's the act of reading. I edit other people's writing all day, and my eyes are tired from work. Emma nibbles away at a peanut butter and jelly sandwich and studies a book, *Readings in French*. Emma is in a French Immersion educational stream, which means she takes all her subjects in French and is theoretically supposed to be bilingual when she graduates from the secondary school system. In practical terms, this means that Emma can't spell in either official language, and Philip and I are forced to attend school assemblies in which we understand only one word in ten.

"Mom, you know all that stuff about Jesus Christ and the Red Sea and God and all that?"

I raise my head from the newspaper. "Uh-huh."

"Are those miracles true?"

Emma is going to be beautiful. Since she's adopted, I can say this honestly and without pride; I have no claim to her beauty. But when I notice it, as I do tonight with the lamp-light catching her face at a lovely angle of inquiry, I'm always surprised. She wasn't a pretty baby. When we first saw her at the Children's Aid Society, she was four months old, bald, mottled like an old porcelain sink, and had no eye-lashes. Her mouth was too big for her face, and she had this odd little nose, thick and upturned at the tip. Her homeliness didn't bother me. In fact I didn't really see it—not after the bitter defeat of infertility and the long gauntlet of adoption formalities. I had waited so long and so yearningly for a baby that I thought, How sweet!

We were introduced to her in a room with a crib, several chairs, and a small assortment of Fisher-Price toys on the floor. The foster mother had dressed her up, but the pink booties had frayed pom-poms and the white dress was clean but stained from the spit-up of many babies before her. She had no teeth but chewed on her fist with her gums, making wet, slurpy sounds. She also wiggled. She was sitting on Philip's knee, and he, who had never even picked up a baby before, had to hold her tight because she arched and kicked and turned her head in every possible direction.

"A real live wire," the social worker said. "The foster mother says she's on the go all the time."

I should have known then, shouldn't I? I should have been forewarned about the possible unruly directions that energy could take, but all I thought was, How charming! How lively!

"Surely she's too young to be crawling," Philip said. He'd known nothing about babies prior to the call from Children's Aid saying they had a girl for us, but in the forty-eight hours since, he'd taken a crash course in Dr. Spock. Now he was a minor authority on infant behavior.

"No, but she's almost there. She's turning over now."

Philip frowned. "That's a bit precocious, isn't it?"

"She's an active baby."

He put Emma down on the rug at our feet and placed her on her back. She scrunched up, she slithered, and the next thing we knew, she'd flip-flopped onto her stomach and, utterly pleased with herself, grinned triumphantly up at us.

I looked down and saw not a homely unknown package but a baby, *my baby,* and thought, How wonderful!

Then Philip and I glanced at each other, and I nodded. It was really my decision. He'd claimed he could live without children; I was the one who had despaired and wept and grieved. And I was the one who, after all the humiliating tests had proven to be so very definite and final, had suggested adoption.

"We'll take her," he said.

I gathered Emma up into my arms. She was warm, surprisingly heavy, and smelled of baby talc. She busied herself trying to pry the watch off my wrist, and I thought, I'm a mother!

Time has altered Emma and obliterated those baby features. Now she verges on beauty like a swimmer poised to leap. Her face holds a promise that will be fulfilled when she loses her too round cheeks and the spray of pimples on her chin. She has striking red curls and pale unfreckled skin. She also has eyelashes now, thick ones a darker red than her hair, and her eyes are long and light green. The nose is still odd, but also oddly suitable, perched about a small, soft mouth. Within the square of her face, her chin forms a smaller square and gives her a look of stubborn determination.

"You've been talking about miracles in school?" I ask.

"I was just wondering if all that stuff about Jesus really happened."

"No records have survived from that time in history," I say, "and no letters or books, so we can't be certain that those Bible stories are absolutely true." I warm to the topic. "On the other hand, I think something must have happened back then, because the story of Jesus had to come from somewhere."

"Well, I was wondering about miracles. Like, do we have any today?"

"I don't know of any."

"Then how come they had them in the old days?"

"Christian miracles are like the myths Daddy studies— stories that got told over and over again. And you know what happens to a story that's passed around. It keeps on growing."

"So there really weren't any miracles, even in the old days?"

"I don't think so, honey."

Emma appears to be thinking about this, and I wait for the next question. "Mom?"

"Yes?"

"Can I stay for the second show at the Mayfair on Friday night?"

"Absolutely not," I say.

Disappointment juts her lower lip forward. "Mom, everyone else can stay."

"I don't care about everyone else."

"Why do you always say that? I hate it!"

"Because it's true. You're the only person I care about."

"You and Daddy are the strictest parents in my whole school."

"I doubt that."

"You know what I have to do?" Emma says. "I have to apologize to my friends all the time."

"That's too bad."

"They laugh at me all the time."

"Come on, Em. Stop exaggerating."

"How would you like to have to tell your friends that your parents are . . . overprotective?" This is her newest word and she wields it like a weapon.

"How would you like me to phone Felicia's mother and ask her what she would say?" Felicia's mother, Alice, is my closest friend, and Emma knows very well that when it comes to motherhood issues, Alice and I pose a formidable front.

Emma slams her glass down on the table so that drops of milk leap out and splatter on the table. "Everyone thinks I'm a baby! Everyone laughs at me, having to call up all the time and tell you where I am. Everyone thinks I'm stupid! It really sucks!"

My problem, Philip tells me, is that Emma and I are too similar. Like bumper cars, we zoom around our enclosed space, crashing into each other at frequent intervals, sparks flying and crackling. "Are you picking a fight?" I ask. "Is that what you want—a fight?"

Emma lowers her head and studies the pattern of bites in her sandwich. These battles have a sameness to them that wearies me. The screaming matches metamorphose into noisy crying or self-pitying tears, then into stormy exits and slammed doors. Emma lifts her head, and tears glitter on her lashes: step one. She sniffs and says, "Well then, can I skip singing practice tonight? I've got too much home-work."

Oh, how Emma hates to lose face. "No."

"If I don't get my math done, Mrs. Waddell will flunk me. She said so. You don't want me to flunk, do you?"

"You can do both."

"She gave us a whole hour!"

"You'll manage," I say, and suddenly remembering that Emma had her singing lesson today, I add, "Plus you'll have new music."

"I don't have any."

"Mrs. Stern didn't give you new music?"

"I didn't go."

We've given Emma flute lessons, skating lessons, and art classes. We've driven her to hockey games and track meets, bought uniforms and attended parents' meetings. Nothing has lasted. Within a few weeks, Emma decides that she isn't interested or it's too hard or she doesn't like it anymore. So when she suggested singing lessons, we balked. She begged and pleaded, she promised dedication and commitment. We finally agreed on condition that she attend every lesson and practice faithfully.

"You didn't go?" I echo angrily. "Why not?"

"Mrs. Stern canceled."

"She didn't call me."

"She told me last week. I forgot to tell you." Emma goes back to eating her sandwich and reading.

But she has said this far too glibly, and a strange expression crossed her face that I read as a combination of fear and complicity.

"Why did she cancel?"

"Mom," she says with a tone of exasperation, "she had to go on a trip. To Toronto. To see her aunt or something. She told me, but I don't remember. Maybe her aunt was sick or something."

"This doesn't sound right," I say.

"Do you think I'm lying?" she says defiantly.

"I don't know what to think."

"I didn't have a lesson!"

"Okay," I say.

"It's true!"

Guilt in Emma is like a clanging persistent bell. The more she struggles to shut it off, the louder it rings. By now even I can hear it. "If you say so," I say.

She stands up, banging the chair leg against the table. "You never believe anything I tell you!"

"I just want to know the truth."

"It is the truth!"

She tries to storm out of the kitchen, but my words—"I'll call Mrs. Stern and check"—hook her in the doorway.

She turns, and I see that beneath the bluster, she's frightened. The skin over her cheekbones is stretched taut and whiter than the rest of her. "Okay," she says, "I didn't come home."

"Then where were you?"

"Listen, Mom, I didn't want to tell you because it would hurt your feelings."

This is a new ploy, and it stops me for a moment. My feelings are of little concern to Emma. "Why don't you let *me* decide if my feelings are hurt?"

Emma has grown rapidly in the past few months, and she's not always sure what to do with her new length. She wraps one leg around the other. She entwines her arms, two thin branches. She hunches her slender shoulders and tucks her chin against her chest.

"You're not going to like it."

I have the kind of imagination that leaps to worst-case scenarios. Is it drugs? I think. Shoplifting? "Let me decide that," I say.

"And you're going to be sorry."

"All right, Emma."

"I mean, really sorry."

"Enough. Spit it out."

"I've been seeing my . . . mother."

I don't think I've heard correctly. "Who?"

"My mother."

Even then I don't get it. "Em, *I* am your mother."

She swallows. "My other one," she says.

 TERRY HAS SMALL, BONY, FRECKLED HANDS that are smarter than they look. She keys in the code for bananas—403—and thinks of the numbers stored in her fingertips. Numbers for lettuce and peas, for zucchini and grapes, for potatoes and lemons. A hundred codes live beneath her skin. She once dreamed she couldn't punch in the code for watermelons. She tried every number, but the machine wouldn't accept them. It beeped and hissed at her. Customers began to line up around her cash, their voices rising in complaint. The manager, Bill, and the head cashier, Flo, screamed at her. In desperation, she sliced her fingertips with a razor. The numbers, black and thick, poured out with the blood and flowed down the checkout counter.

She glances at the register's screen. "That's not right," she says.

The customer leans forward. "What's the matter?"

"I don't think they've coded in the sale price." While

the customer looks suitably impressed and gratified, Terry lifts her phone and speaks into the mouthpiece. Her voice booms out over the store: "Price check, cash four. Price check, cash four."

Terry's one of the best cashiers. At the end of the week, she's usually top of the computer list for speed. She's also won the award for Customer Service and Affability three times. She does that by smiling a lot and chatting people up. "Good price for lemons, isn't it?" she might say, or "Is it still raining outside?" or "Did you notice the coupon in the paper for tomato juice? It'll save you fifty cents."

In the meantime she likes to play her private game of Grocery Guessing. She can sum up a customer by a glance at a grocery cart. Take this one, for example. Imported Dijon mustard, expensive olives, club soda by the case, and crackers cut in the shape of stars—Terry knows a fancy cocktail party when she sees one. Not that this customer was going to eat any of the stuff she'll serve. She's got Weight Watchers and Lean Cuisines hidden in her freezer by the dozen. Problem periods, too. Get a load of the boxes of No-Name maxi pads and super tampons and Midol.

Terry prides herself on her good eye. She can see the customer has plenty of money but it isn't doing a thing for her. No sense of style. Terry herself would take the ugly straps off the shoulders of that white blouse, open it three buttons down, and dress it up with a bunch of chains. She wouldn't be caught dead in that long blue skirt, either. She wears short skirts that hug her hips and leave her thin, freckled legs bare. And she loves bare-back heels, the higher the better so that she teeters slightly as she walks. When she's with a guy and wears her highest heels, she can feel him leaning toward her as if he could stop her from falling.

When Terry gets bored with Grocery Guessing, she gives interviews to Barbara Walters. She doesn't go for the idea of being interviewed by a Jane Pauley type. First of all, there isn't enough time on those morning shows. They zap you in; they zap you out. She wants a long, thorough interview. She may only be twenty-seven, but her life has been chockablock full of drama, mostly tragedy. She's got enough of that for "Days of Our Lives," the "Young and the Restless," and "As the World Turns," all rolled into one. Secondly, those Jane Pauley types have to interview ordinary people while Barbara only talks to celebrities. During her interviews, Terry is either a movie star or famous singer, depending on her mood. She doesn't tell Mic or Charlene about these imaginary interviews because they'd laugh, but the truth is, she knows she's got talent, and she'd be in L.A. right this minute if it weren't for her lack of money and connections. She's a firm believer in it's not what you know but who you know. Look at all those kids of stars—Liza Minnelli, for instance, and Michael Douglas, and she could name dozens more. Who's to say they were born with more talent? They just have an in, that's all.

"That'll be one forty-nine twenty-five."

The customer writes out a check and hands it to Terry with her Loblaws check-cashing card. Terry keys in the numbers, verifies the check, and gives the customer the cash-register receipt. "Have a nice day," she says and turns, smiling, to the next customer.

The interviews with Barbara take place in Terry's New York apartment. She also has a dream house in Malibu, but that's her private place. The New York apartment has pale blue leather furniture on a darker blue expanse of carpet. There are lots of original paintings on the walls and glass tables supporting expensive-looking sculptures. She's seen the exact replica of this room in a color spread in *Canadian Living*. Since she's never been to New York, Terry has only the haziest idea of where this apartment would be. She thinks Central Park, maybe, and Fifth Avenue. Wherever the fanciest address is, that's the location. But she knows it's on the twentieth floor and has a marble foyer. *Foyer*. She loves that word. She found it in an article on budget decorating while flipping through the pages of *Redbook*.

Although some of the stars Barbara interviews dress down for the occasion, Terry dresses right up. She wears a black dress that leaves her shoulders bare, black stockings, black stiletto heels, and silver earrings in the shape of falling leaves. She also has had her hair done, but not by just anybody. She goes to Kenneth or one of those big names who do the stars and who are written up in *People*—the type who charge two hundred dollars for a haircut and you have to call three months in advance. Her hair is spiked in the front, thick and curly at the back and sides—thicker and curlier than in real life. Kenneth raves about the color. He's never seen a red so rich and deep. It's a gift to work on her hair, he tells her, he should be paying her.

Barbara covers Terry's life from A to Z. She likes to linger over her childhood, filled as it was with hardship and brutality and the way Terry's family made her feel as if she never belonged. Barbara leads her through pregnancy, leaving school, the terrible jobs she had until she ended up at Loblaws, the rocky road to stardom.

Barbara leans forward in that way she does when she's going for the dirt. "And there've been a lot of men," she says.

"Yes."

"A lot of bad experiences."

"Yes."

"Why was that?"

Terry shrugs. "Bad luck, bad choices." She's not going to talk on the air about the lousy slime she's gone out with— the one-night stands she never heard from again, the jock who would've traded her in for a football, Roy who went from slaps to belting her across the face before she threw him out.

"But things have changed now, haven't they?" Barbara says.

"Yes."

The camera pulls closer, and Terry feels the naked adoring yearning in the millions of eyes behind its lens.

"There's someone very important in your life right now."

"Mic," Terry says.

"Are you in love?"

"You're packing that bag too heavy."

Terry stares down at the cans of tomatoes she's stacked in one bag. "Sorry," she says. "I don't know what I was thinking about." Rapidly she pulls out most of the cans and replaces them with lighter items like boxes of saltine crackers and spaghettini.

The customer looks mollified. "I couldn't have lifted that. I've got back problems."

Terry makes sympathetic clucking sounds. "Backs can be terrible, can't they? I put mine out last summer."

She has to be careful. Sometimes she falls too deep into the fantasy. Sometimes Barbara and the TV cameras and the cool leather beneath her thighs become more real than her job, and she loses track of where she is and why. Sometimes she has to wipe her brain clean as if she's wiping counters in the kitchen. But in the back of her mind, undisturbed and always ready to move forward, is the knowledge of her specialness. There it gleams, secretly, like a jewel in a blue velvet box.

 AFTER OUR FIRST VISIT WITH EMMA AT THE Children's Aid Society, Philip and I waited two more days while the paperwork was being completed before bringing her home. We were living in our first house then, a three-bedroom bungalow deep in the heart of a postwar Ottawa suburban tract called Elmvale Acres. All around us were houses built by the same developer and deviating only slightly in layout and facade. My attempts to make our house distinctive on two slender salaries involved starkly modern Swedish furniture, large doses of macramé, and shaggy white throw rugs imported from Turkey that smelled like goat—a decor similar to that of half a dozen other houses on the street.

Several months ago when I was cleaning up the basement, I found the last of the macramé at the bottom of a box of toys Emma had outgrown. The wall hanging was made of fuzzy yarns in gray and brown knotted into scrofulous lumps. Once a woman named Jane, who considered herself a person of some taste and refinement, had chosen to hang this on her living room wall. Now a woman named Jane looked upon this work and deemed it garbage. I tried to see it through the eyes of that earlier Jane, but I remained repelled by its ugliness. I had shed my other selves the way a snake sheds its skin, leaving behind passionately held opinions in the form of pale, withered husks. But as I held the wall hanging over the garbage pail, I had a surprising attack of sentimentality and almost didn't throw it out. Ugly though it was, it brought back memories of that Elmvale Acres house and the two frantic but wonderful days I'd spent turning the TV room into a nursery in time for Emma's arrival.

I didn't have time to paint the room the appropriate pastel or find the right curtains or rug, so I went wild in the baby department at Sears instead. If an item had the picture of a smiling baby on it, if the word "educational" appeared on the package, if the object had the slightest functional use, I purchased it. I bought a plate with a raised rim and three little pigs running around its circumference, a small spoon and fork with handles specially made for tiny fists, an electric heating dish for cereal, bottles with deluxe nipples, little dresses with lots of lace, sleepers decorated with teddy bears, quilted baby blankets, terry-cloth bibs, best-quality diapers, hypoallergenic soaps, creams for super-delicate skin, expensive cotton balls, specially designed Q-Tips.

I thought I was done until the saleslady asked if the baby would need any toys. Toys! I exclaimed. Of course! And rushed off to the toy department where my reputation had preceded me and I was welcomed with open arms. I bought soft animals that squeaked, rubber ones that floated, dolls that spoke and blinked, shapes that fit together, dials that turned, and colorful things that popped and rattled. The money flowed through my fingers, and the packages piled up in the car as I made up for lost time and opportunity, releasing in one glorious afternoon all the accumulated and repressed fantasies of two years of trying for a baby and two years of confirmed infertility.

We brought Emma home to a fully equipped nursery, and I was set to leap into fully equipped motherhood. I couldn't wait to share *Pat the Bunny* and "Sesame Street." I longed to wheel her around the neighborhood and brag about her accomplishments. I wanted to hold her in my arms and to exchange smiles of trust and adoration. Instant motherhood. Instant mother love.

But to my shock and horror, it didn't work that way. I didn't feel like a mother. I felt like a baby-sitter caring for someone else's child. Emma's gestures meant nothing to me, her smile was strange and her face foreign, the almost Asian fold of flesh at the corners of her eyes was unlike anything Philip or I could have produced. I thought I'd have the same feelings as a woman who'd had nine months to develop an attachment, but when that bond didn't immediately take hold, I trembled with shame. I desperately wanted to ask the social worker if I was atypical, but we were on a six-month probationary period, and I was terrified she'd take Emma away if she knew the truth.

"Everything okay?" the social worker asked when she came for the obligatory three-month visit.

"Just dandy," I said.

I had strapped Emma into her Jolly Jumper, and she was leaping madly in the living room doorway. She didn't appear to have any knees, only fleshy thighs and fat calves that tapered to small narrow feet. We watched her for a moment.

"Energetic, isn't she?" the social worker said.

"Never stops for a minute."

"She must tire you."

"Not at all!" I exclaimed.

The social worker smiled. "Is that hair I see?"

A fuzz had appeared on Emma's scalp. "I think she's going to be a redhead," I said.

"How's her weight?"

"She's gained five pounds."

"Good." The social worker studied her notes. "Any problem with that diaper rash she was prone to?"

"Gone," I declared proudly. "I cleared that up in no time."

I covered my inadequacy with activities. Emma and I went for walks, we visited shopping malls, we stopped at the library, we enrolled in a Moms 'n' Tots swim class. But I couldn't get over the feeling that there was someone hovering at Emma's periphery. I couldn't see the shape or the face. I saw only a shimmering outline as if this presence were made of the same substance as the soap that children blow into trembling translucent bubbles. Of course I knew who it was. The other mother. The woman who had left her stamp on those small, alien features. She was there when I fed Emma. She was there when I bathed her, diapered her, and dressed her. Since I couldn't make her disappear, I had to ignore her, and I did it the only way I knew how. I talked to Emma as I performed all of those daily tasks. I told her about the sky and the earth, about her father and her relatives, about her fat cheeks and curled-up belly button: "You're my baby. My child. My daughter. My little girl." And Emma would study the movements of my mouth with an infant's intensity, her own lips moving as if to match mine.

"Hello?"

His voice is groggy. "Philip? Did I wake you?"

There's a pause. "What time is it?"

"One-thirty."

"Jesus, Jane."

"I've been trying to reach you all night."

"Tonight was the *Antigone* performance."

"How was it?" I ask.

"Horrible. A modern interpretation—pseudo Salvadorans destroying Aeschylus. The director should have been shot, but he was wandering around the foyer in the intermission all too alive. Wearing a god-awful red bow tie."

"How'd your paper go?"

"They seemed to like it."

"Barnaby didn't try to get you?" Estella Barnaby of the

University of Chicago and Philip have been trading insults in the *Journal of Classical Studies* over the origins of the Oedipus myth.

"She was subdued. Overwhelmed no doubt by the clarity of my rhetoric."

"Maybe you've won her over at last."

"Hmmph," he says unconvinced, and I can see the scowl on his face. Philip is a burly man, and when he scowls, he looks ferocious. When I first saw him, I couldn't believe he was a classicist. Classicists were thin and bookish, weren't they? Pale from spending hours bent over obscure Latin texts? Philip is ruddy with bright blue eyes beneath thick sandy eyebrows. His hair is thinning now, and his face more jowly, but at forty-eight he still has an air of youthful, muscular health that occasionally translates into action. Just before he left for the conference, we attended a lecture on bestiary in Aristophanes at the university, and I was mentally going through a litany of my miseries—the excruciating monotone of the speaker, how stifling the wine and cheese would be afterward, the way Jackson Maynard, the head of the department, would corner me and discuss house renovations, once again drenching me in bad breath—when Philip, who I thought was paying devoted attention to the subject matter, turned to me and said, sotto voce, "Let's get bestial tonight."

Now I say, "Philip, we have a crisis."

"A what?"

"Emma's found her mother."

"What?"

"Her mother. Her birth mother."

There is a silence and then he says, "How the hell did she do that?"

"They met in the second-floor ladies' room at the Rideau Centre."

"Where?"

"They were standing at the counter side by side, combing their hair. Their hair's the exact same color; that's how they recognized each other. Em's been seeing her secretly. Going to her apartment and having milk and cookies." There is another silence. "Philip?"

"Well, this is unprecedented," he finally says.

"You're right," I say nastily. "Dr. Spock doesn't have a chapter on this one."

Philip rarely stoops to my level. "Jane, you're upset."

"Of course I'm upset! And you know what bothers me the most? That she kept it a secret."

"She was worried we'd be angry."

"So now what do we do?"

"We hang up and get a good night's sleep."

"Doesn't this bother you at all?"

"Of course," he says. "It's a very disturbing thing."

"It's more than that," I say, my voice rising. "It's something a lot more fundamental than that!"

"Jane, it's also one-thirty in the morning, and we're both tired."

"I'm wide awake."

"And I have another lecture in the morning."

I relent. "I'm sorry."

He relents. "Will we solve anything by losing a night's sleep?"

"No."

"So the point is to stay calm, right?"

"Right."

"And not get too dramatic. Okay?"

"Okay."

I hang up and sit back against the pillows. In our marriage, Philip is the calm partner while I'm the volatile one who flaps around and takes things too much to heart. When I met Philip, it was the late sixties, and I was in my hippie stage, wearing my hair long and my skirts short. While I was definitely more interested in bashing the establishment than in getting a degree, I was also not so foolish as to flunk out or lose sight of the aim of all middle-class girls brought up in the fifties: to find a professional man and marry him. In my junior year I enrolled in a class on classical mythology, of which Philip was the graduate student instructor.

I had only the faintest interest in the gods and goddesses, but soon developed an avid curiosity about Philip. It was a large class, and it took him a while to notice me, even though I had taken to sitting front row center. I, on the other hand, spent the hour studying the width of his shoulders, the movement of his buttocks beneath his trousers, and what I thought was the deliciously arrogant curve of his lips. The term paper I wrote for his class was a confused treatise on the Freudian interpretation of myth. Philip gave it a C-minus, which enabled me to request a meeting, which further enabled me to ask, helplessly, if I had misunderstood Freud. Hadn't he thought myths were symbolic sexual fantasies of primitive man? Hadn't he believed they were the distorted expressions of savage libidos? Oh, yes, Philip said, but it's going a little far, Miss Simpson, to assume that Cecrops' lower half—that of a snake—was an obvious case of penile wish fulfillment.

The moment genitalia entered our conversation Philip was lost, although he didn't know that at the time. How could the two of us at twenty and twenty-four years of age talk about penis envy and vaginal symbolism without our own private parts clamoring for attention? No matter how dryly or abstractly Philip approached the subject, I was constantly aware of the bulge behind his zipper, and he could not avoid glancing at my breasts pressing against the tight turtleneck I wore or the shadowy triangular zone created by my pressed-together thighs and the hem of my miniskirt.

I never intended this flirtation to end in marriage, but I couldn't help enjoying the way I reduced Philip from his high and serene intellectual plane to a sweaty erection every time I entered his tiny office. It may sound as if I did this coldly with exploitation aforethought, but nothing could have been further from the truth. I was equally enamored and just as hot, sitting in that overheated cubicle, my panties sopping from desire. I loved the way Philip's sandy brown hair curled around his ears. I thrilled to the passion in his voice when he talked about Zeus. The fact that he wasn't American excited me even more. I thought Canada was exotic. I pictured snowy mountain peaks, the broad red chests of Mounties, soaring pines against blue sky.

If I'd known about the reality behind the myth I had created, would that have stopped me? Not likely. Like water, love seeks its level, rising or falling of its own accord. I had no control over it, didn't wish to have any control over it. I rose and fell with it, the ride so swift, so exhilarating that I never even caught sight of the landscape passing me by, the details of sky and earth, of past and future, of cause and event, until it was far too late.

I sigh and click out the light on my night table. Of course, the exoticism paled, and sex inevitably lost its illicit and seductive pull. We might have foundered then like so many other couples. I imagine myself divorced from Philip and see myself flying in loose, wild circles, like some planetary body careening out of control, lost in space. Sometimes I'm afraid of myself, of the depths to which I can plunge and the heights to which I can soar. At times I can even destroy Philip's calm and logic, but never for very long. Philip is my mooring. He's like the plastic inflatable clown we gave Emma to punch around when she was two years old. Bottom-heavy, it would swing back and forth, from side to side, swaying with each blow but never losing its balance. That is Philip, holding steady against the winds of our marriage.

DEAR DIARY,

Friday. Weather—snow and slete. I have three zits and my hair looks terible. Today I put white nail polish on and then dots with red nail polish. It looks weerd but good. In school everyone came up to me and told me that Mark is going to ask me out. I mean everyone even Lisa who hates me. Then Cello wanted to know what I wuld say. I told him its none of your busness. He said Mark thinks your butiful. I said oh sure give me a brake. He said no its realy true. I said fuck off. How stupid do they think I am? I know there lying. I know its a big joke. Ha-ha.

Mom found out about Her. I knew it would kill her. Thats why I didnt tell. You shuld have seen her face. I mean it was like a mask or something from Halowen—realy awful and strange. Then she started asking a million questions like I knew she wuld. Mom always wants to know everything about everything. Maybe I should have told her before exsept I knew it wuld bother her. Anyway she didnt say I culdn't go again so I gess I can. I mean I would anyway, becus I think Terry is real neat and She is my mother right?

Meanwhile I met Mic, Terrys boy friend. He is realy a major babe! Like Tom Cruise only his hair is blond. Terry says she met him at work and like it was imeediat love. There not married but there living together. Maybe they will get married some day and have kids. That means I culd have brothers or sisters which wuld be realy neat. Maybe I could babysit and stuf like that. Eksept theyll have to have more money because there apartmints way too small for kids and its kind of ugly. Its got craks and things like that. Terry says Mic wants her to get another job because she can only get work part time at the grociry store and Mic says she makes fucking peanuts.

Nothing much else eksept I prayed for another miracel even though Mom says there arent any. I prayed for my zits to go away but it didnt work. Shit.

Bye for now.

 MY OFFICE IS IN A CLUSTER OF SQUAT GOVernment buildings with dark narrow hallways and small offices painted in beige and carpeted in brown. The faces of dead and departed chief scientists and directors of the Geological Survey of Canada stare down from the walls in the corridors, their glances resting on signs indicating washroom facilities and detailing fire regulations. They're men of a certain weighty age, bald heads vying with slicked-back silver curls, and they're soberly dressed in dark suits and ties, their features airbrushed into smooth perfection. Sir

William Edmond Logan. Alfred Richard Cecil Selwyn. Dr. George Mercer Dawson. They're a constant reminder to those of us who lean toward irreverence or lack loyalty to the long and distinguished history of the Survey. Behind their spectacles are visions of rocky seascapes, vast prairies, and soaring mountains all neatly reduced to contour lines and map legends. I find their expressions both smug and disapproving, particularly that of Dr. Dawson, who hangs outside my office. What are you doing here? he seems to ask. Where did they find you?

Like the others who work here, I've tried to personalize my office, but nothing really can hide the naked fluorescent lighting, utilitarian filing cabinets, and old wooden desk nicked and marked with ink like the school desks of my childhood. Still, I make the effort. Two African violets struggle to bloom on my windowsill, and I've covered the walls of my office with posters of Greece, where Philip and I went several years ago when he was on a sabbatical and I was between jobs. In these posters the Mediterranean is a glorious aquamarine and the buildings a brilliant white. On days when the snow and ice have been salted to a dirty slop, when the winter light barely reaches the dark corners of my office, and I'm editing a paper with a title like *High Grade Metamorphic Facies Changes in the Cape Smith Orogenic Belt,* those sunny vistas seem to me to be not of another country but of another planet, another galaxy, altogether.

My life's dream was never to become an assistant editor of geological bulletins, a bureaucratic paper-pusher in a drab office, working for a paycheck and a dental plan. I had far more glamorous dreams—princess, figure skater, movie star, ballet dancer. Throughout my childhood I rotated through these, adding others as I grew older—TV announcer, model, President's wife, heroine of it-didn't-matter-what. At thirteen I became enchanted with the idea of becoming a famous writer. I wrote dozens of stories into a thick three-ring binder and regaled my parents and brothers with plot lines. I saw my name in bookstore windows and on the spines of library books and spent most of my thirteenth year in a dreamy haze of fame, until my grade nine English teacher brought my writing career to an abrupt halt.

She read a composition of mine to the class, a two-page story about a pilot who promised his soul to the devil so that his plane wouldn't crash and conveniently forgot this pact until Satan came to collect. Being singled out in the classroom caused me to squirm in an agony of pride and embarrassment, but those emotions were nothing compared to what I felt when, after finishing the story, the teacher turned to me and said, "Now, Jane, tell us what this means."

What it means?

The class turned to me while I kept my head down and studied the stained inkwell in my desk, my bitten fingernails, my knees covered by crumpled plaid cotton. It hadn't occurred to me that stories had to mean anything. I'd written not from any profundity of thought or religious conviction—my family hardly ever went to church—but because I had a tremendous yearning for theatrical moments. I longed for a drama that would take me high above my oh-so-ordinary life, above the boredom of school, the parental decrees, the endless sibling squabbles: "Empty the dishwasher, Murray." "But it's Jane's turn." "It is not." "Is so!" "Is not!" I fantasized about being Audrey Hepburn, Debbie Reynolds, Anne Frank—who cared if she died young, at least she *lived*.

After that humiliation I gave up writing, and the three-ring binder gathered dust in my parents' attic until it disappeared during one spring cleaning. My dreams shifted, narrowed, and focused. I wanted to be prom queen, the football captain's girl, voted most popular in my class. When I went to college I majored in English with a minor in geography, not out of fascination with either subject but because nothing else caught my fancy. By then I was far more interested in being a campus radical than in anything else, and the dreams shifted once again. I would be the wildest, the coolest, incredibly political, the sexiest chick. Of course I achieved none of the heights, being far too conservative to be more than a shallow imitation of the real thing. But then, that was the sixties. Everyone was marching and protesting something, and I didn't want to be left behind.

"Jane?"

Des Miller stands in my office doorway, and I feel a surge of pleasure. We don't often get to see each other during the course of a working day. "Come on in," I say. "Have a seat." As he sits, I notice the depth of the lines cutting his face and the small pouches puffed under his eyes. "You look tired," I say.

"Why does everyone think bureaucrats have it easy?"

"Because they're convinced we're on a perpetual coffee break."

"I don't even like coffee," he says and smiles.

Des has a slow, sexy smile but no knowledge of its existence or its impact on members of the opposite sex. I'm no exception to the seductive pull of those lips as they curve upward, or the way the tilt of them is reflected in his eyes, which are of a blue lighter than Philip's. Having taken a psych course in college in which the professor was fond of reducing human relations to geometry on the blackboard, I've come to think of my relationship to Des in the form of two intersecting silver triangles. Along the three edges of the first triangle lie the three reasons why Des and I should be lovers.

We like each other.

We turn each other on.

We've both been married for twenty-one years. Twenty-one is a significant number: the highest total in blackjack, the year of consent, three times the seven-year itch. And as both of us were married at twenty-one, we've reached that point in our lives where we've been married as long as we were single. Des and I agree this is a sobering thought.

On the other hand—and I'm an expert on other hands, fingering and juggling alternatives, weighing possibilities, always seeing the reverse side of arguments—there are the three sides of the second triangle, each equal in length to that of the first and providing equal argument why we shouldn't fall into bed together.

I socialize with his wife.

We work in the same government department.

I prefer illusion to reality. If Des is anything like Philip, he wears his briefs until the elastic frays and small holes appear at the seams. If he's anything like a lover of my friend Vera, he makes grunting noises at the moment of orgasm that are distressingly similar to the sound of, as she put it, a cow in labor. How Vera, my most urbane friend, knows even the first thing about cows remains a mystery.

Sometimes I twirl the first triangle, sometimes the second, sometimes I throw both high in the air and watch them descend, spinning as they fall. Like leaves separated from a tree, they are subject to contrary gusts. The winds of lust, caution, longing, and recklessness blow them this way and that. Des knows nothing of this hexagonal whirl of geometry. We rarely touch, except for a brushing of hands when one or the other reaches for a restaurant check, the accidental rubbing of shoulders when we walk side by side, and the casual midnight brush of lips at the New Year's Eve party when we have legal license to kiss spouses other than our own. If Des wants to go to bed with me, he doesn't say so, nor do I drop sexual hints. At the moment I have no intention of crossing the line that separates friendship from dangerous indiscretion, and I presume he doesn't either. Our agreement on this issue is silent and mutually understood.

So Des and I are engaged in a pleasurable, comfortable mental affair. Sometimes we meet for lunch or for a drink after work and gossip. Des is a gentleman of both the new school and of the old. He does all the traditional things, like open doors and pull out chairs, his hand hovering within two inches of the back of my waist to catch me should I stumble. At one time I would have been insulted by this behavior, convinced that it demonstrated a belief in female weakness, but age has mellowed me. Since I'm almost five feet ten and built to last, I'm refreshed by the thought that someone finds me fragile and delicate. Des balances this courtliness with a nontraditional sensitivity. He takes me seriously, he respects my opinions, he can discuss emotional intimacies as easily as other men discuss politics or football. Philip has these skills, too, but he's so buried in his work and research and we've been married so long that he neglects to apply them.

"I can brew some tea," I say.

Des shakes his head. "No, thanks."

"How about a large pot of sympathy?"

"That sounds about right."

"What happened?"

"I didn't pass my French."

"Oh, shit," I say.

"Yeah. Precisely." He takes off his glasses and pinches the bridge of his nose between his forefinger and thumb, a weary gesture I haven't seen him make before. I have the urge to walk around my desk and wrap him in my arms as if my embrace could protect him from the cruel absurdities of his position.

Des is a director and under new government regulations will have to become bilingual or else. No one quite knows what the "or else" entails. Demotion? Pink-slipping? Dead-end positioning? Des, who is an excellent administrator, has been caught in the French trap and, not having a facility with languages, can't seem to get himself out. This is the third time he has failed, despite weeks spent in French training, stays in Quebec City, his own money spent on Berlitz lessons and the Alliance Française. The absurdity of it is that Des doesn't have to work in French at all.

"So what now?" I ask.

"I put myself on more training. I don't know when. Sam goes on French next week; then it's Sandra's turn. I sometimes wonder how we get anything done."

"It's ridiculous," I say vehemently, "and unfair."

"This is the price we pay to have a bilingual public service."

"Come on, Des, we have hospital beds closing in Ottawa for lack of funds, and the government's giving fifty-five million to Saskatchewan to help it become bilingual. *Saskatchewan*, for Christ's sake."

He puts his glasses back on. "Darreau wants twenty-five percent francophone representation in the department."

"You're kidding."

"Would I kid about stuff like this?"

Darreau is our minister, the politician in charge of our department. He has nothing to do with day-to-day operations, but mixes and agitates the broth of government science policy. He's exceedingly temperamental and rabidly Quebecois. He screams at his underlings in French; all meetings with him have to be held in French; even the most trivial memos have to be written in impeccable French. When he arrived a year ago, he decided that everything, from letters to scientific publications, had to be issued bilingually, even if they were only being sent to that last anglophone stronghold, Alberta. Although government austerity has forced severe cutbacks in scientific programs and personnel, each division and sector has been forced to hire translators to satisfy his demands.

"Twenty-five percent francophone representation?" I say. "He can't do that, can he?"

"He thinks he can."

"But it would be prejudicial to bilingual anglophones, wouldn't it? And against equal-hiring policies?"

"I haven't looked into it yet."

"The man's a maniac," I say.

"You know what I dream about? A woman trained in geophysics with a French father, an Inuit mother, and a limp. That would cover all the fucking bases: francophones, women, visible minorities, and the handicapped."

Des rarely swears. This is how I know he's really reached the end of his tether. I feel so bad for him that a gust of desire sends the triangles that form our relationship on an updraft.

"And then there's Maureen," he adds.

I think of Maureen whom I last saw several months ago at a barbecue at a neighbor's. In addition to being husband and wife, she and Des are cousins many times removed. Certain traits have crossed that familial distance. They possess the same long, inquisitive nose. They are both tall and lean and, when they were younger, had the appearance of elegant racehorses moving in tandem. But I'd noticed at the barbecue that middle age is slowly turning Maureen stringy, her smooth long limbs revealed as bone and rope. Des, however, is becoming patrician, fashionably gray at the temples, distinguished creases cutting down his cheeks.

"She doesn't like real estate?" I ask. Maureen has started a new career selling houses in old but trendy neighborhoods.

"No, she's fine. It's probably me."

"Des, what's the matter?"

"Our marriage seems to be—I don't know—unraveling."

Des and I usually talk about our marriages as if they're states of weather and we're weathermen reporting on conditions of far-off zones. Conditions can be calm, everything's fine, or unsteady as if the barometer were vacillating widely. In general, Des's marriage falls into far more turbulent zones than mine.

"I thought you had a wonderful time in Bermuda," I say.

"It didn't last."

"You've got to make more time for each other."

"It might help."

"A romantic candlelight dinner. Flowers, preferably roses." I'm getting enthusiastic now. "Wait—diamond earrings."

"I gave her a pair for her fortieth birthday."

"Oh, Des," I say, shaking my head. "A woman can't have enough diamonds."

"Jane, what would you do if you and Philip hadn't talked for weeks?"

"Sit him down and tell him we have to get to the bottom of what's wrong."

"What if he wouldn't sit?"

"I'd get him in bed where he's a captive audience."

"What if you weren't sleeping in the same bed?"

My glibness deserts me. "Oh, Des—" I begin.

"The truth is," he says, looking away, "Maureen and I haven't slept together for two months."

We may try to peel our marriages as if they are onions, stripping layers to reach their unfathomable cores, but we rarely mention details of physical intimacy. I'm taken aback, and in my silence Des gives an uneasy laugh and, with a quick unhappy motion, brushes aside a lock of graying brown hair that has fallen across his forehead. I know he hasn't intended to say this. I also know that if I don't, in the next moment, divert the conversation along safer lines, he will leave embarrassed and ashamed at his loss of restraint. It will be months before we can once again enjoy that comfortable combination of flirtation and friendship.

I hastily search for a change of subject and find the one crisis I know will work. "Guess what happened at our house?" I say. "Emma found her birth mother."

I've been successful. For a moment it's clear he doesn't know what to say. "When?" he finally asks.

"She found her last month. I found out yesterday."

"How?"

I tell him how it happened. "Sheer coincidence," I conclude.

"The birth mother doesn't have any legal rights over Emma, does she?"

"Not that I know of."

Des has a teenage daughter of his own. "Emma is at such a volatile age."

"Tell me about it."

"What're you going to do?"

I'm the one whose laugh is uneasy. "Emily Post doesn't have a chapter on this one."

Des puts out his hand and places it over mine, which is resting on the top of my desk. It's the first time he has deliberately touched me, and the triangles of our relationship start a slow silvery spin.

"Let's run away together," he says.

"Sounds good to me."

"Which South Sea Island do you prefer?"

"The one farthest away."

"Does Air Canada go that far?"

"I doubt it."

He bestows that unconsciously sexy smile upon me, and as I bask in its warmth, the triangles whirl around and around, faster and faster, until the six points seem to form one continuous silver blur.

 EVER SINCE SHE FOUND EMMA, TERRY'S HAD A recurring dream about work. In it, Emma has been purchased by a customer—only she's a baby, not a thirteen-year-old. Terry keeps trying to drag her naked body across the small glass window that reads the universal code, but Emma's wiggling too much. The harder Terry tries, the more slippery Emma becomes until she finally slides off the counter and hits the floor. The customer screams at her, Flo brings a broom and starts sweeping, and Bill says, "You broke the merchandise."

She tells Mic about the dream one morning at breakfast. "You think I'm under stress?" she asks.

"They're dreams," he says as he pours himself a cup of coffee.

"You ever have dreams like that?"

"I sleep like a fucking baby."

Terry doesn't tell him that he cries out in his sleep and only stops when she pulls him into her arms. "I read this article in *Woman's Weekly* about dreams," she says. "They mean something. They're like keys, the article said, to a part of your brain. They're important."

Mic takes a sip of coffee. "What's important, babe, is that Buddy and I clinch that deal today. Then you can quit that lousy job and stop dreaming about it. It could be the big break. L.A. and points south."

L.A. and points south. Terry's never met a man who can spin dreams like Mic. Sometimes late at night, after they've made love, Mic lights a cigarette, leans back against his pillow with Terry tucked into the crook of his shoulder, and talks about the ranch he means to own someday, except he just doesn't say ranch and then go on to something else like most people would. Instead he paints that ranch for Terry as if his words are tiny brushes stroking colors and sounds onto the dark ceiling of the room so she can see the turquoise of the sky and the greeny brown of the earth, and she can hear the low snorting of horses and the tramp of cattle's feet on the barn floor.

She sips her coffee and says dreamily, "You think we'll ever really get there?"

"Didn't I just say Buddy and I might make the big deal today?" She nods. "If it goes, we're outta here, babe. We're history."

Terry believes that she loves Mic more than she's loved anyone or anything in her life. If Barbara Walters came to interview her, Terry knows that the camera would keep slipping from her face to focus on Mic's. He's movie-star perfect. When she first saw him, standing in her line at Loblaws, both hands jammed into his jeans pockets, his thumbs straddling the bucking bronco buckle on his belt, she could hardly pack her customer's groceries. He had blond hair—almost white—that curled to his shoulders, and blue eyes framed by thick light lashes. He wasn't tall, but compact the way middle-sized men can be when they're mostly muscle and bone. And his face had a smooth beauty that took her breath away. Terry remembers everything he bought that first time—Pepperidge Farm cookies, Crest toothpaste, a case of Coke, and Kraft's Tuna Helper. The Tuna Helper made her even more fluttery. The box sat in his cart like a mute plea. I'm all alone, it said. Would you help me?

"Having a party?" she said when he came up to the cash.

He smiled. "Does this look like a party?"

"For one," she said. She hated how fast she was on cash. He was going to be packed and gone in minutes.

"That's 'cause I'm new."

"You just moved to town?"

"Yesterday. Don't know anyone yet."

"Wrong," she said.

"Wrong?"

"You know me."

Then he looked her over the way guys did when they came to the magazine rack by her cash and studied the *Cosmopolitan* cover. It was a narrow-eyed glance that was sexy and dangerous. "Yeah," he said slowly, "now I know you."

She pressed the total button, and the register made clicking sounds. "That'll be eighteen dollars," she said, looking right into that thin blue gaze, "and sixty-three cents."

Although he moved in with her right away, it turned out he did know people in Ottawa. Friends of friends of his back in Vancouver. People who, like Mic, didn't have jobs but always seemed to have money. Mic first told Terry he was on unemployment, but Terry knows there's not enough money from the dole to pay for his hand-tooled leather boots and the black leather jacket or for the gifts he showers on her when the "money's in": a gold bracelet, a green silk scarf, a delicate blue sweater with pearls at the neckline. She worries about where the money is coming from, but the gifts have the power to bewitch her. Few boyfriends have ever given her presents, and no one has done it with Mic's flair: the fancy wrappings, the gleam of anticipation in his eyes, the way he nods when she tries something on. "That's great," he says. "When we go to L.A., you're going to turn heads, babe. Shit, you're going to break necks."

But even if the gifts dazzle her, even if Mic's dreams of L.A. dovetail so beautifully with her own dreams of stardom, Terry knows that Mic doesn't love her in the same way she loves him. She doesn't have to do the compatibility questionnaire in *Redbook* to understand that she wants more from Mic than he's willing to give her. She wants to know everything about him, and while he's always willing to talk about the future, he's secretive about the present and the past. She gets bits of him thrown at her the way animals get thrown scraps of food so they're hungry all the time. Terry only knows he's from British Columbia, his father married a woman he didn't like, he's never been married, and he loves cars. On one of his deals with Buddy, who works part-time at a garage, he got a flame-red Camaro with bucket seats, four on the floor, and the power of a "fucking nympho in heat." *Redbook* calls these "outside interests."

*Does your significant other include you in his outside
    interests?*
a. All the time
b. Some of the time
c. Rarely
d. Never

"When I was a kid," Terry says, buttering a piece of toast, "I used to think dreams came from God. Good dreams were rewards. Bad dreams were punishments." She laughs a bit. "I was always in trouble so I had a lot of really lousy dreams."

Mic is sipping his coffee, and those blue eyes are looking at her, but his hands have tensed on the cup he's holding, and she knows he's seeing something else, somewhere else. Terry wants to follow him there, but he won't let her. She's tried, and he laughs off her question with the same carelessness with which he wards off questions about the past. Suddenly he shakes his head as if mentally denying something and then says, "You doing a laundry today?"

"Yes." Their apartment building is an old one, and Terry does their laundry in a Soap 'n' Suds on Bank Street.

"Check out that new shirt of mine, will you? It has a spot on the sleeve." Terry's never known a man who's as fussy about clothes as Mic. It's as if his skin is more sensitive than other men's, as if it can only stand beautiful fabrics.

Mic stands up and stretches. "You working this afternoon?"

"No. Emma's coming by." She pauses. "You think that's why I had the dream last night? Because she was coming today?"

"You got her on the brain."

"Sometimes it feels like we come from different worlds."

"She's fucking rich, for chrissake."

"But she's my kid."

Terry watches as Mic pulls on his leather jacket and then slips his hair back over the collar. His jawline is so pure it makes her throat ache. She loves Mic's beauty, but it also confuses her. It draws her to him at the same time as it holds her at arm's length, and she can't figure out what part of that beauty is Mic himself and what part of it is a mask, concealing another, different Mic. Even though she knows he'll come home at the end of the day, even though she knows that when they sleep together he will give her pleasure, sometimes when she watches him she has a frightening sense of not knowing.

When your significant other leaves you, are you sure you know where he is?

When your significant other cries out in the dark, do you know what he's saying?

When your significant other makes love to you, are you sometimes scared, but don't know why?

a. *Always*

b. *Sometimes*

c. *Maybe*

d. *Never*

Terry doesn't do the laundry right away. Instead she drives past the Soap 'n' Suds, over the Bank Street Bridge, and into the suburb of Ottawa South. It wouldn't be Terry's first choice of neighborhood. Her ideal is one of the newer suburbs with the stretched-out bungalows and wide expanses of green lawn shadowed by elms and weeping willows. The houses here are taller, closer together, and have old-fashioned porches and narrow driveways. She notes that some of them have been done up nice while others need new roofs, windows, and paint jobs.

She turns right at the corner of Brighton and Bristol,

passes Fentiman, turns right again onto Belmont, and parks in the middle of the block. Snow has started falling, and the street is deserted. Small gusts of wind pick up the snow and hurl it against the windshield. She sits in her car and looks at the house across the street. It has two stories and a porch that spans the width of the front. The porch has white-painted rails and a gray-painted floor. The yard is a small square dotted with a few bushes that have been cut down for the winter. Terry studies the drapes in the picture window and the brass mailbox that gleams against the dark red brick. The edges and corners of white and brown envelopes poke out of the mailbox.

Barbara looks down at her notes. "You grew up on the wrong side of the tracks, didn't you?"

"Mechanicsville," Terry says and, understanding that the gleam of stardom shines ever brighter when it's placed against a gray and drab backdrop, adds, "It was very poor. Very ugly." Even when she was five years old, the houses offended her. She hated the garish colors, the phony stone-and-brick facades, the dirty cracked windows, the tiny lawns filled with weeds and rusting bicycles.

Barbara looks appropriately grim. "You didn't feel as if you fit there, did you?"

"I'd walk until I was out of the neighborhood and onto some nice streets—the ones with pretty lawns and real brick houses. Then I'd look for For Sale *signs. When I found one, I'd run home. I'd grab my mother by the skirt and try to pull her out the door. 'You gotta buy this thouse,' I'd say. 'Right now. Right now!' "* At the memory, tears spring into *Terry's eyes.*

"And what would your mother do?" Barbara asks.

"Push me away," she says, delicately dabbing at her eyes with a hankerchief—pale, pale pink with her initial embroidered at one corner. All the real stars choke up when Barbara talks to them, and Terry knows the crying is an important part of the interview. It brings that star out of the TV and right into the living room.

"She pushed you away because there wasn't enough money?"

"We were on welfare."

Now the full force of the past sweeps over her, and Terry cries hard but beautifully for that unhappy little girl, the tears a poignant symbol of the distance she's traveled and the people she's left behind.

Terry only meant to come and look, that's all, but the brown and white envelopes beckon to her so powerfully she can't resist. She looks up and down the street and gets out of her car. She steps over the crack, up the steps, and onto the porch. Then she lifts the mail out of the box and walks quickly back to her car. All around her the houses watch, their windows accusing dark rectangles. Her heart is pounding, and her hands trembling, but she manages to switch on the ignition and drive away. It isn't until she's several blocks away that she feels safe enough to stop.

Then she goes through the mail. There are bills addressed to Dr. Philip Wastenay from Bell Canada, Consumer's Gas, and Ottawa Hydro. There are two letters to Jane Wastenay—a bill from the Tall Girl Shop and an envelope postmarked South Carolina with the address written in an elegant script in blue ink. The rest of the mail consists of circulars from Regal Realtors, Ottawa South Drugs, and Mr. Fix-it: "Dear Homeowner, It's that season again. Time to clean out your gutters, caulk your windows, and protect your home from the onslaught of winter!"

Terry doesn't know why she's crying. It's stupid, that's what. When she cries, her skin turns blotchy and her face feels puffy. She takes a wad of tissues out of her purse and blows her nose. She glances in the rearview mirror, mutters "Shit," and blows her nose some more. When she finally feels composed, she drives to the Soap 'n' Suds. Along the way she stops at a mailbox and drops the letters through its slot.

I HAVE TWO CLOSE FRIENDS, VERA AND Alice, with whom I share most of the details of my life. Unlike the mirrors in my house, they reflect my image back to me in ways I don't expect. They see what I can't see—interesting angles and shadows—and use language I would never think of using. After I've talked to them, the events of my life take on a different quality. If they were sad or depressing, the gloom surrounding them lifts slightly so I see the irony or poignancy. If the events were happy or unusual, they become fascinating and brighter as if my life were more highly charged than that of ordinary mortals. Nor does my need for Vera and Alice end there. Their own lives are windows through which I peer into dramas other than my own. No matter how long I've known them, no matter that I think I understand them well, their dramas constantly unfold in startling and amazing ways. Vera's is like a roll of rich, vibrant silk. Alice's is more subdued—a pure cotton—but no less rich in color and subtlety. Over the years, they have pleated and gathered, wrinkled and crumpled, yet all the while, somehow, they run straight and true.

I tell Vera about Emma at a small bistro in Hull where we are having lunch. Hull is across the river in Quebec, a stone's throw from Ottawa. It's a French-speaking city, and its restaurants are as Parisian as the owners can afford. The one we're sitting in may be tiny, its tables covered with worn checked tablecloths and plastic carnations, but its walls are gloriously Left Bank, covered with poorly painted murals of bookstands, beret-topped pedestrians, Notre Dame, and a Seine of choppy little waves that glint in the sun. The menu is also rigorously French—no translations—and I have to wade through the *à la florentines, à la bonne paysannes,* and *aux poivre verts* to find a soup and salad.

"So what are you going to do?" Vera asks.

"What can we do? It's like a broken egg. There's no going back."

"Have you talked to Emma?"

"She just clams up. She says it's private."

Vera sips her wine. "I suppose she's trying to keep her two lives separate. I know I would if I were in her shoes."

"But I think we should meet this . . . woman," I say.

Vera nods. "Then you'd know what you're dealing with."

"The question is, how do we do that without telling Emma?"

"You can't. You have to ask her permission. This sort of thing should be open and aboveboard."

"Suppose Emma says no."

"Cross that bridge when you come to it."

"Actually," I say, "I'm afraid to meet her."

"Of course you're afraid," Vera says. "I'd be afraid."

Not beautiful Vera. Today she is a watercolor portrait—thick blond hair, creamy complexion, apricot silk dress, scarf the color of pale green grapes. Her delicacy conceals a steely composure and a philosophy of never backing down. "Would you?" I ask.

"Of course. She's threatening."

"Very." I sigh.

"What does Philip think of all this?"

"On the last day of the conference Barnaby told him she was writing a monograph on Zeus that was going to blow him out of the water. What do you think he's thinking about?"

We exchange smiles. We're old friends and go back eighteen years. We met when we lived in Elmvale Acres and Vera was married for the first time. We were both newly transplanted Americans, eager to understand Canada, and were recruited into a neighborhood book club whose mandate was to discuss only novels written by Canadian authors. I don't remember any of the titles, only that most of the books were marked by a dismal, inward-turning tone, as if the Canadian literary soul was caught in a perpetual state of winter.

When I look back at pictures from that era, the casual photo taken at parties and picnics, I find that Vera's the only one of us who didn't look ridiculous in the absurd fashions of the day: the bell bottoms that made us look hippy and knock-kneed, the hot pants designed by some sadist that exposed our legs to the freezing Canadian elements, the blouses with big collars shaped like upside-down elves' ears that pointed directly at our breasts. I look rigid in the photos, tall and uncomfortable, my brown hair unable to stay smoothly in the style of the times. But Vera is always relaxed, even when caught in an awkward pose, and elegant, as if her bones were sheathed not in mere muscle and flesh but in graceful satin.

Our conversation switches to Vera's job. She's a director general in the Department of Indian Affairs and Northern Development, in charge of environmental audits. "We have a new deputy minister who's a workaholic, but I'm not letting that bother me," Vera says.

"Good," I say.

"And I'm planning a major lifestyle change."

I think of the serenity of Vera's apartment with its cool glass sculptures and pretty arrangements of flowers. I think of the serenity of her personal life, undisturbed by the demands of husband and child. Both her marriages were short-lived, and while I have always believed that Vera was far too intelligent for her husbands, a part of me has always been convinced that she must also be too self-centered, too intent on her creature comforts, to share them with anyone else. I have no evidence for this, only the care she takes to surround herself with perfection and clarity.

"You're going to move to a bigger apartment," I say.

"No."

"Quit the government?"

"And bite the hand that feeds me?"

I'm running out of ideas. "Vote Conservative in the next election?"

"I'm going to get pregnant."

I can't answer because the waiter arrives with our soup, but I'm sure my face says it all. I can feel the stretch of disbelief, twisting my mouth out of shape.

"Don't look so shocked," Vera says calmly, unfolding

her napkin. Her nails are manicured the exact same shade of apricot as her dress.

"You've got to be kidding."

"No, I'm absolutely certain."

"For God's sake, why?"

"I may not have been meant to be someone's wife, but I'm sure I was meant to be someone's mother."

"At forty-one?"

"I know all the risks. My doctor has given me a long list of hideous possibilities. I studied them carefully and decided it was worth it."

I can't even touch my soup. "What about your career? I thought that was the most important thing in your life."

She calmly sips hers. "It's important, but it isn't everything. Besides, other single women can do it. Why shouldn't I?"

"No one's saying that they're doing it well or happily or easily. It's hard enough bringing up a kid with two parents."

"I know every objection you can throw at me. I've spent hours arguing with myself. The thing is, I want a baby. You can understand that, can't you?"

She looks at me, and I see that she wants this more than she has wanted anything in her life. And Vera is a ferocious wanter in a delicate but insistent way. When she wants a certain piece of clothing, she buys it, no matter what the price. When she wanted a holiday in Hawaii, she took it, even though her second husband had left her and cleaned out her bank account. When she decided she wanted to be a high-level bureaucrat, she climbed her way up the ladder, scheming and plotting on every rung. I had always assumed that she achieved this goal by being smarter and shrewder than everyone else, but she shocked me once at a party by saying casually with that small brittle laugh that she gets when she's been drinking: "I want to reach a position so high that men will have to screw *me* to get ahead." I never dared to ask her if she was joking.

Vera leans forward. "Jane, why do I have to be everybody's favorite aunt? The one who brings gifts and dotes on other people's children? I don't want to be the old lady who has nothing to cherish but her china knickknacks and some mangy cat that she's dragged in to keep her company.''

"Children are no guarantee for your old age."

Vera sighs. "I know, but I don't care. That's the point, you see. I've got to have my chance."

"And there's one other thing," I say. "Babies don't stay little forever. They turn into children who turn into adolescents. Then they're not cute anymore. Tell me, if you were going to give birth to a teenager, would you still do it?"

"That's ridiculous."

"No, it isn't."

"No one thinks that far ahead. Why should I?"

The soup, half eaten, is whisked away, and the waiter brings our lunches, which I ignore. "I think you're crazy."

"I know."

"And who are you going to get to be the father?"

"There's a man I often see when I go to those regional meetings in Manitoba. He's attractive and intelligent. Married, of course, but that doesn't matter. He'll never know. And he does have children, so I know he's fertile."

"Is it fair for a child not to know its father?"

"Is it fair for me to go through life without a child?"

"And are you going to tell this child about its father?"

"Of course. I wouldn't hide such vital information."

I'm startled by my sudden anger at Vera, at her managerial composure and her smooth, cool beauty. "You know something?" I say. "This is a selfish thing you're doing."

She gives me a serene smile. "We're all selfish, aren't we? Why do you suppose people have children? For the unborn child's sake? Come on, Jane, you can't condemn me for wanting what everyone else wants."

Words bubble angrily, awkwardly, out of my mouth. "I *know* what it's like for children who aren't brought up in the normal way. Who don't know their parents. Who have that . . . that empty place."

"What are you talking about?"

That empty place. I've never spoken of it before, I've

never even articulated it to myself, but suddenly I am very sure of what I know. "The one in here." I place my clenched fist on my chest. "The one I can't fill in Emma no matter how hard I try."

"You've done a wonderful job with Emma."

I shake my head. "You and I really can't understand it. We know our parents."

"Jane, you're not going to change my mind."

Nausea rises in my throat, and I push my plate away. "Oh, Vera."

"There," she says, touching my hand again with her tapering apricot fingertips. "There. It won't be so bad. You'll see."

While Vera is my most beautiful and glamorous friend, Alice qualifies as my most famous one. She writes novels, thin but smoldering books about love and passion. She's Ottawa's only published romance writer and a minor celebrity, being called upon to give interviews on occasions like Valentine's Day. When that happens, Alice gets her makeup done, has her hair elaborately twisted into a knot, takes off her glasses, and has interviews in the *Ottawa Citizen* and on the CBC. Her fame has even spread as far as Montreal where she had a big spread last year in the *Gazette*.

Alice doesn't look like a romance writer. She has the appearance of a harried, overworked secretary whose salary doesn't stretch far enough to cover the cost of stylish clothes. She's a small person with a small face closed in around a thin short nose and a perpetual frown that narrows her brown eyes behind their big round glasses. I didn't like Alice when I first met her. She struck me as secretive, aloof, and too busy to be friendly, but I got to know her better when we car-pooled for Brownies. The frown, I learned, had to do with having three children, paying off a huge mortgage, living with a permanently discontented husband, and pursuing a career with no stability. In short, she's much like the rest of us in one way or another.

What I like best about Alice is that, despite the frown,

she isn't the sort of person who lets herself be limited by the burdens of her own life. If she likes you, she simply adds you to the heaped-up pile of her concerns. She worries that I'm not ambitious enough, she thinks I don't appreciate my own talents and achievements, and she frets about my health. When I was on antibiotics for a bladder infection and didn't eat yogurt, she scolded me. "Vaginitis," she warned, "is lurking right around the corner." She was right, of course. It took me another two weeks to clear that up, all together a month of misery and no sex.

Now when I tell her about Emma, she sits very quietly, but my past emotions flicker across her face. I see my worry, shock, and fear replayed as if in a silent movie. "What a terrible thing," she whispers. "Oh, Jane, you must have felt awful."

We're sitting in Alice's dining room, trying to thread pipe cleaners through narrow loops of gray felt, while the children are upstairs. In early anticipation of the annual Hopewell Elementary School Christmas concert, Emma and Felicia's teacher has already chosen "A Visit from St. Nicholas" for grades seven and eight to perform. Emma and Felicia will be house mice, which means that Alice and I have to sew mouse costumes, and since neither of us is good at sewing, we've decided to pool our meager talents. The pipe cleaners are intended to make upright ears that will be attached to gray hoods, which in turn will be attached to gray capes. Or so the instructions say.

As the end of my pipe cleaner tears through the felt, I say, "It feels as if my life is a pool of water and someone just heaved a huge stone into it."

"Maybe Emma will handle it better than you think."

"I've got to learn to handle it. I got only three hours' sleep last night."

"Philip's away, isn't he?"

"He's back. He sleeps like a log."

"It always amazes me that when Rob goes to work, he forgets the children exist. I never forget. In the back of my mind, I'm wondering whether Felicia gave her little talk in

English without being too nervous or whether Marshall is coming down with another cold or whether Sylvie is going to get in a fight on the playground."

"Why are mothers so vigilant?" I ask. "Why can't we sit back and relax?"

Alice yanks the pipe cleaner out of her piece of felt. "I don't think we have a choice. When we have a baby, we're hard-wired into nurturing."

"But I didn't have a baby."

Alice puts down the pipe cleaner, and her forehead puckers into a fierce frown. "It's not any different for you than it is for me. You brought Emma home and you loved her like she was yours. You fed her and took care of her. No one can take your place. *No one.*"

What I can't take from my own mother, that sympathy and scolding, I take from Alice. It's the delivery, I think, that makes all the difference. When Alice speaks, she reminds me of high school slumber parties when the lights were switched off. We'd settle under the covers and smoke, matches flaring and subsiding, the red-hot tips of cigarettes moving in the air. Eventually our eyes would become accustomed to the lack of light so we could see the pale ovals of our faces and the glint of hair rollers. Then we'd talk, hours and hours of whispers and laughter, the secrets flowing under the safe cover of that barely lit darkness.

"Alice! *Alice!* Where's the wrench? It was in the basement yesterday."

Rob appears in the doorway of the kitchen. I'm always surprised when I see him because, as a male specimen, he's so far removed from Alice's romantic heroes. He's narrow-shouldered and slightly potbellied. His legs, above the socks and below the pants hems, are white and almost hairless. To compensate for this perhaps, his head is exceptionally hairy. He has thick sandy curls, furry nostrils, and a heavy dark brown beard. He's an engineer who does something with electrical circuits, and as we can never find a topic that's mutually interesting, he and I have stilted conversations at dinner parties.

"The wrench? How should I know?" she say.

"How can I fix the dishwasher without the wrench?"

Like Philip and me, the McGaskins live in one of those old houses with high ceilings and plumbing that's in constant need of repair. Right now the dishwasher has been pulled out from under the counter because a pipe had burst behind it, causing water to flow out over the linoleum floor and down into the basement.

"Good question," Alice says.

"Hi, Rob," I say.

"Oh, hello, Jane. Alice, if one of those kids has taken my wrench, there's going to be hell to pay." He stalks off, stamping back down the basement stairs.

"How's Rob's new job?" I ask.

"He had a fight with his boss. I think he's going to quit."

"Oh, Alice, not again."

She gives an unhappy shrug.

"He doesn't seem to have trouble finding jobs."

"No, just in keeping them."

"Maybe he's having a mid-life crisis," I suggest.

"He's had one already," she says. "He doesn't get any more."

Vera can't understand how Alice can be married to Rob and write romantic stories filled with hot kisses and steamy sex. "She must have some imagination," Vera says grudgingly. "She can't be doing a lot of research at home." At first, like Vera, I was mystified by the incomprehensible balance that Alice seems to have struck in her life. When I read her books, *Angel's Passion* and *To Love Again,* I sought the Alice I knew behind that curtain of words and found someone quite different, an Alice beyond children and husband, car pools and broken dishwashers, an Alice rich in secret yearnings and dramatic desires. I've come to believe that if it weren't for her novels absorbing this richness like a blotter, the needs would overflow into her marriage, flooding it in a torrent.

Alice is studying the instruction sheet again. "I'm going to switch to the cape," she says gloomily. "The ears are beyond me."

"How's your book going?" I ask. "The last I heard, your heroine was pregnant from a one-night stand."

Alice always perks up when she talks about her books. "Oh, she's really in trouble," she says with a smile. "You see, she can't care for the baby—she has dizzy spells and no way to earn a living—and finally, in desperation, leaves it on the hero's doorstep when it's eight months old. Of course this breaks her heart, and five years later, when she's finally over the dizzy spells and has established a career, she goes back to kidnap it."

"How does she do that?"

"She gets hired as the child's nanny. The hero's incredibly rich, of course. A CEO type. Sits on the board of directors for a zillion multinationals. And incredibly handsome. Dark hair, gray eyes, et cetera, et cetera."

"Why doesn't the heroine just go back to him and say she's the mother? Wouldn't that be easier?"

"What kind of romance novel would that be?"

"But doesn't the hero recognize her?"

"Of course not. She's in disguise. She changes her hair color from blond to brown and wears shapeless clothing."

There is the clatter of feet on the stairs followed by a loud voice and an angry scream. Felicia rushes breathlessly into the kitchen. Like Alice, she is slight and already wears glasses. "Mom, Sylvie is bugging us again!"

Sylvie arrives right on her heels. "She hit me, Mom! And it hurt!"

"She's a liar. I didn't hit her."

"You did, too!" Sylvie plants her hands on her hips and glares at Felicia. She is a solid child and has Rob's thick curly hair. "Mom, she did!"

I see Emma hanging over the stair railing, watching with interest. Being an only child, she's always intrigued by sibling squabbles.

"Did not!"

"Did too!"

"*Did not!*"

"Did—"

"Girls," Alice says calmly, "if you don't stop scream- ing, you're both going to go to your rooms. And if you go to your rooms, you'll miss the end of Disney."

"But, Mom," Felicia says, "she keeps switching chan- nels. She won't *stop*."

"I mean it.

Sylvie has already run back up the stairs, yelling, "I'm going to get the best sitting spot! So-o-o there!"

"Back to your heroine," I say, when they're gone. "How does the hero recognize her?"

"She goes for an early morning swim, skinny-dipping, of course. He's there too, and they have one of those romantic encounters."

"He's naked too?"

"Of course. At the end of it, she runs away from him up the beach."

"They don't screw?"

"Jane!"

"Well, I would."

"Anyway, he catches a glimpse of the sun glinting on her pubic hair and realizes she's a natural blonde."

"God," I say, "why don't exciting things like that ever happen to me?"

"This is real life, remember?"

I hold up an ear. I've finally managed to get the pipe cleaner through the fold of fabric, but the gray felt is looking the worse for wear, and the wire is twisted at a peculiar angle. "What do you think?"

"I think a bent ear is better than no ear at all."

We smile at each other.

"You're a solace to me, Alice."

"What are friends for?"

DEAR DIARY,

Saturday. Weather—frezing. The wart on my knees getting bigger!!!

Nothing to do today and its real boring. Dana went shoping with her Mom. Cello and Peter are playing hockey and I dont know what Mark is doing. Thinking about me??? Like Im thinking about him???

I put more pictures from Sassy on the walls. I like the ones best when the girl is looking like she isnt too happy. I think maybe she had a big fight with her boy friend and they broke up. I think hes probably a major babe and shes sorry and wants him back. But I know thats just the picture. The girl is really happy because shes getting to ware such great close and shes real skinny and beautiful too. I had this dreem last night I was a model and got to be on the cover and had a limozeen and neat stuff. Actualy I was the most beautiful model in the world and my hair wasnt messy and my thise werent fat. Lisa was so jelous she tried to break the window on my limozeen but she couldnt and my body-gard told her to fuck off. I laffed like—

Diary, I just got interupted by my jerky father because of my science project. Like it isnt doo for a million years but he wants to start today!!! I said no Im too busy cant you see that? He said I was procras-something—a real long word. I said so what. He said he was disapoynted. So who cares? You know something? I once thot my father was cute like Sean Penn or something. Isnt that weerd? Hes getting fat and bald and his eyebrows are real thick and the hairs go all over the place. Gross and grosser.

I wish something wuld happen. Like Im so bored I could screem!!!

Bye for now.

"EVERYONE ELSE'S ALLOWANCE IS MORE than mine."

"I doubt that."

"Lisa gets twenty-five dollars."

"Daddy and I can't afford twenty-five dollars a week," I say.

"You know what my allowance is?" Emma says. "Fucking peanuts."

"I don't like that expression. Where did it come from?"

"Nowhere."

I continue pegging Emma's jeans. Her legs are so thin we can never find tight enough. I'm reminded, as I pin the legs, of the fights my mother and I had about my skirts when I was the same age as Emma and hemlines were rising. Our fights were loud and bitter. I would stand, angry and impatient, in a half-finished skirt, while my mother knelt before me, her mouth spiked with pins. She had a hemmer, a tall metal device with a floor base and upper calipers shaped like the beak of a crane. This beak grasped the bottom of my skirt and allowed my mother to insert a pin at the length she had decided was appropriate and I always thought too long. The territory over which we battled was measured in inches, half inches, quarter inches, and finally thread widths. We screamed until my father was forced to intervene. "Now, Jane," he would say, "you're upsetting your mother. Let's take it a little easier now, shall we?"

How proud I am that I don't fight with my daughter over the shortness of her skirts or the tightness of her jeans. Proud that I'm not petty. Proud that I don't repeat the patterns of the past.

Mother love. While I sought it, unhappily wondering if I was different from everyone else, it was actually growing and flourishing right under my nose, hidden in the nooks and crannies of my daily life. Who could guess that love was folded into the freshly washed pile of diapers? Or that it was caught in the drops of water that glittered on the wall when Emma splashed in her bath?

"Here," I say, inserting the last pin at the bottom of one leg, "try them on now."

"Those pins are going to scratch me!"

"Inside out, Em. Try them on inside out."

She puts them on gingerly, hopping from one foot to the other. Her legs are the longest part of her. Her feet are pale and narrow.

"Okay," I say, when she's finally standing still, "how does that feel?"

"They're too baggy."

Not knowing that love was so close by, I was ignorant of the moment when it became a part of me. I only noticed that I had gradually stopped feeling like a baby-sitter, that I no longer had the sensation I was feeding and dressing some- one else's baby.

I refrain from pointing out that each pant leg is one-half inch from stopping her blood circulation and obediently kneel on the floor beside her and begin to adjust pins. As I do so, I give in to my curiosity and ask, "How was Terry yesterday?"

"Terry's okay."

"What did you do?"

"Nothing different."

"You do the same thing every time you go there?"

"It's right after school, Mom. How many things can we do?"

"I don't know. I was just wondering. Does she give you a snack?"

"I told you she did."

"Milk and cookies," I say. "You should tell her that car- rot sticks are healthier."

"I hate carrot sticks."

And then one day, about six months after we'd brought Emma home, I discovered that the other woman, the one who hovered just beyond Emma's face, was no longer present. I didn't celebrate this disappearance. I didn't trust in magic anymore. I thought she might come back, and I was right. She returned now and then, elusive and dreamlike, just beyond my vision.

"Do you talk?"

"M-o-m."

"Well, about what?"

"Just things."

"Such as?"

"I don't remember."

"Do you talk about school?"

"Yeah, I guess so."

"And family?"

"I told you, I can't remember everything. I'm not a tape recorder, you know."

"Well, does Terry work?"

"Yeah."

"At what?"

"At Loblaws." Emma studies her reflection in the long mirror on her door. "It's too loose below my knee."

"Does she like it?"

"I guess so."

I move a pin. "What's she like—personality-wise?"

"She's nice. She's kind of like me in a way."

"What way?"

"She likes the same music."

I like Emma's music too. Sometimes. "What else does she like?"

"Lots of things, I guess."

At first her visits were regular, but then like postcards from some friend who has moved far away, her presence became less frequent and more sporadic. These later visits were hardly noticeable at all. Her substance had thinned, her outline fading into the air.

"Daddy and I would like to meet her." Emma's leg jerks away and I rock back on my heels. "What's the matter?"

"I don't want you to meet her!"

"Why not?"

"I just *don't*!"

"Em, what could be bad about it?"

"Mom, I don't want you to. Isn't that enough?"

"If she's important to you, then she's important to us."

"Mom, this is my thing! It's mine!"

"We aren't going to interfere."

"*Mom!* I don't want you to!"

I work carefully through a thicket of words. "Em, put yourself in our shoes. This isn't just something we can ignore."

"No!" There are tears in her eyes. "*No!*"

"Emma! Please. I'm just trying to figure out what's the best thing to do. That's all."

"*Mom!*"

"It is not necessary to yell. My hearing is not impaired."

"Mom?" I can hear the effort Emma is making to sound reasonable. "Maybe later, okay? Just not right now."

I can be reasonable too. "Fine," I say reluctantly.

"Just promise me you won't try to see her now."

"Emma, I said I wouldn't."

"Promise?"

"Emma, for heaven's—"

"*Promise me!*"

By the time Emma was thirteen, I hadn't seen her real mother for several years, and I'd almost forgotten she existed. What a fool I was to let down my guard. To think that there was no such thing as magic or coincidence. When my back was turned, when I no longer looked over my shoulder, she reappeared, conjured up out of nowhere, the translucent made solid, illusion formed into flesh.

"I promise," I say. "Now come back here and let's finish these pants."

Emma studies her reflection again. The flush on her cheeks is slowly subsiding, but her hands are still clenched tightly at her sides. "They're still way too baggy. Pin them tighter. No, Mom, I told you—tighter!"

"All right!" I snap. "All right."

On the night of Emma's outburst, Philip and I are lying in bed. Our bedroom is my favorite room in the house. The floor is carpeted in pale blue, and the space is large enough to accommodate a queen-size bed, dressers, two wing chairs, and a small table. We had a fireplace put in during the renovations, and we have a fire almost every night during the winter. Climbing into my warm and toasty bed (courtesy of an electric blanket), while a fire spits and crackles, throwing an orangey yellow light on the walls, is as close to real luxury as I'm ever going to get, and I usually savor it. But tonight neither the room nor the dying fire soothes me.

Philip is reading the Men's Fashions supplement of the *New York Times*. He sighs frequently as he flips past pouting men, smiling men, and windblown men with unruffled hair. Generally, they are younger than Philip, or if they're middle-aged, they have thick gray hair and the photogenic skin of youth. I wonder if we're about to enter one of those twice-a-year periods in Philip's life when he decides to revamp his wardrobe. During these periods he rummages through his closet and drawers. Our bedroom is transformed, the chairs and bed piled high with pilled sweaters, worn pants, and jackets that he declares to be outdated and threadbare. Everything, he says, should go to the Sally Ann. But I am wiser and suggest we wait. I know what will happen when we go shopping: thrift will overtake fashion. Philip will be so horrified by the prices that he'll purchase one jacket—a blazer to go with the pants he already has—and some underwear.

"Philip?" I say.

He takes his eyes from a picture of a half-naked man with striking pectorals in a red leather jacket. "What?"

"I wonder if Des and Maureen might split."

"Why?"

"Des is pretty unhappy."

He turns a page. "Power Dressing," a headline announces. "Hmmm."

I study Philip's profile, the curve of his neck, the expanse of his bare chest, shaded with graying sandy hair. Age is thickening him in some places and thinning him in others. His chest is no longer flat and hard but slightly rounded, and his jaw has lost its fine edge. But his nose is more hawkish, the flesh tighter over the bridge, and the skin over his Adam's apple lies in folds, as if his neck has shrunk in width. On the days when Philip is very dear to me, I don't examine these details in a dispassionate way. I mark them sadly; I feel a gushing tenderness. On the days when he's just the stranger I sleep with, I notice the wrinkles, the creases of flesh, the sagging skin, in a clear-eyed way. So that's how it's going to be, I think. Well, too bad.

The emotional stage of my marriage is like a pendulum, its rate of swing capricious, unpredictable. Months can go by when I find Philip pleasurable. We make love more often, I laugh at his jokes, I take a proprietary interest in his work. Then, without warning, the pendulum swings and I find myself cohabiting with a stodgy, patronizing bore. Small things about him irritate me, we fight more often, I turn away from him in bed. There are also moments in our marriage—tonight is one—when the pendulum is not at either extreme and Philip is my closest friend, the repository of many of my most private thoughts and a good many of my friends' deepest and darkest secrets.

"Des told me his sex life is shitty."

Philip turns and looks at me. "He tells you things like that?"

"Not usually. That's why I think it must really be bad." Philip goes back to reading, and I put my hand over the page. "Philip, it would be like a death, wouldn't it? If their marriage ended?"

"If you want to know the truth, I've always thought Maureen and Des were ill-suited. They're too much alike. A typical pair of uptight English Canadians."

"You're English Canadian," I point out.

"I'm not half as uptight as Des Miller. The man walks around with a spike up his ass."

"He doesn't."

"I've never seen him laugh either."

"He has a quiet sense of humor."

"You've always liked Des more than I do." Philip removes my hand from the page and sighs as he looks down. "You know what it says in here? That these pants would go well with the white linen dinner jacket in my closet. There must be something wrong with my closet."

I glance at the page but say, "I told Emma I wanted to meet Terry. She got really upset. She made me promise we wouldn't."

Philip closes the magazine. "Emma's afraid we won't like Terry."

"She said that?"

"Jane, it's obvious. There's also a probability that *she* won't like *us*. Which would put Emma in a difficult position."

"But we have to meet her, don't we? She's going to be a major influence on Em."

"Maybe. Maybe not."

"Oh, Philip, how can she not? And what do we know about her and that . . . that boyfriend of hers? Where's he from, anyway? And what does he do for a living?"

"We'll find out eventually."

"And Emma's behavior is getting worse. I got another call from the school. She mouthed off to Mrs. Jonté and had to spend an afternoon in the principal's office."

"I agree it's troublesome and we'll have to talk to the teacher, but the behavior isn't necessarily related to her birth mother. It's teenage stuff."

"Maybe if she'd found her father instead of her mother, you'd feel differently."

"Maybe."

"Maybe you'd want to see that other father with your own eyes."

"Perhaps."

"Maybe you wouldn't want to be told to sit back and take it like a lump on a log!"

Philip ignores the rising crescendo of my voice. "Take what, exactly?"

But now I'm crying tears that have suddenly risen out of nowhere. Philip pulls me into his arms, and I sob for a while against his warm flesh.

"I don't know why I'm taking this so hard," I finally say, blowing my nose in a tissue.

"It'll be all right," Philip murmurs, kissing me.

"Am I building this up into something bigger than it is?"

"I think so." He pulls up my nightgown so that he can cup one of my breasts in his hand.

"But . . . bad things can happen. Can't they?"

"You're a pessimistic broad, but sexy. Does that help?"

I sniff. "Maybe."

He bends his head and takes one of my nipples in his mouth. Sex with Philip is like slipping into a pair of well-worn, comfy slippers. The look is no longer novel or intriguing, but the fit is just right.

I make one of those deep, shuddering sighs that come after a hard cry. "Would you turn off your light?" I ask.

When he does, the only illumination left in the room comes from the dying embers of the fire, a deep red-orange glow with glints of gold in the center.

DEAR DIARY,

Friday. Wether—sunny but cold. A zit on my nose. Gross.

Lisa was passing nots to Mark in school today. She thinks he likes her. Ha ha no chance. I told Peter she had a crosh on Cello. He told the Jello. The Jello laffed like a manyack. Then Dana told her who told Peter. She had a shit fit. What a nerd. There all stupid nerds. Yesterday the Jello said I was titless. Weener dick. Mom says I shuld give it time and Ill have brests soon. I say—how long? A million years? Lisa—that asshole doorknob—is always wearing see-threw to show off her bra.

Terry doesnt have much brests either. I guess thats wear I get it from. Heres all the ways I look and dont look like Terry—

LOOK LIKE   DONT LOOK LIKE

red hair   only frekles on my nose.
green eyes   longer hair
nose   more eyelashes
feet with narow heels

Theres the singing too. Terry says she wanted to be a singer her hole life long—just like me. Also she realy likes close and jewlrey and things I realy like. Mom and Dad read books all the time and Mom talks about the goverment and Dad talks about the univercity and they go to work and have realy boring lifes. They never go dansing or anything like that. When I grow up, Im never going to have a boring life. Never!

Bye for now.

I HAVEN'T BEEN ENTIRELY FAITHFUL TO Philip, and I don't know whether he's been faithful to me. When we were young and not yet married, we had one of those passionate discussions after making love in which we agreed that we would never be able to tolerate adultery, *never*. We were, we said as we lay naked in each other's arms, far too possessive. Philip said infidelity would kill his passion forever. I said my love for him would be utterly destroyed. If we were going to marry, we agreed, we were talking about vows of trust, total commitment, one hundred percent faithfulness for life. This did not, at the time, seem too much to ask.

I committed adultery during a conference I went to in Montreal in the early 1970s. It was sometime after we'd found out I was infertile, and I hated everything then: the house we lived in, my job, my supervisor, my clothes, my friends who were having children, and Philip because he had a normal sperm count. But most of all I hated myself and my inadequate loathsome body, which had fooled me for so many years. Years of messy menstrual cycles. Years of careful birth control. And all for nothing. I was a wasteland of useless tubes and organs. I'd long since stopped enjoying sex, and Philip had buried himself in work. I was unhappy, lonely, and isolated, unaware that I was easy pickings for an aggressive man with the right moves.

Stuart was unmarried and Australian, a big man with dark, springy hair, a strong accent, and a rough, familiar way about him. He liked to drink, laugh, and handle women. He was far more physical than the men I knew, patting me on the back when we first met, touching my arm when he wanted to make a point, brushing my cheek with his knuckles when I amused him. I responded to him because I like to touch, too, although I am generally careful not to do so. Canadians often misunderstand that sort of gesture.

At first I didn't take him seriously, but the conference went on for a week, and he made me laugh. I had almost forgotten how. My face felt like a mask that had hardened into place, and when Stuart made me laugh, lines cracked along my cheeks and at the corners of my eyes. We tumbled into bed on the fourth night of the conference, laughing at some joke he had made, and I didn't care that he wasn't as good a lover as Philip. For the first time in months my body responded to a man's touch, and I remembered that my female parts existed for a reason that had nothing to do with procreation. We made love three times, and then the conference was over. Stuart went back to Australia, and I returned to Ottawa, all the ends of the affair tied into a neat and tidy package.

Although I often forget about this act of adultery for long stretches of time, when I do think about it, I still feel guilty. I never planned to be unfaithful, and I believe I betrayed my marriage vows and abused Philip's faith in me. An innocence I had about marriage has also been destroyed. I don't trust myself anymore, and paradoxically I don't trust Philip, either. If I'm capable of adultery, I reason, then he is, too. I watch him more closely now, and when he goes to conferences I'm aware of all the temptations that might cross his path and all the pleasures in which he might indulge. Yet he usually returns home hungry for sex, and my suspicions disappear until the next time.

On the other hand, if Philip has ever been distrustful of me, he's never shown it. Not even when I returned from that conference in Montreal and seduced him as soon as he came home from work. Not even when I began to smile again and laugh and start talking about adopting. He never questioned the changes, only accepted them gratefully and gave me diamond earrings for our anniversary. Of course I didn't completely change overnight. I didn't give up being angry or grieving for the children I would never have, but it was as if I had walked through a doorway from a dark house into the shade of a tree. Now and then a ray of sunlight would work its way through the leaves to touch and warm my face.

I've never seen Stuart again. Occasionally I wonder where he is and how he's doing. I wonder if he's married and has children. Sometimes, when I'm in a crowded place like a shopping mall on Saturday or the theater lobby at intermission, I see a head of dark springy hair and a pair of broad shoulders and I get a shock of recognition. The sensation fades after the head turns and the face revealed is someone else's. But sometimes the shock lingers, like the taste of a heavy dark spice, and several days must pass before I forget him once again.

"WOULD YOU LIKE TO KNOW ABOUT YOUR father?" Terry asks. She and Emma are sitting at the kitchen table. She's drinking a beer and smoking a cigarette. Emma's drinking milk and eating from a plate of Oreos, Cinnamon Swirls, and Rainbow Chocolate Chips.

Emma's face lights up, and Terry knows she's hit pay dirt. It isn't easy being a mother to a kid you haven't seen in thirteen years. It has drawbacks, like the first time Emma came to the apartment and Terry could tell she'd never seen such a dump in her life but was too polite to say so. She sat with her back straight and her ankles crossed and asked if she could help clean up. Manners right out of a magazine like *Redbook* or *Family Circle*.

"What would you like to know?" Terry asks.

"Do you have any pictures of him?"

"No."

"Oh."

Emma lowers her eyes to avoid showing her disappointment, but her lower lip moves slightly forward and Terry recognizes one of her own expressions. It's weird when that happens, like she's been hit with a tiny bolt of lightning. The sensation goes right through her, leaving her breathless and slightly dizzy. Of course, it's nothing compared to what happened in the Rideau Centre. She was standing there brushing her hair, looking in the mirror but not really seeing herself. She was thinking about going to Eaton's and buying stockings when a motion in the mirror caught her eye. A girl with hair the same red as hers passed by and stood in front of the adjoining mirror. Terry knew who she was instantaneously, just like that. All the years of remembering and wondering, of marking birthdays that might have been and Mother's Days that passed uncelebrated, of holding close to her thoughts the daughter she'd never known, joined together into one moment that suddenly slipped from the real into the horrible when Terry believed that Emma had materialized from her own imagination.

Then Emma turned and Terry felt a hook catch in her

throat, snared by the way Emma's hair was held back from her temple by a white plastic barrette decorated with two pink hearts. It was like mirrors at the fun house. It was you—face the same shape, eyes the same green, noses with the same blunt thickness at the tip—but not you. Your face but not yours. Familiar features out of context, their lines altered, twisted, and changed. Emma had different eyebrows, fuller lashes, a squarer chin, fewer freckles.

For a moment they stared at each other. Emma was terrified. Terry recognized the way the skin stretched across her cheekbones and felt another of those minor bolts of lightning.

"How old are you?" she asked.

"Thirteen."

"Oh, my God," Terry said.

Emma burst into noisy sobs, and Terry put her arms around her. "It's okay, honeybunch, it's okay."

Now Terry pours Emma another glass of milk and watches while Emma drinks and then carefully wipes her mouth with a napkin. "I went to high school with your father. We were in history together. I thought he was really cute, and I wanted to go out with him. I told my friend, Charlene, and she told Bruce's friend Dennis, and that's how Bruce found out."

Terry doesn't tell Emma about going with Charlene to Bruce's house. It was on a quiet crescent a mile from Mechanicsville—a two-story house with brick on the first story and white clapboard on the second. The living room window had blue gauzy curtains looped to frame a large potted plant. Terry wore her tightest sweater, shortest skirt, and reddest lipstick. As they passed back and forth in front of the house, she and Charlene laughed loudly and shoved each other. Then a curtain flicked in one of the second-story windows and they broke into a run, giggling hysterically, stopping only when they reached the corner and could lean against a light post.

"That was his bedroom," Charlene said, gasping. She was a heavy, sloppy girl with a spray of pimples across her chin. Her blouses were always edging out of her skirts, and her shoes were worn at the outside edges because she walked with a slight waddle. Charlene never had any boyfriends of her own and got a vicarious thrill out of Terry's love life.

"It was his bedroom," Charlene said again.

"It was not."

"It was so."

"How can you tell?"

"I just can."

"You're full of it."

"He was up there dreaming about you."

"Fuck off, Charlene."

Charlene closed her eyes, held a clenched fist to her ample breasts, and swayed in imitation of an imagined Bruce. "Terry, my love, my darling, my sweetheart."

"Asshole," Terry said and shoved Charlene off the sidewalk.

Now she says to Emma, "He asked me to a party. It was wonderful. We danced all night. First in the living room and then out onto the balcony in the moonlight." Terry punches out her cigarette, gets up, and demonstrates slow-dancing with an imaginary partner. When Emma laughs, she embellishes on the dance, dipping and swaying and twirling. "He was a lot taller than me, and my head came below his shoulder."

Terry hums and remembers. She couldn't quite believe she'd made it to this party and into his arms, because it wasn't the sort of party Terry Petrie got invited to. She also remembers the bottles of gin and the cooler full of beer and the joint that was passed around, and growing dizzy from the drinking and the sweet, acrid taste of the smoke in her mouth and the way Bruce started feeling her up as the lights got lower and the music got louder.

"You gonna come to the football game on Saturday?" he murmured in her ear.

She looked up at him and, oh, his eyes were so blue and their lashes so dark and his shoulders so broad and she knew she was in love. "Maybe."

He kissed her, his tongue filling her mouth, his erection pressing against that concave spot just above her pubic bone, and the beat of the music entered her, throbbing, throbbing in that place between her legs. Somehow they drifted into the bedroom, just recently vacated by another couple, and somehow, without her being quite aware of it, they fell onto the bed and out of their clothes.

"Did you love him?" Emma says.

Terry closes her eyes and dips and sways again. "I was nuts about him," she says.

"Did he love you?"

"He gave me a ring. I wore it on a chain around my neck."

She also remembers what a big secret that was, because Bruce said his parents didn't like the idea of him going steady at such a young age. Terry knew what they wouldn't like was Bruce going steady with *her*. But she told Charlene she didn't care that they had to sneak around, because Bruce really loved her and had told her so a million times.

"How does he say it?" Charlene had asked.

"What do you mean, how does he say it?"

"Like is he really emotional?"

"Jesus, Charlene. What do you think? He says it like he's talking to his dog?"

Actually Bruce never said he loved her. He just wanted to make love to her. So they didn't go to the movies too often or out to dinner. Mostly Bruce would park on a dirt road outside of town, and they'd climb into the back seat and start kissing, although Bruce didn't have much time for preliminaries because his parents believed in early curfews. So pretty soon her blouse was unbuttoned and her bra was up around her throat and her panties were down at her ankles and she was lying at an uncomfortable angle with her head jammed in between the back of the seat and the door handle. She didn't cry out when he bit her nipples too hard or at the sharp pain in her back when he pounded into her, because it was a small price to pay for the privilege of being his girl and being able to hang around with the other girlfriends at football practice, complaining about the cold and the bleachers' hard seats and the boredom.

"And then I got pregnant with you," Terry says. She sits down, lights another cigarette, and blows two jets of smoke out of her nose.

Emma has her hand over her mouth, and the tears are starting. Terry feels her own throat constrict. She hasn't cried about this in years, although she cried buckets then. Buckets when her mother cried. Buckets when Charlene dropped her and latched on to another friend. Buckets when her father slapped her so hard she fell backwards against the kitchen counter, gashed open her upper arm, and had to go to Emergency. But she didn't cry when she told Bruce one night while the car sat idling on the dirt road. He went completely ashen, his skin taking on a sickly gray tone.

"You can't be," he said.

"Well, I am."

"We used rubbers."

"They're not a hundred percent."

"Fuck," he said. "Fuck. Fuck." And with each "fuck," his fist slammed against the wheel. "Can't you get something done?"

"It's too late."

"What do you mean, it's too late?"

"I'm almost five months." Five months because she had ignored all the signs, hoping that it would go away. Of course, it hadn't.

"What am I going to do?"

"What about me?" Terry asked. "I've got a life, too."

"My parents are going to kill me," he said, and leaning his forehead against the steering wheel, he began to cry.

But Terry doesn't tell Emma this, either, or how Bruce was whisked out of Ottawa so fast that it was now you see him, now you don't. His parents shipped him to somewhere in northern Alberta, and when Terry's father went to see them, they said they couldn't be sure the baby was Bruce's because Terry had a reputation for sleeping around. Terry doesn't tell Emma about dropping out of school right after that and the horrible boring months of being at home, fighting with her mother, and spending hours watching the soaps. Nor does she tell Emma that she ripped Bruce's class picture into pieces and flushed it down the toilet, watching his left eye, right nostril, a section of blemished cheek, and the curl of brown hair over his forehead swirl around the bowl before being sucked into the sewer.

"Did you want to get married?" Emma whispers.

"We had to break up," Terry says.

"But you loved each other."

"We were too young to handle it."

"It's so sad," Emma says with a wail, but she's crying so hard now that the words are mixed with the tears and a half-chewed Oreo, and Terry's crying, too, and when Mic comes in, he stands in the doorway to the kitchen and stares at the two of them, hugging and rocking back and forth, their faces wet and shiny.

"Jesus frigging Christ," he says. "Who turned on the waterworks?"

THE MORNING AFTER PHILIP AND I MADE LOVE, I wake up with a sore throat and a headache. "That's why I was so emotional," I say to Philip as he is dressing. "That's what it was all about."

"Mom! M-o-m, where's my sneakers?" Emma throws open the door to our bedroom.

"Have you ever heard of knocking?"

"Sorry. Do you know where my sneakers are?"

"No."

"Mom, I need them for gym!"

"Then you'll have to go look for them."

She's reached the point of wailing. "But I don't know where they *are*!"

There have been too many last-minute panics, too many cries of "Wolf!" for me to be concerned. Besides, I feel feverish. "That's your problem," I say, turning over and curling back up under the blankets.

After Philip has gone to work and Emma has finally left for school, sneakers discovered in the downstairs closet, the house is quiet and I get up. It's snowing out, but there's no wind and the flakes fall thickly and straight down. Our street has very little traffic, and the peace is broken only once by a Francis Fuels truck delivering oil to a neighbor. I call in sick to my office, take aspirin, and stare out the windows. The wind has picked up, and the snow is blowing almost horizontally now, hitting the glass like small pellets. I contemplate the weather and feel the weight of a customary depression. I followed Philip to Canada with enthusiasm and curiosity only to receive in return the dreary Ottawa winters. At first I tried to enjoy myself. I took up skiing, I went to skating parties. But nothing helped me with the tediously gray days, the long cold nights, and the unrelenting, vehement, pervasive chill. After Ulan Bator, Outer Mongolia, Ottawa is the coldest capital in the world. A dubious distinction. If I'd known that, I wonder, would I have married Philip and come here? Probably. Love was so hot then, I thought it could melt anything. I hadn't counted on the reality: blowing snow that pricks and cuts the skin, Arctic blasts that turn the inside of the nose numb, frozen fingers and dry itchy skin, snow piled to the height of a man, and salted streets that rot boots and cars.

My winter depression is like a flock of migrating birds. Every November it arrives and settles heavily onto my spirit until late spring when it lifts and flies off. I lack energy in the winter. I'm subject to headaches and colds and anxieties. As I wander upstairs, I think that maybe Philip is right, maybe I am making too much out of this business with Emma and her birth mother. Nothing has changed, has it? Emma still goes to school and comes home. She does her homework and practices the piano. And the defiance is just a natural part of adolescence. I think of the ups and downs Alice has with her two teenagers. Emma's no different, is she?

I open the door to Emma's bedroom and am assailed by the mess and the darkness. She's decided to redecorate and create, as far as I can make out, a cave. The white of the walls is blocked by hundreds of pictures cut from *Sassy, Elle,* and *Mademoiselle.* The pictures feature slender pretty girls modeling clothes. They stand with legs outstretched, arms flung high, and heads tilted back. Emma had Philip put up a full-length mirror on her wall, and she's draped its corners with necklaces and chains so that she sees herself framed in gold and silver. I stand in front of the mirror and see that I am surrounded by reflections of beautiful women. I imagine Emma imitating modeling postures, trying on the smiles and sexy pouts.

The pale pink and green colors I once chose as charming and girlish have been replaced by opaque, light-denying shades. Her bedspread is a dark green duvet, and her curtain is a huge Indian black and mauve paisley scarf she found in the basement. This scarf is never pulled back but filters the light in such a way that the room appears to be in eternal dusk. My own need for sunlight is so strong I can't understand why Emma finds it an intrusion, but I do remember how I, too, at thirteen decided to make my bedroom my own. Prior to that it had merely been a place to sleep in and change my clothes. Then, suddenly, it became an extension of myself, the only part of the house that I found comfortable. Like Emma, I spent hours in my room. The only thing is, I can no longer remember what it was I did there, only that when my parents and brothers knocked on the door, I'd scream, "Leave me alone!"

I restrain an urge to pull the scarf back from the window and instead start to tidy up. There are clothes in bundles on the floor, and the desk is piled high with papers and cosmetics. I make the bed and find a book under the pillow— Emma's diary. When we gave Emma the diary, she was entranced by the tiny gold lock and key, opening and closing it a dozen times. I wonder if she realizes how flimsy the lock is and how vulnerable her secrets are. I wonder if the contents of the diary would shock me.

My mother once read a letter written to me in high school by a lovesick boy, which she had discovered while cleaning my room. When she couldn't resist divulging one of its more flamboyant phrases to me, I became furious.

"Oh, for heaven's sake, Jane," my mother said. "I just thought it was funny."

"Who said you could read it?" I screamed.

"It was sitting plain as day on your desk."

"Who said you have the right to go through my *things*?"

My father arrived on the scene and told me to go straight to my room until I came to my senses.

"It was private! She didn't have permission!"

"Right now, young lady. I mean immediately, do you understand?"

I vowed then that I would never do that to a child of mine. I wouldn't go through drawers and shelves. I'd never read anything without asking permission first. With my fifteen-year-old self carefully watching, I put the diary back under the pillow, unopened and unread, and pulled up the sheets and blankets, smoothing the bedspread and tucking in the edges.

Emma's room is like a mountain made of sedimentary rock that has heaved and faulted. The accumulation of her past interests and ambitions lie not one on top of the other in an orderly time sequence but jammed together, their chronology broken and jumbled. Ceramic and glass animals, a collection begun when she was five years old and wanted to be a veterinarian, lie next to a stack of Broadway show albums and tapes of singers like Tiffany, Madonna, and George Harrison. Stuffed animals, former confidants and sleeping companions, sit on a shelf, their backs against posters of current heartthrobs like Michael J. Fox, Tom Cruise, and Don Johnson.

Although my headache is getting worse, I can't resist the urge to bring order out of chaos. I place several batches of paper in neat piles. I put loose pencils and pens in a drawer. I uncover our long-lost kitchen stapler and my spool of white thread languishing beneath the top of a shoebox on her dresser. I sigh but refuse to allow my irritation to rise above a low murmur. I plug in her lamp—where does she do her homework?—and move it back to the left-hand corner of the desk. A notebook falls to the floor, and as I pick it up, more papers fall out of it, scribbled notes and scraps with cartoon drawings on them. Sighing once again, I kneel down to retrieve them. I find an old Mother's Day card, handmade by Emma when she first started school. I open it and read the poem inside, written in big block letters:

MY MOTHER

These are the things my mother does.
She takes care of me.
She helps me when I'm hurt and crying.
She washes my clothes and makes sure I eat right.
She tells me stories.
She tucks me into bed.
She kisses me good-night.
When I have bad dreams she comes into my room and
    gives me a big hug.
I love my mother very much because she is a special
    person.

XOXOXOXO

Love, Emma Wastenay
Age 7, Grade 2

Tears come to my eyes, and I think Alice is right. How can Emma forget these things just because another woman has entered her life? Why should I feel so threatened? I put the card in my bathrobe pocket and lean over to pick up a photograph lying face down on the carpet.

It is a fuzzy Polaroid of three people: a man, a woman, and Emma. It isn't a good photograph; it's been taken by someone with no skill in composition. The scene is too crowded and shot at a slight angle. The man and woman are standing side by side against a background of cluttered kitchen counters and open cupboard doors. They are barefoot, their toes pressing on white linoleum patterned with gold swirls, and they are smiling into the camera lens. The man is dressed in tight jeans and a blue T-shirt that has "Molson's Lite" in black script across the chest. He has blond hair that curls to his shoulders. The woman, who is the same height as Emma, is dressed in jeans and a white T-shirt and has long hair the shade of hot red pepper.

Emma stands between the two of them. She is wearing a red turtleneck and her white corduroy pants with the huge blue and green swirls.

I think, I really can't stand those pants.

Emma and the woman are smiling, and the woman's left hand rests casually on her shoulder.

I think, That linoleum is so ugly.

Then I find I am crouched over the photograph, aching head bent, knees brought to my chest, breathing shallow and uneven.

I think, This is utterly ridiculous, but I'm gripping the photograph so tight the muscles in my hand begin to shake. I try to stop the shaking, but my hand won't unclench, and a sharp pain shoots up into my wrist. In the meantime, their smiles flutter at me like trembling crescent moons, and their faces shift rapidly back and forth in ever wider swings until the edges of their flesh blur and the smiles merge into one.

Part II

DECEMBER 1988

ONE EVENING WHILE I'M WATCHING A DOCU-
mentary on the Baby M trial with Philip, I
remember the first time I realized that all
mothers were not the same. It was the winter
I was ten years old, and a school friend,
Susan Felsher, invited me to go sledding on Prospect Hill.
This hill, which wasn't in our town but a half hour's drive
away, was steep and wide and had a reputation as the best
sledding hill for miles around. My mother didn't know the
Felshers very well, but I begged her to let me go and offered
to take my brother Derek. Derek was then four years old, an
annoying tagalong whose presence I rarely tolerated. My
unexpected generosity tipped the scales in my favor, and
mother phoned Mrs. Felsher and confirmed the arrangement.

As it turned out we were a foursome—Susan and her
twelve-year-old sister, Janet, Derek and I. We all wore
woolen snowsuits, caps with earflaps, mittens on strings,
and rubber boots that fit over our shoes. Mrs. Felsher drove
a large blue station wagon with plastic panels on the sides
that looked like wood. Janet sat up front reading a book
while Susan, Derek, and I sat in the back seat and played I
Spy and a numbers game based on the license plates of other
cars.

What do I remember about Mrs. Felsher? Very little. She
smoked and drove and listened to the radio. The noise we
made, the occasional screeches at pinches and shoves,
didn't bother her. She never once looked back. She had
brown hair carefully styled into a flip I admired, and she
wore perfume with a musky smell I didn't like. She was
neither big enough nor small enough to make an impression.
She was just another friend's mother, a pourer of milk and

a donor of cookies, the shadowy figure behind Susan who either obstructed or facilitated our plans. I remember Susan much better. She had enviable braids, thick and a lustrous brown, lots of freckles, and the ability to stick out her tongue and curl it. She and Janet also had gleaming new sleds, which they'd gotten for Christmas. My sled had once belonged to my older brother Murray and was made of wooden slats with the name Easy Glider written across them in flowing but chipped red paint. It also had crossbars, for controlling the rusty iron runners, which I had to push either to the left or to the right with all my might to make the sled turn. But I was determined not to let the superiority of Susan's sled ruin my afternoon. When Mrs. Felsher let us off, saying she would be back in an hour, I was the first out of the car, the first up the hill, and the first to whoosh down its icy slope, my eyes tearing from the wind.

Time meant very little to me then, and I wasn't aware of the lowering of the sun and the lengthening of the shadows until Derek came up to me and said he had to go pee. Even I could tell then that more than an hour had passed since Mrs. Felsher drove away. I found Susan and asked her when her mother would come back. "Soon," she said and took off down the hill again.

Then I looked for Janet, who had joined a group of girls. "Is it time for your mother to come?" I asked.

"I don't know," she said with a shrug and turned her back on me.

"Janey? Janey, I hafta pee," Derek said. His nose was running, yellow mucus dribbling onto his upper lip. His mittens were wet, and his teeth were chattering.

"Put a knot in it," I said and, throwing myself on my sled, left him behind in a spray of snow.

But there was no getting away from him. When I got back to the top of the hill, he was waiting for me, crying, his tears mixing with the yellow dribble. "Janey," he blubbered. "Janey."

"Crybaby," I hissed.

"I gotta go!"

The shadows of the surrounding pine trees were mauve on the snow, and the wind had picked up. My pants were sodden, my toes were cold inside their casings of leather and rubber, and I also began to feel that pricking of pressure inside my bladder. I spotted Susan, arriving at the top of the hill, pulling her sled behind her. "Susan! We want to go home," I said.

Susan readied her sled on the snow and then glanced at Derek, who was now wailing. "What's wrong with him?"

"He has to go to the bathroom."

"Oh." She flopped down on the sled.

"Your mom said she'd be here in an hour!"

Susan pushed off with her foot, the words flying in disjointed syllables over her shoulder as she picked up speed going down the hill. "May . . . be . . . she . . . for . . . got!"

I remember that I stood in horror, as if a dark chasm had opened just before my feet. *Forgot?* How could a mother forget? *My* mother would never forget. I was too important; even whiny, irritating Derek was too important. Our mother never stopped thinking of us. Oh, she might do other things when we weren't there—shop, cook, clean—but those activities were only sideshows to the main event in her life: *us*—me, Murray, Derek, Brent. Worrying about us, thinking about us, taking care of us. When I thought about me not being important to my mother, I had the same terrifying sensation I felt when I contemplated the stars through my father's telescope. He'd bought the telescope at an estate sale, and for a while we were all struck with a frenzy for stargazing. I would look and look into the blackness, at the glittering stars, dizzy from trying to understand the distances and afraid when I realized I could keep on looking deeper and deeper and never see an end. . . .

The television flickers with images as figures pour out of a courthouse. First the camera focuses on Elizabeth Stern, then Mary Beth Whitehead. If I squint at the screen, they could be sisters. Mary Beth's hair is the same color as Elizabeth's, only fuller. She has the same bangs on a broader brow, the same chin-length cut framing a prettier face. Mary

Beth stands before a bank of microphones. A reporter asks her if it's true she once separated from her husband and worked as a go-go dancer. She shakes her head, and her dark hair swings from side to side. "I did nothing I'm ashamed of," she says. "We've had our problems, but not anything we haven't been able to deal with." I think of Mrs. Felsher, who drove a station wagon, who served plates of cookies, who had a comfortable, unexceptional appearance.

"Did I ever tell you about the time Derek and I were abandoned on a sledding hill by my friend's mother?" I ask Philip.

"Uh-uh," he says.

"She forgot to come and get us because she was drunk. She was a secret drinker. Vodka. Bloody Marys. My mother found out later."

"Hmmm," Philip says, his eyes on the screen.

I solved the problem that afternoon by taking Derek by the hand, walking down the hill into a subdivision of houses, and knocking on doors until a sympathetic woman (a mother?) let us use her bathroom and telephone. Her house was warm, and she offered us chocolate milk and crackers, but Derek and I knew better than to accept food from a stranger. We walked back to the bottom of the hill and stood there shivering until my mother arrived in her station wagon, bearing a thermos of hot cocoa and warm blankets, and wrapping us in concern and indignation.

Now I watch as Elizabeth Stern hurries past the reporters, clutches her husband's arm, and ducks her head. Mary Beth Whitehead turns toward the courtroom and shifts to avoid walking into a cameraman. Her hair swings and swoops, hiding her profile and then revealing it, hiding then revealing. It's like the game mothers play with their children: *now I see you, now I don't.*

DEAR DIARY,

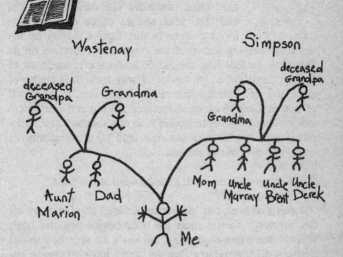

Wastenay

deceased Grandpa   Grandma

Aunt Marion   Dad

Me

Simpson

deceased Grandpa

Grandma

Mom   Uncle Murray   Uncle Brent   Uncle Derek

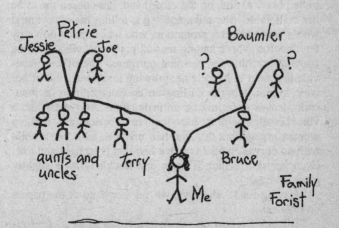

Petrie

Jessie   Joe

aunts and uncles   Terry

Me

Baumler

?   ?

Bruce

Family Forist

Bye for now.

OTTAWA IN DECEMBER: A COLD TEDIUM OF gray skies broken by the occasional day of hard clear sunshine. The canal froze solid early this year, and my office window overlooks a scene of tiny figures skating on the ice. I'm studying a map of the Arctic and reflecting on its absurdity. In real life, the Arctic landscape is made up of rocky plains broken by the jut of gray rock and patches of snow and ice. Cartographic reality is different. In the world of mapmaking, geological features are colored in tropical shades. Tundra is the turquoise blue of a southern sea, rocky plains as hot pink as a tea rose, and bleak mountains as warm and brilliant as the sun.

"Jane?"

I look up and see Madeleine Kendall at the door.

"Can I come in?"

I don't answer, but Madeleine Kendall slips into my office anyway. As she shuts the door behind her, my heart sinks. I don't like Madeleine, but she's the secretary to our division director, Barry Pearson, and I have no choice but to be pleasant. She, on the other hand, has chosen me to be her confidante. She talks and talks, telling me everything: who's going to get a promotion, who was dressed down by the director, who's having marital problems, who used the copying machine for personal purposes. The office grapevine is rooted in Madeleine, growing luxuriantly out of her wide mouth, tendrils curling on an exaggeration or innuendo, leaves unfurling on an insinuation. And she's like a vine herself, twining into the chair beside my desk, a woman my age but thin and half my size, built like a child with no curves and pale orange hair that is straight and fine. Even her skin, which is pasty and freckled, has a slightly greenish hue.

"Having fun?" she says, waving her hand at the papers on my desk.

"Bilosky's report on the Arctic. It has to go to peer review."

"Bilosky's such a windbag."

"I've got to get it done," I say. "Deadline's tomorrow."

Madeleine doesn't take the hint. She yawns and then sighs. "What a day."

I'm not deceived by her show of exhaustion. Madeleine has bright blue eyes, and when her sap runs thick with gossip, they gleam through their orange fringe of lashes. I put down my pen to listen.

"You're not going to believe this," she says. "After all those cutbacks last year, they're planning to chop another twenty PYs from the branch."

A PY is a person-year, governmentese for a job.

"Well, that's nothing new," I say. Treasury Board always wants the department to cut back; our directors are always trying to maintain or augment their turf. Meetings are frequent, and memos fly back and forth in a blitz of paper. This is the bureaucratic way.

"It was crisis time at the executive meeting this morning," Madeleine says. "Of course it's the ADM's fault."

ADM is governmentese for assistant deputy minister, the bureaucrat who tops our division the way a maraschino cherry tops an ice cream soda.

"He didn't fight hard enough for the branch," Madeleine goes on. "That's what Barry told him. He was so furious he said it right out. To his face. 'Science always has to take it on the nose, while goddamned policy gets fatter every day. We're getting shafted.' "

Madeleine doesn't attend executive meetings, but she always knows what goes on behind their closed doors. I haven't been able to figure out where the leak is. Is it Celine who works in an office adjoining Madeleine's and who's a close friend of Marie-Jeanne, the ADM's executive assistant? Is it Pierre Tremblay, division director of geophysics, who fancies himself a ladies' man and is often indiscreet? Or is it much closer to home—our own director, who should know better but likes to be affable and chummy with staff?

"When isn't there a crisis?" I ask.

"And Belson and McGregor refuse to take retirement." Madeleine wears a large collection of silver bangle bracelets, and they are clinking as she waves her thin hands in the air. "Barry's practically begged them on hands and knees, but no, after thirty-five years and a full pension they still want to keep doing science. Puttering is more like it, really. Belson is so arthritic he can hardly walk down the hall, much less go out in the field. And McGregor, I swear he's an alcoholic. You walk into his office and the smell could knock you over."

"No one can force them to retire," I say. "It's against the law."

"Barry can't count on attrition this time, and he's trimmed just about everywhere already. So, I ask myself, where can he turn? Well, it's obvious, isn't it? Between the hiring freeze and letting go so much support staff, we're already short secretaries."

I'm slow today. It takes me a moment to realize that, despite the funereal downturn of Madeleine's mouth and the concerned, querulous tone of her voice, the characteristic gleam in her eyes has intensified—a high-octane flare of rumor and speculation. It takes me yet another moment to understand that gleam is focused directly on me.

"Are you trying to tell me," I say, "that Barry is going to cut editorial staff?"

"He hasn't said so directly, but Jane, what else can he do? Cartography is down to the limit and Printing isn't much better, so what's left?"

I won't give her the satisfaction of seeing my sudden alarm. Instead I give a careless shrug. "I'll believe it when it happens."

Madeleine doesn't like having her gossip refuted. "The memo came from the top. Signed and sealed. Twenty PYs and that's that."

"It can come from God," I say, "but until the pink slip arrives on my desk, I won't believe it." The metaphorical pink slip, announcing that one's services were unfortunately no longer required by the Government of Canada / Gouvernement du Canada. What could I do if a letter of dismissal actually arrived? I'm not bilingual, I'm not Canadian, and English editors are a dime a dozen.

Madeleine leans forward, her bracelets clattering against my desk. "If I told Barry once, I told him a thousand times he should get you off term and into a permanent position. It's a crying shame—you'd have had some union protection that way."

I'm thankful Madeleine's grapevine hadn't yet wound its way into Barry's office on the day I asked to be given permanent status. He had hemmed and hawed, fidgeted with his pen, refused to look me in the eye. "Yes, well, I know what you're saying . . . would love to do the right thing by you . . . budget constraints . . . austerity programming . . . unfortunate decisions . . . nothing personal . . . highly valuable to our division . . ." and on and on and on, while I seethed with fury and frustration.

"If you were permanent, they'd be forced to give you six months," Madeleine continues. "They'd have to put you on the surplus list. Now you know what's going to happen?"

There's no need to answer. I glance out the window as the sun breaks through the clouds. The ice glitters like diamonds.

"You'll get fired." Her bracelets are jingling like crazy. Her lashes flutter, little orange brushes gone mad. "And all you'll get is two weeks' notice."

"Madeleine, I've got to get this paper ready."

She stands up and walks to the door. "Oh, I know I don't win any popularity contests being the bearer of bad news. You know what they did in the old days? Killed the messenger. Cut off his head. But would people rather wait and find out at the last minute when the ax actually falls? Oh, no. Then they're angry and put out. 'Why didn't you warn me, Madeleine?' they say. 'If I'd known, I could've prepared myself.' I never get any real thanks, that's what I've discovered. No thanks at all." And she makes a dramatic, flouncing exit, leaving behind a faint scent of honeysuckle.

But I don't go back to work on Bilosky's paper right away. The wind rattles my window, and I look at those posters of the Mediterranean. I really should take them down, I think. They're old and dated. Maybe the sea isn't that blue anymore; maybe the sky has turned gray and dismal. Maybe it's snowing in Greece, white flakes falling on those timeless white ruins.

I reach out to pull the first one down, but my fingers just brush the shiny paper surface. I know it's not snowing in Greece. That sunlit reality is as fixed in its place as mine is held in this room, this job, this life I have chosen. What an odd word, I think. *Chosen.* The girl with all those fantasies never chose this. She simply followed something: a pathway? a line provided by fate? No, nothing even as dramatic as that—just the trail made by Philip's own ignorant footsteps. And she was such a stumbler, that girl. She tripped and lurched from one moment to the next, barely noticing the important junctures, only dimly aware of the crucial turns.

But if, through all the following and stumbling, I've arrived at a questionable destination, this doesn't mean I have any intention of moving on. My shackles are firmly, if invisibly, in place. I'm the product of my parents, and I know that while an apple may roll and bounce a bit, it doesn't fall far from its tree. My father sold insurance—"Be prudent with Prudential"—and my mother was a vigorous nester, turning each of our houses into her version of a *House and Garden* home. I was brought up to plan for the future, to appreciate nice things in orderly circumstances. And I swallowed, along with the tall glasses of milk and the cinnamon toast, aphorisms coined in other, more naive eras. A penny saved is a penny earned. The early bird gets the worm. Can I help it if I like a solid savings account? A regular job? Friends I've known for years? A husband who comes home after work?

I look down at the papers spread out on my desk and words jump up at me: *terrain, sedimentary, glacial till.* I think about stone sliding on stone, about layers of rock, about the millennia of Canadian Shield beneath my feet. From that angle of perspective, my life seems to be nothing more than ordinary debris—dust ground by time into a powder so light and fine that if I were to blow on it, the particles would rise and float forever, fanning endlessly outward into dark space.

MIC'S FRIEND BUDDY SHOWS UP FOR DINNER just about three or four nights a week. It drives Terry crazy, because he doesn't wait for an invitation or call in advance to ask if he's welcome. He just shows up at the door, walks right in, and sits at the table. Neither he nor Mic notices the way Terry slaps the plate of macaroni and cheese down in front of him.

"Get Bud a beer, will you, Ter?" Mic says, and the two of them immediately fall into a deep conversation about vehicles. Terry can't stand Buddy. She can't stand his narrow pale face, the acne scars on his cheekbones, the dark grease under his fingernails, and the way he pulls his dark hair back in a ponytail to cover a bald spot. Most of all, she can't stand the fascination he seems to have for Mic. Lately Mic's deals seem to revolve around cars, and it's always Hondas this and GMs that, and cylinders this and carburetors that. He and Buddy talk about buying and selling motorbikes, cars, and trucks: "moving wheels" is what they call it.

"Lloyd knows a guy with a Caddy. He says it's in really good shape," Buddy says. He takes a big forkful of macaroni and chews with his mouth open. Terry looks away in disgust.

"That motherfucker can't tell the difference between his ass and a hole in the ground," Mic says.

"He got that great LTD."

"He's a bigmouth."

"His connections are good. His father owns that insurance company."

"Lloyd isn't one of us, Bud. I don't want to deal with him."

"Okay, okay," says Buddy, throwing up his hands in surrender, but he gives Terry a sly smile as if he knows something she doesn't, and that makes her hate him even more.

"Ter, the beer."

"He knows where it is," she says.

Buddy shakes his head as Mic goes to refrigerator. "You think this woman is a slave, man?"

Mic grins at Buddy, leans over, and pats Terry on the cheek. "This woman is going to be in the big time. This woman's got talent."

Buddy sits down and opens his beer. "So, Ter, how's the checkout factory?"

"Still standing," Terry says.

"And the kid?"

Mic has taken out two bottles of beer. He puts one in front of Buddy. "That kid's no good for her. They were bawling their eyes out the other day."

"About what?"

"None of your business," Terry says.

"Excu-u-use me," Buddy says, wiggling an eyebrow at Mic. "That would've freaked me, a kid coming back like that."

Mic opens his beer. "It freaked her. It's all she talks about."

"I'm handling it," Terry says. "I'm getting used to it."

"She has these weird dreams," Mic says. "She keeps me up half the night."

Buddy leans back in his chair. "I got a girl pregnant."

"That must've been a miracle," Terry says.

Mic laughs, but Buddy ignores her. "I wanted her to keep it, but she had an abortion." He shrugs.

"I got a kid somewhere," Mic says.

"No shit."

Terry looks quickly down at her plate, because she doesn't want Buddy to see from the expression on her face that this is how she finds out the important things about Mic—not by asking, not by being told, but in bits and pieces, at unexpected moments, in front of people she detests.

"Yeah, somewhere in B.C."

"A boy or girl?"

"I didn't stick around long enough to find out." Mic pushes away his half-empty plate. "Bring any stuff?"

"Yeah," Buddy says, reaching into his pocket and pulling out a couple of joints. "Fresh as a fucking daisy."

When they light up, Terry leaves the kitchen. She doesn't do pot, and she wishes Mic didn't either, but he likes it; he says it relaxes him. She sits on the couch and picks up the TV remote. She flips through the channels. CBC: boring Afghanistan. PBS: another special on whales. "Wheel of Fortune": she looks at the clues and guesses "Never say never" four spins before the woman who's spinning the wheel. "The Cosby Show": Claire and Cliff are lying together in their pajamas on their king-size bed.

Buddy's voice rises in the kitchen. Mic laughs. Buddy's voice gets louder: ". . . two grand . . ." and then subsides.

The doorbell to the Malibu dream house rings, and she hears the maid opening the door. "Hello. No, I'm sorry, she's very busy. Can I ask who's calling?" The maid comes to her room. "Miss Petrie? There's two women at the door. I think one of them is the press." Terry takes off the coat— thick white fur tinged with black—and apologizes to the furrier who has brought a rack of them for her to try on. "Excuse me, please."

He bows his head. "Of course, Miss Petrie."

She crosses the foyer, her high heels clicking on the marble floor. She doesn't immediately open the door. Instead, she glances at her image in the huge mirror that covers the wall. Black leather pants, a fiery red silk blouse, her hair in becoming disarray. She opens the door, and the cameras start whirring.

"Yes?"

The reporter carries a notepad. "Miss Petrie? I'm Lena Miles with CKVU. We'd like to talk with you and Mr. Avery."

A naked Mic is in the hot tub, waiting for Terry to join him. "I'm afraid he's not available."

"Miss Petrie? Do you know who this woman is?"

Terry glances at the girl standing beside Miss Miles. She is blond, not very pretty, and carries a bundled-up baby in her arms. "I've never seen her in my life."

"Do you know who this baby belongs to?"

"What are you getting at, Miss Miles?"

"Mic Avery is the father of this child."

"Miss Miles," *Terry says,* "have you any idea of the number of young women who claim that Mr. Avery has impregnated them?"

"Mary says she met with Mr. Avery on his trip to British Columbia."

"Miss Miles, I was with Mr. Avery on that trip." *Terry is too much the star to give away the stab of pain that pierces her through the heart at the memory of the night Mic didn't come back to the hotel.*

The reporter busily scribbles in her notepad. "Are you denying this woman's allegations?"

Terry stares directly into the cameras. "Absolutely."

The girl bursts into tears and holds the baby out to her. "It is his! It is!"

"Ter?" Mic stands in the hallway with Buddy right behind him. "We're going to see a guy about a truck."

"Okay."

"Delicious meal, Terry," says Buddy.

She ignores him, and they start to head out the door. "Mic?" she calls.

"What?"

"Maybe she had an abortion."

"Who?"

"The girl in B.C."

"Yeah, maybe."

The doorbell to the Malibu dream house rings, and she hears the maid opening the door. "Hello. No, I'm sorry, she's very busy. Can I ask who's calling?" *The maid comes to her room.* "Miss Petrie? There's two women at the door. I think one of them is the press." *Terry takes the ring—*

a diamond encircled by sapphires—and apologizes to the jeweler who has brought a box of rings for her to try on. "Excuse me, please."

He bows his head. "Of course, Miss Petrie."

She goes to the door. The reporter carries a notepad. Beside her is a young woman. Behind them is a camera crew.

"Yes?"

"Miss Petrie? I'm Lena Miles with CKVU. We'd like to talk with you and Mr. Avery."

"He doesn't live here anymore."

The camera whirs. The reporter writes frantically in her notebook. "You and Mr. Avery have separated?"

"Irreconcilable differences," Terry says.

"Where is Mr. Avery now?"

"I couldn't say," she lies. She knows exactly where Mic is—licking his wounds in a rented room in Beverly Hills, begging her forgiveness, vowing he'll get rid of Buddy, and promising he'll tell Terry everything she wants to know.

"Miss Petrie, do you know who this woman is?"

"Not at all."

"Did you know Mr. Avery got her pregnant?"

"Mr. Avery's flings don't interest me."

The woman bursts into tears. "But I had an abortion. I did what he wanted."

"You'll have to excuse me," Terry says haughtily. "I'm extremely busy."

The door closes behind them, and Terry turns back to the television. Claire and Cliff are cuddling together on the bed, and as usual, Claire is determined to find out something Cliff is hiding from her. This time it's the results of his latest physical. Terry knows Claire will get it out of him. She lights a cigarette and settles back.

EVERY YEAR BEFORE CHRISTMAS, MY mother makes her annual visit to Ottawa. This trip is actually part of a month-long trek around North America during the holiday season, in which she visits all of her children and spreads largesse to her grandchildren. My brother Murray lives in Wisconsin with his wife and three girls, Derek is in New Jersey with his wife and two boys, and Brent, who is divorced, has custody of his son and owns an apartment building in Maine. My mother spends the other eleven months of the year in South Carolina, where she moved ten years ago after my father died. She plays golf and tennis, is studying Spanish, and goes on frequent cruises to such places as the Galapagos Islands and Antarctica.

This year I'm second on the list, sandwiched as I was in birth order between Murray and Derek. Her visit throws me into the usual throes of anxiety. I get my hair cut and permed, I diet a week before she comes, I clean the guest room and actually dust the woodwork. I think I'm fully prepared, but when I pick her up at the airport, I find she has two surprises. The first I see immediately as she emerges from the customs area—a mink coat and a matching hat. "Isn't it gorgeous?" she says as I lean down to hug her, my head immediately enveloped by her familiar floral scent. "I just got it."

"Gorgeous," I echo. My mother could model for one of those magazines that extol the virtues of the older woman. No effort has ever been spared to keep her as petite and pretty as she was at nineteen years old and about to be married to my father. At forty she looked twenty-five, at sixty she looked fifty, and as she approaches seventy, you would swear she's not yet sixty. Her secrets include expensive creams and rinses, regular visits to beauty salons, stays at health spas, and cosmetic surgery. She has had her eyes done twice and her chin and neck once. "You look fabulous," I say.

My mother pats a curl of ash blond hair that lies beneath

the dark fur edge of her hat. "Am I extravagant or am I extravagant?"

I know what she wants. "You only live once."

"Exactly. I said to myself: Helen, this life is not a rehearsal for the performance. This is it. So go for it. Splurge. You deserve it." She gives me a meaningful look. Her eyes are brown like mine, but she dresses hers up in purple eye shadow and false lashes. "Of course it was on sale."

The second surprise now emerges from the customs area, carrying a suitcase and looking around. My mother smiles and dimples like a schoolgirl. "I didn't mention this on the phone," she says in a low voice. "It's sort of a last-minute thing."

The last-minute thing is tall and lean, tanned and silver-haired. He wears a furry gray fedora with a jaunty red feather and a black leather trench coat. The hand that shakes mine has manicured polished nails and liver spots. "Ted Barowsky," he says, smiling. He has dimples, too. "Pleased to meet you."

"Hello," I say.

"Ted and I met a week ago," my mother says.

"When you were with Murray?" I ask in disbelief.

My mother tucks her hand in the crook of Ted's elbow. "At the church," she says, looking up at him. "Isn't that right?"

"I was standing in the pew right behind her, and I thought, Who is that pretty little lady?"

"And I turned around," my mother chimes in, "and thought, Who is that dashing fellow? And would you believe it? Ted's son works with Murray. Wasn't that a coincidence?"

I smile. Ted smiles. My mother smiles. We're into a frenzy of dimpling. "Amazing," I say.

"So we got to know each other."

"Church suppers and all that," Ted explains.

"And the day before I left," my mother says, "I thought to myself, Helen, you only get one kick at the can. So I said to Ted, 'Live it up and come with me to Ottawa,' and he said"—she pauses for emphasis—"'yes.'"

I say, "Well, that's wonderful."

"Now, Jane," my mother adds quickly, "Ted doesn't want to impose, do you, hon?"

"Absolutely not."

"So we made reservations at the Chateau Laurier."

I'm no fool; I can read between the lines. Our guest room has only one bed, a single covered with a virginal white counterpane.

Ted pats my mother's hand, the one tucked into his bent arm. "Helen thinks of everything," he says. "She's a regular little general. That's what I call her—Generalissimo Simpson."

My mother gives Ted another flash of dimple. "Isn't he the cutest?" she says to me. "Isn't he sweet?"

The first few times my brothers and I heard about my mother's boyfriends, we were shaken by the news, and there was a flurry of agitated phone calls among the four of us. My brothers believed that my mother's life revolved so completely around my father she would never notice another man. I thought I knew better. As the only other female in the family, I'd recognized early that, in the competition for my father's attention, I would never be a winner. My mother was our family's goddess, and my father worshiped at her feet. I was convinced that my mother would be like the *univira* of ancient times, a Roman matron who never married again because no living man could ever equal her dead husband in adoration. For whatever reasons, we all naively assumed that Helen would cloak herself in the mantle of sexless widowhood with dignity and grace. Which just goes to show how little any of us know about our mothers. Since my father died, Helen has been picking up men with the effortless speed of a lint brush going after fluff.

Time has dulled the shock, and distance allows us to keep our children ignorant of their grandmother's affairs. But Ted's arrival brings Helen's sex life front and center, and I worry how Emma will take it. She adores my mother and can't wait for her yearly visits. When they're together, they talk incessantly. I'm not sure whether my mother drops to Emma's level or Emma rises to hers. Perhaps the distance between them is a short one anyway. They are both obsessed by the same things: clothes, cosmetics, and men.

On the night of my mother's arrival, Emma and I drive Helen and Ted to the hotel after dinner. Emma and my mother sit in the back seat while Ted sits next to me in the front. I point out landmarks, trying to talk over the whispers in the back and the bursts of giggles. Snatches of conversation make their way through my words: "So curly. I can't do anything . . . and then I saw the cutest T-shirt and . . ." "What's his name? Come on, Em, you can tell me. . . ." "Grandma! I don't love him! I only like him."

When I pull up in front of the Chateau, my mother and Ted get out, and Emma moves into the front seat.

"Good-bye," my mother says gaily, "we'll see everyone tomorrow."

"Great dinner, Jane," says Ted for the fifth time.

As we drive away, Emma watches them walk through the Chateau's revolving doors. She's frowning. "Is Grandma going with Ted?" she asks.

"You know, Em, Grandpa's been dead for a long time, and Grandma gets lonely. We can't expect her to want to be by herself all the time. Much as she loves us, she sometimes needs to be with friends her own age."

"I don't mean just that, Mom. I mean, is she *doing* it?"

"Doing it?" I ask, carefully negotiating through the heavy traffic in front of Confederation Square.

"You know," Emma says impatiently. "Sex. That stuff."

I clear my throat. "Grandma and Ted are over sixty, and they've both been married once and brought up families and done what they had to do. Now they're old enough to please themselves. It's not like they're young and have their whole lives ahead of them the way you do." I glance over at Emma to see how she takes this and find that she's looking out the window, her forehead creased into a frown. "Now," I add brightly, "let's pick up some brown sugar and make butterscotch cookies."

"Well, I hope she's using condoms," Emma says, child of the late eighties. "I hope she's practicing safe sex."

Sunday after lunch. Emma is watching a Christmas special. Philip and Ted are in the basement; they've found a common interest in renovations and carpentry. Helen and I are cleaning the kitchen, and she's chattering away. It's not necessary for me to keep the conversational ball rolling when my mother is around. She bounces it, twirls it, and spins it: a one-woman verbal juggling act.

"So I didn't say anything. I wasn't going to interfere between a husband and wife. If Sally wants to be rigid about the children and Murray isn't going to do anything, it's not my place to step in the middle, is it? Of course I feel sorry for him, but he doesn't look to me for advice. If I try to say the littlest thing, he gives me one of those drop-dead glances. Well, you know what I always say, don't you? 'A daughter's a daughter all your life, a son's a son until he takes a wife.' "

I rinse off a plate and put it in the dishwasher. My mother gives me another one and makes a scolding sound.

"You should wear rubber gloves," she says. "Your hands are rough. And your nails! Heavens, Jane, you're letting yourself go. Would you like me to give you a manicure?"

"No, thanks."

"I brought my polish."

"That's okay."

"You never liked wearing polish, did you?"

"Not really."

"It makes a woman's hands pretty."

"No, thanks."

My mother sighs but forges on. "I hope you don't mind my mentioning this, but I've noticed Philip's put on a bit of weight. Not that he isn't a nice-looking man still. I've always thought Philip was handsome, but he tends to be on the burly side. You'll have to watch him, you know. Make sure he's not eating so much fat and carbohydrates. Your father was like that. As he got closer to fifty he began to thicken around the middle. I tried to tell him without hurting his ego, of course. I tried to get him to eat more fish and less roast beef. I wanted him to join the Y and get some exercise, but he just wouldn't. He was such a stubborn man! Maybe if he'd known the stress he was putting on his heart, he'd have done something about it. Well, what can you do but try?''

As my mother chatters on and I wrap slices of roast beef in wax paper, I think of my father, Harry Simpson, commercial insurance agent. He worked long hours in the city, leaving the house before I woke in the morning and coming home after my brothers and I had supper. In the evenings he read the newspapers and watched television, falling asleep in front of the television, his head tilting down and to one side, his mouth hanging open. I have a photograph in my album from a summer long ago in which my father is on his hands and knees in the backyard, and my brothers are tumbling over him. When I see this photo, I remember that he was more comfortable with boys than he was with me, especially when I began to physically change from a girl to a woman. When I conjure him up now, he's always turning a corner away from me so that I see only his back. I see his suit jacket with its rear double flaps, his neck, which was thick and reddish, and his hat, the businessman's fedora that covered his bald spot. I hear him coughing his heavy-smoker's cough and spitting phlegm into his handkerchief.

I do have one different image of my father. I'm standing in my college dorm room only minutes after arriving for my freshman year. I'm nervous and excited and trying to make awkward conversation with my roommate whom I've never met before. My mother, who has orchestrated my departure from home with numerous lists and shopping expeditions, has still not yielded control. She is energetically bustling around the small room, unpacking my suitcase, hanging up my clothes, opening drawers, deciding where this item and that should go.

"Underpants here, bras here, slips here," she says. "Did you remember to bring the sachet?"

I look at her and my glance slides past her, out the door to where my father stands in the hallway. For once, his back isn't to me. For once, he isn't walking away, turning a corner, disappearing. He is leaning against the wall and holding his hat by the brim, turning it around and around in jerky circles. The corridor lights gleam on the freckled skin of his skull and catch the silver in the fringe of hair above his ears. Our eyes meet, and he gives me a small helpless smile as if to say, Women's stuff. But I see something else in the lines of his face, in the sad heavy pouches. I see what he has never been able to show me. I see what I have known all along. I see that he loves me.

My mother's voice is rising in decibels as if she senses that I've drifted off. "Have you thought about building out on this kitchen? It's a little on the narrow side, isn't it? You could put on an addition the way Derek has on his. Did I tell you about it? No? It's very nice and adds a lot of light. I'm sure it cost them an arm and a leg. Not that I asked, of course; it's none of my business. Still, to tell you the truth, I thought maybe there was a bit too much light, since the back of the house faces south, and they're going to roast in the summer, but I didn't say anything. Melanie is so sensitive. The slightest criticism gets her back right up."

I make the appropriate noises and put the bottles of ketchup and mustard back in the refrigerator.

Now my mother lowers her voice dramatically. "So what do you think of Ted?"

"He seems very nice," I say.

"At first I thought he was Mr. Right. I turned around in that pew and my heart just went pitter-patter. Then when I found out he had money, I couldn't believe it. Imagine finding a healthy man with his own income. You know how hard that is to do when you're sixty-nine? All the good men are dead or married." She sighs again. "But you know something, Jane? All you have to do is travel with someone to find his flaws." She glances at the basement door and lowers her voice even more. "He's not quite a man."

"He's not?"

"You know what I mean."

"He can't get it up?"

"Jane! Not so loud. So maybe's he's not Mr. Right. It was worth a try, don't you think?"

"Absolutely," I say.

"Life is never giving up, Jane. That's my motto. The day I give up is the day I die."

"The day you give up is the day you die." How often had I heard that? It was the refrain of my childhood, brought out and flown like a banner at every opportunity. Homework too hard? A flute piece too difficult? Hair that wouldn't flip? Stubborn pimples? My mother reduced all my complaints to this do-or-die level, leaving me with only two choices: to conclude that everything was worth fighting for or, conversely, to decide that nothing was worth all that effort. Most of the time I opted for nothing, and that drove her wild. We argued over my messy appearance, my low grades, my disorderly room, my lack of organization, my failure at music and dance lessons.

I understand now that I got an enormous pleasure from enraging her, while paradoxically wanting very much to be as lovely and ladylike as she was. And looking back, I find myself reluctantly admiring her stubborn courage. She never gave up trying to make me over, despite my resistance and the lack of appropriate material. It wasn't entirely her fault. She was petite and perfect while I was large and imperfect, having inherited my father's build, his too strong features, his dark coloring, his thin fine hair. I was also surrounded by noisy rough brothers with whom I played ball, climbed trees, and wrestled until I was almost sixteen.

I wasn't a complete tomboy; I wanted to be pretty and fragile and feminine, but it wasn't possible. I was big-boned, long-limbed, and awkward. I wore braces and needed glasses. I knew how hopeless my mother's quest was, but she never acknowledged defeat. She struggled with me, trying to make me over in her image. That was where she went wrong, but neither of us knew it then. In fact, she doesn't know it now. Her colors are pastels, her movements delicate, her sense of style honed by small bones and neat flesh. I'm none of these things. I'm entirely separate and distinct, so different from her that sometimes it seems incomprehensible that once her blood passed through my veins and her heart beat for mine.

On the last night of my mother's stay, we sit in the living room and open the Christmas presents she has brought. Helen doesn't believe in letting us wait until Christmas morning, she likes to give gifts and wants the pleasure of seeing them exclaimed over and enjoyed. Helen also has an instinct for gift-giving—for some people, that is. Philip receives a black leather belt and a biography he's been eager to read. Emma is equally delighted with hers: earmuffs, an oversized black shirt, silver peace-symbol earrings—"Just what everyone's wearing at school!"—and a huge Miss Clairol cosmetics kit with twelve different shades of nail polish and lipstick.

"Thanks, Grandma," she says, throwing her arms around my mother's neck.

"Heavens," my mother says breathlessly, "but you're too strong for me."

Ted, who has grandchildren, steps in. "Come here, young lady," he says. "Let me test that muscle."

Emma obediently walks over to him and, clenching her fist, forces her biceps into a tiny mound.

"Wow," Ted says, testing it with his fingers. "You a weight lifter?"

Emma giggles; she's decided she likes Ted. "Uh-uh."

"How about you, Phil? You do weights?"

Philip is lying on his side on the carpet, watching the flames in the fireplace. " 'Fraid not," he says with a yawn.

"You should," my mother jumps in. "It's very good for your heart."

"I'm faithful," Ted says, "and my last EKG was A-plus."

"It's good for your lungs, too," Helen says. "You have to take deep breaths. It causes expansion."

Meanwhile, I'm opening my gifts with trepidation. The choices my mother makes for me are always inappropriate. This year proves to be no exception. She has brought me a gift certificate to a beauty boutique—"Maybe you'll get your nails done now"—a large scarf in an overblown floral pattern that jars my sensibilities, and a nightgown too sheer for Canadian winter and, I suspect, too narrow in the hips to accommodate my flesh.

I hold up the nightgown. Philip and Ted whistle. My mother says, "Every woman should have one."

"It's lovely, Mom," I say, getting up and kissing her powdered, perfumed cheek. "Thanks."

"And you wear the scarf over your shoulder. Like this." She stands up, takes it from me, folds it into a triangle, and drapes it over her black dress. "With one end at about elbow length and the other two tucked into your belt, front and back." She adjusts it and then swivels, bending one knee and then the other, like a fashion model, so we can see how it should go.

I've sunk back into my chair. I look up at my tiny perfect mother, and it occurs to me for the first time that Helen may have felt about me, her daughter, in fact may still feel about me, much the same way I feel about Emma. She may have the same sense of bewilderment, the same sense of fate having worked against her, the same sense of resignation. Did she also dream pink and misty visions? Did she picture a daughter as pretty as she was? Did she want, in that family of rough-hewn males, someone small and delicate and hers alone?

Ted is applauding as she dips and struts, and my mother has a flush on her cheeks beyond the boundaries of her carefully brushed-on rouge. I discover an ache spreading in my chest, wider and wider, until I can hardly breathe for the pain of it. Is this daughter love? This hurtful, breathtaking sorrow?

DEAR DIARY,
Guess what Diary? I had my first kiss!!
With Mark!!!
We FRENCHED!!!!

He was at the dance and we danced a lot together. He danced with Lisa too and she thought he was realy intirested in her but he wasnt. He kept looking at me! I was waring my realy tite blue cords my black shirt and silver earings. I used my Moms blue eye stuff and made my lashes realy big. Anyway Mark had beer hiden in the playground. He drank some and I drank some. It was pretty disgusting—yuck. Then he kissed me. He had that thing with his brases in—that plat—and it was all sorts of goobery. But still neat!

Then after that Cello passed me a not saying Lisa hated me realy bad and was trying to make me jelous but Mark had a crush on me and was in love with me and talked about me all the time. I read it in the girls room and then flushed it down the toylet. Then Lisa came in and said—dont you think you overdid that crap on your eyes? I told her no I thot it was really good. She said well I think its gross. I said well go suck hokey sticks you bitch and she left.

Other IMPORTANT news—Terry asked me if I wuld like to come to there New Years Eve party. I culd help with the food and stay overnight. Then She could introdus me to all her friends. Isnt that neat? I havent asked Mom yet. All shell do is ask a lot of questshons like she always does. Like I know she realy hates Terry. She says she doesnt but I can tell. Well I dont care. Terry is my mother too. And shes realy neat and does things I like. You know what I mean Diary shes not egsactly like a mother shes more like me. We culd be twins sort of. And she doesn't tell me what to do all the time like Mom whose realy getting on my nervs lately. Speshialy for stupid little things like leaving close on the stairs. Like who realy cares? I mean she culd give me a brake but all she does is yell. My Mom must have the biggest vocil cords like in the hole world.

Oh I forgot. Thursday. Weather—bad—too much snow.

Me and my Dad made a snowman in the front yard. Its pretty bad looking but Dad liked it. I used the crimper on my hair and now I have the frizzies. It looks neat. My back is all broken out and disgusting.

Bye for now.

 CHRISTMAS IS A SEASON THAT SEEMS TO GO on forever. The parties begin in early December and run until New Year's Day when, in a last festive gasp, some hardy soul throws a brunch. By then I will be sick of fruitcake, butter tarts, and shortbread cookies. I will have drunk too many glasses of sherry and other wines and been forced into too many inane conversations with people I see only at Christmas parties. "Is that David (Sarah, Scott, Lindsay)? I can't believe how much he/she has grown," I will say of children in their party clothes, dashing around underfoot and stuffing their faces with cookies and candy. Maybe that's what I dislike so much at Christmas—the children. I can ignore the aging of my acquaintances—gray hair and wrinkles are slow encroachments—but I can't ignore the children. They grow like crabgrass, tall and lanky and ceaseless, evidence of the years flowing by.

This Christmas I'm more misanthropic than usual. I've left everything until the last minute and am forced to join the hordes of other last-minute shoppers. I spend too many evenings driving through the slush to yet another shopping mall where I stand in line, weighed down by purchases, sweating into my coat and boots and thinking sour thoughts about our Visa balance. I'm not even pleased when Philip is given tickets for a performance of *The Messiah* by another professor who can't attend. I'm tired from work and go reluctantly, my displeasure mounting when we discover that our seats are in the last row, last balcony. Miles below (an exaggeration, but I'm in that frame of mind) is the stage with its miniature orchestra and rows of dwarf singers. Next to me a lady unwraps a mint and noisily sucks on it. A cougher sits beside Philip and hacks into a tissue.

My Christmas malaise is compounded by my feelings about Philip. The pendulum that is our marriage has made its inevitable swing downward, carrying me with it. I'm angry with him but not angry enough to pick a major fight, at least not yet. Instead I'm in a state of constant annoyance. I'm irritated by the way he clears his throat several times before settling in his seat, I'm provoked by the precision with which he straightens the crease in his pant leg. When he opens his mouth to comment on the orchestra, I think, Oh, shut up. We've already had minor words. Words about Emma and Terry. Words about my tendency to exaggerate and his inability to comprehend my feelings. These words have been spoken in short unsatisfying exchanges. I complain about this to Des, but to my further annoyance he takes Philip's side.

"He doesn't want to get crushed."

"Crushed?"

"Caught in the middle of monumental motherhood forces."

"All I want him to do is understand why I'm worried."

"Forgive me, Jane, but if I were in his shoes, I'd run like hell, too."

I can't pick a fight, because my anxieties don't center around arguable specifics. Instead they swirl sluggishly around in the dark waters of my imagination, coming to the surface now and then, their shapes threatening and sinister. I envision Emma moving in with Terry. I imagine Terry taking Emma to Toronto and never coming back. I'm fixated by Toronto, and in my mind it becomes Sodom and Gomorrah. I see myself walking down strange streets, peering into dark unsavory corners until I finally come to the glass-enclosed Eaton Centre. Suddenly I see Emma going up one escalator and then another, her red hair a beacon. I run. I push through the crowds. *Emma!* But I'm caught in an endless series of slowly revolving doors. Around and around I go, and with each revolution she's farther away until she disappears altogether.

I told this to Philip, making a joke of it. "The Eaton Centre," I said. "That den of iniquity."

Philip wasn't amused. "You're doing it again," he said.

"I can't help my imagination!"

"You're driving yourself crazy."

"You know what's making me crazy? Talking to a wall! That's what's making me crazy!"

Now I sit, too disgruntled to listen to the music of Handel soaring around us. Instead I peer down at the first ten rows of orchestra seats and notice that four seats in the third row center are empty. I imagine the pleasure of seeing the singers full size and nudge Philip with my elbow. "Look," I say, pointing downward. "Empty seats." He looks down and then back at the stage.

I twist around, cup my hand by his ear, and whisper, "If they're still empty at intermission, let's take them."

He shakes his head.

"Why not?"

"No."

"Why *not*?"

"No."

"You think the owners of those seats are going to arrive in the middle of the performance? They've missed too much."

He ignores me.

"In New York theaters," I say, "empty seats are up for grabs at intermission."

"This isn't New York."

"But we'll be able to see!"

"*No!*"

By now we're hissing at each other, and both the mint sucker and the cougher are glaring at us. I sit back in my seat, and my anger sizzles and bubbles like water drops in hot oil. Not that I'm surprised. I knew Philip wouldn't move. I knew he'd cringe at the possibility of a confrontation with strangers. I knew that taking over those seats would offend his Canadian decorum, that exquisite sense of appropriate behavior. *We didn't pay for those seats, did we?*

We don't deserve them. I've been married to Philip for so long I can predict what he'll do, and I'll be accurate ninety-nine-point-nine-nine percent of the time. How my anger hardens! It metamorphoses like the formations I read about in my geological bulletins. It solidifies into stone, smooth and hard. Like a squirrel gathering nuts, I collect such stones, store them, horde them, greedily count them. And when the pendulum of our marriage reaches its lowest point, the nadir of pure fury, I will use them.

As weapons.

DEAR DIARY,

Terible cramps yesterday!!! Right in the midle of supper. Mom says there a warmup for my period. Im going to be the last girl in my class to get her period. Its so imbarrasing. Sometimes I pretend I have it so Lisa the bitch wont say, Oh realy Ive had mine for ages.

Terry got her period real early, like when she was 11. Mom got hers at 12. But Mom says theres nothing rong with me. She says every girl is on her own skedool. She gave me a heeting pad for my stomack and we talked abot sex and risponsibility. She talked about AIDS and diseeses and scary things like warts in terible places that you can get by doing it. She said I had to take care of myself because nobody else wuld. She said lots of boys will tell a girl they love her just to get her to do sex and stuff. She said boys are bilt differently than girls and there erges are real strong. I told her the boys in my class were so uncordinated they culdnt do it anyway. She laughed and said Id be surprised. I wuld be surprised. There such jerks! Even Mark. Somtimes he can be such a jerk!

Then Mom asked if I had any questshons and I asked if Daddy was a major babe when he was yung and if they slept together on there first date. She said he was very handsom and they wated until they knew each other better. I asked if she and Daddy had sex when she had her period and she said they did. I said gross. And she said not when two people love each other. She said love is the most important thing and that when a man and woman love each other everything they do is all right because they do it with rispect. So I said, do you and Daddy do it with your mouths? She said yes!!! Is that gross, Diary or what!!!

Today, Dana said only hookers do it with there mouths but I told her no way. She said she read it in a magazeen. I said magazeens arent always right. She said how do you know, bitch? I said because my mother told me that she and my Dad did it. You shuld have seen her face. It was wicked!!!

Bye for now.

LATELY I NOTICE THAT EMMA IS BEING LOVing and attentive. Although I suspect she has ulterior motives—she's given me a list of things she wants for Christmas, and she's angling for permission to go to Terry's for New Year's Eve—I've also noticed that her feelings toward me go through cycles. Some days we recapture the connections of preadolescence when she likes to be around me, wants to share her life with me, and is curious about what I am doing. Other days I seem to be her greatest enemy, destroyer of her dreams, and an obstacle standing in the way of her happiness. There's no predicting the cycles. She can go to bed friendly one night and wake up hostile the next morning. Nor can I guess at how long a cycle will last. I've learned that all I can do is enjoy the good times and live through the bad.

For the past few days Emma has taken to following me around the house in the evenings. She sits by me while I'm reading the paper or watching television and hovers over me when I pay the bills.

"What's that?" she asks.

"The gas bill."

"It only costs a hundred and thirty-five dollars to heat the whole house?"

"That's for one month, Em."

"Oh."

We grocery-shop together, a task she usually hates, and she insists on coming with me when I go to the store to buy a New Year's Eve dress. She sits in a chair by the dressing rooms and studies me each time I emerge in a new outfit. She tilts her head to one side and narrows her eyes as I turn in front of the mirror.

"That doesn't look right on you," she says. "The color's no good."

"Is that so?" I say, slightly affronted. The dress is a green shot through with silver threads, and I think it's pretty.

The saleslady, who has disappeared into the back room, now returns and flutters around me. She adjusts a shoulder, straightens the waist. "A perfect fit," she says.

I squint at the mirror to soften the edges of my angles and lines. "Hmmm," I say.

"Very flattering to your shape, ma'am."

"Mom, that green makes you look"—Emma tilts her head the other way—"yellow."

"Yellow!"

The saleslady gives a sour smile. "Quite the fashion consultant, isn't she?"

Our companionship is glued together with chatter. Emma talks incessantly and fills silences with breathless rushes of confession and gossip. Aware that a misstep on my part threatens these moments, I tread carefully, talking very little, offering no advice, and allowing her to take the lead.

"So everyone told Cello that Lisa had a crush on him, and he went up to her and said, 'I hate you, you fucking bitch.' Oh, sorry, Mom. So you know what Lisa did? She stole his *science* book and put it in the girl's *bath*room."

"No," I say. We're folding laundry. This is a job Emma usually avoids, but now she's contentedly matching socks.

"Cello had to *sneak* in before school to get it. But I mean he deserved it, don't you think, Mom?"

"Uh-huh." I think two wrongs don't make a right, but I've learned that my opportunities for moralizing are few, and I must save them for critical issues.

"He thinks he's a *real* dude. But he's not, he's just a *jerk*. Mom, there's only one of these." She holds up a brown sock of Philip's.

"The other one will turn up," I say.

"Anyways, then Lisa thought she could get Mark to take her to the dance. So she asked Nicky to ask Dana if we were still going out. Dana told her she didn't have a chance. Mark's asked me."

"I like Mark," I say. "He's a nice boy."

"I can say anything to him. He always understands."

"That's good," I say, but I'm thinking with an unexpectedly sharp pang that motherhood seems to inevitably thin with time, full-bodied in a child's infancy but losing substance with each passing year, its richness diluted and drained. What is left feels to me like a frail shell, untethered and light enough to float into space.

Emma chatters on. "Mrs. Waddell told everyone they were going to have to go see the principal. She thinks she runs the whole school. She thinks she can tell everyone what to do."

As I fold a sheet, I suddenly notice how Emma has changed. Her face has lengthened, the roundness of childhood almost gone. In its place are angled cheekbones, a sharp jawline, the square little chin. She also wears makeup now, continuously, even when she isn't going anywhere. She's chosen a jarring assortment of colors: blue eye shadow on her green eyes, hot pink lipstick that clashes with her hair. Emma insists these colors suit her, and I don't argue. I see through them and past the changing geometry of her face to the adult she will one day be. I savor that future, knowing there will be a time when I don't have to control and she doesn't have to test the edges of that control.

". . . caught Dana smoking in the school yard behind the gym and yelled at her in front of everyone. She was so scared . . ."

I think, Maybe we'll be friends.

TERRY IS SITTING ON A STOOL IN THE KITCHEN with a sheet wrapped around her and held at her throat by a safety pin. Her wet hair hangs down her back. Charlene is carefully trimming her hair. They've moved the television into the kitchen since Charlene doesn't want to miss "Cheers." She has a thing for Ted Danson. Charlene hasn't changed a lot. When Terry ran into Charlene at the St. Laurent shopping center, she recognized her right away. She was still heavy and still waddled. The difference was she didn't have zits anymore and her hair was great instead of frizzy—spiked into big waves at the front and a mass of long curls at the back. She works as a hairdresser at Hair Galore on Rideau Street.

"If I was Rebecca," Charlene says, "I'd sleep with Sam. He's so sexy."

"He'd cheat on you."

"I wouldn't care."

"That's your problem," Terry says. "Guys know they can walk right over you. You must wear a sign on your forehead: Trample Here."

Charlene sighs and snips. On the screen Rebecca flounces into her office and slams the door. Sam's face fills the screen, and Charlene looks at him longingly. "I'll bet Ted Danson's a great lover."

"Why?"

"His mouth. It's so sensuous."

"That doesn't mean a thing."

"It does to me."

"There's no outside thing that can tell you if a guy's going to be a great lover or not. The sexiest guy I ever knew was lousy in bed."

"Which one was that?"

"Roy."

"The guy who beat you up?"

"I told you, Charlene, he *tried* to beat me up. I kicked him out."

"You're so tough," Charlene says. "Just like Carla. I get such a kick out of her."

Charlene annoys Terry, like she always did. She's still naive, silly, and clinging, but now she has a way of pricking those bubbles of annoyance so Terry can't remember what irritated her so much. To her surprise, Charlene's become her closest friend and confidante. She came back into Terry's life about the same time that Mic arrived, and in Terry's mind, the two events are entwined with Charlene reflecting back to her all the excitement and satisfactions of her relationship with Mic.

Charlene combs the front of Terry's hair. "Is Buddy coming to the New Year's Eve party?"

"I told you, Buddy is slime."

"I thought he was kind of cute."

"Honest to God, Charlene, your taste must be in your toenails."

"He's unattached, isn't he?"

"For good reasons."

"Just tell me. Is he coming?"

"Mic invited him."

"I'm going to wear that blue silk."

"The one with the low-cut back?"

"And front."

"It'll be your funeral, Charlene. Just don't come crying to me when it falls apart."

"Is Emma coming too?"

"I think so."

"Have you met her family?"

"No."

"How come?"

"There are stages in these things. We haven't gotten there yet."

"Aren't you curious?"

"Not really."

"Jeez, I'd be dying to know what her parents are like."

"Well, you're you and I'm me."

Charlene may be her best friend, but Terry doesn't tell

her about the times she's sat in her car in front of Emma's house. She's got it memorized: the pleats in the sheer drapes, the slight tilt to the brass number five on the mailbox, and the way the brick changes color around the door frame. She knows now that Emma's room is on the second floor in the back, and that the professor and his wife sleep on the second floor in the front. She knows the professor, *Philip*, has an office in the basement that is only partially finished. She knows the second-floor shower leaked into the dining room ceiling and the professor's wife, *Jane*, had to call in a plasterer. She knows these things, but she's never seen either of the Wastenays. In her imagination they are tall, well-dressed, substantial, and faceless.

"Who else is coming?"

"People from work, a couple of neighbors—oh, and you won't believe this—Roberta and her husband, John." Roberta is Terry's older sister, and the only other Petrie left in Ottawa. She works as a secretary for the city. The rest of the family is out west: Terry's mother in Calgary, two brothers in Edmonton, and another sister in Vancouver.

"You invited her?"

"I didn't think she'd accept, but they have a couple of parties so they're going to stop in."

"How's she doing anyways?"

"The same." The last time Terry saw Roberta was during the summer when she and Mic went to a barbecue at Roberta's house, a semidetached in the west end of the city. Roberta and John, who is an accountant, talked money all night long. How much they had, how much they planned to have, how much they needed before starting a family, how the cost of living was cutting into their paychecks, how their pension plans worked, how they'd halved their electricity bill by switching to those new light bulbs and timing their showers, and so on and so forth until Terry was ready to scream.

"Does she know about Emma?"

"Not yet."

Charlene stops snipping and puts her hands on her ample

hips. "Terry Petrie, do you mean to say you haven't told anyone in your family about Emma?"

"That's right."

"Well, that'll make New Year's Eve a big surprise, won't it?"

"I'm counting on Roberta. She's such a blabbermouth she'll tell everyone, so I won't have to."

Charlene shakes her head admiringly and goes back to trimming Terry's hair. "You're so clever," she says. "I'd have blurted it out and spent the rest of my life explaining."

Charlene can sometimes hit the nail on the head in spite of herself. You can't explain when you don't have the answers. Not to why she sits in a cold car and stares at a house that doesn't belong to her. Not to why the flickering of firelight in a sliver of window on the second floor is so memorable she dreams about it. Not to why in the dream the faceless professor is making love to her in the firelight and when she pushes his head down, it goes willingly, down and down, until her body is shivering and expectant. Or why she suddenly realizes his mouth isn't sliding over her body but is slipping down the cold hard surface of the grocery counter.

Terry woke from that dream still trembling, still open and wet. She turned to Mic, wrapped herself around his curved back, and cupped her hand around his scrotum. He emerged slowly from sleep, his penis rising from the base of her palm.

"What time is it?" he mumbled.

"I don't know."

"Christ, it's still dark." She stroked the tip of his penis. "You want it now?"

"Now," she said fiercely. "Right now." And thank God, Mic isn't the type to ask questions, because she couldn't have told him why.

LATE ONE SATURDAY AFTERNOON I RUN INTO Alice at the Bay in the Rideau Centre. We are both weighed down with packages, and I know the harried expression on her face is a mirror image of mine. We try chatting over a rack of lingerie, but customers mill around us.

"I have a suggestion," I say, remembering the quiet secluded bar in the hotel attached to the shopping center.

"Anything," she says.

"Let's go to the Westin and drink."

The bar has wing chairs, elegant little tables, and a view of the Parliament buildings. We divest ourselves of our packages and our coats and order martinis.

"This feels decadent," Alice says, lifting her glass.

"Isn't this what glamorous romance authors are supposed to do?"

"Supposed to but don't. Instead, we spend an afternoon shopping after spending a morning arguing with our editors on how to write about impetuous reckless romance in the era of AIDS."

"How're you going to do it?"

"We have to discreetly and euphemistically mention birth control. For example, if you have to say something, 'sheath' is preferable to 'condom.' "

"We like euphemisms at work too: restructuring, refocusing, consolidation, downsizing."

Alice peers at me over the rim of her glass. "You worried about your job?"

"There's gossip."

"You could go free-lance, couldn't you?"

"I'm a sucker for a regular paycheck."

"Mmmm." She sips delicately. "The other thing glamorous authors do is go to meetings with teachers to find out their children are skipping classes and flunking math."

"Felicia?"

"No, Matthew. You know what's so strange, Jane? A year ago he was a little boy and still liked to be cuddled. Today he's growing a mustache and is hardly civil."

I think of Emma, whose mood has shifted yet again. This latest mood swing reminds me of a cold front that has blasted in from the north, driving the mild temperatures before it. "Children are hard," I say with a sigh.

"And Matthew wants to do weird things, like shave only one side of his head."

We both smile, but I am reminded of something. "Speaking of weird," I say. "I found groceries in Emma's closet."

"Chips and cookies?"

I shake my head. "Canned corn and a package of sponges and a box of Minute Rice."

"She bought them?"

"She took them from the kitchen."

"Are they open? Is she eating the stuff?"

"You know what I think, Alice? She plays grocery clerk. She stands in front of her desk with the food on one side and a paper bag on the other, and she runs the cans and boxes over an imaginary—what do you call it?—code window." I don't say what else I imagine: the rapt, private expression on Emma's face and the three-note tune she used to hum to herself when she played house with her dolls.

Alice gets it right away. "Like the birth mother," she says. "Making believe she's the birth mother."

"I left the food in the closet," I say. "I didn't know what else to do."

Alice frowns and I feel her take me mentally under her wing. "You must feel like that woman is right in your house—all the time."

"And now Emma wants to spend New Year's Eve with her."

"Jane, you have to talk to the mother. It'd make you feel a lot better."

"I promised Emma I wouldn't."

"Why did you do that?"

"I felt I had to be aboveboard. So I asked her and she got very upset. I said I wouldn't."

"I had a heroine once who had to find out a secret from the hero's past, but the only person who could tell her was the Other Woman. The hero had forbidden her to see the Other Woman, and she'd promised, but without knowing the secret, she knew their love was threatened.''

"So she talked to the Other Woman."

Alice nods. "And had a happy ending."

"If only life was like fiction."

"Well," Alice says, "you don't have to deliberately plan to meet Terry. You could just happen to *see* her."

"How could I do that?"

"Go to where she works. Isn't it Loblaws?"

"That's devious."

"She might have one of those faces you immediately like and trust. That would help a little, wouldn't it?"

I sip my martini and imagine myself skulking around the aisles at Loblaws. "Suppose she looks untrustworthy and dislikable. Where would that leave me?"

"At least you'd know."

I've always thought of Alice as the friend whose outlook, whose beliefs, and whose morality were most like mine. Which just goes to show how little we know about our friends. I put down my glass. "You'd do it, wouldn't you?"

"Without hesitation."

"Alice, you take my breath away."

She leans forward and gives me an intense look from behind her glasses. "Jane, if a plot's stalled, you've got to get it going."

Philip is in the middle of marking Christmas exams when I interrupt him. This isn't a good time for a discussion, but we've reached that point in our marriage when the pendulum has swung so low there never will be a good time. When Philip and I were first lovers and then young marrieds, we couldn't bear to be angry with each other. We sought, like blind moles, for pathways to each other through the darkness we had created. Fights always ended with reconciliations—hugs, tears, pleas for forgiveness—and reconciliations always ended with passionate sex. But we're no longer newlyweds, and now the sun can rise and set on our anger, creating a sour, unpleasant atmosphere, which we hide to the best of our ability. The running of the household doesn't come to a halt, and I doubt if Emma even notices that we are barely speaking. Philip and I go about our daily business as if nothing has occurred. Errands get run, clothes washed, meals made. Nor do we sleep in separate rooms. Instead we pull the blankets up and curl away from each other into our separate spaces, backs turned, like strangers on a bus. When we reach this stage of mutual dislike, the width of a queen-size bed becomes infinite.

He looks up as I enter. "Philip—" I begin, but he says, "I'm marking papers, Jane."

"We have to talk."

"We've talked enough."

"I don't want her to go."

He puts his pen down and swivels on his chair so that he's facing me. I note that his hair needs washing and his belly is pressing against his sweatshirt in an unpleasant fashion. I can't imagine feeling even a smidgen of sexual interest in him.

"I was just in Emma's room," I say, sitting down. "She's supposed to be doing her math, but she was trying on eye shadow."

"Has the school said anything about her math grades?"

"Not yet, but—"

"Honest to God, Jane, you look for trouble."

I think of the argument Emma and I just had. I talked, my voice rising in shrill decibels, and she lowered her head until her hair fell over her face. I had no way of knowing if anything I said registered. I remember the way I blotted out my own mother. When she yelled at me, I'd fall into a dreamy haze, pleasant thoughts mixing and flowing at random until Helen would disappear—first her voice, then her face, and finally her body. Eventually, when the silence was complete and the air in my room was still, I would lift my head and find that my mother was gone altogether.

I wonder how infuriated Philip would feel if Emma blotted him out. "I think you're deliberately blind," I say. "You ignore trouble until it hits you in the face."

"One night with Terry is not a crisis."

"But one thing can lead to another. Suppose she likes it so much she wants to spend a lot more time there."

"That's unlikely."

"Suppose she wants to move in. What would you think then?"

"I don't see any evidence of that."

Nothing enrages me more than when Philip's calm rationality verges on pomposity. "Don't lecture me," I say, my voice rising. "I'm not one of your damn students."

"Any one of my damn students," he says, each word deliberately enunciated so that I don't miss a nuance, "would be clever enough to realize that not letting her go will simply make her want to go even more."

"You really don't care, do you? You'd rather bury your head in the sand."

"What do you want from me? Paranoia? So I can sink down to your level?"

"Oh, now I'm paranoid."

"Paranoid and jealous."

"What a shitty thing to say."

"It's true, isn't it?"

"And you're so perfect? Sitting up there in your ivory tower?" Furiously I throw the stones of my anger. "Looking down your nose at the rest of us like some goddamned intellectual snob?"

"Why should I sit here and take this?"

"Go ahead! Leave! That's what you always do, isn't it? Walk off when the going gets tough!"

Now his voice matches mine in volume. "You know something, Jane? You've got some desperate, sick need to believe that your problems are more dramatic, more interesting, and more significant than anyone else's."

"Now it's a personal attack."

"You started it."

I stand up. "No, I didn't."

"Yes, you did."

"I didn't."

"You always do. You can't resist it."

"Did I call *you* desperate and sick?" I yell.

He stands up and yells back. "You called *me* an intellectual snob. Do you think I enjoyed *that*?"

I march out of the room and slam the door behind me. This is how Philip and I fight. We start off with a legitimate issue and, if it's unresolvable, are soon reduced to a ridiculous childlike exchange that provides a safety valve for our anger and frustration. I don't know how other couples fight. Perhaps they're more vicious and savage; perhaps they throw dishes, hit each other, attack with obscenities, speak the unspeakable. We stop short of violence and never say what we really think. I call Philip an intellectual snob, knowing it will make him furious, but also knowing that if I call him a pompous asshole I'll have gone too far. What epithets he holds in reserve for me I don't know. We don't say them, drawing the line at some invisible boundary beyond which lie words so sharp that they could, knifelike, sever our marital tie.

Which isn't to say that such fights are easy. I shake with fury; my face gets hot and flushed. I clench my fists so tight my hands ache, and if I've screamed loud enough, I'll have a sore throat. Philip not only tightens his fists but also juts his jaw forward and clenches his teeth. I've seen him in the aftermath of a battle, working his jaw to release the tension. Somehow these aftereffects are comforting. We know, without ever saying so, that it is far safer to inflict this violence of self than to go at each other in the blazing heat of the moment. Like the effects of those unspeakable epithets, the damage given and received could be irreversible.

DEAR DIARY,

Wether—boring.

Mom and Dad had a terible fite about me going to Terrys for New Year's Eve. I culd here them through the door to Dad's ofice. First there voices were loud. Dad said just because I wasnt doing homework I shuldnt be allowed to go. Mom said she was afraid I wuld want to go to Terrys a lot more. Then they screemed and yelled. Mom said Dad doesn't understand. Dad said she was realy paranoyd. I looked that up in the dictionary. It says—A PSYCHOSIS CHARACTERIZED BY SYSTEMATIZED DELUSIONS OF PERSECUTION OR GRANDEUR USUALLY WITHOUT HALLUCINATIONS—thats what it says!!! So I asked Mrs. Dixon, my English teacher, and she said a paranoyd person thinks everyone is going to do bad things to them.

Anyway I hate it when they fite but I hope my Dad wins because I realy realy want to go and Ill be mad if Mom trys to stop me.

Bye for now.

 BINS OF BROCCOLI, GREEN BEANS, AND beets. Net bags of grapes sit next to boxes of mandarin oranges. I stroll through the fruit and vegetable section, studying the eggplants and zucchini. I find a plump, smooth eggplant and put it in the cart. I disregard the zucchini—too bruised. I pick up a cantaloupe and squeeze its ends. Not ripe enough, I judge, and put it back. Suddenly I'm outside my body, watching myself. I notice the care with which I examine the produce, my head tilted slightly. I admire the delicate suppleness of my wrist as I turn over an apple. I'm a master shopper. Years of supplying and feeding the Wastenays have given me these skills. It wasn't always so. When I married Philip, I didn't know how to cook. He'd had far more experience, having lived on his own when he was in graduate school. We used to shop together then, and he would tell me the Latin names for things.

"*Cerasum*," he'd say, holding up a cherry, or "*Uvae*," presenting me with a cluster of green grapes.

"*Uvae*," I echoed. I was delighted with Philip's ready store of obscure knowledge.

"*'Terra feracior uvis,'*" he quoted. "'The earth rich with grapes'—Ovid, *Amores.*" Philip had a resonant voice, and after we made love, he would read to me from the Latin love poets: Ovid, Propertius, Catullus. " '*Vivamus, mea Lesbia, atque amenus. . . . Da mi basia mille.*' " Let us live, my Lesbia, and let us love. Give me a thousand kisses.

"Should we buy some grapes?" I asked, but by then he'd gone on to the meat department, and I followed him.

"A *gallina*," he said, picking up a package of chicken thighs. "Well, parts of a *gallina*."

"Shall we broil those for dinner?" I asked.

"No, I hate thighs. Actually, I'm a breast man." He stood there, staring down at them, a perplexed look on his face.

"We need eggs," I said, "Philip? Philip?"

"A breast man," he muttered. "Ah—*mammarum amator.*"

And I would smile at him, the enchanted smile of a lover.

As I remember this, an apple in my hand, I see her. She's walking briskly, carrying a cash-register tray. Her hair—the color of hot red pepper—is pulled up into a ponytail, and it sways from side to side, the tip of it sweeping her back between the thin shoulder blades. She disappears down an aisle, and I find myself gripping the apple so hard I've bruised it.

Alice's idea, which I once found distasteful, no longer repulses me. I've lost the battle of New Year's Eve, not because I'm wrong, but because I don't have enough evidence to convince Philip it would be a mistake, especially since Emma, who is adept at manipulating her father, is being particularly cooperative and pleasant at home. My failure has rankled and festered like an unhealed sore, and I've applied a righteous balm of indignation at what I believe to be an impingement on my rights, feelings, and sensitivities. I've brooded on these wrongs and slowly whipped my indignation into determination mixed with pragmatism. We need bread and milk, don't we? And toilet paper and dishwasher soap? And this Loblaw's isn't that far away from the house, is it? And if Terry isn't there, the trip won't be a waste, will it?

So here I am—the master shopper. Oh, I know exactly

what I'm doing as I turn the corner and push my cart down an aisle of canned soups. I'm making her territory mine. She may work here, but I'm also on intimate terms with the brand names, the plastic-wrapped packages of meat, the varieties of yogurt. I make my way to the dairy case and pick up a carton of eggs. I open it, notice a cracked egg, and put the carton down. I open another and run my fingers over the eggs, making them rock back and forth in their card-board cradles. One sticks, and I know it's cracked at the bottom and has leaked. Finally I find a perfect dozen, smooth and unbroken.

And so it goes. Up one aisle, down the next. Jars of juices, boxes of pet food with pictures of grinning dogs, sharp-scented bathroom deodorizers, pristine sponges and mops, packages of rice gleaming as if varnished, canned pears—Canada Fancy/*Canada De Fantaisie* (far more inter-esting in French). My cart fills, my head fills: Philip needs ham for sandwiches. We're out of English muffins. Is there a jar of peanut butter left? I'll cook a pork loin for dinner. Finally I reach the checkout counters and place my cart in number four where Terry is finishing another customer's order. I pick up a *Ladies' Home Journal* and leaf through it, but I'm not really studying the pictures of an apartment decorated on a budget. I'm surreptitiously watching Terry, spying on her. I know she's twenty-seven years old, but she looks younger with her hair pulled back. She wears the uniform of the Loblaws checkout girl: gray pants, orange and white checked shirt, brown-orange tunic. The shade doesn't suit her no matter how much blusher she has ap-plied. It accentuates the pallor of her skin, the freckles across her cheeks.

Although her resemblance to Emma is strong—they have the same coloring, the same square face—she isn't as pretty as I think Emma will be. She's too thin, too angular, her cheekbones too sharp. There's something crude about her, I think. The bitten fingernails perhaps. The too bold applica-tion of rouge and green eyeliner. Or the teeth, which are not quite straight and not quite white.

"That'll be fifty-nine sixty-three," she says to the woman in front of me. She takes the bills, snaps them efficiently between her fingers, and takes change from the cash drawer. "Thank you and have a nice day." Then she glances at me. "Will this be a car order, ma'am?"

A car order: picking Emma up at the Children's Aid and bringing her home. We didn't have a baby car seat yet, so I sat in the back holding Emma on my knee. She was too young to realize she'd just had a major shift in family, and she wiggled this way and that, peering first at me and then at the passing landscape. She was dressed in pink shorts and a white shirt with pink giraffes marching across it in tiny rows. Her feet were bare. Although we had the car windows open, the circulation of air barely cut into the heat, and her skin stuck to mine wherever we touched.

"No, no car order," I say, but I have to clear my throat to get the words out.

She's a good cashier. Bags are quickly doubled, vegetables weighed, awkward packages dragged smoothly over the electronic eye. Her wrists are bony and freckled like Emma's, and she wears a no-nonsense digital watch with a stainless-steel band. On her chest is a button with her name and a slogan: Terry—First in Affability.

The manager stops beside her. "When's your break, Ter?"

"In five," she says without interrupting the rhythm of her packing.

"Cukes have been marked down to four for ninety-nine. It isn't on the computer yet."

"Okay," she says.

When he's gone, I say, "Not a bad price for cucumbers."

"They were sky high," she says. "About time they came down."

"You must save money on food," I say, "working here." She looks directly at me for the first time, and I'm struck by the clarity of her eyes. They're greener than Emma's, more crystalline. I clear my throat again. "Don't you get a discount?"

"That would be nice, wouldn't it?"

"You mean you don't?"

She shrugs and lifts a bag onto the counter. "That's the breaks."

"Well, I hope they pay decently."

She punches in the price of the loin of pork. "We have a union."

"Really?" I say.

"And the work's steady."

And through the inanity of the conversation, I'm thinking; This is easy. This is a cinch. What was I so worried about? Terry and Jane—First in Affability. I could say, By the way, we haven't met, but I'm Jane Wastenay. And she would smile at me and say, Nice to meet you. I've heard so much about you.

She puts the toilet paper, the final item, into a bag and totals the register. "That's thirty-two nineteen," she says. "Will that be cash or a check?"

"Cash," I say, and I'm about to say more, but something begins to happen. As I open my purse, my heart starts to pound, a jolting heavy lump in my chest. My breath comes short as if my lungs have filled and there isn't enough space for air. Suddenly I'm panting and can feel the heat rising in my face. Sweat breaks out on my forehead.

Then I feel an odd sensation in my right hand, not a tingling exactly, more a . . . loosening, and I discover that my fingers have acquired a life of their own. I try to open my wallet, but they shiver and jiggle and dance. The effort to control them makes my heart pound harder and my breath come shorter. I feel a trickle of sweat between my breasts. I clench my right hand and open it again. My palm is wet, and the whole hand trembles. I manage to open my wallet but can hardly pull out the money. Bills and noisy coins fall between my fingers onto the counter and the floor.

"I'm . . . sorry," I say, bending over. I can pick up the fallen bills, but both hands are shaking so badly I can't manage the dime and quarter. In desperation, I kick them under the counter. When I stand up, I feel dizzy, and the sparks in my eyes flash with every thud of my heart.

"Are you okay?" she asks.

I push two crunched-up twenties at her. "I'm fine."

She straightens out the bills, glancing suspiciously at me, and puts them in her cash drawer. Then she holds out the change.

"Just drop it in here." I hold my purse open.

"You sure you're okay?"

"In here. Please."

She shrugs—I hear her thinking, Crazy customer—and drops in the change. "Thirty-three, thirty-five . . . forty dollars. Have a good day."

I escape with my groceries clutched to my chest and my purse dangling open from my arm. I stumble out the door and to my car, where I lean against the back fender, my head bent, and suck in deep breaths, forcing the cool air into my lungs. Other customers get into and out of their cars, and I feel their eyes on me, but I can count on their Canadian reserve. They may glance at me, but they immediately look away, far too discreet to show curiosity, too polite to interfere where they might not be wanted.

The steadiness of my breath eventually forces my heart into a regular rhythm. My hands become my own again—palms dry, fingers steady—and I can pull on my gloves. But I don't feel like myself. I'm exhausted, as if I have run up a flight of stairs, and my eyes are gritty, as if I've been crying for hours.

I put my groceries in the trunk. I get into the car and turn on the ignition. As I drive home, I focus not on the panic attack I've just experienced but on the details of driving: the car in front of me, my hands on the wheel, the pressure of my foot on the brake. *Turn, slowly now,* there's no rush, red light, step on the brake, slowly, that's it, ease to a stop, green light, foot on the gas, gently, slowly, start rolling, carefully, smoothly, that's it. . . .

We always celebrate New Year's Eve with the same people, rotating hosts from year to year. Our group is formed of ten couples, some of whom we seldom see outside of this

annual gathering, others whom we go out with during the
year. Among the latter are Vera, the Millers, and the Mc-
Gaskins. The format of our New Year's Eve parties is always the same. We have a potluck supper, drink whiskey
sours, stand in a circle at midnight, and throw streamers
when the clock strikes twelve. Then the men go around the
circle kissing the women. If we've imbibed enough whiskey
sours, the kissing becomes a little more enthusiastic than
our marital status warrants. This is about as Dionysiac as
we ever get.

This year we gather at Des and Maureen Miller's. Their
house is dressed up for the holidays, the colored lights
strung like a glittering necklace across the roof and over
the front porch. Inside the house, shiny red and blue letters
spelling New Year's Eve have been pinned across the foyer
wall, and bursts of laughter come from the living room. The
air is redolent of scents, the sharp pine of the Christmas tree
almost blanketed beneath the rich aroma of roasting beef.
From the hall closet, already packed with coats, I smell the
potpourri of perfume and after-shave that lingers on the
wools and furs.

Maureen swoops down on us, wearing a dress of brilliant
red that conceals her ropy neck and arms. "Here you are!"
she cries. "Last but not least. Boots in the paper bag. Your
name is on your bag. I know, I'm so organized it's disgusting. Your coats will have to go up on the bed in the guest
room. Then come down and have a drink. We've got quarts
of whiskey sours. Here, Jane, I'll take that salad and wine.
My God, but we have wine. We're going to be plastered."

Philip and I separate as soon as we can. He heads toward
a group of men standing before the fireplace talking and
looking into the flames. I go into the kitchen where the
women are working on dinner. They're as pretty as butter-
flies in their party dresses, alighting here and there, moving
bowls from refrigerator to table, fixing trays of hors
d'oeuvres, their voices high, their laughter delicate. Maureen presides over us, queenlike. "The dessert forks are in
the silver chest. . . . Saran Wrap? It's in the third drawer

down. . . . No, turn it down as soon as it boils. . . . I don't like those napkins, but they'll have to do. I couldn't find any to . . ." She is so much more animated than usual and laughs so frequently at next to nothing that I suspect she started on the whiskey sours long before the party began. I also notice her laugh is grating and that, when we all go out into the living room, she never directs it at Des. In fact, I notice that she and Des, like Philip and me, circle each other, planets in different orbits.

TERRY'S NOT ENJOYING HER OWN PARTY YET. Charlene hasn't arrived and she's supposed to help set up, a run is starting in the stocking on her left leg, and she hasn't dared drink because she's afraid of screwing up the food. In spite of that, she can smell her crab-cheese-mayo nibbles on English muffin halves burning in the oven. Plus, she has Emma shadowing her wherever she goes. From the bedroom to the bathroom to the living room to the kitchen. She looks as sweet as can be in that Laura Ashley dress with its tiny pink and blue flowers, but Terry wishes she'd leave her alone for just five minutes.

Emma sniffs. "Terry? I think something's burning."

"I think you're right." There's a loud rapping at the door. "Check those cheesy things, will you?"

Terry rushes down the hallway. She's already kicked off her heels, and she's so hot from working in the kitchen she can feel perspiration creating a pathway between her breasts. As she passes the entrance to the living room, Whitney Houston suddenly blares forth from the speakers. She looks in and sees Mic standing by the stereo, laughing with Buddy and drinking a beer. "Turn that down!" she hollers, and then mutters, "Shit," when Buddy leans over and turns the volume up higher.

She throws open the door to find Charlene standing there. "You were supposed to be here an hour ago," she says.

"I had to repair a seam on my dress." Charlene takes off

her coat and boots and pulls her high-heeled shoes out of a bag. "How's it going?"

"Buddy's here with two friends. Margo and her boy-friend—she's from work—and Sylvia who lives down the hall."

"There," Charlene says. "How do I look?"

"Fabulous." Actually, Terry thinks she looks like a blue and gold cream puff. The turquoise silk barely contains her white rolls of flesh, and she's adorned herself with gold chains and bangles and sprayed gold sparkles in her hair.

Charlene professionally assesses Terry's hair. "It held up."

"You could varnish a house with the amount of spray I used."

"And I love your dress. Turn around."

Terry turns. Her dress, which is emerald green, has a short, tight skirt and a filmy long-sleeved bodice that is high in the front but plunges to the waist in the back, revealing Terry's bony spine and freckled skin.

"Sexy," Charlene says. "Very sexy."

"And how do you like this?" Terry points to her choker. It's silver and has a small emerald embedded in the V at the front.

"Mic gave you that?" Charlene asks. "Wow."

"Terry?" Terry turns around to find Emma standing behind her. she's got on an oven mitt and is holding out the tray of blackened hors d'oeuvres. "They're all burned."

"Oh, my God!" Charlene exclaims. "Is this Emma?"

Emma nods.

"Ter, it's unbelievable! Like two peas in a pod or something."

Terry hasn't felt like smiling all evening, but now she feels an unaccustomed pride lift up the corners of her lips. "Didn't I say it was amazing?" Now Emma is smiling, and Terry thinks how pretty she is. Prettier than she was at that age.

"You know something, Emma?" Charlene says. "Your mom said you looked alike, but I didn't believe it!"

Emma's smile suddenly disappears. "My mom?" she asks with alarm, and looks beyond Charlene to the still open door.

Startled, Terry also looks at the open door. It frames a view out into the hallway, a rectangle of wall and floor, of cracked beige paint and speckled black linoleum. Charlene continues to gush over Emma: ". . . just like her! Like twins! It's incredible, really incredible. I knew your mom when she was your age. Did you know that? That's right. We were best friends, weren't we, Ter?" Her voice, loud and cheerful, fills the awkward silence and even the empty space where the professor's wife, *Jane*, could have been standing. Terry closes the door. "Come on," she says. "We've got work to do."

As they walk back to the kitchen with Emma in the lead, Charlene whispers in her ear, "She doesn't look like Bruce in the least. She's all you, Ter. All you."

DINNER IS BUFFET STYLE, AND I SIT BEtween Rob, Alice's husband, and Vera, balancing a heaping plate on my lap. Vera, who has two other parties to go to, eclipses us with her usual elegance. She's wearing a dramatic black dress with a silvery sequined bodice and black sandals with the highest heels in the room. Rob, who always dresses down, is in a blue sweater, turtleneck, and jeans. At first we talk sporadically, the way people do over plates full of food, and the conversation is idle. We talk of the holidays, plans for the coming year, what we face when we go back to work. I mention the peer review of a paper I'm editing on glacial retreat, which has been so negative and vicious that steps are being taken to suppress it. This leads us to professional jealousies, competitive pressures, our unfortunate place in the demographics: we're well-educated baby boomers with too few jobs at the top, and we agree we'd have had better opportunities if we were ten years older and had entered the job market earlier. In the mid-sixties, Vera says. I point out that the government was wide open even in the late seventies. There were more permanent positions, more upward mobility, easier French requirements. Rob insists he knew someone then who got a bilingual bonus on the basis of being able to say *oui* and *non*.

"Oh, come on, Rob," Vera says. "It was never that easy."

"I'm not shitting around. The guy couldn't string three French words together."

The conversation shifts to abuses, boondoggles, scandals. We talk of the constant redecorating of the prime minister's residence at taxpayer expense, the rumor that Mulroney had a special closet built to house his Gucci loafers, an ADM in Vera's department whose son had illegally been awarded a huge contract.

"Great nepotism," I say as I pick up a piece of roast beef on my fork. "Will he get pink-slipped?"

"Hell would freeze first," Rob says.

"It's been suggested he take a long sick leave or think about retirement," Vera says.

"Those fat cats kiss up and shit down," Rob says. "He'll end up with a pension and a consulting job in another department."

We move to the economy, denouncing high taxes, the cost of living, and the free trade deal with the Americans.

"We'll be eaten alive," Rob says. "The Americans don't give a damn for anybody but themselves."

When I first arrived in Canada and came up against anti-Americanism, I was shocked. I was patriotic then, back in the early seventies, and blinkered by my loyalty. Like most Americans, I held this truth to be self-evident: that everyone worldwide agreed on the rightness of the United States of America—especially those quiet, peace-loving, English-speaking (weren't they just like us, even with that funny money?) neighbors to the north. It took me a while to get used to angry Canadians, particularly those who demanded to know how I could live in one country, work for its *government,* for Christ's sake, and reap its benefits—clean air,

peaceful cities, universal health care—while remaining a
citizen of another. Even Vera couldn't understand it; she
renounced her American citizenship in 1976 and became a
Canadian as fast as she could. "The U.S. is sick," she said.
"It's a violent and brutal place."

"Come on," I said.

"You've been brainwashed by the Pledge: 'One nation,
under God, indivisible, with justice and liberty for all.' See
how I reeled that off? Permanent brain damage."

"What about having to sing 'O Canada' every time you
go to the movies?"

Vera dismissed this as trivial. "You know what we had
to write about for my grade eight graduation essay?
'America—The Land of Liberty.' My English teacher practically had an orgasm because I said we lived under blue
skies that rang with freedom."

"It was poetic."

"A Canadian kid would write about 'Canadian Culture
—Holding Fast against American Imperialism.'"

"You're exaggerating."

"At least Canadians are in touch with reality, Jane.
Americans are lost in their own myths."

But I'd swallowed the myths, and unlike Vera, I've never
entirely disgorged them. I'm only an armchair patriot,
though, sinking deeper into the cushions with each passing
year. I've never had to fight for my country, I don't vote in
any American election even by proxy, I've given up defend-
ing the United States from verbal attacks like Rob's. What
difference will it make? Who even cares? And I make a joke
out of my silly, illogical refusal to change my citizenship. I
say it's an escape clause in my life contract, that when the
Ottawa winter and Conservative taxation policy finally
break me, I'll have somewhere warm to go with a higher
standard of living. I say this even though there's nowhere
in the United States I want to live, and when I cross the
border, I have no sensation of coming home.

Rob is still talking about the free trade agreement. "The
trouble is, Canada isn't tough enough. We'll lose every sin-

gle dispute. The next thing you know, we're going to be living in a country ruled by the National Rifle Association.''

"Now, Rob," I say, "that's a bit of an exaggeration."

"Rob!" Maureen is standing over him. She is carrying a full glass of wine, and I see that her face is now flushed right up to the hairline. "Is that an empty plate I see? You have a responsibility here."

He gives her a mock salute as he stands up. "Aye, aye, Capitano."

"Come on," she says gaily. "Let me lead you to the seconds."

"This was my seconds."

"Thirds, then!" She pats Rob's sweatered belly and winks at us. "He needs a little meat on him, doesn't he?"

As they walk away, Maureen swaying in her high heels, I frown and start to say, "She doesn't usually drink like that, does she?" when Vera grabs me by the wrist and leans forward. "Jane, it's going to happen!"

"What's going to happen?"

"I've got a trip to Manitoba at the end of January."

My first whiskey sour warmed me, the second is beginning to have its fuzzy effect. "Manitoba?"

"The baby, Jane. My baby!"

Suddenly I have a vision of Vera in a hotel bed with a man lying beside her. She is elegant even in coitus: limbs graceful, blond hair spread alluringly on the pillow, the blue of the sheets matching her eyes. "Oh," I say.

"I called him, we're having dinner, and the timing's perfect," she says. "My period's due in the middle of January so I should be ovulating while I'm there."

"And he thinks you're on the pill."

She frowns. "With this AIDS business, he might insist on a condom." Her hand tightens around my wrist. "Pray for me, Jane."

"You know how I feel about this. I don't like it."

"You're the only person I can tell. Please?"

"Vera, I—"

"Please?"

"All right," I say, "I'll pray, but I hope to hell nobody's listening."

 TERRY IS STARTING TO ENJOY HERSELF. She's on her third gin and 7-Up—but no more, the drawback of having your kid at your own party—and the edges of New Year's Eve are blurring in a pleasant way. The apartment's filled up with people. There is a clump of women talking about post-season sales in the kitchen, and a clump of men talking about football in the hallway. Beneath the beat of the music, Terry can hear the clatter of glasses and the occasional sounds of laughter. Emma is busy circulating bowls of chips and dip, nuts and whatever they could salvage from the cheesy nibbles that burned. Whenever she catches sight of Terry, she smiles.

Mic has been deep in conversation with Buddy, and Terry decides that enough is enough. She perches on the arm of his chair and begins to twirl a strand of his hair around her finger. "Is that all you guys can talk about?" she says. "Cars?"

"We could talk hockey," Mic says.

"Or baseball," Buddy says.

Buddy's wearing a suit and tie, and he's cleaned his nails and washed his hair. Terry considers him marginally presentable, but he can't hold a candle to Mic, who looks fabulous in the hunter green sweater with leather shoulders she gave him for Christmas. It cost her almost three weeks' worth of salary, but she knew she'd done the right thing when he opened the box. For a moment, he didn't do anything. Then he said, "Beautiful, babe," and stroked it with his hand. And then he gave her the choker. "That emerald matches your eyes," he said, and Terry had almost been able to ignore the little voice inside her that fretted about where the money had come from. When she put the choker on and felt the silver grow warm from the heat of her body, she'd given a light laugh and said, "What'd you do, Mic? Rob a bank?"

"Sure," he drawled. "The Royal, the Toronto-Dominion, and the Bank of Montreal. They know me so well, when they see me coming, they put the money right out on the counter."

Now Terry touches the emerald with the tips of her fingers as if it were a talisman and catches sight of Charlene hovering nearby and looking anxious in that cowlike way she has. Taking pity on her, Terry beckons her over. "Buddy wants to know what you've got in your hair."

Buddy gives her a look of disbelief while Charlene settles on the couch next to him. "Sparkles," she says, bending her head.

"Very nice," Buddy says.

"They come in a spray can."

"Hey, Bud," Mic says, "you should spray that on the Mercedes."

"Or the BMW."

The two men laugh, and Buddy winks at Terry. "An in-joke."

Terry ignores him and says to Charlene, "We rented *Ghost* last week."

"I loved that movie!" Charlene turns to Buddy. "Didn't you?"

"All that Demi broad did was cry."

"Of course she cried," Terry says. "The guy she loved died."

"I cried too," Charlene says, "I *love* Patrick Swayze."

Buddy looks disgusted. "The guy can't act his way out of a paper bag."

Terry raises an eyebrow and gives Charlene an arch smile. "We don't care how well he acts, do we?"

"Women are all alike," Mic says to Buddy. "They don't respect a guy's mind."

"We would," Charlene says, "if there was anything in it."

"Whoa," Buddy says. "Get her."

Emma has come over, and Terry puts an arm around her waist. "Having a good time?"

"Oh, yes."

"The thing that got me about that movie," Mic says, "is that even though there was a heaven and a hell in that movie, nobody helped him. Did you notice that?"

"What movie?" Emma whispers, and Terry whispers back, *"Ghost."*

"Oh," says Emma, "I saw that."

Mic is continuing, "You know what I mean? There was this heaven with all the light, and then there were all these dark shadows that took the bad guys away to some hell. Only, there wasn't any God. Swayze had to fight the evil himself. It doesn't make sense, does it? That a God or something would have made the heaven and hell but left it up to a ghost to do all the work?"

There is a silence during which Charlene stares down at her nails and Buddy takes a long swig of his beer. Then Emma pipes up, "What I think is they put in a heaven to make us feel better at the end because they couldn't really bring him back to life."

There is another silence. Mic shrugs. "Yeah, maybe."

Charlene says, "I love happy endings. They make me cry."

"I love sad endings," Terry says. "They make me cry."

Buddy says, "Women," and takes another swig of his beer.

Terry has been idly wrapping individual curls of Mic's hair around her finger, but now she takes a handful. She spreads her fingers and pulls them slowly outward from his head so that the strands, thick and coarse, are pulled straight. For a second she holds them there, and then she lets go. They immediately spring back into curls and waves. She tries to take another handful, but Mic shakes his head away from her. "Time for a fill-up," he says, holding up his beer can. "Any of you women want to do the honors?"

"I'll get it," Emma says, spinning out of Terry's arm. "I'll be right back."

AFTER DINNER I BOOGIE WITH DES. THE food has been cleared away, and the dining room table moved to a far wall so that we have a place to dance. Someone has brought a tape of the Beach Boys, and "Surf City, U.S.A." is playing. It is nostalgia, I think, that keeps us from dancing to modern hits. New Year's Eve evokes for us rock and roll, high school proms, gymnasiums draped in streamers and balloons. Like the adolescents we once were, Des and I twitch and sway, circling each other, bobbing in time to the beat, hips thrusting, arms waving. If I narrow my eyes and let their focus soften, I might be able to distort reality enough to imagine that we are sixteen years old again, but Des is talking about a science conference he is organizing, and I'm trying to hear him over the sound of the drums.

"So I've got the commissioner of official languages on my back."

"Who?"

"The commissioner of official languages! He says we have to provide simultaneous translation even though only five people used it at the last conference, and the translators quit halfway through because they couldn't handle the technical terms."

"Can't you tell him there aren't enough qualified translators?" Des shakes his head. "Well then, just don't supply any. Who'll know?"

"The language police."

I echo him in disbelief. "The language police?"

"Someone will report it," he says glumly. "You can count on that." To cheer him up, I move to his side and give his hip a smart bump with mine. For a few minutes we do a comfortable hip-bump-grind to the beat, and then the music changes to something slow, and Des holds out his arms. "Shall we?" he asks.

I've never slow-danced with Des before. We tend to do that with our husbands, not our friends' husbands. But tonight there's something in the air, something making the

banners and balloons that hang from the ceiling bob and
sway as if a hand were pushing them. It adds a hint of recklessness to our laughter, an unusually frenetic quality to our
gestures. Maureen, I see, is dancing with Rob. Alice has
moved into Philip's arms. I wonder how many of us are not
speaking to our spouses, how many have drunk too much,
how many would like to go home with someone else's husband or wife. Not for the first time I speculate on the marriages around me. Who has been faithful? Who has not?
We may have suspicions, but our gossip doesn't extend its
tentacles deep into our sex lives. No one here knows about
Stuart, and our only scandals have been provided by Vera.
As I begin dancing with Des, I imagine stripping away their
encrustations of Canadian reticence and politesse. What
would I find quivering beneath that rectitude? Sexual quirks
and perversions? Philandering and peccadillos? Ménages à
trois?

Des and I circle slowly. He's more slender than Philip,
his shoulder beneath my hand less broad. I feel his thighs
moving against mine, and he hums to the music, a pleasant
melody in my ear. We turn and turn, different parts of the
room, different couples, swimming in and out of view.
Vera's dancing with Bill Fraser, a neighbor of the Millers',
and whispering in his ear. Maureen has closed her eyes.
Philip's back first appears in my sight with Alice looking
over his shoulder. She gives me a slow smile; then they
turn. Philip and I look at each other, and our glances slide
off and away, frictionless, as if we're strangers.

As we circle once more so that Philip disappears from
view, I sigh, and Des asks, "Anything the matter?"

"Marriage," I say with a light party laugh. "I've decided
you're right. It's hell."

ROBERTA WAS ALWAYS A LOUSY DRESSER, and Terry is happy to note that New Year's Eve doesn't make a bit of difference. Her dress is a tacky mustard-gold that makes her skin look pasty and has see-through sleeves that reveal her heavy upper arms. Roberta's fatter than she was in the summer, and so is John. He's got a gut on him a mile wide. It hangs over his belt and lifts his blue and red striped tie forward. Terry imagines John naked, his belly as round as his bald head but with more hair. She swallows a bubble of laughter, chokes on it, and is coughing as she leads them into the living room where Mic is lounging on the couch, one arm thrown over the back, his legs stretched out in front of him. Terry checks out the angle of Roberta's glasses to make sure she's looking at Mic. Does she see how the muscles bulge in his shoulders, the flatness of his stomach, the length of his legs?

"Mic," she says. "It's Roberta and John."

He raises a glass to them. "Hey," he says. "Want a beer?"

John takes a step toward Mic, but Roberta puts a hand on his arm. She has plump white hands with nails the color of cherries. "Remember what the doctor said." She looks at Terry. "High blood pressure."

"Oh," Terry says.

"Job stress," Roberta says. "He's under a lot of pressure."

John's mouth pouts beneath his dark sliver of mustache. "Come on, Berta, a beer isn't going to kill me."

"John," Roberta says warningly.

"Just one little beer."

Roberta turns to Terry. "A club soda with lemon."

"She doesn't want me to make her a rich widow," John says to Terry with a grin. "I tell her I'm worth more dead than alive."

"We got soda in the kitchen," Terry says. As they head into the kitchen, she feels her smile fix into position, a rigid curl whose tips tremble with tension. She knows Emma's there. The kid's been a busy little beaver, passing food around, bringing the dirty glasses and plates back to the kitchen, and stacking them by the sink. Now she's started washing, and Terry would bet a million she never does that at home. She'd bet Emma and Jane fight like cats and dogs over stuff like that. The thought makes the laughter rise again, not one big bubble this time, but a fizzy, continuous pressure.

She makes a little skip that puts her well ahead of Roberta, puts her arm around Emma, and whips her around. Emma's hands leave the sink and spray soapy water over the floor. "My daughter, Emma," she says.

Roberta gives a satisfying little screech and slaps her hand to her mouth. Her tight brown curls shiver, and Terry feels the hilarity break through the barrier of her throat. She laughs out loud, ignoring the way Emma's shoulders stiffen beneath her hands.

"I'm speechless," Roberta finally says. "I don't know what to say."

"Em, this is your aunt Roberta. My sister. And her husband, John."

John nods. "Emma."

"Well, Emma," Roberta says, "you're a surprise for sure."

"Looks just like you, Terry," John says.

Emma drops her head and looks at the floor.

"Aren't you going to say hello, hon?" Terry says to the nape of Emma's neck. "They're family."

"Hello," Emma replies, her voice almost indistinct. Terry feels the stiffness spreading in her, from the shoulders down the back and into her legs. For a moment she feels bad about springing Roberta on Emma. Maybe she should've warned her first. Maybe she should've prepared her for the ugly way Roberta presses her lips together.

"I would've appreciated a little warning," Roberta says.

"What was I supposed to do? Send a birth announcement?"

"Have you told Mom?"

"You're the first to know." The hilarity bursts out again, and Emma shudders.

"This isn't funny," Roberta says. "This isn't a laughing matter."

"Oh, come on, Roberta, lighten up."

"We can't stay, can we, John?"

"Uh? I thought . . ."

But Roberta is already walking away—"Don't worry, we'll get our own coats"—and John has to follow. He winks at Terry. "Nice seeing you," he says.

Terry's hands fall from Emma's shoulders to her sides. She has a feeling in her throat like pop that's gone flat and sour. Emma looks at her with eyes that are wet. "It's okay, hon," Terry says. "Roberta's always been a lousy bitch."

 IN MY EVENING BAG, I CARRY A COMB, LIP-stick, wallet, keys, and a piece of paper with Terry's telephone number on it. I slipped this in at the last minute. It lies at the bottom of my purse in much the same way Emma's overnight visit lies in the back of my mind, forgotten for periods of time but always there when I start rummaging. When I'm in the bathroom, intending to apply more lipstick, the paper appears in my fingers. I hold it as I redden my lips and pat down my hair. I hold it as I walk into Maureen's office, which is filled with the paraphernalia of her real estate business. House For Sale signs are stacked up against the desk, and thick loose-leafs with MLS listings lie on top of the computer monitor. The beat of "Yackety-Yak" comes up through the floorboards. I dial the number. No sign of panic, I notice. My hands are quite steady.

The phone rings several times before a man answers, "Happy New Year!"

In the background I can hear blasts of music, laughter, voices, and the clinking of glasses. "Hello?" I say.

"Well, hello there, sweetie. How're you?"

"I'd like to speak to—"

"Anything you need, just ask. Buddy will provide."

"Excuse me, but—"

"Hey, you got a name?"

"I would like to speak to Emma Wastenay, please."

"You're breaking my heart, babe. This coulda been love at first ring, you know."

"Emma. Please."

"Hold on, sweetheart, Hey! Anybody named Emma here?"

I hear garbled sounds and then he's back. "What does she look like?"

"Red hair. Skinny. She's thirteen."

"Oh, her."

The phone clatters down onto some surface, and I have to hold the receiver away from my ear for a minute. Then the receiver bangs in my ear and I hear "Hello?"

"Em? It's Mom."

"Oh, hi." She pauses. "How come you're calling?"

"I just wanted to see how you're doing."

"I'm okay."

"Having a good time?"

"Yeah."

"Did you have any supper?"

"Sort of. Well, there wasn't any *real* supper, but we're going to have pizza soon."

"You know where you're going to sleep?"

"The couch, but if I get tired before the party's over, I'm supposed to go into Terry's bedroom."

"So it's going okay?"

"Yeah."

"Her friends are nice?"

"Yeah. Real nice."

"That's good. Well, I'm glad to hear that you're having a good time." I know there's nothing more to say, but I can't bring myself to break the connection. I cling to the thin sound of her voice. "Don't drink too much."

"Mom!"

"Just teasing. And make sure you get some sleep. You

know how you get sick after sleep-overs when you try to stay up all night. Daddy and I aren't going to be very happy if you come home sick."

I hear Emma's sigh. "Okay, Mom."

"And call us tomorrow when you're ready to get picked up."

"Okay."

"Bye . . . oh, Em?"

"What?"

Brush your teeth. Wash your face. Eat a good breakfast. Remember I'm your mother. "Don't forget to thank Terry for her hospitality," I say. "It's important to be polite."

"Okay."

"Bye, hon. Happy New Year."

"Bye, Mom."

 TERRY'S FLYING HIGHER THAN A KITE. SHE hadn't meant to drink more, but someone's always pressing a glass into her hand, and she finally thinks, The hell with it, it's New Year's, isn't it? Now she's had a brainstorm —it's wild, really wild— and she pulls Emma into the bedroom.

"Let's sing something at midnight."

"You and me?"

"A mother-daughter singing act."

"But I won't know the words."

"We'll lip-sync. It's easy."

"In front of all those people?"

"They're friends."

"I'd feel silly."

"You want to be famous? You want to be on the cover of *People* magazine?"

"I suppose so."

"You want to make millions of dollars and have all the clothes you want and be in movies like Madonna?"

"Yeah."

"This is how we start."

"I don't want to."

"This could be our big break." Terry imitates an interviewer and holds an imaginary mike up to Emma. " 'Tell me, Miss Wastenay, how'd you get your start?' "

Emma giggles.

"We'll do a Shirelles number, but we gotta practice the moves."

Humming, Terry flings open the closet door, revealing a sagging wooden pole supporting a jumble of clothes. She pushes the door to the wall and holds it there by leaning a chair against it. The mirror on the inside of the closet door reflects the dimly lit room—the pale green wall with the butterfly-shaped crack in one corner, the bed with coats piled high on it, the dresser with makeup bottles and jars scattered across its surface.

She kicks off her shoes. "Come on," she says. Emma stands next to her so that they are both facing the mirror. "Imagine the two of us, all in black. Short skirts, black tops with holes cut out at the shoulders, leather jackets—"

"With those metal things?"

"Studs. Matching belts. Silver bands on our necks."

"High heels?"

"The highest. Hair out to here." Terry demonstrates with her hands.

"Black hats."

"Black eyelashes."

Emma's really getting into it. "Lots of earrings."

"Silver. Five in each ear."

The image in the mirror wavers, readjusts, transforms itself. Gone are the sweet Laura Ashley floral, the cheap green polyester, the backdrop of old apartment, the crack, and the clutter. In their place, a stage, bright lights, the glitter of instruments, two women in black, hair redder than anything, rippling down their backs, the emerald winking . . . an audience wild with applause. . . .

Terry blinks and the room returns. She looks into Emma's mirrored eyes. "We're going to be a major hit," she says. "We're going to be dynamite."

MIDNIGHT. WE'VE FORMED OUR CIRCLE LIKE priests in some ancient religious ritual. The rules are as follows: we must stand next to our spouses, we must wear silly pointed hats, we must count down the minutes along with the radio announcer. At midnight we cross our wrists, clasp hands, and sing "Auld Lang Syne." Swaying back and forth like one large entity, we sing. Alice has the best voice of the group, and it soars sweetly above us: "Should auld acquaintance be forgot, and never brought to m-i-n-d?" At this point tears always come to my eyes, and I see my friends through a soft, generous mist. It makes us look younger than we are, as if time hadn't etched the lines of trouble and worry in our faces.

When the song is done, we're finished with sentimentality. We give a loud whoop and throw skinny streamers, red and blue curlicues, that fall like benedictions onto our hair and shoulders. Then, with as loud a racket as possible, we blow toy trumpets and noisemakers, pointing them in one another's faces and ears. When we have no breath left, the men begin their inner circling. Philip's lips brush mine, dry and noncommittal. Bill, then Tim. Rob, wet and mustache-bristle. David. Garth. Ian. Des. "Happy New Year," he says in a low voice and presses his mouth against mine. His lips are warm and full, and I give myself to the kiss (what is it in the air?), enjoying it until I feel the tip of his tongue touch my teeth. Then I pull back quickly. Des gives me a sexy enigmatic smile as he moves on to Alice.

The music is turned back on. "All I Have to Do is Dream." The Everly Brothers croon loudly, and couples are dancing again. Rob turns to me. "Dance?" he says, and I'm just about to move into his arms when there's a scream and everyone turns. Maureen is standing on a chair and reaching toward the chandelier, intending to drape it with streamers. But she's too drunk for accuracy, and her arm has swung out too far. We rush toward her, but no one reaches her in time. The chair tilts at a dangerous angle, the streamers fly upward, one end of the red and blue and green strips up at the ceiling, the other clenched in Maureen's hand. For a breathless second she appears to be hanging by these paper threads, dangling precariously in space, a woman-bird in brilliant red, poised for graceful flight. The next second, just as Des tries to grab her, Maureen screams again and crashes to the floor.

Part III

WINTER 1989

IF I THOUGHT THE NEW YEAR WAS GOING TO be easier or gentler on any of us, I'm quickly cured of that illusion on its first day when Des calls to say he took Maureen to the emergency room at the Civic Hospital where they discovered she has two cracked ribs. That, despite picking herself up after that fall, brushing off any offers of concern, and dancing until three in the morning.

The following week Alice's son Marshall, who's fifteen, goes to a party where there's drinking, a fact that Alice discovers the next day when she's phoned by a concerned mother.

"I wasn't home and Rob gave him permission to go. I was furious, Jane, I could've killed him."

"How could Rob know there'd be alcohol there?"

"The kid who was throwing the party was eighteen, and there were no parents home. What did Rob think they were going to do?"

"Did Marshall drink?"

"He says he only took a sip of someone else's drink. He says he doesn't like the taste of beer or gin."

"Marshall's a sensible kid," I say.

"Why am I always the one who has to say no? Why do I have to be the heavy? The thing that gets me so angry is Rob won't take any responsibility. He leaves everything to me."

Then in mid-January Philip learns via department gossip that Jackson Maynard, the chairman, doesn't favor him for a promotion to full professor. There are three things that can make Philip lose his cool: sex, which brings out the hidden passionate side of his nature; a fight with me, which provokes the slow burn of his anger; and Jackson Maynard, an old ham with bad breath and, according to Philip, bad scholarship.

Conflict with Jackson Maynard—he and Philip often disagree on department policy—fills Philip with a seething mass of frustration that has no outlet. He speaks to Emma and me in indifferent monosyllables and withdraws into himself, turtlelike, pulling his head beneath a carapace of grim resignation. Sometimes this reaction irritates me intensely, but the marital pendulum has swung once again. When this happens, when the venom collected between us has been spent, its discharge leaves a vacuum into which the old affection inevitably seeps. Our marriage feels like a ship that has righted itself after listing dangerously to port, and I begin to look at Philip with kinder eyes. I decide he's handsome and intelligent once again; my interest in sex rises sharply.

The reasons for the venom collecting in the first place haven't entirely disappeared. I still believe Philip is burying his head in the sand about Emma and Terry, and in an ideal world we would all meet and have a civilized and affable conversation, discussing expectations and setting down guidelines. But the world falls far short of ideal. While I think that Philip's motives are suspect, based on his Canadian reticence and his fear of emotional situations, I've come to realize that, all along, he has understood something I ignored until my visit to Loblaws: we have invisible personal boundaries, which we cross at our peril. For the first time, I respect Emma's insistence that she keep her two families separate, and I begin to suspect Terry hasn't contacted us for the same reason. In this situation in which there are no rules of appropriate behavior, I was the only one brash enough to march headfirst into the wilderness and the first to trip and fall. I decide Philip may be right and that, for a while, we should just give the situation time.

With a harmony of sorts restored to our marriage, I do everything I can to cheer Philip up.

I take the car to the car wash.

I make a batch of chocolate chip cookies.

I try to give him a different perspective. "Jackson can't block a promotion," I point out. "He's only one on a board of three."

"He can do his damnedest. He can really screw it up."

"The other board members like you, don't they?"

He shrugs.

"Isn't one of them Lorraine Henkler? She told me she was impressed with your publications."

"Lorraine," he says dismissively. "She bends with the wind."

Then, just when I think our run of bad news has come to an end, the vice-principal at Hopewell Elementary phones me at work to say that Emma and a group of eighth grade boys were at the convenience store on Aylmer Avenue during the lunch hour when another boy collapsed in the back alley from inhaling spray.

"Inhaling *what*?" I say, my voice too shrill.

"A cooking oil spray. Out in the back behind the store."

"Who is he?"

"A high school student from the Alta Vista area. None of our children knew who he was, but the four of them were apparently watching when it happened."

"My God. Is he going to . . . ?" My voice trails off. I can't say it. Not out loud. *Die, dying, dead, death*—words like bees buzzing too close to Emma, swarming around her head.

The vice-principal is cool about this. "They've taken him to Emergency. In the meantime, our children are quite upset. The police are coming here to talk to them, and we thought it would be a good idea if we could get some of the parents here as well."

When I get to the school, I find a small unhappy gathering in the library. A police officer is addressing the four children, the vice-principal, and two other parents. No one says anything to me as I slip into a chair, but Emma glances at me and I see how scared she is. I don't want to be there either. I've spent too many hours in this school, in this very room, listening to bad news about Emma: that she's argumentative, a class disturbance, not achieving to the level of her abilities and "she's such a bright child, Mrs. Wastenay, but not well focused." For years I've envied my friends with daughters who fit the mold, colored within the lines, played quietly, and liked school.

I stare at Emma's pale profile, and her fear is communicated to me so completely I feel it as if it's my own. This is the conditioning of motherhood, built on thousands of needy cries: "Mommy! I cut my knee. . . . I had a bad dream. . . . That boy hit me. . . ." "Here, let me kiss it better." But I'm forced to sit a half a table away. I take off my gloves and put them neatly in front of me.

"Mrs. Wastenay," the vice-principal is saying to the police officer. "Emma's mother."

The officer nods and I nod back. He wears a uniform, a holster, and a gun (the official man), but he's also middle-aged with a bald spot and a graying mustache (a father, a husband). He is visibly upset.

"So, let me get this straight now," he says, addressing the children. "The boy started jumping around. Then he screamed and fell to the ground."

All the children nod, and Nicky says, "I thought he was just fooling around."

Vincent adds, "I thought he was showing off."

"Had any of you seen him before?"

The four heads shake.

"Emma, why did you go out into the back with him?"

Her voice is high and trembling. "He asked if we wanted to try something really neat."

"You knew he meant sniffing spray?"

"Not . . . Well, sort of."

"You know it's dangerous to sniff spray?"

I hear the tears rising within her. "I wasn't going to do it," she says. "I was just going to watch."

"And after he fell, what did you do? Mark? What did you do?"

Mark is the thinnest and reediest of the boys. I notice his voice is breaking and his upper lip has a shadow. "When he didn't get up, I thought maybe something was wrong, but it was time to go back to school.''

''Who told the store clerk?''

Nicky raises her hand, ''I did, sir.''

The officer goes on at length about the dangers of certain kinds of sprays, cites statistics about injury and illness, pinning each child with a solemn look, and ends by saying the boy is in critical condition in the intensive care unit. Do they know what that means?

''He's really sick?'' Nicky ventures, his voice wobbling.

''It might mean brain damage,'' the police officer says and then nails his case shut, ''or death.''

One of the children—they're all so frightened now it's impossible to tell which—makes a noise between a moan and a sob.

Now the vice-principal gets up and says the school will expand its discussion of the dangers of cooking sprays and glues in its drug awareness program. Nicky's father, who is active in the parent-teacher organization, says the PTO will devote a night to these dangerous substances. Mark's mother suggests the children might want to contribute money for a card and flowers for the boy. This aftermath of well-meaning doesn't permit smiles, but it does allow for a release of tension.

The police officer finally leaves, and the children are sent to their classrooms to get their coats and books, as all of them want to go home rather than stay in school. As we put on our coats and gloves, the other parents and I express our shock and distress to one another, our voices subdued— ''Terrible . . . unbelievable . . . a dreadful business''—trite and vapid words that conceal the workings of our imaginations. We've watched too many television dramas; we're conversant with emergency rooms, heart monitors, oxygen tents, tubing that enters the body like an obscenity. We see our own children in that unknown boy's place, silent and unmoving.

We don't linger long. The ritual of distress has its own schedule, which we instinctively understand. The vice-principal says good-bye to us, but when I turn to go, her hand falls on my arm, forcing me to stay behind. She's a tall, bony woman with pale blond hair and lots of silver jewelery. She doesn't smile often, and I've never warmed to her.

"Such a shame," she says.

"Yes."

"It's no consolation, of course, but at least our children will have learned something from the experience."

"I hope so."

"You know, I was looking at Emma's file," she begins, and I feel a familiar tightening of my facial muscles. It's the motherhood mask: a small rigid smile, eyes that don't give the dismay away. "These school problems are escalating."

"I'll have a talk with her." I say.

"She's a delightful child."

"Yes."

"Full of talent."

"Yes."

"A lively, interesting girl."

I try to leave, but her fingers once again graze my sleeve, and the rare smile she gives me is far too tender and curious. I know what's coming, it's happened before. "Don't tell them," another mother once advised me. "They'll pity you. They'll think it's the reason for everything."

"She's adopted, isn't she?"

"Yes," I say.

"Adolescence can be especially hard on adopted children. That search for identity is so critical."

"Yes," I say.

"Well, I just wanted you to know, Mrs. Wastenay, that we're with you. We understand where you're coming from, we have a feel for the issues, and we're onside all the way."

"Thank you," I say and flee.

"Mom?"

"Mmmm?"

"Mom, why did he have to die?"

"I told you, Em. He had a heart attack. There's a chemical in the spray that hurt his heart."

"I didn't think he was going to *die*."

"Nobody did."

"Do you think if a doctor had been right there, he wouldn't have?"

"I don't think so."

"But why did it happen?"

"No one knows the answer to that, Em. Fate, I guess."

"Cello says it was God punishing him for lying or something."

"I don't believe that."

"You'd believe it if we went to church."

"Let me put it this way. If there is a God, I can't believe he would kill a boy because he told a lie or wasn't nice or skipped school."

"But there has to be a *reason*."

"It was an accident. He was foolish and reckless and thought he knew better than anyone else."

Pause.

"Mom?"

"Mmmm?"

"Why don't we go to church?"

"Daddy and I don't think we need an organized religion to tell us what to do. We think we know how to live a good life."

"Do we believe in God?"

"Well, Daddy studies the gods of the Romans and Greeks. And then there's the Jewish God and the Christian God and the Muslim God."

"Do you believe in any of them?"

"No, not really."

"Well, I do, even if you don't."

"That's fine."

"I mean, things can't just *happen*."

"Okay."

"And I'm going to start going to church, too."

"Really? Which one?"

"The Catholic one on the corner near the school."

"Okay."

" 'Cause I'm Catholic."

"I didn't know that."

"Terry's Catholic, so I am, right?"

"I guess so."

"You don't believe me."

"If you say you're going to do it, I believe you."

"No, you don't!"

"Em, I said I did."

"I *hate* it when you treat me like a little kid."

"I'm not treating you like a little kid."

"Yes, you are. You always do. You think I'm going to forget all about it. Well, I'm not."

"Okay."

"And I'm going to pray, because Cello said that boy is going to go to hell and burn there. And that he has to stand in the middle of hot flames and his skin turns all black."

"I'd sure like to know where Cello gets his facts."

"His dad told him."

"Hell is a myth, Em, just like the myths Daddy studies. It's not real."

"Are you the smartest person in the world, Mom?"

"Of course not."

"So how can you know what's true and what isn't all the time?"

"I can't."

"And how come Cello's dad says one thing and you say another? How come nobody ever agrees about anything? You know what I hate. You know what I really hate? That nobody ever ever, *ever* has the same answers!"

When Emma was a baby and needed comforting, I could hold her in my arms. She might wiggle and squirm—she was never a quiet baby—but her body molded itself to mine. Her legs automatically straddled my hip, a hand would clutch my blouse, and her round cheek would press against my shoulder or neck. Her hair, a fine red-gold fuzz, smelled of baby shampoo, and her scalp always felt like velvet.

When she was around eight years old, Emma wanted to be hugged on her own terms. She chose the time and the place; she decided on the duration. She would come to the chair in which I was sitting, perch on its arm, and slowly descend backwards onto me until she was in my lap. Then she would snuggle under my chin, and I could put my arms around her. For all her thinness then, Emma wasn't uncomfortable to hold. She fit on my lap, a neat package of head and torso, cornered by elbows and knees. When she'd gotten what she wanted, she slithered away, often leaving by the route that she'd arrived: off my lap, up the arm, and down over its side until her feet reached the floor.

Now that she's thirteen, she doesn't want to be touched by me at all. She doesn't flinch when I put my arms around her, but she stands still, her arms hanging at her sides. She's not quite rigid but not flexible, either. Sometimes I feel her lean into me the slightest bit, but I can't always be sure. Taking courage from the fact that she doesn't actually pull or duck away, I rub her back, swaying with her from side to side. Emma is so tall now her shoulders are just beneath mine and her hair tickles my chin. Her back is thin and angular, the jutting vertebrae sharp beneath my fingers. I hold her until I sense she can stand no more, and then I let her go.

This is what is left of the baby who clung and the child who curled to me. Emma no longer wants that physical comfort, and even though I understand that this was inevitable and she will naturally seek it from someone else—a boy and, finally, a man—I still mourn what I've lost. And when I hold her, so reluctant and awkward, I close my eyes and smell the soap on her skin. It has a floral scent: soft and pink and yielding.

THE RINGING OF THE PHONE WAKES TERRY but not Mic, who grunts and turns over. She glances at the clock—6:00 A.M. on Sunday, *shit*—slips out of bed, pulls on a robe, and makes her way into the kitchen.

"All right. All right," she says and lifts up the receiver. "Hello?"

"Terry?"

Terry's been dreading this call. "Do you know what time it is here? Six in the morning!" she says, as if by going on the attack, she'll be able to stop what's coming.

"I've been up all night, on my knees, praying for you."

"And it's three o'clock there!"

"Ever since Roberta called me, I've searched my soul trying to understand why you couldn't tell me about finding my granddaughter."

"Mom—"

"And I just don't know the answer, I really don't. But ever since you were a little girl, you've been a stranger. I've been able to look into the hearts of all my other children, but never yours. It's closed, that's why. Closed hard. You have a hard heart, Terry. You always did. I'll never forget when you broke your auntie Grace's best crystal vase and . . ."

Terry sits on the floor and closes her eyes. She knows what's at the opposite end of the phone line—Jessie Petrie, dressed in a floral bathrobe and threadbare slippers, hugging the phone to her ear. Her mother is a small spider of a woman: thin in the arms and legs and fat in the abdomen and face. Her hair, once as red as Terry's, is thin, white, and permed into tight curls. When she's angry, she narrows her eyes and purses her mouth. Terry believes she can hear the pursing through the phone lines. It makes a hissing sound, like air seeping through a small hole.

When Joe Petrie died eight years ago, Jessie was the beneficiary of his small life insurance policy. The money was enough to get her back to Calgary, where she'd grown up, and to purchase a tiny house, which she immediately filled

with crucifixes, pictures of Jesus, and a collection of porcelain knickknacks: deer, frogs, babies, gnomes, and miniature landscapes. Jessie lives on old-age pension checks and
the generosity of her children, except for Terry, who never
made enough money to contribute. Not that she would have.
There was too much lousy blood under the table for that.

". . . and then all that trouble at school, fighting with your
teachers, getting detentions, failing everything. Nothing I
said made the slighest bit of difference, did it? You were
just heading right down the road to hell, and nobody could
stop you. I remember that time your father caught you
climbing out the window at two in the morning with a purse
full of drugs and . . ."

*Barbara and Terry are walking, barefoot, arm in arm, on
the beach in front of the Malibu dream house. Terry loves it
when Barbara walks with her like that, although she knows
it's only for looks. It makes Barbara seem motherly rather
than just hard as nails. But Terry still likes it. The hand at
her elbow is warm and firm.*

*"What was your relationship with your parents?" Bar-
bara asks.*

"Difficult."

*Barbara nods in sympathy. "Often the most talented or
brilliant child in the family is the odd one out."*

"Well, that was me. I never fit in."

"What was the atmosphere like?"

*"Arguing, fighting. I was always in trouble for some-
thing."*

"Did they encourage you at all in your ambitions?"

"They didn't even know I had any."

*Barbara sighs. "Gifted children need an outlet for their
talents or they get frustrated and cause problems."*

*Terry tries to imagine what her life would've been like if
Barbara Walters, instead of Jessie Petrie, had been her
mother. She superimposes elegance over shabbiness, compassion over indifference, and serenity over turmoil. But
they don't last. Jessie intervenes, her small, round face*

puckered with anger, and Joe steps forward, belligerent as hell.

"My mother said I was a shit disturber."

Barbara takes on her deep look. "Sometimes one child in a family becomes the lightning rod for all the family's frustrations."

"Yeah," Terry says. "My father used to beat the crap out of me."

". . . so I asked Jesus, what did I do? Why did I deserve this? I taught her right from wrong. I taught her how to behave. I brought her up Christian."

Terry knows better than to remind Jessie that the Petries weren't religious. No one went to church, and Joe hated priests and nuns. He called them *sweeties* and *crows*. Jessie's born-again religion came after Joe's stroke, when she met a fundamentalist preacher in the parking lot of the funeral parlor and he converted her.

"I'll send you a picture of Emma," Terry says.

"Roberta says she's a Petrie through and through. And a nice girl. Very well brought up. Does she come from a Christian family?"

Terry rolls her eyes to the ceiling and notices dust dangling in threads from one corner. "Yes," she says.

"Thank the Lord."

"Yes."

"And how's work?"

"Going fine."

"And Mic? Does he have a job yet?"

"Yes," Terry lies. "He's driving a truck for a bottling company."

"Well, that's good honest work."

"Yes, Mom."

When the call is over, Terry goes back to bed. Mic is awake. He has one hand under his head and he's smoking a cigarette, looking up at the ceiling. Terry takes off her bathrobe and, shivering, slides in next to him. His body is warm and solid.

"Driving a truck for a *bottling* company?" he says. "Jesus, Ter, is it beer or what?"

"I couldn't think of anything else."

Mic leans over and butts out his cigarette in an ashtray by the bed. Then he pulls Terry into the crook of his arm. "Do I get to wear one of those uniforms with my name on the pocket?" he asks. "And when I come home at night, do I say, 'Where's my dinner? I just drove three hundred and fifty klicks to Cornwall and back'?"

Terry laughs. She loves it when Mic is in this kind of mood—amused, affectionate, and slightly ironic.

Are there moments when you feel particularly close to
  your significant other?
  a. All the time
  b. Most of the time
  c. Some of the time
  d. Not at all

"You know what that reminds me of?" Mic says. "My old man. He had a bread route—that was his job. He got up at four o'clock every morning and went down to the bakery and picked up the bread. Then he'd go door-to-door and deliver it."

Terry lies very still, because she knows if she moves he might stop talking.

"He had a jacket with his name on the front and the name of the bakery on the back. He drove a pickup truck and kept a clipboard on the dash with the names of his customers and whether they'd paid or whether they owed him. When I was little, he'd let me go with him sometimes. You shoulda seen me, sitting on the edge of the seat and thinking I was king of the road. I thought delivering bread was hot shit.

"And he always bragged about the nice neighborhoods on his route and how friendly everyone was and how he'd tell jokes to the housewives and they'd smile when they saw him coming. He'd say to me, 'You know what those smiles are, Mikey? They're money in the bank.' I musta been ten years old before I figured out that he made shit money and the only reason he didn't quit was because he'd been fired from every other job he'd ever had. And you want to know what his really big ambition was? Get this. My old man thought the top of the shit heap would be to drive a truck for Molson or Labatt's.''

What kind of tears can your significant other bring to your eyes?
a. Copious
b. Plentiful
c. Scanty
d. Next to none

Mic sits up and reaches for another cigarette. "Want one?" he asks. Terry nods, and he lights one for each of them. As he's exhaling, he adds, "And it didn't take me long to figure out that those rich bitches in the big houses didn't give a flying fuck for people like him. When the bakery quit delivering bread door-to-door, he was out on his ass. That's when I learned you can't buy fuck-all with smiles."

JANUARY SLIDES INTO FEBRUARY, THE worst month of the year. There are enough post-season sales and pleasures to be found in gifts and purchases to make January tolerable, but February lacks any charm for me. It's no longer the cusp of winter but the beginning of its slow, blurred finale. I drag myself out of bed in the morning and am sometimes asleep before Emma at night. I'm always tired: tired by the heaviness of my winter boots, tired by the seemingly endless assault of snow and sleet, tired of the long, dark nights that begin before dinner and end after breakfast.

At work I stare at the piles of paper before me—the scientists' reports, the peer reviews, the maps with legends that need checking—and my head swims with exhaustion. When Barry informs me the GSC intends to cooperate with the United States Geological Survey in publishing *The Decade of North American Geology* for its hundredth anniversary, I feel the weight of work on my shoulders, bending me over my desk. The only aspect of this new project, which at first heartens me, is that it will require an English editor and my job can't be cut. Then it occurs to me they could hire an outside consultant. In short, I am dispensable.

Dispensable. This is my word for the new year. It echoes in my ears.

When Emma came back from Terry's New Year's Eve party, I was taken aback by her enthusiasm and excitement. For once she was not reluctant to talk. The party was great! The food was *really* good! Everyone was so neat! She just loved it! When those superlatives had finally boiled themselves dry, she explained that she and Terry had sung together—a mother-daughter team—and that they had been, according to all those present, stunning and terrific. I found it hard to be congratulatory. My face hurt when I smiled, my mouth ached when I said "How nice." Jealousy has invaded me, a physically aggressive act. I feel it pressing painfully against my gut, where it lodges like an unwanted guest. I don't want to be jealous. I want to be understanding and generous in spirit. Jane, patron saint of adoptive triangles.

"But you're not a saint," Alice points out one Saturday afternoon when we're putting together a mailing list for Emma and Felicia's Pathfinders troop. "Why should you feel like one?"

"Jealousy is so ugly."

"Romance wouldn't exist without jealousy. I wouldn't have a job."

"That doesn't mean I have to like it."

"Terry doesn't have any real claim. She has only what Emma is willing to give her. Nothing more, nothing less."

"And what if Emma gives her a lot? Then what do I do?"

Alice puts down her pen. "Do you think years of mothering are going to go down the drain because of a little show-biz glitz?''

"Emma loves singing."

"So what? She comes to you when she's worried, doesn't she? You get the life-and-death questions. And did the school call Terry over that spray business? You're the bottom line for Emma. Not Terry—you."

Emma at three years old.

"My other mommy took me to Baskin and Robbins and bought me a chocolate-strawberry-vanilla ice cream."

"Did it taste good?"

"It was yummy delicious!"

Emma at four.

"You're so mean!"

"It is very bad behavior to throw your clothes down the stairs."

"My other mommy wouldn't be mean."

"All mommies punish children who misbehave."

Emma at five.

"Tell me the story of how you got me again."

"Well, Daddy and I went to the Children's Aid, and we said to the lady there, 'We're looking for a little girl.' And the lady said, 'Mr. and Mrs. Wastenay, I have just the little girl you're looking for.' 'You do?' we said, and when she brought you out and Daddy held you in his arms, we said, 'She's absolutely perfect. We'll take her right now.' "

"Where was the other mommy?"

"She wasn't there."

"How come?"

"Well, I guess she'd gone back home."

"Does she live on our street?"

"No, she lives far away."

"Can we visit her?"

"We don't know her address."

"When we find out, we should visit her."

"Why?"

"Because she misses me."

Emma at six: in the park near our house.

She goes up to an elderly neighbor who's sitting on the park bench near us and says, "I have one mommy and another mommy."

This neighbor, a grandmother and used to children, gives her a smile. "My, my," she says.

"But one mommy doesn't live in our house."

The neighbor smiles at me. "They have such imaginations, don't they?"

Emma is persistent. "She lives far away."

"Is that right?"

"My mommy told me."

"My, my."

"So what I want to know is"—Emma takes a deep breath—"are you that other mommy?"

Emma at nine.

"It's *bad* to give a baby away."

"Not everyone can keep her baby. Not everyone has that choice."

"She could have."

"She was too young. She wasn't ready to be a mother yet."

"I wouldn't give up *my* baby, if I had one. I'd love her and keep her. I'd hug her and kiss her all the time."

"It's not always that simple."

"I hate her!"

"Honey, you don't even know her. I'm sure she thinks about you. I'll bet every time you have a birthday she thinks about the day you were born."

"Oh, sure."

"Em, she gave you up because she loved you and wanted the best for you."

"I hate her, Mom. I don't care what you say. I *hate* her!"

Like a shimmering, trembling, translucent bubble, she has floated in and out of my life, alighting for a moment, rising on a breeze, dissolving into the air. You wouldn't think a bubble, elastic and pliant, could give pain, would you? But it does. Oh, yes, it does—even when it rests, for the briefest second, against the skin.

DEAR DIARY,
Wednsday—blizard condishions. A gross zit on my nose. Also—looking into the miror. One brest bigger than the other! Grosser.

Good news—Terry took me shopping for maching outfits to wear when we sing. We got black pants and slinky black tops and black hats—like cowboys with silver bands. Were going to wear lots of silver jewlery and silver high heals. We tried on the close at her apartment and practiced some singing. Terry said we were hot like profeshionals and we should pik out stage names like maybe Black Magick or something.

Mark and I are sort of going steady. I realy like Mark. Maybe I even love him I don't know. But sometimes he acts so stupid. Like a real jerk. Like throing his pudding on the cafateria floor. I dont want to go out with him if hes going to be jerky speshially at the movies. They kick you out at the Mayfair if youre realy stupid.

School realy sucks. We have to do reports on countries and I got pared off with guess who? Dana the doornob thats who. We have to do South Africa which my Mom says is realy good because of all the problems with black people. She says they are being discrimanated against and jailed and shot at and stuff. She says it shuld be very intiresting. Like I realy care.

I am broke Diary! I only have sixty-three cents because I spent all my money at McDonald's. I had to pay for the Jello because he didnt have any money at all. We got kicked out of McDonald's because Nicky kept saying this gross poem over and over again and we culdn't stop laffing.

> There once was a geenie with a ten foot weenie
> And he went to the lady next door
> She thot it was a snake and cut it with a rake
> And now its only two foot four.

Ha. Ha. Ha.
Bye for now.

 ON THE LAST DAY OF FEBRUARY AN ECSTATIC Vera is confirmed as pregnant. She tells me this one evening over a celebratory cup of coffee in her apartment.

"Wonderful," I say. "It's just what you wanted."

"I couldn't believe it!"

I've decided to put a good face on a bad business. "It's probably the only decent news we've had around here in a month."

"First time around, too," Vera says. "I must be one of those women who get pregnant the minute a man drops his pants."

I envision a man's pants falling to his ankles and look down at Vera's gleaming cream-colored floor. Her condominium is in a new building on Sussex Drive, a hefty stone's throw from the prime minister's residence. It's a fashionable address and home to ministers and members of Parliament. Vera bought it when her mother died and she inherited enough money to absorb the cost of marble flooring, a Jacuzzi in the bathroom, and mirrors everywhere. There isn't a speck of dirt to be seen or a dish or towel out of place. I think of a baby in here, throwing pureed peas onto the finely waxed floor or regurgitating strained peaches. Once when Emma was ten months old, she chewed on a deck of cards after eating lunch. She then crawled back into the kitchen where I was still working, smiled at me, and threw up mashed liver, squash, blueberries, and the corner of the jack of diamonds.

"It was so easy," Vera goes on, "that it makes me shudder when I think of the risks I've taken, like going bareback with my boyfriend from high school."

"You didn't," I say.

"Of course I did. Didn't you?"

"My boyfriend got condoms from his older brother." Sweet Danny Thompson, my senior-year lover, with his shy, endearing smile.

"We practiced coitus interruptus."

"When I went to college, the nurse gave a talk to our dorm and said that women could get pregnant from the sperm in the precoital drop. Half the audience went white."

Vera laughs. "And what about broken condoms? I've had a few of those, too."

I'm smiling as we reminisce about those dangerous pre-pill days, but as I stir my coffee, something sour stirs inside me. An infertile woman doesn't remember her birth-control struggles with any fondness.

"Anyway, the doctor says I'm as healthy as a horse and, barring the unexpected, should do very well. I don't even have any morning sickness."

"That's great."

"Oh, Jane, I'm really excited about this."

"I'm happy for you."

"It still has to be kept a secret, though, as long as possible."

"Can I tell Philip?"

"Philip's okay." Vera reaches out and touches the back of my hand. Her nails are a pale pink shade that matches a pink in the swirling blue and mauve paisley of her blouse. "Jane, you're my closest friend. You know that, don't you?"

I'm embarrassed because I can't reciprocate this statement. I'm closer to Alice than to Vera. "Vera, I—"

"No, I mean it. I have a lot of acquaintances through

work, but you're the closest thing I have to a sister. And we've been through a lot together."

Eighteen years of job problems, my infertility, Emma's adoption, marital ups and downs, her divorces, lovers come and gone: gossamer strands in a web of friendship.

"And my parents are dead, so I have no family left at all."

I get her drift. "Philip and I will be godparents if you want. Or aunt and uncle."

Vera shakes her head. "I know you'd do that. I have another favor to ask. A big one."

"Ask," I say, lifting my coffee cup to my mouth.

"Would you be my labor and birth coach?"

Coffee burns its way down my throat.

"It's a big commitment," she says quickly. "I know that."

That sour something inside me recoils and rises, and my mouth floods with it. The bile of anger and disappointment. The bitter taste of experiences desperately desired but capriciously denied. Who am I, the junk queen of useless tubes and worthless parts, to help another woman in childbirth? What do I know? What advice can I give? What succor can I offer? I don't want any part of this, but how can I refuse? The web of our friendship, woven of tears and laughter, of intimacies and confessions, tightens around me.

Vera is continuing, "There'll be classes and the delivery."

I take a deep breath. "I don't have any qualifications."

She laughs her glittery laugh. "Do prospective fathers?"

"Of course . . . I'll do it."

"Just a warning—I'm terrified, I hate pain, and I'm a rotten patient." She gives a rueful laugh. "Now you're going to want to back out."

Yes! "Nope."

"You're sure?"

No! "Absolutely."

"Oh, Jane, I knew I could count on you."

I dream about Vera's unborn baby. I dream the baby is inside me, and we're in the hospital, but it isn't quite a hospital, because there are desks instead of beds, like a classroom at the university. I'm taking a math test, and I know I won't have the baby unless I pass. I'm worried about this because I don't understand the questions, and the baby is pushing down hard between my legs. It feels like a large wooden club pressing against my genitals. It's pushing so hard I have to pee, and if they don't let me pee, I'm going to explode all over the chair. "I have to go!" I say, but Vera is shushing me: "Don't talk or they'll think you're cheating."

I wake up to the sensation of a full bladder. The bedroom is dark and cool, and I glance over at my radio: 5:14. We've turned the thermostat down at night, and I dread the thought of getting out of my warm bed to go to the bathroom. The uncarpeted floors are icy, the outside walls chilly to the touch. Although it's March, Ottawa has been bitter cold for the past week, temperatures in the minus twenties, a windchill factor close to minus fifty. I think about the alarm due to go off in two hours, the cold wait for the bus, my suede gloves that have a split in the seam by the thumb. When it's as frigid as this, the cold seeks out those rents and tears, searching for bare skin. Shivering, I turn to curl up next to Philip's warmth and discover he's not there.

I know what Philip's absence means. He found out several days before that he hadn't gotten the promotion, and he isn't sleeping well. I pull on my quilted bathrobe and sheepskin slippers. I visit the bathroom and go downstairs. I find Philip lying on the couch in his bathrobe, his eyes closed. The curtains are open, and a wan morning light spreads itself into the room, fingering the frame of a picture, illuminating the dust on the glass-topped coffee table. That ghostly touch also brushes along the top of his head, revealing the thinness of his hair.

At the sound of my footsteps, his eyes open. "What's the matter?" he asks.

"I had a bad dream," I say.

"I couldn't sleep," he says, "again."

"Want some tea?"

"That would be nice."

Tea is an elaborate procedure in our household, based on British rituals brought to Canada by Philip's parents when they emigrated before the war. We don't throw tea bags into coffee cups and add boiling water—my uncivilized American habit. First we fill a teapot with hot water to warm it. When the kettle is whistling, we pour out the hot water, add loose tea, and steep the leaves in boiling water for the appropriate amount of time. In order to keep the teapot warm throughout this process, we enclose it in a tea cozy shaped like a rooster's head with a red cotton crest. The spout of the teapot emerges from its beak. When I bring the pot into the living room, we pour the tea through little individual sieves, which rest on top of our teacups. Philip adds a bit of lemon to his tea. I, who used to douse orange pekoe with milk and three teaspoons of sugar, now take the delicate Earl Grey straight.

I sit next to Philip and switch on the light. "Let's have a worry exchange," I say.

"You think that's going to work, do you?"

I pour tea into his cup and mine. "It might."

We haven't had a worry exchange in years, but we were big on them when we were first married, eager to hear each other's problems and convinced, in the bloom of our youth and health, that there was a solution to every difficulty. And it was true then. A worry exchange worked wonders when each partner was afflicted with a misery whose heaviness could be lightened by intense conversation, mutual sympathy, and lovemaking. To me, a worry exchange was like a full-course meal with a dessert at the end: a luscious dessert, rich and sweet and satisfying.

"Come on," I say. "You first."

"Well, there's the damned promotion, of course. Then it struck me I was eighteen yesterday, and I'm going to be fifty tomorrow. I think the director's running the film too fast."

"*Tempus fugit,*" I say, working in the little Latin I know in hopes of making Philip smile.

He doesn't notice. "Then I started thinking about my eighteen-year-old self and what he was like. He was an idiot. Ninety-nine percent of the time he thought about girls. In the brief time he devoted to thoughts of his future he decided to become a classicist. You know why?"

"He was good at Latin."

"He won a prize in sight reading, he didn't want to do history like his mother—that would've been a bore—and he liked those silly stories about Hercules. The fact that he didn't make the football team had something to do with it, too. Plus he had a thing for this girl in his Latin class. What was her name? Sally? That's right. Sally." He gives an unhappy laugh. "So now I'm almost forty-nine and have to live with the decisions of that kid."

I study the fragrant depths of my tea. "Is there something else you'd rather be?"

"I always wonder if I would have made a good lawyer."

"I didn't know that."

"You know what I realized? It doesn't matter that I didn't get the promotion. It's not going to change anything. I've got tenure. It's a nice, safe trap. And there aren't a lot of openings for classicists anyway. Besides, how many places are going to hire someone who's due to retire in ten or fifteen years? I feel like I've reached the wrong end of the telescope, everything narrowed down to one point and nowhere else to look."

A good wife is a problem-solver. Hungry? I'll feed you. Need a shirt? I'll iron one. Bothersome tooth? I'll make an appointment with the dentist for you. But what happens when a good wife is confronted by a problem with no solution? She becomes a cheering section of one.

"You're a good scholar and a great teacher," I say. "Nothing is going to change that."

Philip sips at his tea and sighs. "I suppose."

We're silent for a while. I hear the furnace fan click on and feel the rush of warm air. I remember when we bought the house and had it renovated. Its skeleton was revealed, and I could look from one room to another without the obstruction of walls. Light flowed around the bones, those pale beams and joists, and wherever I walked, my shoes raised swirls of plaster dust. The empty house was too small for echoes, but when Philip called out to me, I could hear his voice ringing out from basement to roof, clear and round as a bell.

"Philip?" I rearrange myself, kicking off my slippers and tucking my feet beneath me. "Are you sorry that we couldn't have children of our own?"

"No, not at all."

"Really?"

"That eighteen-year-old kid didn't have fatherhood in his dreams. That was the farthest thing from his mind. Actually, you know what he wanted most? He wanted to get laid."

I can't be diverted. "What about the almost-forty-nine-year-old?"

"He's happy with Emma."

"Be *honest*," I say fiercely.

"Jane, I am being honest. I don't mind; I never have. What brings this on anyway? It's ancient territory." He pauses. "Ah, Vera's pregnancy."

"All those feelings about not being able to get pregnant, they're coming back." Tears rise and seep hotly from the corners of my eyes.

Philip puts his arm around me. "Jane, honey—"

"It's infertility raising its head again like . . . like something from one of those movies from the fifties. Those Godzilla things?"

"I remember. The monster emerges from the ocean after being awakened from a long sleep."

"And tramples Tokyo." I give a little laugh and wipe my eyes.

"You don't have to coach her."

"She needs me."

"Let her find someone else."

"She doesn't have anyone else, and I can't let her go

through it all by herself. We've been friends too long. But I'm going to hate it. I just know I'm going to *hate* it."

"Jane, you're a fine mother, a fine wife, and a good friend. Nothing is going to change that."

What else can a good husband, a cheering section of one, say when his wife presents him with an unhappiness that can never be erased? Offer her words of support. Give her a show of stalwart loyalty. And all the while conceal that overwhelming sensation of helplessness. So much, I think sadly, for the worry exchange, that lovely three-course meal with its grand finale, sex jubilee.

I replace the sieve on his cup, put my hand on our crowing pot, and lift. "More tea?" I ask.

"Please."

DEAR DIARY,

Tuesday—sun and I slept on my hair real bad and it looks terible.

I hate Felicia!!! I just hate her. She came over yesterday to do our cards on the boys in grades 7 and 8. She loves Nicky and thinks hes the most sexy boy in the hole school!! Even though hes got all those zits on his chin. But she didnt want to put anything about the zits on his card because it wouldnt sound good. I said whats the point of the cards if there not the truth? She said why are we doing them anyways. I said because its important, thats why, doorknob. Aktuly I didnt call her a doorknob but thats what shes like sometimes. Shes such a stupid bitch!!!

But I dont hate her because of the cards. I hate her because of when I was cutting up my close. Im doing that to put holes in them like Madonna. She said wont that make your Mom mad? I said I dont care. She said it doesnt matter because my Mom isnt my real Mom anyways. Then she said it must be neat to have two Moms. I wanted to realy screem at her because she doesnt know anything, the stupid asshole bitch!!!

And, Diary, I dont like Mic and his friend Buddy. I never told anyone but on New Years I saw Buddy give Sharlene something that looked like a sigaret but wasnt. It was drugs!! And she liked it because she smiled and let Buddy rub her nee with his hand. It was disgusting!!! And I think Mics mean. Even though hes realy good looking, hes always watching peeple in a funny way. And one time he put his hand on my shulder and scueezed until it hurt. I dont know why Terry loves him so much.

Bye for now.

 I'M SITTING IN MY OFFICE WORKING OUT A printing schedule for the latest Survey bulletin when Madeleine gives a small knock and walks in without waiting for an invitation. She never enters my office in a frontal fashion. She sidles in, her head appearing first, her body wrapping itself around the doorjamb.

"Busy?" she asks.

"Very," I say.

"Aren't we all," she says with a sigh, slithering down into the chair by my desk.

She looks different today, and I realize that she's gotten new glasses. The old ones had gold metal frames; the new ones are a speckled tortoiseshell. The combination of beige freckles and yellow-brown speckles haloed by the pale orange hair is overwhelming. I have the sensation that I can no longer actually see her face, that I have to search for her features through an irregularly beaded curtain.

"You've got new glasses," I say.

"Invisible bifocals. You like them?"

Madeleine is also wearing a vivid purple dress with wide shoulder pads that emphasize the flatness of her chest and the thinness of her arms. "Very attractive," I say.

"Thanks." Madeleine leans forward. "Did you hear about the executive performance evaluation meeting?"

"No." Nor do I have any reason to. The meetings are

only for ADMs, they're held behind closed doors, and their sole purpose is to determine the merit pay for directors and directors general. They are marked, or so the gossip goes, by bitter political in-fighting as the department, under current government quotas, can only give five percent of its executives the coveted Outstanding rating.

"Apparently they were going at it hammer and tongs."

"Really."

"I'll bet Des Miller is on tenterhooks."

"Oh?"

"After that increase he got for the department, you'd think he'd deserve an Outstanding, wouldn't you?"

This was Des's managerial triumph, a two-year effort of lobbying Treasury Board officials and ministers' executive staffs that paid off, despite austerity and PY cuts, with a five million dollar annual increase to the Survey's operational budget for the Northern Logistics Project.

"You'd think so," I say.

Behind the glasses and orange lashes, Madeleine's blue eyes gleam. "Well, the word on the street is that they're only going to give him a Fully Satisfactory Plus Plus Plus. Isn't that ridiculous? Of course everybody knows the ADM is such a yes-man he won't fight for his directors, but even so . . ." Madeleine's voice lingers on the "so," but her mind has moved on to more interesting gossip. She pauses, glances at the closed door, and says in a low voice, "Have you heard about the corruption?"

"Corruption?" I say with surprise.

"Upstairs." She bobs her head toward the ceiling and beyond, in the direction of the minister's office. "At the highest levels."

"Come on," I say. "What corruption?"

Madeleine twines herself tighter in the chair, and her orange lashes flutter with pleasure. "You know how we decorate the minister's offices with samples from the Permanent Mineral Collection?"

"Yes."

"Well, as ministers change and the staff comes and goes, the samples have been disappearing."

"Like souvenirs."

"Barry got angry and sent the word upstairs that he wanted a label on each sample saying it's from the collection."

"But it didn't work."

"Worse than that." Triumph sends her freckles and speckles into a shivery jig. "The word came down from the top. He was told to forget it. We're supposed to consider the stolen samples *gifts*."

"Nice," I say.

"And to think they have a screaming fit if there's so much as a paper clip missing down *here*." She stretches and stands up. "Oh, by the way, it's really hush-hush, but I heard Darreau's going to announce a cut of four hundred sixty-two PYs for the whole of EMR."

I'm aghast. "Four hundred sixty-two?"

"Of course it might not be a good rumor."

"Where'd you hear it?"

The beaded curtain has a way of closing. "Oh, here and there."

"But—"

"Got to go." Madeleine slips out the door sideways, with her feet first and her head second. "See you later."

The last I see of her is the tips of her pale narrow fingers waving a good-bye.

"Four hundred sixty-two?"

"That's what she said."

"How did she get that number?"

"She wouldn't say."

Des sighs. "That woman probably knows more than the prime minister."

"You mean she's right?"

"I have no idea. That stuff is confidential. Cabinet level."

Des and I are having coffee in the employee cafeteria. It's too late in the afternoon for the lunch crowd and too early for afternoon breaks, so we have the room to ourselves. Even so, we huddle over our cups, our voices low and conspiratorial.

"Anything new on the language front?" I ask.

"The commissioner of official languages met with the translators and the French Canadian scientists. The translators told him they can't handle the technical terms; the scientists said they listen to English anyway. Wouldn't the taxpayer be thrilled to know we spent five thousand dollars for nothing?"

"So he'll let you off the hook?"

"It's a matter of bypassing Darreau. He doesn't care if it's useless or costs a million for French translation. But the commissioner makes recommendations directly to Parliament. He can go right over Darreau's head."

"Sounds like a good strategy to me."

"I'm keeping my fingers crossed."

"And how about *your* French?"

"I've scheduled myself for two weeks of intensive training in May. The good news is the examiner who was flunking everyone has been fired. There've been complaints from other departments." Des stares into his coffee cup, then lifts his head and gives me a small smile. "In the meantime, Maureen and I are in counseling."

I pause. "That's good, isn't it?"

"I don't know. According to the counselor, I feel neglected, which has something to do with my mother not giving me enough affection. And Maureen feels I try to be too dominant, which has something to do with the way her father used to boss her mother around."

"Does knowing that help?"

Des rubs his hand across his face, and I hear the scrape of his shaven beard against his fingers. He has a nick on his chin, and I imagine him in the morning, standing before the mirror, his face outlined in lather. When Philip and I were first married, I loved to watch him shave. We had a small apartment with a bathroom so tiny Philip insisted he could shit and shave at the same time. I used to sit on the edge of the tub, wishing I could be his razor and lie so close to his fragrant skin. Now we stand side by side in the mornings, follow our personal rituals, and rarely speak. Or if we talk, the subjects are always mundane: a problem with the thermostat, theater tickets that need to be purchased, the fact that we've run short of milk.

"Maureen thinks it helps," Des continues. "I think we're going around in circles. And it's exhausting. After every session we're up past midnight talking about it. Or rather Maureen talks about it. I listen."

"That's better than not talking."

"Sometimes," he says. "Sometimes I just want to get out and run so fast no one will ever catch me."

I'm taken aback by his sudden desperation and the raw look of appeal he's giving me, but am saved from a reply when a voice interrupts us. "Hey, Des!" We look up to see Brian, one of Des's staff, weaving his way among the tables and chairs as fast as he can, waving a newspaper. "Wait till you see this! You're not going to believe it!" Brian is out of breath as he arrives at our table and throws the early edition of *The Citizen* on the table. We look down and the headline screams at us: "462 POSITIONS TO GET THE AX AT EMR."

We stare at it in silence for a few seconds, and then Des speaks. "Jesus Christ," he says. "Jesus fucking Christ."

DEAR DIARY,
Wether—realy cold. Zits—terrible.
I went to the movies with Mark. We held hands and kissed again—a couple of times— but there were other kids from school and they make gross jokes. Their such dweebs its disgusting. Mark says his parents are real cruwel to him. Like he isn't alowed to go to the park after dark and his father makes him do a lot more stuff than his brother. I said he should hear my Mom if he wants to hear cruwel. Last night she got realy mad because she found the clothes I cut up. She screemed and hollered just like I knew she would and about how my

room is such a mess, and she made me emptee my draws and put everything away again. I was realy mad too and when she left my room I dumped out three draws and crumpled everything up and threw it back in.

I have to read Anne Frank for school. Anne Frank is a very sad story that takes plaice during World War II about a girl who gets killed by the Germans just because she's Jewish. I know the ending already because Dana told me. Its pretty horible about the Jewish people and the Germans. I saw a picture in a book of dead people piled up. They were all bones and stuff. It was called the Holocost. Dad says we cant ever forget it because we dont want something like it to hapen again. He says were very lucky to live in a country like Canada where things like that don't hapen.

Bye for now.

 IN MARCH PHILIP'S MOTHER COMES TO VISIT for his forty-ninth birthday. Like my mother's visits, Barbara's are rituals. She comes twice a year, in March and August, stays for a week, and then flies back to Thunder Bay, where she lives in the same small house she and Philip's father, Martin, bought when they emigrated from England. Martin died of a heart attack when Philip was in college, and Barbara has never remarried or, as far as we know, even dated. She's a stout, imperious woman with iron gray chin-length hair and is given to wearing suits with dark floral blouses and shoes with low, sensible heels. Her abiding passion has always been politics. When she comes to see us, Barbara visits Liberal headquarters, talks to Philip about government policies, and smokes many packs of cigarettes. Since she never raises a hand to help me and we have nothing in common other than her son and granddaughter, her visits are always a trial.

Still, I do my best. I buy air deodorizer. I stock the coffee table with the latest issues of *Macleans* and *Saturday Night*. Since Barbara is a hearty eater, I make hearty meals: roast beef, loin of pork, roast potatoes, carrots, peas, pies, and cookies. I always weigh five pounds more at the end of one of her visits. And I don't complain to Philip about how she provokes me. Instead I try to ignore the small surges of fury that overwhelm me from time to time and smile, smile, smile.

"Mother? Some more soup?" I say.

"No, thank you. Emma, it's not necessary to slurp like that. And your spoon should not move toward you but away from you. Like this."

Emma obediently follows directions. She dislikes this grandmother, and I don't blame her. When she was six years old and told us Grandma was a horrible bossy cow, Philip explained to her that Barbara had once been a teacher and was used to being in charge. Emma reluctantly accepted this explanation and made faces behind Barbara's back. Now she's much more adept at deception and is so exquisitely polite that Barbara recently informed me Emma has lovely manners for a child of her age.

"After those cuts to VIA Rail, we've established a cross-country Mulroney Watch," Barbara says to Philip. She's president of the Thunder Bay Liberal Seniors, a post bestowed upon her after her activism in the fight against the government's attempt to de-index old-age pensions. "We have to keep an eye on him."

"It's the CBC next," Philip says.

"That's on the top of our agenda," Barbara says.

"And the civil service," I say, but I don't expect Barbara to respond. She doesn't consider me politically astute.

"There are days," Barbara goes on, "when I can't believe the people of this country voted that man in. He'll always be a used-car salesman to me."

Emma pipes up. "Did Brian Mulroney used to sell cars?"

"I was using a metaphor," Barbara says, "to explain how I feel about the prime minister. Do you know what a metaphor is?"

"Mother, white meat or dark?" Philip says.

"White please."

"Mashed potatoes?" I ask.

"Thank you. A metaphor, Emma, is a way of describing a thing or person by the use of imagery. So, for example, I could say clouds are cotton balls, which they're not, but you would know exactly what I mean."

"But did Brian Mulroney really sell cars?"

"A used-car salesman is a metaphor often used to denote a person whose honesty is in question. So when I compare the prime minister to a used-car salesman, I am implying that the head of our government is not an honest man. He promises one thing and does another. Now, would you call that honest?"

"No, I guess not."

"Can you see why it's very important that when you get older and can vote, you thoroughly understand the character of the men and women who want to run our country?"

"Yes, Grandma."

"At any rate, the real question is—can we get Mulroney out before he destroys every single one of our national symbols?"

"The bureaucrats hate Mulroney," I say. "Ottawa is almost completely Liberal."

Barbara ignores me again. "And he's opened a Pandora's box with Quebec and the constitutional talks," she says to Philip. "There's trouble ahead."

I tamp down the anger, smile as I pass the green beans, and wonder for the thousandth time why I keep on trying.

When I was first introduced to Barbara, I was impressed with her intelligence, her firm no-nonsense approach to life, and her ignorance of most things cosmetic. She didn't have a dressing table cluttered with makeup and perfume, and an investigation of her bathroom cupboard yielded a pragmatic assortment of household remedies and nothing more exotic in toiletries than an unopened bottle of rose-scented cologne. Her library, on the other hand, had the sort of books my mother would never read—biographies and autobiographies, political studies, historical analyses—and her house was cluttered with pamphlets, mailing lists, and policy papers.

My admiration for Barbara was not reciprocated. Try though I might—and I did, reading the same biographies, watching the CBC, absorbing as much of the alien Canadian political landscape as I could—I never rose above the status of an intellectual lightweight in her eyes. After all, I haven't given up my American citizenship, and I can't vote in Canadian elections. My understanding, she once told me, is skewed by a lack of commitment and an ignorance of Canadian history. She said this early on in my marriage when I was attempting to hold forth about something or other. Her tone was kind but impersonal, as if I were one of her fifteen-year-old students. When I fumed about this to Philip, he comforted me by kissing my mouth, caressing my breasts, patting my ass, and saying he'd learned to ignore his mother years ago. But I wasn't comforted easily. In the first years of our marriage, I even cried at those times—family gatherings, mostly—when her indifference seemed overwhelming and painful. Philip couldn't understand my anger or grief.

"She likes you," he said. "She thinks you're good for me."

"She's never interested in what I do or what I think."

"She isn't interested in me either. She's always loved the Liberal party far more than she's loved me."

"That's not true."

"Look, she doesn't interfere in our lives, does she?"

"No."

"So she could be a lot worse, right? Think of it. She could be like your mother."

I laughed shakily. "God forbid."

I didn't understand my anger or grief either. Both had depths more profound than a mother-in-law seemed to warrant. Eventually I grew a protective armor. I learned to dismiss her as an intellectual snob. I laughed at her as a dreadful bore. I said to myself, What do I care what she thinks? But beneath the surface, the hurt still rankles, stinging me now and then, like the remembered feel of an old cut or burn.

On the third day of her visit, I arrive home from work and find Barbara sitting on the couch in the living room. She's been there for quite a while; the ashtray beside her is filled with the butts of dead cigarettes, and the air holds the stink of smoke.

"I thought Philip would be home," I say as I take off my coat and hang it in the hall closet.

"He called to say he had a student conference that was running late."

"I hope you found something to do."

Barbara lights up another cigarette. Her fingers are like Philip's, short and thick, and she keeps the nails cut blunt. "I wasn't bored," she says, indicating a document lying beside her. I glance at it as I sit down: "Government Practices: The Auditor General's Report."

"How's Marion?" I ask. Marion is Philip's older sister, a pediatrician who lives in Edmonton with her lawyer husband, Daniel, and their two sons.

"She's doing very well. Her practice has expanded to include another doctor."

"How nice."

"And Daniel's law firm is involved with the Lubicon Indian land claim. It's an absolutely fascinating case. I'm appalled at the way the provincial government has acted on that one. Of course, Mulroney's Tories haven't acted in good faith either."

I refrain from pointing out that the present Conservative government inherited many of the problems of sixteen years of Liberal rule. "How old are Marion's boys now?"

"Seventeen and twelve. Sean's going to go into geology, I believe."

"That's nice."

A silence threatens us. Barbara leans forward, her steel gray hair falling on either side of her broad face. If I narrow my eyes, I see a softer, older version of Philip.

"I'm curious," she says. "In your job, do you see much government waste?"

I can't resist. "We wallow in it."

"This isn't a laughing matter, Jane," she says, tapping the report beside her. "Government overspending threatens our economic stability. It's a matter of grave concern to the taxpayers of this country."

"We do try, Mother."

"I'm afraid the reputation of our civil service leaves a lot to be desired."

I think of Barry, illegally keeping me on a term contract to hold down the branch budget. I think of Des, sparring with the commissioner of official languages to save translation fees. I think of the slow turnaround time on maps because Cartography has already lost one PY and will probably lose another. How I wish that every taxpayer could spend one week working in a government office, watching us scramble to complete more work on shrinking budgets with fewer people.

"Time to make dinner," I say, jumping up. "I'd better start the potatoes."

I wonder if, for once, she'll take the hint, but Barbara is already lifting up her report. She starts to read it, the cigarette dangling out of her mouth, squinting against the smoke, which spirals up to her eyes.

We celebrate Philip's birthday at home. The dining room table is set with linen, sterling silver, the good china, and two tall red candles. We have a dinner of lobster, green salad, and white wine, followed by a chocolate birthday cake that Emma has decorated with lopsided red roses and shaky handwriting. I present Philip with a new watch; Emma gives him cologne. Barbara's gift is the inevitable political biography and a sweater. Philip is flushed with wine and makes toasts. To Barbara: "May the Liberals win the next election." To Emma: "The next Tiffany or whoever." To me: "Jane, wife and editor supreme." And to himself: "Half a century, here I come."

I laugh—what else can I do?—we all laugh, and Barbara, who's not quite sober herself, begins to tell Emma stories about Philip when he was a little boy. The stories start with his innocence—"Your father was the prettiest baby in the hospital; he had the most beautiful long lashes"—and gradually sink into tales of childhood depravities. Emma learns that Philip never brushed his teeth, didn't take showers with soap, skipped school in the seventh grade, almost flunked Spanish in grade ten, crushed in the fender of the car two days after he got his driver's license, and got drunk on his eighteenth birthday.

"Really drunk?" Emma asks with delight.

"Smashed," Philip says.

"He couldn't walk straight," Barbara says. "He staggered into the house at three in the morning."

"Singing at the top of my lungs."

"He woke everyone up."

"They all came out in their pajamas and stared at me."

"Then he threw up on the kitchen floor."

"Oh, gross."

"And I was sick for two days. I thought I was going to die."

"You lost your driver's license for a month."

"And you gave me a talking-to when I was sober." Philip gives Emma a look. "Your grandma really knew how to cut a guy down to size, let me tell you."

Barbara gives him a smart rap on the wrist. "You were a straight-A student. I wasn't going to have my future classics professor turn into a drunken bum."

"I didn't get A's in history."

"Yes, you did."

"Remember when I got a C in Canadian history? Remember how mad you were?"

And on and on and on, while I clean up. I've never seen Barbara so motherly or Philip so filial. They're laughing, talking too fast, interrupting, catching each other on the hooks of reminiscence. The shadows of their former selves seem to dance over the plates and napkins, around the tall flickering candles. Emma is excited, giggling at the stories and jokes. Philip gives her a sip of wine, fills up Barbara's glass, and finishes the bottle himself. When the laughter really gets raucous, I sink into my chair and look at them: at Emma clapping her hands, at Philip, who has thrown his head back, and at Barbara, whose heavy cheeks are stained red with wine.

Mother-in-law.

Daughter-in-law.

Mother. Daughter. In law.

At a time when I was emotionally severing ties with my own parents in order to become an adult, *a wife*, I acquired a second mother. For the first time it occurs to me that I've invested Barbara with far too much significance. I've allowed the word "mother" to provoke in me the needs of a child, even though she's not my mother and I'm not her child. I wanted her love, and when I couldn't have that, I craved her affection. When that wasn't available, I desperately sought her approval. When, finally, I couldn't have that, either, I raged at her, anger and grief mixing a potent brew.

Philip is describing to Emma the fights he and Marion used to have over television programs. Barbara is gazing at Philip with pride and love, her smile broad, the twin flames of the candles reflected in her glasses. I remember my wedding, a small affair held in my parent's house. After the ceremony, Barbara took me by the shoulders, held me firmly away from her, and gave me a cool kiss on the cheek. For the first time I understand that, at an age when Barbara didn't want any more children, she found herself saddled with a second daughter.

Mother-in-law/*daughter*-in-law.

What is this relationship foisted on two reluctant women who are strangers?

Adoption, I think. Adoption by another name.

TERRY AND CHARLENE ARE IN THE BAY-shore Shopping Centre on a Monday morning when the mall is just about deserted. Terry is just window-shopping—she spent all her money on Christmas—but Charlene has gifts to buy: a wedding gift for one friend, a baby gift for a woman who works in the beauty shop. They browse through the housewares section of Eaton's, idly discussing coffee makers, toaster ovens, and corn poppers.

"If I buy one of these," Charlene says, "she'll probably get two more."

"How big is the wedding?"

"Huge. Six bridesmaids and six ushers. Two flower girls."

"Expensive," Terry says.

"Twelve thousand dollars, would you believe?"

"Shit. What a waste."

"Oh, I don't know," Charlene says, staring dreamily at an electric frying pan.

"It's a down payment on a house."

"Terry, you don't have a romantic bone in you, do you?"

"I'm realistic, Charlene. That's all."

As they drift out of housewares and take the escalator to the third floor, Terry expands on the theme of being realistic—how life is rough and full of hard knocks, how expectations can get your hopes up too high, and how high hopes create ideas about other people that aren't true. These false ideas, she explains, make you act toward these other people in the wrong way, and then they don't do what you want them to do. The result? People end up treating you like shit.

"And you come full circle," Terry says as they enter the baby department. "I read about it in *Cosmo*."

"I'm realistic," Charlene says. "I don't even think of owning a salon. I'd have to marry a millionaire or something."

They stop at a table piled high with winter baby clothes. Baby Woollies Spring Sale, a sign announces, 25% Off. "If you were really realistic," Terry says, "you'd get rid of Buddy tomorrow."

"He's sweet," Charlene protests.

"Sweet? You must be blind and deaf."

"You don't know him, Ter. Not really."

Terry picks up a tiny pink sweater with a hood. Pinned to it are matching pink booties. She thinks of the last time Charlene and Buddy came over to watch a hockey game and the way he fondled the top of Charlene's heavy pink leg through all three periods, including intermissions and advertisements.

"He's only out for sex," Terry says.

"They're all like that."

"Charlene, if you don't aim for something better, you're never going to get it."

"Buddy has potential."

Terry shakes her head. "Jesus."

For a few minutes they pick through the tiny sweaters, caps, mitts, and booties. Terry watches Charlene examine a pale yellow scarf with tassels, slowly turning it this way and that, reading the price tag several times. There is a bovine quality to Charlene that she usually finds soothing, but today it's having the opposite effect. Charlene's big round eyes irritate her; the fat fingers drive her crazy. Terry has an overwhelming desire to poke her hard, as if Charlene were a balloon and she could let the air out of that stupid romanticism and complacency.

"Buddy is crude."

With a surprised look, Charlene puts down the scarf. "That's not very nice, Ter."

"He has disgusting table manners."

Charlene's round cheeks start to flush. "I like Buddy."

"He's low-class."

Charlene clutches her purse so hard to her breasts that the tips flatten and the tops bulge against her blouse. "People who live in glass houses shouldn't throw stones."

Terry's eyes narrow. "I don't spend my days drinking beer, watching hockey, and farting."

"You're just jealous because Buddy doesn't blow all his money!"

They are now faced off on opposite sides of the table. From a distance, a saleswoman glances at them. Terry lowers her voice. "Mic does not *blow* all his money."

"Oh, no? Then how come you still live in that lousy apartment?"

"He helps."

"Buddy says he's never seen anyone spend the way Mic does."

"Buddy's taste is in his asshole."

Charlene is now bright red. "Well, let me tell you something, Terry Petrie. Have you ever asked yourself where Mic gets all that money? Have you?"

Terry, shaking with rage, turns her back on Charlene just as the saleswoman arrives. She walks to the far corner of the baby department and stares at the picture of a mother and a plump naked baby on a package of newborn Pampers. She thinks, That's not what newborns look like, and she remembers it all: the hateful, scorching pain, the pursing of her mother's lips as if she deserved the pain, the nurse who said she shouldn't hold the baby if she was going to give it up, and Emma at the moment the doctor lifted her from Terry's body—raw red, streaked with blood, her back arched as she let out a wail.

The woman lies on the hospital bed, her eyes closed, her hair fanned out around her head. She is pale almost to the death, her lips bloodless and dry. As the doctor had warned her, the delivery was almost too much for her delicate system to bear. Around her, the doctors and nurses work in a frenzy, attempting to keep her alive, because she is far too young and beautiful to die now, when her life and the baby's stretch out like glittering threads. Behind the emergency room doors are her parents and her husband. They pace, they cry, they pray, but there's nothing they can do. Her parents' money will not be able to buy her back if she slips away. Her husband's passion will not be able to reclaim her from the grave.

The doctors inject her one more time, and her eyelids flutter.

"She's coming around!"

She murmurs, and a nurse leans forward.

"Mic," *the woman says.*

"Get him in here!" *the doctor orders.*

Through her closed eyes, the woman senses her husband above her. She feels him take her hand and press it. She knows he is willing her to live with every part of his being.

"Ter," *he says urgently.* "Ter, I'm here. I love you."

The power of his words affects her eyes. The lids move slowly, and the camera swoops down to catch the gleam of green as the thick, dark lashes lift. She looks up into the lights, into the tears that well in her lover's eyes.

"Cut!" *the director hollers.* "It's a take!"

"Ter?" Charlene says. "I'm sorry."

Terry turns around. "Mic's going to take me out of this," she says, sweeping her hand so that it takes in the baby department, the store, the mall, Ottawa, Canada. "You understand that, don't you?"

Charlene blinks her round eyes. "Yeah."

"I mean it, Charlene."

"I know you do."

"Otherwise there'd be nothing. Get it? Absolutely nothing."

 AT THE END OF MARCH WE HAVE A WARM spell that brings with it a tantalizing promise of spring. The snow piles begin to recede, the air has that rich smell of fertile earth, and the sun's rays are warm and as yellow as butter. But just as quickly as it arrived, bringing us false hope, the warm spell is overtaken by the winter's worst blizzard. Snow swirls on the bare pavement and open patches of dead grass, building quickly into sculpted drifts. The flakes are big, and fifty-mile-per-hour winds drive them against windows and into faces with the force of knives. During rush hour, cars stall and die or pile up in slow-motion collisions.

When the storm is over, Ottawa has gained ten inches of snow and I've hurt my lower back shoveling our front walk. When I limp into work the following day, an office mate reports to a group of us during coffee break that a few crocuses in this backyard had poked their heads above the soil before being buried beneath a drift. We have a moment of silence, mourning for them as if they were children.

Everything combines to make me irritable: the blizzard, the sharp twist in my back whenever I bend over, work that piles up on my desk as high as the drifts, and Emma. This time the cycle of anger seems to have no end. She is constantly impatient with me, annoyed at whatever I say or do. We've had confrontations over bedtime, the duration of showers, the state of her bedroom, her newest habit of cutting up her clothes, her marks at school. She argues with equal vehemence over trivialities and matters of vital importance. I'm at a loss whether to attribute this to normal adolescent behavior or Terry's presence, or whether it's a difficult mix of both. I've taken to reading magazine articles with titles like "Dealing with Your Teenage Children" and "The Angry Adolescent."

One evening when Philip is teaching, Emma provokes an argument with me about Mark. Mark has developed from a pudgy, talkative boy into a tall, silent adolescent with a smooth olive complexion, brown eyes, and straight dark hair that falls over his forehead. Emma thinks he's cute; I find him alarming. His hands are enormous, his shoulders thin but broad. His voice has changed and has a husky Bogartian quality. It's not the physical changes that make me wary exactly, but the fact that they are part of the other changes—the long silences and the way his eyes follow Emma. When he's in the house, there's a scent in the air, a sexual scent. It has no odor but hovers around him like a halo.

I've become aware in the last month that Emma is going steady with Mark. He phones her every day after school. They go to the movies on Friday night. Their outings are rarely private. They're usually part of a larger swirl of children, traveling in a noisy crowd. But once, I stood unnoticed in the doorway of the TV room and found them sitting together on the couch, watching a rerun of "Welcome, Back, Kotter." On the screen, one student was trying to stop another from jumping off a ledge.

"Arnold's going to get her off," Mark said.

"He's got this really dorky voice," Emma said.

"He's a fag."

"No, he isn't. He's married."

"On the show?"

"In real life."

"I still think he's weird."

"I hate his pants," Emma says. "They're disgusting."

The television flickered, Emma leaned against Mark, and he began to play with the strands of her hair, winding them around his fingers. They never looked at each other but stared at the screen and laughed with the sound track as if each was unaware of what the other was doing.

On this particular evening, when Emma and I are alone in the house, she informs me that since there is no school on Friday, which is a professional development day for teachers, she intends to go to the movies with Mark on Thursday, Friday, and Saturday night.

I've been reading the newspaper, but now I put it down on my lap and look at her. She's standing by a bookshelf, idly running her fingers over the tops of the books and looking bored. She no longer wears clothing that I consider normal or attractive. Everything—skirt, sweater, tights, shoes—is black, held together with safety pins or dotted with holes.

I may have given up on the clothing issue, but I have strong convictions about thirteen-year-olds dating. "I'm sorry, but the answer is no," I say.

"I don't have any school."

"That makes no difference."

"But I can sleep in."

"What about your father and me? We have to get up and go to work."

"You don't have to wait up for me."

"You are *not* going to the movies three nights in a row."

"Why not?"

"I just told you. Besides, who are you going to go with? Your friends aren't going to be allowed either."

"Mark can go."

"Oh, no," I say. "Absolutely not."

"Mark's a friend."

"Mark's a *boy*friend."

Emma is no longer in that casual stance. She's standing straight with her chin forward in a defiant jut. "What's the matter? Don't you trust me?"

"You know the rules. Daddy and I don't believe in dating at thirteen. A group of friends is fine. The two of you going out alone night after night is not."

"What do you think we're going to do? Have sex?"

I think of Emma's lanky body with its slight swell of breasts and small pale nipples, its tiny swatch of red pubic hair. Despite several bouts of cramps, she hasn't yet started menstruating. How odd to think of that body engaging in sexual intercourse, even odder to envision it amorously entangled with that of Mark, equally lanky, equally unfinished.

"No," I say evenly. "We've agreed on that, too, haven't we? Thirteen is too young to be having sex."

"So why can't I go, then?"

"Rules are rules."

"You're so unfair! Mark will think I'm a baby!"

"He'll think you have parents who care about you."

"You're ruining my life! You don't want me to have any fun!"

"Em, go to your room!"

She storms out of the living room and stamps up to her bedroom. When her door slams, the whole house shakes. I don't see her for the rest of the night, but when Philip comes home, I give him an angry earful.

He's tired, but he rallies. "She's not ready for dating," he says. "That's crazy."

"That's what I told her, but she wouldn't back down."

"I'll have a word with her."

He walks out of the living room and goes up the stairs. I hear Emma's door open and an exchange of voices in that brief moment before it closes again. A half hour later, Philip returns.

"Well?" I say.

"She says she knows she went too far. She knows she's not ready to date."

"What did you do?" I ask incredulously.

Philip settles into a chair and picks up the newspaper. "It's just a matter of being reasonable."

"I *am* reasonable until she makes me crazy."

"Maybe you go crazy too fast."

"Oh, now it's my fault."

"I don't fight with Emma the way you do."

"She doesn't want to fight with you. She waits until you're gone and then comes after me."

"That may be true."

"It is true! You get the good behavior. But I'm the mother, I get the garbage."

Philip opens the paper. "Calm down, Jane. It's over."

The fights come and go, like the inhalations and exhalations of some god of war. Emma seems to forget them once they're over, but for me they accumulate one on top of the other, the weight of them pressing me down, making me more irritable and quicker to react. Emma accuses me of being mean and cruel. Of course, I deny this but secretly acknowledge its truth. Motherhood has honed my cruelty to a fine art. I know, with the instincts of a tyrant, every possible twist and turn of my power. I can hassle, aggravate, and nag. I can hold back, refuse, set rules, make impossible demands.

Tuesdays are my cruelest days. I wake up angry, go to

work angry, come home feeling angry and defeated. Philip is so busy marking papers and attending committee meetings he doesn't notice, but Emma is fine-tuned into my moods. She isn't deceived by my solicitude and comes back from her weekly visits with Terry defensive and defiant.

"How was school?"

"Okay."

"What did you do?"

"Nothing much."

"What about your geography assignment?"

"I did it. I told you."

"And Terry, how was she?"

"Okay."

"Did she buy you those earrings?"

"I saw them in a store and liked them."

"She takes you shopping?"

"Sometimes."

"Does she buy you other things?"

Pause. "No."

"So what did you talk about?"

"Nothing much."

"You sat there like two bumps on a log?"

"Mom, I thought we said my times with Terry were *private.*"

"I just asked a question."

"It's none of your business!"

"Set the table."

I make dinner with a singular lack of grace. I bang the pots and pans. I throw lettuce into the bowl and chop the tomatoes into crude lumps. Emma sets the table, clattering the silverware and smacking the plates down on the place mats. She doesn't fold the napkins properly beneath the forks, but tosses them helter-skelter onto the plates.

"I think we should ask Terry and Mic to dinner," I say, tossing the salad furiously.

"M-o-m!"

"Well, why not?"

"You promised."

"That was months ago."

"I don't want you to."

"You know, Em, I'm wondering what you're trying to hide."

"I'm not trying to hide anything."

Emma's fine-tuning capability isn't superior to mine. I can sense the tiniest change in her, the most minute shift or deviation. Take that earlier pause of hers, that slight hesitation. I registered it immediately.

"So how come Terry is buying you earrings?"

"I don't know."

"It's not your birthday."

"She liked them. Is there anything wrong with that?"

"You told me she doesn't have much money."

"They weren't expensive."

"Oh? How much were they?"

"I don't know. I didn't ask."

"And that was it? Just a pair of earrings?"

Emma is close to tears now. "I told you. She didn't buy me anything else."

"If you say so."

"Mom, why can't she buy me things? She likes me!"

"I didn't say she couldn't."

"Maybe she even *loves* me!"

"Maybe she does." I turn toward the refrigerator, and a pain jabs my back. "Stop throwing those napkins around. Since when do we do that in this house? Fold them properly. I said *properly!*"

I don't enjoy the exercise of cruelty. I hate it. I loathe myself. And I've learned that the sharp initial sweetness of cruelty never lasts. The taste immediately turns bitter, and no matter how hard I try to spit it out, the flavor lingers, acrid and unpleasant, on my tongue.

DEAR DIARY,
Zits, zits, ZITS!

I am so MAD! I culd screem and screem! Mom is realy angry at me just because Terry bought me earrings. God but shes such a BITCH. She picks on me all the time and treets me like CRAP! She never understands anything. Shes always screeming and yelling. Living at home realy SUCKS!! I wish I could live with Terry. Shes realy neat. She wuldnt be overprotektive and she understands me because shes my real MOTHER. If I lived with Terry I wuldnt have to explane things all the time to someone who is a real BITCH!!! A realy horible BITCH!!!! The thing is theres no room in Terry's apartmint and besides she doesn't have much money because of her lousy job. So Im stuck in this SHITTY house for my whole LIFE!

School sucks too and all the dweeby nerds in my class like Lisa and Dana and all the teachers who think they know everything and are realy just big assholes. And I dont care I wasnt invited to Lisas stupid party. It was a lousy party anyway. Everybody said it was real boring. Also Lisa got her hair permed and she looks like a total asshole.

The only good thing in my hole life is that Mark and I are going realy stedy.

Bye for now.

ALICE DROPS BY UNEXPECTEDLY ON A SUNday afternoon when Philip has gone to the office to mark essays and Emma is at a movie with Mark and some other friends. As I bring us coffee, she sinks onto the couch and heaves a sigh. I haven't seen her for a while, and she isn't well. Her voice is hoarse, and her eyes look red and puffy. She coughs into a handkerchief and sighs. "Lousy flu. This is my third bout this winter."

"In the old days," I say, "they died of catastrophic illnesses. We just get ground down by flus, viruses, and stress.''

"Marshall has decided he's a party animal," Alice says. "He wants to go out every night possible and stay out late. We're always fighting. Felicia is getting her period and is bitchy. Sylvie is cranky, and I hate having Rob at home." After Christmas Rob quit his job, became a free-lance consultant, and set up an office on the third floor of their house. "I want to leave or kick him out. Whatever's easiest. I have a deadline and he's driving me *crazy*."

"You know a good definition of middle age?" I say. "Lurching from one crisis to another."

"You know how all of us have a personal space that's usually about to here?" Alice demonstrates, waving her hand a foot from her face. "Well, I've discovered mine includes the whole house. I can't think straight when anyone else is in it."

"Isn't the third floor far enough away?"

"He works to music. The sound comes down through the vents."

"Get him earphones."

"And Rob just doesn't walk. He stamps down the stairs. He slams the doors. He rattles things. Oh, I don't know, maybe I'm too sensitive. Or maybe my marriage wasn't intended to be a full-time thing."

I think what it would be like to have Philip around all the time: taking the bus with me to the office, working nearby, interrupting me, listening in on telephone conversations. I get a whiff of claustrophobia. "I don't think my marriage would survive that either," I say.

"You know what I think would be a civilized arrangement? If Rob and I lived separately during the week and saw each other on the weekends. I even suggested it to him."

"What did he say?"

"He said he'd hate it. He said he'd get lonely. But, Jane, he spends his evenings reading and doesn't talk to me anyway."

"He likes to know you're there."

Alice leans her head against the back of the sofa and briefly closes her eyes. "Marriage is the most peculiar institution. Sometimes I think my heroines are out of their minds to want it so badly."

"How is your heroine, anyway?"

"Oh, she's kidnapped her daughter and is living near Baltimore in a crummy apartment."

"How is she supporting this kid without any money?"

"She works as a temporary for a personnel agency." Alice yawns and then coughs. "The thing is, she doesn't know that the hero has put a detective on her trail."

"So he knows where she is."

"He's going to come after her, and all hell will break loose. He'll steal the kid back and threaten her with legal action if she doesn't marry him."

"Aha," I say, "the plot thickens."

"It's just a twist on the old marriage-of-convenience plot. You've got these two people forced to live together, who don't know if they love each other, who may even hate each other sometimes, but who have sex anyway." She pauses and then gives me an ironical smile. "God, that's my marriage. Life imitating art."

It strikes me as I smile back that my life has also imitated Alice's art. I was a heroine once, wasn't I? I had all the qualifications: youth, surging hormones, and a strong belief in the romantic myth that Mr. Right would come riding out of the sunset to claim me for his own. How did I acquire that myth? It was fed to me by my mother who'd met my father on a cruise and was a strong believer in love at first sight. "Someday you'll meet someone," she would say with a nostalgic sigh, "and you'll know. Just like that." So primed was I for love that I recreated that myth for myself when I met Philip, twisting the facts to fit my fiction. A classicist? That meant he was clever. Canadian? That meant he was unusual. Cool and reserved? Still waters run deep, don't they? And I was so sure it was love. What else could all those powerful feelings be?

"I wonder," I say, "if people who've been married as long as we have actually talk about love anymore."

"When Rob and I were first married," Alice says, "I used to call him up at work just to say I loved him."

"I used to talk dirty to Philip on the phone to see if I could get him to come home in the middle of the day."

We both sigh, and I remember an evening, just recently, when I switched on the television and Philip appeared on the screen. I'd forgotten he was substituting for Lorraine, who teaches on Instructional Television and was laid low by the flu. He was lecturing on Juvenal, reading from his notes, glancing now and then at his audience, and ignoring the camera. Our set isn't a good one, and he was slightly off-color, his hair appearing grayer, his skin more orange. The camera and classroom lights weren't any more merciful. He looked heavy and older, and his face was caught in its most naked state: creased, moled, jowled, and sagging. "In the whole of Roman literature," Philip informed the class as I watched him, "there is no more elusive character than Juvenal." Where was that arrogant cut of mouth, the seductive curve of buttock, that had snared me twenty-three years earlier? But who was I to ask? I had pouches under my eyes, a soft underbelly to my chin, skin that trembled on my thighs. Nor was I front row center and hooked by that youthful and incessant desire. Oh, Philip, I thought, where have we gone?

Now I say, "I don't know what love is anymore."

"It's inertia. You don't dislike each other enough to split."

"Splitting would take so much energy," I say. "Moving, lawyers, dividing assets, custody. Just talking about it makes me exhausted. Which reminds me—did you know Des and Maureen are in counseling?"

Alice nods. "I think Maureen has a thing going with someone in her office."

"Really?"

"She didn't say. I read between the lines."

"Poor Des."

"Who says *he's* faithful?"

"Oh, he is," I say.

"How do you know?"

"He's too miserable."

"A significant sign."

The implications of Maureen's affair sink in, and I say, "Imagine being single after twenty years of marriage."

"Who would want to go through all that shit again?"

"Dating."

"Waiting for the phone to ring."

"And sex," I say. "Think about having to break in another man."

"That's one thing," Alice says. "Rob knows what I like."

"And think about having to expose your middle-aged body to somebody who didn't know it in its prime."

Alice grimaces.

"Besides, I read that married people have three times as much sex as singles."

"Okay," Alice says, throwing up her hands, "I surrender. I won't divorce Rob yet."

"Well, that's why you came over here, isn't it?" I say. "To be convinced?"

"I knew I could count on you, Jane."

"What are friends for?" I say, echoing an earlier conversation, and we smile like conspirators.

I recall this talk with Alice on the following Tuesday evening. I'm lying beside Vera on a mat that has been placed on the floor in a small drab room at the Glebe Community Center. We're surrounded by fifteen other pairs of people who are also lying flat, staring at the ceiling and listening to the voice of the instructor, a nurse with the Childbirth Without Pain Association. She's young and cute with the pert enthusiasm of an aerobics teacher. "And a-one and a-two and a-three," she says. "Way to go!" We've already run through a short relaxation program, talked about the physical changes of pregnancy, and been given a brief introduction to proper breathing for labor. Today, she has informed us, we'll concentrate on Kegels, exercises designed to strengthen the pelvic floor muscles. Well, I think, what are friends for?

Vera and I aren't the only all-female partners. Although most are husbands and wives, some frighteningly young, there are two other pairs of women. One pair appears to be a mother and a teenage daughter, the other two friends like us. They're middle-aged, their makeup is stylish, and their sweat suits, like ours, are designer-styled and designer-colored. When we entered the room, our eyes met theirs and we all smiled. I envision us two classes down the line, meeting afterward for coffee and finding acres of common ground. We'll discover we work for the government, have acquaintances in common, probably even share the same gynecologist. Ottawa is like that.

"Now the first Kegel exercise," the nurse is saying, "is a simple one. Basically I want you to tighten the vaginal muscles. I want you to feel the walls contract. Everybody try it." There's a snort from one of the participants, and she gives a little giggle. "Sorry, husbands and boyfriends. Just tighten the muscles around the penis and scrotum. You'll get the same effect. Okay, feel that tightening? Now I want you to do it ten times—slowly. A-one and a-two and a . . . Come on, folks. Pelvic muscles are often neglected and out of shape. And a-three and a—"

"Arnold Schwarzenegger, here I come," Vera whispers to me.

"Very funny," I say.

"Tighten, ladies. Tighten!"

This is a pregnancy exercise class, and Vera's enrolled in it early. "The doctor said I could wait," she told me, "but I want to get it right."

"Get what right?" I asked.

"Everything—the pregnancy, the birth."

"No one's going to give you a grade. Either you have a baby or you don't."

"I'm a perfectionist," she said stubbornly. "You know that."

She's not the only one. There are several other women

who don't look pregnant either. In fact, I could be the expectant mother, lying with a supportive friend, tightening my vaginal muscles, strengthening them for childbirth. I could fantasize about a curl of humanity, a comma of a child, growing deep within me. Oh, the fantasies I had! They were so saccharine, so sentimental, I'm ashamed to remember them. Their backdrops were softly textured walls in pink or blue, and their musical scores were lullabies. There wasn't much of a plot. The action was strong on cuddling, and the air was scented with Johnson's baby talc. I wince at them now, those little dramas with the inevitable menstrual ending, but at the time they dominated my life. I lived by the calendar and the thermometer. I kept charts that marked the most intimate details of my life. And I dreamed of babies, dreams as smooth and oval as eggs that cracked once a month, their contents draining out of me along with my menstrual blood.

For a long time I sought the roots of the anguish I felt at these monthly tragedies as if, once discovered, I could expose and cut them out from my life. But they were too deeply entrenched, planted by instinct, nurtured by family. I remember when my mother was pregnant with Derek. I was six years old and as fully instructed in the mechanics of childbirth as my mother thought appropriate. I'd been told about seeds and eggs: the daddy plants the seed while the mommy grows the egg. Then I'd learned about the mommy's birth canal. The word "canal" evoked an image of Venice, which we were studying in school. The baby, as I understood it, would be borne by some kind of miniature boat down a tiny river bounded on both sides not by buildings but by my mother's firm and solid body.

These concepts worked for me until the day I walked into my parents' bathroom and saw my mother taking a bath. She must have been eight or nine months pregnant then, and as I entered, she reached backwards for the shampoo, her body twisting to one side. I saw the baby take shape below her breasts, the bulge of a head and curved back rising like dough within the cover of her skin. "Get that bottle for me, will you, Jane?'' my mother said. ''I can't reach it.'' She moved again and the baby disappeared, submerged once more beneath its familiar mound. The eggs and planting, the canals and boats, were suddenly absurd, useless, false. For the first time I understood and marveled at the enormity and wonder of what was to take place, and connected my own thin body to the richness of my mother's female flesh.

''Now we're going to do the elevator exercise,'' the nurse is saying. ''What I want you to do is to tighten slowly, counting up to ten, and then relax slowly, counting down from ten. So it's up and down, up and down. Everybody ready? A-one and a-two and—''

''I wonder what they call it when you overdo this,'' Vera says. ''There's tennis elbow and runner's knee.''

''Perineal paralysis?'' I suggest.

''Oh, very good. It's not even obscene.''

''I like to maintain a high tone.''

The nurse is standing over us. ''Are you ladies having any problems? No? All right, everyone, let's go again. Up and down. Up and down. To the count of ten.''

When I was ten, my family went down to Florida to visit my father's parents, who had retired near Fort Myers. My grandfather had gradually become more and more deaf, a condition that I now understand lay behind my grandmother's constant chattering. She talked from the minute we arrived until we left, from morning to night, wherever we went. She talked to anyone who would listen, including me, my older brothers, and even Derek, who was only four years old. When I came down with a sore throat on the day the family was supposed to visit Alligator Island, she volunteered to stay home with me. I lay in a high, thin state of fever on her couch, dozing on and off, while she sat in an armchair and knitted with both wool and words, weaving row upon row of mauve yarn and reminiscence.

''Let's see. . . . Let me think, now. . . . That house . . . yes, we lived in the house on Broad Street the year Arthur was born.''

''Who's Arthur?'' I said drowsily against the backdrop of clicking needles.

"Your father never told you about Arthur?"

I shook my head, and my grandmother sighed as she put the knitting on her lap. She was prone to sighing, heaving huge breaths that lifted the monolith of her bosom and dropped it onto the soft hill of her belly. She's been dead far too long for me now to recall anything but the vaguest details of her face and expressions. I remember best the vast dimensions of her body, her permed white curls, and the heavy, heavy sighs.

"Arthur would have been your uncle, but he died before your father was born."

Surprise roused me from my lethargy. "My uncle?"

"I was working in the kitchen, making a sponge cake and sifting flour, when the doorbell rang. I thought it was the milkman—I didn't suspect a thing—but it was one of our neighbors, Harold Richt—he was retired from the city—and he said, 'Mrs. Simpson, I have bad news about Arthur.' Oh, he sounded terrible, let me tell you. 'Arthur!' I said. 'What about Arthur?' But I didn't wait to listen. I ran right out to the street. I knew, you see. I knew in my heart. I had dread sitting right on my chest. And there he was, lying by the sidewalk." She had started to cry, and her tears were falling onto the yarn, turning it dark purple. "Six years old."

A hard-edged lump was pressing painfully on my already sore throat. "What happened?"

"He was hit by a truck. We'd told him so many times to be careful. 'Arthur,' I used to say, 'don't run so much. Don't be in such a hurry. Watch where you're going.' But he was always a boy in a rush."

"What about the truck driver?" I demanded hotly. "Did you get him?"

"What could he do? He stood there and cried and said, 'I didn't see him, missus. I just didn't see him.' " My grandmother wiped her eyes and sighed. "Oh, it was a long time ago. He would have been forty-seven years old this May."

Long after I'd forgotten everything else about our trip to Florida, this conversation with my grandmother remained. I'd never seen a grown-up cry before, and it made a strong impression on me. I knew all about the power parents had over children—I was subject to *that* every day—but I had no idea of the power children had over parents. It was a two-way street, the tug of connections traveling back and forth, back and forth. Now when my parents made me furious, I fantasized about my own death. I saw my father hiding his face behind his hands while my mother threw herself on my coffin, crying wildly, "Oh, Jane, we didn't mean it! We're *so* sorry! We'd do anything to have you back!" It was very satisfying.

"And now for the ripple exercises," the nurse says. "You start at the front and work back toward the anal area, tightening as you go. Slowly, now." There's a silence as thirty-two of us concentrate on rippling. "Everybody feel it?"

My abdomen aches. My pelvic floor muscles ache. "I feel it," I say to Vera. "I might end up crippled."

"Think what this will do for your sex life," Vera whispers. "It could add new dimensions."

Dimensions: the physical dimensions of pregnancy, the emotional dimensions of having children. I wanted to have it all, to parade my swollen belly down the Ottawa streets, to sit with the other expectant mothers in my doctor's office, to complain about heartburn, leg cramps, swollen breasts, and constipation. I longed for little arms around my neck, middle-of-the-night feedings, a first smile—"Just gas," my friends would say—and dirty diapers. *Primapara:* first-time mother. I prayed to a God in whom I had no belief, and then I ate the fruit of bitterness.

Oh, the tastes, the wants.

My hunger for a baby.

The salt of tears.

The pungency of Philip's semen—oral sex, which he liked, when once again I had failed.

The fat pink leg of a friend's baby, luscious enough to bite.

Foods that obsessed me: avocados, butternut squash, pale pregnant pears.

Would I cry fifty years hence, I wonder, if Emma died?

I stare at the ceiling and feel the old anguish wash over me. Like a wave breaking on rock, it swirls into every nook and cranny, finding even the hidden niches, the long-buried hollows. Tears leak from my eyes and slide down my temples into my hair. The passing of time has had no effect on this anguish. It's as fresh and as painful as it was on the day I learned I would never have children.

DEAR DIARY,

Tuesday—weather condishions. Snow melting. Warmer. Lots of cramps. I had to take Tielinol to school for the pain. Mom says my body is pracktising for being a woman.

Oh and theres good stuff at school. There doing Alice in Wonderland and Im going to try out for Alice. Theres singing and everything. Everybody says Lisa's going to get the part but Im going to try anyways. Felicia wants to be a flower. Mark is going to try for the White Rabbit. Cello the Jello and Nicky want to be Tweedeldee and Tweedeldum.

Not much else Diary except Ive decided I love Mark. Realy. Hes so sweet and nice to me.

WHAT IS LOVE?

What is love?
Is it a heeling?
The symbol is a dove
I do think it's a feeling!

When I am with you I tingle inside
My heart begins to skipabeat
Such a feeling I never denide
I can't wait till we next meet

Your soft hands against my face
We cuddle on the black chair
The one next to the fireplace
You run your fingers threw my hair

Is that what is occuring?
Is it love that is sturing?
                    by Emma Wastenay

Bye for now.

"DES SEEMS TO BE IN A STATE OF QUIET DES-
peration," I say one evening when Philip and
I are making dinner.

"Hmmm." Philip believes himself a spe-
cialist in gourmet hamburgers and is in the
delicate process of spicing the ground beef. He sprinkles
thyme into the bowls, examines the effect, and then sprinkles more.

"Alice says Maureen is having an affair with someone at
her office."

He adds garlic powder. "This is a known and documented fact?"

"An inference, but Alice's inferences are usually good."

"And Des's suspicions are leading him into this state of
quiet desperation?"

"Actually, we're not sure he knows, but we don't think
he's having an affair."

"I see. Another documented inference."

"Come on, Philip. You gossip about people in your department."

"I don't gossip. I impart information."

"Such as that rumor about Lorraine and her husband?
Aha! Got you."

He smiles slightly, acknowledging my shot, and for a second I imagine him not as my husband but as a stranger. I
take off his slacks, his wrinkled shirt, my flowered apron,
and dress him in tight jeans, boots, his leather jacket. I imagine meeting him in some anonymous setting. Would we just
walk past each other or would we notice each other? Would
he strike up a conversation? Would I find him interesting?
More important, would I want him? Would he want me?

"It wasn't gossip," Philip says. "Lorraine and her husband have split up."

"Oh, no."

"Oh, yes. He packed up two days ago and moved in with some woman."

"Oh, no! Did Lorraine know there was another woman?"

"Apparently not. I hear she's collapsed."

I pick up a tomato and begin to slice it. "You know something? We should get a medal from the government—all of us who stay married. Think what we save society by not divorcing. Less trauma. Fewer sick days. More productivity. We're a national resource."

"Or a dying breed. I think this needs more salt."

"I have never seriously considered leaving you," I say, picking up an English cucumber and studying its green ridges. "And you've never seriously considered leaving me." He doesn't say anything but tastes the meat. "Well, you haven't, have you?" He still doesn't say anything, so I give him a poke.

"Kill you, yes," he says. "Leave you, no."

"That's comforting."

We work in silence for a few minutes, and then he says, "On the other hand, if I don't get some sex soon, I might. This definitely needs salt."

"Tonight," I say quickly, guiltily.

"Promises, promises."

Our sex life has been in a slump lately, and Philip has started complaining: I'm not receptive to his suggestions, I don't initiate any action. This is true. I've been preoccupied, although with what I can't exactly say. My mind seems filled with objects, trivial items I see when I'm shopping, like the aquamarine cover of a bestseller, huge crescent-shaped gold earrings, a dress in the window of Holt Renfrew with a jagged, abstract brown and white pattern. I don't want these things, but I can't forget them. When Philip touches me, my mind becomes a road of twists and turns, veering this way and that, and I lose track of what his fingers are doing, what my fingers are supposed to be doing. It isn't only Philip, though. It's happening at work and when I read the newspaper and even when I'm driving. Yesterday I drove several miles down Bank Street, stopping at red lights, starting at green, changing lanes to avoid a parked car, passing a truck, and all the while my mind was on a pair of gleaming white heels with bright red toes that I'd seen at the Bay.

I walk over to him and put my arms around him, pressing my cheek to his back. He's warm, solid, and beneath my fingertips I can feel the steady beat of his heart. I don't know why I've been so absentminded. I don't know why I can't concentrate. And yes, I think, I'd want him. "I'm setting up an appointment," I say, "after the news tonight."

Suddenly the front door is thrown open and a blast of cold air comes down the hallway. "Mom, guess what!" Emma hollers from the foyer.

I can feel the cold air twining itself around my ankles. "Close the door!" I shout. "You're letting in the cold!"

The door slams and the house shudders. "Guess what!" Emma runs into the kitchen, still in her coat and boots, leaving behind her a damp, dirty trail of footprints.

"Your shoes!" I say. "Look what you're doing!"

"Mom, guess what!"

"What? Take off those shoes! Right now!"

Her face is pink from the cold, and I notice she hasn't worn a hat or gloves. I'm about to mention this when she takes me by surprise and throws herself at me, wrapping her arms around my neck and giving me a tight, rough embrace. *"Guess what!"*

"Heavens, what?" I say and put my arms around her. Her tousled hair holds the sharp scent of cold winter air.

"I got it! I got the part! Of Alice!"

"That's wonderful," I say.

She pushes off me, spins around the counter, and throws her arms around Philip. "Isn't that great! Everyone thought Lisa would get it. Nobody thought I would!"

"That's terrific!" Philip says. He is trying to hug her, but also trying to make sure his fingers don't come into contact with her coat. "I'd be more enthusiastic, but you'd end up smelling like a hamburger."

Emma looks at his hands. "Oh, gross."

"I knew you'd get it," I say.

"No, you didn't."

I sigh. Does everything have to be a battle? "Yes, I did. You're very talented."

"But you didn't *know* I would."

"I suspected."

"Well, I did. I did! *I did!*" She's whirling around now, arms outstretched, fingers just missing the cabinets, me, Philip. Whirling faster and faster so that her coat fills like a balloon, her face becomes a pale blur, and her hair forms red-orange streaks, like paint daubed this way and smeared that, wild and exultant.

In his function as a teacher of ancient Greek, Philip has been invited to a cocktail party followed by an ambassadorial dinner at the Greek embassy. Since our social circle rarely intersects with the diplomatic circles in Ottawa, I consider the occasion significant enough to buy a new dress and use the Christmas gift my mother gave me to have a makeover at the Veronica Beauty Boutique.

I take the day off from work and spend the morning in an all-pink cubicle attended to by a pink-clad cosmetician whose beautifully made up face is a living testimony to Veronica products. My face, on the other hand, has just been scrubbed, toned, and left naked and vulnerable. My pores look huge, and there is a spray of fine veins I've never seen before by each nostril. I unhappily consider the secretive nature of my body, doing this and that without permission, springing change on me without notice.

"I'm probably a hopeless case," I say.

She laughs. "Goodness, no. You're fine. You should see what I have to deal with."

How comforting to know I'm not the worst. "Really?"

"Receding chins, overbites, pop eyes, noses beyond belief," she says. "The thing is, if you put the proper color in the right place, you can hide just about anything."

Soon my face is under construction, the tools an array of bottles and tubes, brushes and sponges. The scents and colors take me back in time to my parents' bedroom and my mother's dressing table. She had a kidney-shaped table topped with glass and bounded by ruffles of a pale mauve fabric. In front of the table was a large freestanding mirror whose reverse side magnified her face. On the table were combs and brushes, cut-glass bottles of perfume, tubes and tissue, lipsticks and powders. I refused to sit at that table after I turned twelve, but when I was five, I was seduced by it. My mother would make me up, putting mascara on my pale brown lashes, penciling in my eyebrows, and outlining my baby mouth in bright red. I must have looked grotesque, but at the time I was enchanted with this mask and my mother's reaction to it. "Aren't you beautiful?" she'd say. "You ought to be in pictures." I would spend hours flipping my mirrored face back and forth, patting my skin with the powder puff, and pressing my puckered lips against tissues the way my mother did. I saved these tissue kisses for weeks, storing them in the same shoe box where I kept all my other treasures: a necklace made from Pop-It Pearls, plastic bangles, perfume in a cat-shaped bottle, and a glass ring from a bubble-gum machine.

 TERRY SITS IN HER CAR ACROSS FROM THE house. She's tried to stop watching Emma's house, but she isn't able to quit. It's like an addiction, and her desire can be triggered by almost anything—a For Sale sign, a customer telling her about moving from an apartment to a house, an article titled "Interiors That Fight Winter" in *Canadian Living* magazine, and her dreams.

In the dreams, she's been coming closer and closer to the house. At first she dreamed of flickers of firelight in the window or water flowing from a faucet or a door opening and shutting, but lately the house has taken on form and substance. It sits as a backdrop to her sleep, square and solid. Behind the wisps of remembered dreams and fragmented images, the brass mailbox gleams, the sheers in the window form tight pleats, and the red of the brick is the same color as her hair.

She tries to forget the dream house, but it pulls and tugs at her. She tries to shake it loose, but it has taken up residence in her mind. She understands that visits to the house feed the dreams, and the dreams feed the desire to visit the house, but she can't break the connection. It has strength as if it were a tangible thing like links forged of metal instead of nothing more than the coupling of cells in her brain.

The night before, she'd had the most powerful of all the dreams. The door to the house was open, and the interior beckoned to her. Light colored the windows, and she could smell a sweet scent, like that of flowers, when she stood on the porch. The inside of the house had no living room or dining room. Instead it was one large room enclosing a rock garden and a fountain. The garden had many levels and ledges and was made of large stones with water flowing across their surfaces. The plants were lit by the sun, whose heat flowed down through an opening in the ceiling.

Terry walked into the middle of the garden, and a strange woman came out to greet her. The warm pleasure that the woman felt at Terry's arrival was as palpable as the sun's rays. She put her arm around Terry and pressed her cheek to Terry's so their skin touched. From that point of contact, the warmth spread into Terry's body, expanding from skin to cells, from capillaries to veins, from veins into bones. Then the woman kissed her on the mouth, and their tongues met, quickening the heat of joy into that of sexual desire. "I love you," the woman said, and Terry knew she had come home.

MY CAMOUFLAGE HAS COME WITH WONDER-ful optimistic names. I've been painted with Starlight Bronze rouge, shadowed with Coral Heaven and Velvet Plum, lipsticked with Raspberry Serenade. As I drive home, I sneak looks at myself in the rearview mirror. The face that I see is still me, but it's a different me. If I were to meet myself at a party, I think, I'd be curious and intrigued. Who is this fascinating woman? I'd ask myself. Where does she come from? What does she do? Of course the answers would be the same, I know that. But they'd be slanted at another angle. They'd reflect light and glitter like stars. Living in Ottawa? How exotic! Working for the government? How interesting! Married to a classicist? Imagine that! Has an adopted daughter who's found her birth mother? What an unusual situation!

The only trouble is that I know this veneer is only an illusion conjured up by sleight of hand. My mother enticed me with cosmetics and told me how beautiful I was, but as I grew older, she also told me other things about beauty: that it is only in the eye of the beholder, that it is only skin deep. As I turn off Bank Street and drive into my neighborhood, I think that after the diplomatic dinner tonight I'll come home and wash off these rich, strong colors. And what will happen then? Will I fade back to what I was before? Or will the illusion be strong enough to sustain itself beyond the boundary of night?

TERRY LEANS FORWARD TO TURN ON THE ignition when a car makes a left onto the street. It's going slowly, and instead of passing Terry, it comes to a stop so that the driver is sitting only a few feet from her. Terry realizes the car is going to turn into Emma's driveway, and she ducks her head, but it's too late. The woman in the car has glanced over at her, and now the car doesn't turn into the driveway. The woman and Terry stare at each other through the windows. Terry's pulse beats painfully in her throat. She feels the way an animal of prey must feel when it's caught in the beam of headlights. She wants to flee, she wants to run, but her muscles don't obey her.

The other woman, *Jane,* rolls down her window, and Terry understands she's supposed to do the same. Slowly she does, and they face each other without the intervening glass. Jane doesn't look anything like Terry had imagined. She has fine brown hair that's graying at the temples. It's clipped back with combs, but frizzy wisps have come loose and straggle around her cheeks. Her face isn't pretty—it's too narrow and its features are too strong—but it's made up as if Jane were a model. Her eyes are shadowed with blue and purple, her cheekbones are rouged, her mouth is carefully outlined and filled in with a deep scarlet. This face doesn't match the hair or the ski jacket Jane is wearing or even the car, which is not a new model and has rust marks around the door. Terry has the sensation she's looking at a mask, and that frightens her even more.

"You're Terry," Jane says.

Terry nods.

"I'm Jane Wastenay," Jane says and then frowns. "Are you here for Emma?" She frowns some more. "She's still in school."

Terry frantically searches for an answer. "I forgot about school," she says.

Jane studies her. She has brown eyes, unremarkable and almost concealed behind the thick mascara. They tell Terry that Jane knows she's a liar.

"Why don't you come in for a coffee?" Jane says. "I think it's time we talked, don't you?"

Terry's heart is now pounding so hard she can hardly hear her own voice. "Okay," she says. "I guess it is."

AT FIRST I'M SURPRISED AT MY CALM. THE hand that puts the key into the lock and pushes open the door is steady. My breath comes regularly, and my heart—that vulnerable organ—beats evenly. No panic attacks, I think, not on my own turf. I take Terry's jacket and hang it in the closet. It is a blue wool with toggles, and it's frayed at the collar and cuffs. I watch as she removes her sneakers and puts them neatly on the boot tray in the foyer. She's wearing jeans and a blue sweatshirt with "Los Angeles" written on it in flame-colored letters. Her hair is pulled back in a ponytail while her bangs have been sprayed upward to form a short flag above her forehead. I've forgotten how clear her eyes are, a green you can almost see through. It's also clear she doesn't remember me at all, but then, I don't have the kind of face that makes people sit up and notice.

"In here," I say, waving her into the living room. She pauses for a minute, taking in the room, and then sits carefully on the edge of one of the wing chairs, her legs together, her hands clasped on her knees. "Would you like coffee or tea?" I ask.

"Coffee is good."

"I only have instant," I say.

"That's fine."

"Decaf or regular?"

"Regular, please."

I go into the kitchen and put on the kettle. I come back out and sit opposite her. "I've wanted to meet you for a long time, but Emma wouldn't let me."

"Yeah."

"I guess she was afraid we might not like each other."

Terry gives a polite laugh.

"But it seems to me that it really doesn't matter how we feel about each other. The important thing is that we do what's best for Emma. And I think we can do that by talking, by exchanging information." Terry's stare propels me onward. "For example, Emma's grades have been slipping quite alarmingly this year. I'm not sure why, exactly, but it seems to me that if you talked to her about it, and I talked to her about it, and she saw that we agreed that school is important, then maybe she'd be persuaded to spend more time on her homework.''

I run out of words. In the silence the tick-tick-tick of the clock on the mantelpiece assumes gargantuan proportions. I realize two things almost at once. The first is that my calm is built on Terry's fear, which is growing inversely as I take in her pinched mouth, white knuckes, the way she avoids looking at me, the quick rise and fall of burning "Los Angeles." The second is that I'm treating her abominably. I've skipped all the polite preliminaries: I haven't asked her how she is, expressed an interest in her life, and allowed her to talk about herself, all prerequisites to allowing her to relax and be my guest. I've charged straight forward—Jane, patron saint of personal agendas, bearing my own like a sword.

"I think the kettle's boiling," I say and escape into the kitchen.

 BEING INSIDE THE HOUSE IS OVERWHELMING. Terry doesn't know where to look first. She notes the terra-cotta tile in the foyer and the cream wall-to-wall carpet that extends down the hallway and into the rooms beyond. The living room has high coved ceilings, pale green and royal blue furniture, a glass-topped coffee table, pictures on walls that have moldings in large squares. The sheer drapes let in the light and reveal the shapes of the outside as if through a mist. The dining room, which she can see at an angle through an open door, has a table of gleaming dark wood and a sideboard. She catches a glimpse of white plates with blue flowers on the sideboard and glasses with patterns cut into the stems.

When Jane leaves for the kitchen, Terry runs her hands over the fabric of the couch. It has a glossy feel, smooth and expensive. She leans forward and places her hand on the cool surface of the glass table. She hears Jane coming back and lifts it immediately. To her horror, she can see an imprint of her five fingertips.

"Milk?" Jane asks. "Sugar?"

"Just black, thank you."

Jane hands the mug to her and smiles. Terry grips her mug and looks down into her hot, swirling coffee. She can't bear that mask of cosmetics. She doesn't know what it means, what it hides, what it tells her about Jane. She wishes Jane were a customer in Loblaws, so she could play Grocery Guessing. She imagines Jane on her checkout line, her cart filled with ordinary things like noodles, soup, toilet paper, and Mr. Clean. A husband and kid, Terry would guess, and she's got a job, because of all those frozen dinners. Headaches, too. Look at the boxes of Excedrin. If there were groceries like that in Jane's cart, Terry is sure she'd be able to understand the words that come so fast and furious out of Jane's brilliant red mouth.

"Tell me about yourself," Jane is saying. "I know you work at Loblaws."

"Yes."

"You've been there for long?"

"Three years."

"Is that what you're planning to do as a . . . career? Or are there other things you want to do? Emma tells me that you sing."

"A little."

"Do you take lessons? Emma's taking lessons."

"No, no lessons."

"And . . . um, you live with someone? Mic is his name?"

Terry wonders what these questions are about. She doesn't trust them. They're too personal, too nosy. She bends her head, hardly a nod, but this doesn't stop Jane.

"And what does he do?"

"He's in cars."

"He sells them?"

"Yeah."

"Any special kind of car? Dodge? Chrysler? Japanese imports?"

Is Jane trying to be funny? Terry can't tell. "All kinds."

"That's interesting."

"Yeah."

"Well, as I was saying, I really think it would be to Emma's benefit if you and I could . . . Well, you see, thirteen is a hard age, and what I feel is that Emma is entering that adolescent stage when she's struggling to figure out who she is and . . . Well, having two mothers must make that extremely difficult for her, as I'm sure you'll agree, and . . ."

Barbara leans forward and the camera leans with her. "And did you meet your daughter's adoptive parents?"

"Yes."

"That must have been difficult."

"It was. We're very . . . different."

"They didn't come from Mechanicsville?"

"No, they came from another part of town."

"A better part."

"Yes," Terry says, but she pauses first to let the audience know exactly what Barbara is implying. This is the way an interview should go. The journalist and star feed each other lines; each makes the other look good.

"But Emma must have provided you with a common interest."

"We became great friends."

"Are you close now?"

Terry meets the camera's glassy eye. "Very close. I visit them often."

". . . a good idea if we thrashed these things out." Jane has come to the end, and Terry makes what she considers an appropriate sound of agreement.

Jane sips her coffee; Terry sips hers. The clock chimes two o'clock. They both glance at it. "Would you like to see pictures of Emma?" Jane asks. "We have albums full of them."

WHEN SHE'S GONE, I CLEAN UP THE CUPS, and the adrenaline seeps out of me. I haven't handled this meeting well, I haven't served Emma well. It's no matter that seeing Terry parked across from the house took me by surprise or that I think she was lying about waiting for Emma and I worry what she was doing there. When she was inside my home, I couldn't make her comfortable. I have no sense of having connected with her in any way. The only time she smiled and seemed animated was when I showed her pictures of Emma from our photo albums. That was an inspired choice. It saved the afternoon from being a total disaster.

On the other hand, what else could I do? As I clean up, I mentally present the case to Vera, to Alice, to Philip. Vera, I know, would point out that this is a class issue and Terry and I come from such opposite sides of educational and economic tracks that only a cock-eyed optimist would have hoped for more. Alice would go for the psychological, citing the ways in which fears, mine and Terry's, obliterate reality and put obstacles in the path of any real understanding. Philip would only remark on what he suspected all along: that such a meeting had very little chance for success.

I decide I will ignore these imaginary and negative comments and that once I put aside my feelings of failure, I will be more positive and consider this meeting a first step rather than a conclusion. I will plan informal get-togethers like barbecues. I envision Terry and Mic relaxing on the back deck while Philip grills steak and I toss a Caesar salad. We'll talk about inconsequential things like the weather and shopping.

I walk upstairs and pass the full-length mirror in the hallway, catching sight of my Veronica face. I've forgotten all about the makeup I'm wearing and note how incongruous it looks with my white blouse and old blue slacks—glamour framed in wisps and perched on top of the mundane. I try to imagine what Terry made of it and decide she probably found it funny but was too frightened to laugh. I think of

Helen, whose unadorned face launched a thousand ships, and wonder what my life would have been like had I been not plain Jane but rather a woman who bestowed beauty, launching a thousand male reveries instead of only one. I shrug into the mirror, walk into the bedroom, and then feel the sadness. It is as gray as the sky outside, a heavy blanket of cloud that shrouds my spirit.

Part IV

SPRING 1989

APRIL ARRIVES, LIMPING IN WITH ITS HEAD bent, as if in shame. We've had two more snowstorms and several days of freeze-and-thaw. The end of our driveway is either a skating rink or a pond, and one warm Sunday afternoon the husbands on our street take axes and shovels to the gutter snow piles to free the drains. Women I've hardly seen all winter stand on the slushy sidewalks, watching their children and chatting. Emma is the oldest child on our block; all the others are seven years old and under. They love the puddles and stamp through them, spraying one another with arcs of dirty water. A gang of small boys in rain gear, carrying swords and shields, races down the sidewalk, up a driveway, and back down again.

I put on my boots and step through the wet grass in my backyard to study my newly exposed flower beds. I'm a gardener of flash enthusiasms and easily defeated aspirations. Two years ago I got carried away with ground-cover plants and now must fight the constant threat of takeover by bluebells, violets, and low-lying phlox. Although I'm encouraged by the sight of small buds and tiny green shoots, I'm also disheartened by the realization that I can't remember what plants I moved the fall before. Did I shift the lilies to a sunnier spot? The two peony bushes? Or was it the white Shasta daisies that grew too tall and shaded the dianthus? Alice, a clever gardener, keeps a map of her plants on a bulletin board in her kitchen. She not only knows where her tulip bulbs are located but she's planted them to form interesting clumps of color. I'm just thankful that my tulips come up at all.

Although the air is cold, the sun's rays are warm, and I turn my face in the direction of the sky, closing my eyes against its blue brilliance. The days are longer now, and I'm hoping the extra light will bring about my seasonal change, allowing me to shed the heaviness of spirit I carried all winter. But my sadness is pervasive; I can't shake it. I've come to believe I'm in mourning for the family I once had. Before Terry, I remember a harmony; since Terry, a dissonance has entered our lives. Not that we are or have been a perfect family. We're not impervious to cracks and shifts, to breaks and subterranean faults. We've had illnesses, fights, calamities, failures, unhappiness, infertility, and adultery, but through them all, the core of what we were had never been breached. When I imagined this core, I saw our house standing firm against the weather and the earthquakes, solid and unshakable.

Now I understand we're vulnerable, that nothing I hold dear is safe. One night I dreamed I went to the Pythia, who squatted over her tripod in the inner shrine at Delphi. She was giving birth not to a prediction but to a child who refused to come. She strained and grunted, sweat stains darkening her hair, which hung down before her in strings. The priests wouldn't allow me near her, so I was forced to scream: "Tell me! Tell me!" She lifted her face, and I saw it was Vera. "Go to the window," she said just as the priests blocked my view of her. Then I was running, where exactly I didn't know. Houses appeared, windows sped past me. Finally I stopped before a brick wall and leaned against it, breathing hard. The brick turned to metal, the metal to glass, and then I saw her: Emma standing before the window, arms outstretched, mouth shaped in an O.

Philip once told me that in classical times dreams were thought to come to humans from the cave of Hypnos, the god of sleep. This cave was flanked by two gates. True dreams came through the Gate of Horn, deceitful dreams through the Gate of Ivory. The deceitful dreams could have dire implications, starting the spin of a misunderstanding, which in turn would gather force like a hurricane, whirling itself into catastrophe and finally full-blown tragedy. Deaths would ensue: patricides and matricides, suicides and murders.

"What kind of dreams am I having?" I asked him. "True dreams or deceitful ones?"

"Contemporary dreams."

"You're avoiding the question."

"I'm a classicist, Jane, not a psychiatrist."

But I know what the dream means. It's a rerun of an actual event. I've seen it before. It's the nymph, bringing doom on the House of Wastenay.

"Mom! Can I go over to Mark's?"

Emma stands on our back deck, and I notice how much she's grown this winter. Her jeans are too short, her wrists hang below the cuffs of her sweater. She's thinner and lankier. It's even possible she'll be as tall as I am. When we went to buy her sneakers for the spring, I was shocked to discover she wears a size eleven shoe.

"Don't you believe in socks?" I say.

Emma glances down at her bare bony ankles. "It's *warm*."

"And a jacket."

"Mom! It's practically summer."

"Hardly."

"Nobody wears socks anymore. I'm going to look like an asshole."

I may tolerate bad language when Emma's reporting on what other people say, but I don't allow it in direct conversation. "I beg your pardon," I say.

She's not apologetic but juts her square chin at me. "Everyone will think I'm a geek."

"You just got over a cold."

"I'm not wearing socks!"

"Then you're not going to Mark's."

Emma studies me for a minute, her eyes narrowed. "Why should I listen to you?" she demands. "What right do you have to tell me what to do?"

I think, *The message of the Pythia.* I say, "Because I'm your mother," and watch the silent struggle within her. She wants to throw Terry in my face, she wants to say the horrible, hurtful words, but I see she also understands the power of those words and that once she speaks them, they'll change everything, even the very air we breathe. As we teeter on this precipice, the abyss yawning before us, I wonder if she'll step back. Since my meeting with Terry, Emma's behavior has gotten much worse. The school has phoned with more complaints, she spends hours in her room with the door shut, and I can't hold a reasonable conversation with her.

"Terry's nice, isn't she?"

"She is."

"You don't like her."

"I do."

"I can tell you don't."

"I certainly do."

"You think she's bad."

"Em, for heaven's sake, why would I think that?"

"Because she's different from us, that's why!"

I don't know if I'm incapable of hiding anything from Emma or whether she merely projects her own emotions and fears onto me. Either way, our house has become a war zone with few cease-fires. I once believed Emma had exploited everything in our lives that was capable of causing battle. Now I know that the realm of possible battles has no limits and is ever-expandable. Every step I take, every word I speak, is fraught with danger.

Emma turns on her heel and stalks into the house, her back rigid with fury. I close my eyes for a brief minute, but my victory, if I can call it that, does not lift the sadness. As the weight of it descends, I make a determined effort to shrug it aside. I take out my gardening equipment and study the seeds left over from last year. I put on gloves and brush patches of snow off what I hope will be peonies and daisies. Suddenly I have a vivid memory of the spring when I was thirteen years old. I'd spent most of February and March out of school because of a bronchial infection. I was on penicillin, Vicks VapoRub, foul-tasting cherry cough syrup, and steam. My mother would pour boiling water into a bowl and make me sit over it, my head covered with a towel. I was tall at thirteen and, like Emma, growing fast. I got many colds, and my mother considered me frail. She was always trying to shield me from germs, wrapping me in scarves and hats and gloves. I was allergic to wool, which made her nervous. She didn't trust man-made fibers to protect me.

The first day I returned to school after that marathon of bronchitis was a lovely sunny day in April. The air held a bit of chill so my mother insisted, over my angry objections, that I wear my winter coat, hat, and gloves. Her will prevailed until lunch when, like everyone else, I ran outside hatless, gloveless, and, even better, coatless. A group of us, boys and girls, ran toward the bushes in the hill behind the school grounds, where we played an erotic version of hide-and-go-seek. The girls would hide, crouched behind trees and shrubbery like wild birds, until flushed out by the boys. Then we'd take off, running as hard as we could, arms fluttering as we swooped and turned to avoid capture. We were only officially caught when the boys grabbed hold of us and pressed their hands against our skirts in the vicinity of our crotches. I remember how breathless I would get, laughing and screaming, falling and tripping, fearfully and eagerly awaiting that grasp of a hand.

The illicit thrill of the game was enhanced by my freedom from the stranglehold of scarf and hat, the warnings of my mother, the medicinal prison of pills and syrups. I felt so light I could almost fly. The boys would catch me, hands pressing against my pubis, which tingled with pleasure, and then I'd be off again. Soon we were no longer really hiding but merely darting between the bushes or slipping behind tree trunks. "Here I am!" we'd shout. "Catch me if you can!" The breeze with its sharp edge lifted my hair and whistled past my ears. Whenever I paused, it would evaporate my sweat until I shivered, but I kept on running, gulping great swallows of air until my throat was raw. I knew what was going to happen, but I couldn't stop myself. I was too intoxicated to care that the next day I would be sick again, shaking with fever, my head aching, my chest painful and tight.

Emma appears in the doorway. She's wearing her jacket unzipped and a pair of tennis socks with pom-poms. They're cut so low they leave her ankles almost as bare as before.

"Okay?" she says defiantly.

I'm incapable of fighting the same battle twice and facing the precipice again. I also think of my brief but glorious liberty on that April day, and the sweetness of my nostalgia subdues my irritation. "Call if you and Mark decide to go someplace. I want to know where you are."

"Okay."

"And you have to be home by five-thirty."

"Okay. Okay."

As she runs into the house through the sliding doors, Philip emerges, carrying a cup of coffee from which steam rises and curls in the air.

"How's the digging?" I ask.

"We freed the drain. Where's Emma going?"

"To Mark's."

Philip sits down on the steps that lead from the deck to our garden and sips the coffee. "Isn't she spending a lot of time with him?"

"They're going together," I say. "That's what she told me."

"And what precisely does that mean?"

I study the tiny gray-green mound of leaves on my artemisia and think of the innocent eroticism of my childhood. "They hang out together. They hold hands. Maybe they kiss."

"The trouble is, I remember being fourteen." Philip sighs. "Lust galloped through my veins."

"I've told Emma the facts of life," I say. "What else can I do?"

"Talk about the moral aspects."

With no warning, a hole suddenly opens within me, and the sadness, the weariness, the sweet nostalgia are sucked into its void. Rage rushes in to fill the emptiness, waves of it colliding and crashing, its level rising to my throat.

"I've done that!" I snap. "Damn it, I've done all that!"

I list the items off on my fingers, my voice rising in crescendo. "The importance of love, respecting oneself, health issues, sex, the—"

"Hold it," Philip says, his voice rising, too. "Just hold on a minute."

"What kind of mother do you think I am?"

"Jane—"

"And besides, why am I responsible for everything? *You* could talk to her about"—my throat fills with sarcasm—"the moral aspects."

"What's the matter with you?"

"You always put me in charge! The buck"—I hit myself in the chest—"always stops here!"

"Jane, you're exaggerating."

"Then why am I the only one held responsible?" I say.

"You're not," he says. "I put it badly. I'm just as responsible for Emma as you are."

"If you were, you'd worry more."

"I do worry. Mark has hormones, you know."

"I'm not talking about Mark. I'm talking about Terry."

"Jane, for God's sake, we've been over *that* a million times."

"You didn't meet her."

"She sounds like an uneducated frightened girl."

"Why was she sitting in her car in front of our house?"

"I'm sure there's a reasonable answer."

"You don't care what she's doing to Emma."

"I do care."

"I just had a fight with Emma, and she just about told me to fuck off because I'm not her mother."

"She said that?"

"She *almost* said it."

"Even if she said it, she wouldn't really mean it. You know that."

"I don't know it!"

My rising voice makes Philip nervous, and he glances at the neighbor's house. "Jane," he warns.

"You're such a goddamned . . . Canadian," I say.

"All right," he says with a deadly calm, "that's enough." And with that, he walks down the steps and out of the backyard.

I storm into the house and slide the glass door shut with as much force as I can, regretting that it doesn't make a satisfying slam the way a regular door would. Then I stand in my dining room and hate Philip for his adroit ability to sidestep discord. I remember our first real fight, which occurred three weeks after we were married. Being a terrible cook, I scorched the steak and onions, and since we were on a graduate-student budget, this ruined meal had all the proportions of a financial disaster. I was extremely upset and expected sympathy and understanding, the lavish kind my father showered upon my mother, whatever her misdeeds. But Philip, arriving home from the university tired and hungry, was only annoyed. He said something critical, I said something back, and he made a sarcastic remark. Cut to my vulnerable quick, I flared up, screamed at him, and stormed out of the house.

I marched around the block several times. Each time I passed our apartment, I glanced up at the lit window, expecting to see Philip's anxious face. Each time the window was blank, and I finally went back, chilled and unhappy, to find he had made a peanut butter and jelly sandwich and was calmly eating and reading the paper. I stood in the doorway, shivering from the cold, and burst into tears. Philip immediately put down the paper, came over, and hugged me, murmuring that he was sorry; he hadn't realized I was so sensitive, that I took things too hard, that . . . of course, by this time, we were no longer in the kitchen but on the bed, stripping off each other's clothes.

I can upset Philip now and then, I can prick him into sarcasm and goad him into battle, but I've found too much comfort, too much safety in his stolidity. Now I long for someone different, someone wild and impulsive and reckless, someone quick to erupt into anger and violence. We'd scream brutal things at each other, slam doors so the house shuddered on its foundation, throw glasses and plates until the air was filled with splintering shattering sounds. We would never turn silently away from each other in the expanse of our queen-size bed, but instead we'd grapple with each other, wrestling, twisting and turning, rolling over and over, our breath coming short and fast.

We'd let everything out in a bubbling, erupting, spouting, gloriously exploding Vesuvius of emotions.

Wouldn't I feel better after that?

Wouldn't I?

"Children's Aid Society of Ottawa-Carleton. La Société d l'aide à l'enfance d'Ottawa-Carleton."

"Can I speak to an adoption worker?"

"Is there something I can help you with?"

"Are you an adoption worker?"

"I'm the receptionist, but if you tell me what the problem is, I'll put you in touch with the right person."

"It has to do with . . . It's about a birth mother."

"Are you an adoptive parent?"

"Yes."

"I'll put you right through to Mrs. Keneally, one of our workers."

Click. Ring.

"Hello?"

"Mrs. Keneally?"

"Yes?"

"I'm calling about . . . We adopted a child from you—a girl—thirteen years ago."

"Yes?"

"She's . . . uh, found her birth mother."

"Found her?"

"By mistake."

"A *mistake*?"

"She goes to see her."

"How old's your daughter?"

"Thirteen."

"And she's seeing her birth mother regularly?"

"Every week."

"How do you feel about that?"

"Well . . . that's why I'm phoning."

"Have you met the birth mother?"

"Yes, I have, and—"

"Are you all right?"

"Fine. It's . . . just a cold."

"Tell me, are you a single mother?"

"No."

"And your husband? How's he taking this?"

"He isn't worried about it."

"Is your daughter acting out, picking fights at home?"

"Yes, but it's mostly . . . it's . . . me. I can't seem to—"

"What we like to do is see the family as a whole. That would mean all of you coming in for family counseling—your husband, your daughter, and you. I can set up an appointment with a counselor who deals specifically with this issue, and I think you'd find it very . . . Hello? Are you there? Hello? . . . Hello?"

DEAR DIARY,

Three more zits on my cheek—weather nice.

Terry and I are doing lots of songs now. Like for a hole concert. Terry says Mic may know someone who has a stoodio and we culd make a demo tape and hear how we sound. Mic says we sound like real profeshionals and we culd be a big hit in LA which is ware all the big stars go.

I told Nicky about the demo and he told Cello who told Lisa. She said she didnt beleeve it and I was dreeming if I thot that I culd be a real singer. She said real singers dont have zits. I said suck mikes you bitch, you have more zits than me by a million.

Meanwile Dana's parents are going away next month and leaving Dana with her older brother whose in college. She says shes going to have a party when hes out and well all be invited, boys too. The girls can sleepover afterwards. She says her parents always have beer and stuff in the basement.

Bye for now.

 I'M BUSY ON THE PHONE WITH ONE OF THE contributors to *The Decade of North American Geology* when Des appears in my doorway. I wave him in as I talk.

"The first of May," I say, "that's when it's due."

The contributor, an academic from the University of Calgary, was flattered to be asked but like most of his colleagues is having trouble meeting the deadline. Barry has hired a second English editor on short-term contract to handle the work I used to do, and now I spend most of my hours of work on the phone, hassling contributors and listening to lame excuses.

"Yes, I understand," I say soothingly, "but we have a publication date, and we've already booked the printer."

Des, who's now sitting opposite me, raises an eyebrow, and I shrug. The last is a lie but I'm getting desperate.

"I don't care if it's rough," I say. "I'll smooth it out. That's my job."

When I finally get off the phone, Des gives me that sexy, sympathetic smile. "Fun and games?"

"I'm part editor, part nursemaid, part psychiatrist. You should have heard Nickerson in Vancouver. I had to get the story of his life, his wife's new business, his children's school grades, his house renovations, the fact that his dog's in heat, the . . ."

Des is enjoying my outraged recitation. I can tell by the way his head's tilted, by his amused smile. I ponder, as I have many times before, whether Des would have made a better husband for me than Philip. I speculate on what he would be like in bed. I wonder if, beneath that conservative exterior, Des contains a streak of wildness. It's hard to tell.

Even in his casual clothes, he carries an air of restraint, as if he were wearing a three-piece suit.

"Well, I've got a good one for you," he says when I finish. "The ADM refused to approve the monthly budget report."

"Why?"

"Because I'd done some clever accounting with the Oceans Exploration Program, moving half of what we owe the Americans into the next fiscal year."

"He didn't like that?"

"He accused me of having a fiddle with the books."

"A *fiddle*?"

"He said he was honorable and didn't want to get into shady practices."

Des says this in a light, bantering tone, but I know how much he prides himself on his honesty and integrity. "What a bastard," I say.

"It's stupidity, Jane. He couldn't see I was legally saving the department close to half a million."

"Wonderful."

"And he's supporting the minister's push for privatization."

"Privatization? Since when?"

"You haven't heard? Darreau would like to sell Mapping and Surveys to the highest bidder."

"I thought he was after Meterology."

"That too. Think how Canadians are going to feel when they have to pay a monthly bill for their weather reports. Thatcherite Britain, here we come."

A flash of orange catches my eye, and I see Madeleine hovering in the doorway, her fingertips in frantic motion. Her glasses glint in the fluorescent light, and she's wearing a loose filmy dress that exactly matches the shade of her hair. The effect is quite blinding.

"Yes?" I say.

She sidles in and puts a file on my desk. "A love letter from Barry. Well, hello, Des. We don't see you too often down here."

"I miss it," he says. "It brings back my youth. I used to work in Mapping."

"Really? When?"

"Four summers in the late sixties. The Survey paid my way through graduate school." He gives us a slightly lop-sided, appealing grin, and Madeleine inches closer to him.

"I hear the ADM got rolled over the coals by the minister," she says, lowering her voice into a conspiratorial whisper, "because his French is so bad."

"Where'd you hear that?"

"I hear," she says, "he was so shook up by Darreau screaming at him that he threatened to resign, and the big M backed off."

"You know something, Madeleine?" Des says. "You should write fiction."

The speckles on her glasses shiver indignantly; even her freckles look affronted. "Come on, Des. He's flunked three language tests after five months and fifty thousand dollars in training."

"Short stories about the Survey."

"His French is so bad, the francophones ask him to speak English."

"No, a novel. You'd have a best-seller on Booth Street."

"Are you saying it isn't true?"

Des leans forward, and Madeleine does, too, her orange lashes blinking hard, her eyes taking on that fanatical blue gleam. "What I hear," he says, "is that he can't whistle and shit at the same time."

She straightens up. "Oh, very funny. Very, very funny. Jane, Barry wants that file back this afternoon. *Tout de suite,* or as those who can't speak it say——" and she gives Des an angry glance—"toot swit."

When she's gone, Des sits back in his chair. "I couldn't resist it. God help me, but I couldn't."

"Is she right?"

"She's always right." He leans forward again. "Jane, I came down because I wanted to tell you something before you heard it through the grapevine."

My job, I think, and steel myself.

"Maureen and I are separating."

For a moment I'm speechless. "Oh, no," I finally say.

"The counseling was getting us nowhere. I'm moving out this weekend."

"You mean, lawyers, papers—"

"Maureen's seeing someone at work—another real estate agent. I don't know why I find this surprising, but she's been sleeping with him for six months." He says this in the same neutral tone in which he's said everything else, as if none of it has the power to hurt him.

"Oh, Des," I say.

He shrugs. "So, if you have any furniture or Melmac in the basement—"

"You've rented a place?"

"A one-bedroom, not too far from here. I'll be able to walk to work."

"What about Samantha?" Samantha is Des and Maureen's eighteen-year-old daughter.

"You know what she said? 'I can't believe it took you this long.' Anyway, she's off to university this fall. I'm going to buy a sofa bed so she can sleep over when she's back on holidays." He stands up and heads toward the door.

"Des, this is going to be hard," I say.

In the doorway Des pauses and then shrugs his shoulders as if to smooth the line of his suit jacket, even though he isn't wearing one. "It'll have its moments," he says, but as he turns to walk out, I see that the motion has been an attempt to camouflage something else: a downward slump of his shoulders, a hunching forward, as if the weight of separation has fallen on the back of his neck.

DEAR DIARY,

So much has hapened and some of it is terrible! First bad thing—the PARTY! It was Danas party this weekend and we were suposed to watch a movie but Cello brought a case of beer and people got really really drunk. Nicky had 8 beers and threw up all over Danas mothers best chair. Then Lisa got really really drunk and took off her close and was naked in the bathroom and the boys were trying to open the door and the girls were trying to keep it shut and somebody broke the lock on the bathroom door. And a lot of people were really gross and I culdn't stand it anymore because I don't really like beer and they were playing the stereo loud so Mark and I went upstairs and hid in the closet in Dana's bedroom. It was dark in there and we started kissing and he touched my brests. But I shoudnt have let him, Diary, as you'll SEE!!!

Then we herd a big slam and we ran out of the closet and downstares which was a big mistaik because it was Cello's father who'd found out about the party and was he mad! He turned off the music and had everybody pick up the beer and pour it down the sink and he said he was going to call our parents and if this ever hapened again he would call the police. So I had to go home and Mom and Dad were really really mad and screemed at me about not being reesponsible and using other peoples things without permishion and how they can't trust me and all that shit. I said I wasnt the only one but they said they didnt care about anyone else. They said I was going to be grounded for a month, weekends and everything. I said what about Terry and babysitting jobs and Alice in Wonderland reheersals and graduashion and Mom said she was sick of me acting like a loiyer and trying to wiggle out of everything. Dad said everything would be on a case by case baisis.

Second bad thing—I think Mark and I are BREAKING UP! I found out after the party that he'd been flirting with Lisa and wanted to see her naked. I said how could you? She's such a bitch and so ugly. And he said youre just jealus and I said go suck bricks. I thought maybe wed make up but now Mark doesnt want to talk to me! Diary, my life is ONE BIG HUGE MESS and all I do is cry and cry.

Bye for now.

 THE CALL COMES AT FOUR-THIRTY ON A SATurday morning when I'm in such a deep sleep I incorporate the ringing into a dream. Then I realize it's the phone and have to untangle myself from the blankets and grope for the switch on the lamp beside my bed.

"Jesus," Philip says thickly, turning away from the light, "answer it."

But when I finally get the receiver to my ear, all I hear is crying. "Hello?" I say. "Hello? Who is this?"

"Jane?"

"Vera? *Vera?* What's the matter?"

She manages to get the words out between sobs. "I'm . . . I'm bleeding."

"Bleeding? Where?"

"I have terrible cramps," she wails. "I think I'm losing the baby."

"Hold on! I'm coming."

I dress, get into the car, and race toward Vera on the almost deserted roads, slowing down only when I come to patches of fog. The mist is heaviest near the canal, and when I drive down Colonel By Drive, I can barely see the dark water or the embankment on the other side. At the Praetoria Bridge the traffic light is red, and I stop. I'm the only car at the intersection, and I wonder if I should ignore the light and just go. I tap my fingers impatiently on the steering wheel and rev the engine. Suddenly a canoe and paddler emerge from the fog, sliding silently along the water. My fingers stop, and I lift my foot off the gas pedal so that the car's roar subsides to an erratic hum. The paddler raises his hand, as if in acknowledgment, just as the billows of fog, which have parted before him, swallow him up again. The light turns green and I step on it, the car shooting forward.

Vera's building is also wreathed in fog. I stop in the no-parking zone, run into the lobby, and jab her doorbell several times in quick succession. When she doesn't buzz me up immediately, I search for the superintendent's bell. Suddenly the door buzzes, letting me in. On the trip to the twentieth floor, my imagination, which I've kept in a mental straitjacket, slips out of its restraints and swells with awful visions: Vera doubled over in pain, near fainting, incapable of walking, incoherent and disoriented, almost comatose from hemorrhaging, requiring an ambulance, and so forth and so on until I'm so replete with worst-case scenarios that, when she opens the door, I'm speechless at the sight of her. Her hair is smooth, she's wearing an ivory silk bathrobe that falls in elegant folds to her toes, and she's smiling—*smiling!*—almost gaily, as if she's welcoming an honored guest to a dinner party.

"Jane," she says. "Hello."

"Are you okay?" I ask. The only evidence of that phone call is the weary, chapped skin at the corners of her eyes.

"It's over," she says and then sings, "Over. Over."

"Over?"

She leads me into the bathroom. Vera's bathroom is usually a marvel of pale green Italian ceramic and creamy marble with brass fixtures polished to an expensive glitter. Now crumpled towels are lying on the floor, red-stained Kleenex are stuffed in the small brass garbage pail, and there's a heavy fetid odor in the air. Vera holds out a piece of paper towel. On it lies a lump of bloody tissue in the shape of a monstrous teardrop. She rotates the drop, and I suddenly see a tiny white hand with minuscule fingers reaching out of that raw flesh.

"Oh, God," I say.

But Vera seems immune to the sight. She tilts her head and says, "You wouldn't think it have hurt so much to lose it, would you?"

"Are you sure you're all right?"

"The doctor will want to see it, don't you think?" She thrusts the paper towel at me, and I automatically take it. "That's why I didn't just flush it. And I'll probably need a D-and-C. I've decided on the General. I hear the food there's better than at the Civic." She turns to the mirror. "God, but I look ghastly. Have you ever noticed that when you're past forty your face just *collapses* at the smallest thing? It falls in on itself and *rumples*." She opens a bottle of foundation, pours some onto a sponge and begins to apply it to her skin. "I wouldn't want to go to the hospital looking like death warmed over, so I'm putting a good face on it. Jane, don't look so down in the mouth. That was a pun. You're supposed to laugh."

I don't laugh, I can't, but I take that sad and incomplete morsel of humanity into the kitchen and wrap it carefully in a plastic sandwich bag. When I go back to the bathroom, her makeup is complete and her hair is combed. She turns to me with a flourish. "Almost the old Vera, wouldn't you say?"

"Almost," I say.

"Now, what to wear, that's the question."

I follow her out of the bathroom and into her bedroom. This is another ordinarily immaculate room, decorated in icy blue and cream with touches of Vera's elegance: satin pillows, chic little prints from Toronto boutiques, fragrant pomander balls hanging by ribbons from her four-poster bed. I sidestep a pile of sheets and blankets that cascade over the edge of the bed and trail along the carpet, which is littered with books, magazines, and tape cassettes. Two mugs, still half-filled with coffee, are making rings on her night table. I pick one up and put a Kleenex underneath it.

Vera flings open her closet doors. "The occasion calls for something somber but not dull." She pulls out a pair of dark green slacks and a burgundy pullover sweater, holding one up against the other like a salesclerk. "And a green scarf to tie it all together. What do you think?"

"Perfect," I say, not mentioning the obvious: that only the hospital admissions clerk and those in the waiting room would witness her bravado. The doctors would see her in a hospital gown: white, anonymous, and unflattering.

She takes off her bathrobe and tosses it onto the bed. She's naked except for high-cut silky white panties and a sanitary pad. I avert my eyes, not because either of us is shy—we've seen each other naked before—but because there's something private and intimate about that pad curved snugly against her pale brown pubic hair. When I finally lift my eyes, Vera is tying the scarf around her neck in a jaunty bow. She looks so good, and I look so bad—I rushed out of the house without makeup, hair barely combed, and wearing an old blue sweat suit—that when we arrive at the emergency room at the General, I'm mistaken for the woman who's just had a miscarriage.

Vera is taken down a hallway while I sit in the waiting room. I'm not alone in my boredom and apprehension. A young couple sit behind me, the boy holding his arm close to his chest as if it's broken. An older man paces back and forth, his hair as uncombed as my own. I close my eyes and try to ignore the television mounted above our heads, which is playing a music video. I don't understand music videos. I've tried to watch them because Emma loves them, but I'm confused by the lack of plot, the zooming of the camera—in, out, the faces looming and then shrinking—and the raucous music. I think my dislike is a sign I'm getting old, and it depresses me. The waiting room depresses me. Vera's miscarriage depresses me. I open my eyes and try to find some humor in the incongruities of the room: chairs uncomfortable enough to cause back spasms, fluorescent light that makes the healthy look sick and the sick sicker, a vending machine with high-cholesterol candy bars and heavily salted snack foods.

"Mrs. Wastenay? Could you come this way?" The nurse is short and energetic, and I have to walk quickly to keep up.

"How's Vera?" I ask.

"Oh, just fine. We've got her all lined up for a D-and-C just as soon as we can slot her in. Five miscarriages rolled in here between four and six. It must be something in the air.''

I find Vera in an examining room, lying in a hospital bed. Her clothes are folded neatly beside her, and she's wearing a hospital gown. Now I see why she never wears white; the gown, the pillow, the sheet, drain her face. Beneath the makeup I see the true color of her skin: a pale, flat ash. And the surroundings have destroyed her putting-a-good-face-on-it facade. Her eyes are closed, and tears are slipping into her hair.

I sit down beside her and take hold of her hand. Her fingertips are icy. "Do you want me to get another blanket?" I ask.

She shakes her head.

"I'll stay here until they take you in," I say.

She doesn't open her eyes. "He said it was for the best."

"The doctor?"

"He said it was like a bad apple. It fell off the tree early. He said when it's a good apple you can shake and shake and it won't budge."

I squeeze her hand.

"So I'm lucky, he said. *Lucky*. Except that it wasn't just an apple to me. That's the problem, isn't it? I never thought of it as an apple." She sits up and blows her nose. "I thought of it as a little girl. And I had this cornflakes fantasy. We'd sit down at breakfast, and to show me what a big girl she was, she'd try to pour cornflakes into my bowl. The box would be almost as big as she was, so she could hardly handle it, and the cornflakes would overflow onto the table. Then we'd eat the cornflakes right off the table with our fingers and laugh and laugh." Vera has a small, twisted smile. "My mother was such a fanatic for cleanliness that I wasn't allowed to mess up anything, not even my damned dollhouse. Oh, I know it's a *lousy* fantasy. Why not throw the cornflakes into a mud pile and then walk on them in our bare feet? Why not get down on our hands and knees and squish the mud and cornflakes through our fingers? You know why not? Because it's too messy." The tears spill over and run down her cheeks. "An apple. You wouldn't cry like this over an *apple,* would you?"

I shake my head and think of Vera's baby, slipping in and out of life the way the canoeist slid so silently in and out of the fog. I think of him lifting his hand, of that fetal hand reaching. I think of the phantom hands of all the children I've never had. None has left anything behind to mark its passing.

 MIC SITS ON THE COUCH DRINKING A BEER while Terry and Emma perform a number. Terry wears a bright red halter top, a tight black skirt, and black net stockings. Emma wears black pants and a black tank top. They both have on black cowboy hats with silver bands around the crown. The stereo plays "Get into the Groove" by Madonna, and Terry and Emma sing along, using beer bottles as imitation mikes. At first Terry thought it was silly, but Mic insisted, saying they had to get used to holding something in their hands and singing into it. While they sing, they also practice their moves: dips, sways, turns to one side and then the other. They've reached the point where they can do most of these moves simultaneously, but Emma occasionally falters and has to watch Terry before she picks up the steps. Nor can she entirely duplicate the way Terry can move her hips and thrust her groin. Emma's hips lack sexual knowledge and don't have the same oiled ease.

When the music stops, Mic says, "Looking good."

"I think we should turn more when the music goes dadum," Terry says and looks at Emma. "Want to try it again, hon?"

"I'm thirsty," Emma says.

"The baby-o wants a beer," Mic says.

Emma looks alarmed. "I'd rather have a ginger ale."

"Get her a Seven-Up and, Ter, you're going to have to zap up the middle. You gotta come on stronger. You know what I mean?"

Terry loves the way Mic has taken charge. At first he ignored the singing and dancing, but once she and Emma bought the clothes and began to practice regularly, he took more interest. Now he doesn't leave when Emma comes, but stays home, watches, and makes suggestions. He's turned thumbs down on the twin look as too cute, and has been experimenting with their outfits. He started studying the music business in Ottawa and put feelers out. Recently he's discovered a guy with a studio and musicians where they could make a demo tape. It's pretty expensive, as far as Terry can make out, but Mic has cut some sort of deal.

Mic explains the purpose of the demo to Emma while Terry gets the ginger ale. "You practice a few times with the backup," he says, "and then you make the demo. Once we got the demo, we're in business."

"Do we do concerts then?" Emma asks.

"We send the demo to producers," Mic says. "They're the guys who make records."

"When we get a producer," Terry says as she brings Emma a glass. "Then we do concerts."

"Oh." Emma pauses. "Could we sing at my school?"

Mic laughs. "Christ, fucking peanuts."

Terry sees Emma's crestfallen face and says, "But we could go to her school, couldn't we, Mic? It'd be good publicity."

Mic thinks as he opens another beer. "A sort of sentimental thing?"

"Yeah."

"Okay," he says slowly. "I like it. It could be good for the image."

Terry also loves the way Mic has taken to Emma. He no longer thinks Terry's wasting her time when she's with Emma, and he's come to the conclusion Emma may have some potential for the rock-star business. "When I squint, the two of you are so alike it's really weird," he said. "That could play well. Really well."

"But the thing is," Mic says now, "to get on the charts and have a song go gold. Then you're megastars. Then we're rolling in it."

The singing and dancing started out as just a game, a way for Terry to have some fun with Emma, but when Mic talks about it, anything seems possible. He paints pictures the way he did with the ranch, making dazzling patterns with words: *cuts, percentages, tours, promos, labels.* The talk is seamless, forming one continuous scene that plays in brilliant colors. The bedroom becomes a stage, the lamp turns into a thousand hot lights, and the mirror on her closet door becomes an audience. She sees not herself, but thousands of faces, mouths chanting her name: *"Terry, Terry, TERRY, TERRY!"*

"And when did you realize that you and Emma together were something special?" Barbara asks.

"It was just a joke," Terry says. "We sang at a party."

"And Mic Avery arranged a demo for you."

"He knew someone who knew someone."

"And then you went on the road."

"That's right."

"You and Mic got married then, didn't you?"

A small photograph of Mic appears in the right-hand corners of millions of television screens across the country. Terry believes she can hear the collective sigh of millions of women.

"We got married just before our first concert tour."

"And Mic managed you straight into stardom."

Terry nods. "He always had a vision."

Mic takes a piece of paper from his pocket. "I called the guy, and the first chance we can use the studio is Sunday morning two weeks from now—the twentieth."

Emma gives him an unhappy look. "I don't know if I can go."

"I had to really scramble to get that date." Mic folds the paper. "Studio time doesn't grow on trees."

"My parents are going away that weekend, and I'm staying with Felicia."

"Does that matter?" Terry says. "Couldn't you do it anyways?"

"I don't know," Emma says. "I'll have to ask."

Terry turns to Mic. "If she can't go, we can get another date, right?"

But Mic doesn't answer her. "The whole weekend?" he asks idly and lifts the beer to his mouth.

Terry has the feeling something's changed, as if the quality of the air in the room has become closer, heavier to breathe. She can't pinpoint what has caused this. Perhaps it's the tone of Mic's voice, the way he lifted the bottle, or the look he gave Emma just before the bottle reaches his mouth. Something has caught Terry, something has frightened her, but that something is so fleeting, so momentary, it disappears before she can identify it.

When your significant other speaks, do you always understand what he is saying?
a. Absolutely
b. Usually
c. Sometimes
d. Never

Mic lowers his bottle. "Everybody watered?" he says. "Good. Then let's hear it one more time."

Terry and Emma stand up, and Mic reaches over and turns on the stereo. Their hips begin to rotate, and their lips move so close to the mouths of the bottle-mikes, it's as if they're bestowing soft kisses on the hard curved glass.

 ALICE HAS RENTED A TINY OFFICE IN THE Glebe, right on Bank Street, two narrow flights up from Square Root, a bookstore, and the House of Happiness, a tea and coffee shop. The room is painted a revolting shade of green and has crooked floorboards, a door that doesn't shut properly, and a solitary bulb hanging from the ceiling, but Alice is taking a positive attitude. She loves the location, she says, and she's going to paint the walls off-white, put a dhurrie on the floor, and hang stained glass in the south-facing window. "It's going to be charming," she says. "Wait and see."

I ignore a cracked windowpane and sedimentary layers of grime on the sill. "You'll have to give yourself a charming corporate name to hang on the door," I say. "Something trendy."

"Of course," she says with delight. "The House of Romance."

"Glebeside Writer."

"A Room of My Own."

"Very good," I say but I'm really admiring Alice, who's recently gotten a haircut and a permanent. The softness of curls around her narrow face makes her look younger, prettier, less anxious.

She steps into one corner. "I've got it all planned. The computer goes here with the filing cabinet." She moves to the adjacent wall and spreads her arms wide. "Shelves over here."

"And then you'll be able to finish your book."

"I finished it."

"Alice, you never told me what happened."

"I told you about the marriage of convenience, didn't I?"

"The hero hadn't married her yet."

"Well, he does and they have great sex, but they're suspicious of each other. Then she discovers she's pregnant and runs away."

"But he finds her."

"And he confesses he loves her madly, always has, always will and he says he'll take care of her and cherish her for the rest of her life."

I sigh. "And he's rich, too. Some people have all the luck."

"I put in an epilogue this time. A touching birth scene."

"It was a boy," I venture.

"Of course."

We smile at each other. "And you've got the next book already in mind?"

"A desert island theme with a writer and an artist. Each decides to rent a cabin nowhere from nowhere to finish a project. They're both highly sensitive individualists with strong opinions about art. By some computer error, they both rent the same cabin at the same time. They're either going to have to learn to get along or kill each other."

"Oh-oh. Sounds like real life."

"Well, it's not going to require much research," Alice concedes.

"How *did* you convince Rob the office wasn't a complete waste of money?"

"I wore him down, like water on a stone. Drip, drip, drip. Actually, I think he likes the idea of having the house to himself. But think, Jane! When the kids are sick, he's going to get to play nurse. When an appliance goes, he's going to have to wait around for the repairman. He hasn't figured that out yet, and I'm not telling him."

We go down the stairs to the House of Happiness where, in addition to buying numerous blends of tea and coffee and a wide variety of pretty pots and cups, customers can sit at the small tables, on chairs with wire scroll backs, all painted white, and have a genteel and civilized afternoon tea. Silk lilies in mauve and yellow decorate the tables; light classical music is softly piped in from hidden speakers.

Alice and I sip tea and talk. About Marshall pushing to get his driver's permit while Rob and Alice stall: "He's so irresponsible. How can we trust him with a car?" About Felicia's problems with her math teacher and about Sylvie needing glasses: "At five years old, poor thing." Alice adjusts her own glasses on her thin nose and sighs. We discuss *Alice in Wonderland,* in which Emma has the lead and Felicia is a flower. There's been a call for costumes and costume makers, mothers of the cast especially. Alice and I shudder, remembering the mouse ears, and decide that the mere thought of the sewing requires a large plate of scones with sweet butter and an extra helping of raspberry jam. After we order, our conversation turns to Vera.

"She's really taking it hard," I say. "She figures it was her last chance."

"It was a terrible idea," Alice says.

"Vera thought she could do it all."

Alice shakes her head. "I don't think it matters how much love and care a mother can give, she's never going to be able to take the place of a father."

This subject is a wheel with many spokes. We spin it around and around, stop it here and there, finish one pot of tea and start another. We agree that Vera's need to have a child is selfish, that we all have children for selfish reasons, that children are objects that we use for our egos and pleasure. "Just strip the whole concept of parenthood of its sentimentality," Alice says, "and see what that leaves."

We talk of history, of children as economic necessities, of six-year-olds working in factories and fields. I remember a photograph from the 1930s of boys who worked in the coal mines, sooty, thin boys with sickly faces and haunting eyes.

"At least we're more humane," I say. "At least we allow children to be children."

Do we, though? Alice asks. Haven't we just applied a slick veneer of concern over indifference and cruelty? Cruelty not in a physical sense—we have labor laws and social agencies—but in a psychological sense, a cruelty condoned by governments: cutbacks in education, welfare, and day care. "You know where children are on the government priority list?" Alice says. "Down near the bottom next to sidewalk repair and the environment."

We nod solemnly and take sips of tea as the waitress arrives with the plate of scones and jam, and the conversation shifts back to Vera. "I tried to tell Vera how hard it is to bring up children with *two* parents," I say, "but she wouldn't listen. Not even when I told her about Emma and Dana's party."

"I'm so glad Felicia was too sick to go," Alice says.

"We made Emma write a note of apology to Dana's mother, but I also phoned her," I say. "It was awful. She told me that when she got home and saw the damage, she cried. She said there was vomit all over a chair and the dining room rug, that the lock on the bathroom door had been pulled out of the wood, and someone had drawn disgusting nudes in her hallway with a Magic Marker. She said she felt violated by her own kid.''

Another wheel, more spins and spokes. We sigh and agree these are good kids, brought up in nice homes, taught manners, instructed in proper behavior and morality. But we also remember our own teenage sins: drinking too much beer, fumbling experimental sex without birth control, drag races down open highways. We thank our lucky stars we made it through adolescence in one piece, unscathed in body if not in spirit. "The mental scars," Alice says with a shudder. We recall embarrassments and humiliations, rejections and shame, and lament the long arms of our teenage selves that reach persistently, tentaclelike, into our adult personas.

"My mother told me my virginity was my most precious possession," Alice says, "and I believed her. I felt guilty for years, even *after* I was married."

"I still have the ugly duckling syndrome," I say. "My mother was beautiful, and I could never measure up."

Alice studies me for a second. "You're a perfectly nice-looking woman," she says.

"But not beautiful."

"How many people are really beautiful? Most of us have to content ourselves with being average. Anyway, you have dark, expressive eyes and a lovely smile."

I'm touched by this and, not being used to compliments, immediately shy. I shrug. "You have such a nice way with words."

She picks up a scone and starts to butter it. "I'm a writer, remember?"

"Tell me, Alice, have you ever wondered what happens to your heroines?"

"They get married and live happily ever after."

"No, after *that*."

"There is no 'after that.' That's the nice thing about romance novels."

"But if there was," I persist. "If there was the long
haul—kids, mortgages, mid-life crises, back problems, bifocals. Could your heroines deal with that and still be heroines? Wouldn't they have to turn into something else?"

Alice is about to take a bite of her scone, but now she
stops, holding it in midair. "I don't know," she says, frowning. "I really don't know."

DEAR DIARY,
Friday—sunny and nice. Two zits on my
nose. More on my back!
Having terible cramps. Just awful. I had to
have the nurse phone Mom at work and ask
if I culd come home from school. Mom says if the cramps
get worse shell take me to her doctor. Meantime I took ty-
lenol and hope it gets better. So far Im the only girl in my
class who doesn't have her period yet except for Dana. Felicia started at Christmas.

Diary, Mark and I are definitely BROKEN UP!!! He
asked Lisa the bitch if she wanted to go to the movies and
she said yes. Cello said he did it on a dare but I dont beleeve
it. Its just like the Young and the Restless!!! Everybodys
lying to everybody!!! Lisas been sucking up to him and
flirting with him and everything. I told him if he goes out
with Lisa then its all over. He can just fuck off. He says he
thinks I'm getting too crazy. I said, I thought you loved me.
He said, I did but all youre interested in is being a rock star.
Well, go suck your dick jerk, I said. Hes a dork a nerd a fag
and I HATE him!!!

Meanwile, rehersels are terrible. The Flowers cant sing at
all, there just terible. Felicia is the only one who can carry
a tune but the truble is she isn't loud enuff. I know my hole
part but Im the only one. Mrs. Waddell is just mad all the
time.

Bye for now.

PHILIP AND I ARE DRIVING BACK TO OTTAWA from a weekend at an inn on the St. Lawrence River, where we celebrated our twenty-second wedding anniversary. This is an annual tradition, a getaway from home and work, a time set aside to talk and make love, sleep and make love again. Except this weekend was marred by a paper, "The Origins of Aphrodite Worship," that Philip is to deliver at a conference on the cultures of ancient societies in Detroit when we get back. New facts published in the *Journal of Archeological Studies* based on a recently discovered medieval manuscript have thrown the thrust of Philip's talk out of whack, and he spent most of the weekend worrying about it. Not out loud, but I could tell what was on his mind. He was too quiet, too caught up in his thoughts, too distracted even to successfully make love on several occasions.

"I'm sorry," he said when his penis went limp. "I can't seem to concentrate. I keep rewriting that damned paper in my head."

I lay back. "Is Estella Barnaby going to be there?"

"That's not the point. Everyone will have read the manuscript."

"But it isn't really evidence," I said. "Some monk copied some other monk's work, which was already a copy of something else."

Philip grimly shook his head. "It throws a new slant on what happened after Aphrodite was born, suggesting she didn't just visit the Peloponnese after Cythera, but that her influence went much deeper into the mainland at a much earlier time."

"Too bad she was such a lousy correspondent. The least she could have done was keep Zeus informed."

"All right, Jane, poke fun if you like."

"Can't you just say that these new facts cast an interesting light on already completed research and require further verification?" I ran my hand down his belly into the coarse graying nest of hair at his groin.

He sighed. "That's what I'm trying to decide."

I worked Philip in my hand, kneading his softness. "What I'd like," I said with my own heavy sigh, "would be to have Aphrodite with us in spirit."

"Uh? Oh, sorry, Jane."

It wasn't our worst anniversary weekend. It didn't hold a candle to the one we spent in Château Montebello after I found out I'd never have any children. "Polycystic ovaries, Mrs. Wastenay," the doctor had said. "Very poor or no egg production."

"But how? From what?"

"It's something you're born with."

"Is there anything—"

"I'm afraid not."

I cried for a long time after that—the whole of our anniversary weekend. Philip tried to comfort me, assuring me that he still loved me and, when that didn't work, took long walks.

No, this weekend wasn't the worst, just unsatisfactory in its own way. We've driven back without talking, without even turning on the radio, each of us wrapped in a heavy silence.

We pick up Emma who spent the weekend with Felicia. "Did you have a good time?" I ask her as we drive away.

"Sylvie is a pain," she says. "She kept bothering us. We had to lock her out of the room. She must've pounded on the door for hours."

"Poor Alice," I say.

"We didn't do it when Alice was there, Mom. We waited until she was gone."

"That was nice of you," I say.

"And is Marshall ever mean to Felicia. You wouldn't believe it. They had a big fight on Saturday night over the television, and he called her a little cunt."

"Emma," Philip says.

"Dad, I'm just telling you what I heard. I'm not *saying* it."

"Where does all this swearing come from?"

"Everybody talks that way."

"Everybody does *not* talk that way," Philip says. "Plenty of people can converse without using bad language."

Emma shrugs. "Not in our school."

"And did you make your demo?" I ask. Arrangements were made with Alice for Terry and Mic to pick up Emma on Sunday morning to make a singing demo. Emma is convinced this demo is going to bring her and Terry fame and fortune. She's chattered excitedly about producers and concerts and going to Los Angeles. For a while I worried about the power of this fantasy, but then I decided it's harmless fun, and I keep my mouth shut. "It got canceled," she says.

"That's too bad," I say. "Can you do it another time?"

"I think so."

We're finally home. Philip parks in front of the house, because a neighbor has left his second car in our driveway to make it look as if someone has been there for the whole weekend. This is standard practice on our street. We have a Neighborhood Watch program, and we've had the police come and talk to us about precautions and friendly surveillance of one another's houses. We've put distinguishing numbers on our VCRs and televisions with a special vibrating pen, installed lights at doorways, and put Neighborhood Watch stickers on our doors. The stickers have a red stop sign that says "Warning!" and informs all burglars: "The contents of this house have been marked for police identification."

While Philip unloads the suitcases, I go to the side door and put my key into the lock. I'm starting to turn it when I realize the door has been open all along. "That's funny," I say to Emma. "The door's open."

Even then I think the door has been unlocked by another neighbor who keeps a key in case of emergency and brings our weekend newspapers into the house when we're not there. I'm thinking how careless he was not to lock the door when he was finished, when I step into the kitchen and come abruptly to a halt. The room is not as I left it: the counters wiped clean, the canisters in a neat line, the drainboard empty. Chaos has swept through the kitchen, trailing mess and dirt and litter in its turbulent wake. The drawers and cupboard doors are open, dirty dishes fill the sink, flatware is strewn everywhere, canned goods have been tossed onto the floor. A spider plant has been upended, and dead foliage and soil fan out on the stove top next to a pool of liquid, dark and thick. I take a deep breath and gasp at the smell. Then I see the bottles on the floor and the dried tributaries of beer that ran together into one river of liquid, flowing into a heat vent.

"Mom!"

"Oh, my God," I say.

"Who did it?"

"Go get your father and don't touch anything!"

The police, replete with guns and holsters, are sympathetic but neither surprised nor encouraging. They look around and take notes. They tell us there's been a spate of burglaries in Ottawa with the same kind of vandalism, although that doesn't necessarily point to only one perpetrator. Our particular burglar, they say, must have known when we were coming back because he took his sweet time going through every nook and cranny of the house. He searched through my jewelery, picking out the good pieces; he found Emma's cache of Christmas money, hidden in the bottom of her closet with the old Barbie clothes; he discovered our sterling silver in the basement behind a stack of wood. He even played our CD player—his taste ranged from "The Best of the Classics" to Pink Floyd—drank half a case of beer, and consumed a jar of olives, a jar of cheese spread, and a box of crackers. He'd taken nothing marked with our distinguishing number.

"What about fingerprints?" Philip says. We haven't touched a thing in the house, only gone from room to room and noted the destruction.

"We'll dust for fingerprints," one of the policemen says, "but I doubt it'll tell us anything. It rarely does in cases like this. Neighbors are a better bet; they may have seen something out of the ordinary." And he asks us how many people knew we would be gone on the weekend.

"My colleagues," says Philip.

"People at work," I say. "The neighbors."

"Some of my friends," Emma says.

"Anybody else?" he asks.

We look at each other and shake our heads. We look pale and drawn. Philip is the most controlled. He makes a list for the police of what is missing, he signs their report, he sees them to the door and says good-bye. I'm less able to hold myself steady, being buffeted by gusts of a shaking wild anger every time I think of my panties and bras pawed through and dumped onto the floor. Emma has been crying on and off. The burglar tore the posters off her wall, dumped out shoe boxes filled with her treasures, and walked over her glass and ceramic animals, crushing them into the carpet.

The job of cleaning takes us all that day. Philip tapes sheets of plastic to the broken glass in the sliding door. I wash dishes and mop the kitchen floor and reorder the cabinets. I try to find solace in the fact that I'm discovering long-lost utensils, but the irony falls flat. I'm too tired, my jaw aches, my lower abdomen throbs as if I've been punched in the stomach. When I find a stained semen-smelling dish towel wedged between the refrigerator and the microwave stand, a guttural animal sound comes out of my throat. I jam the cloth as deep as I can into a garbage bag.

When the main floor is cleaned, I go upstairs to Emma's room. She's slowly hanging up clothes to the loud blare of rock music. She doesn't acknowledge me, even when I turn her radio off and the room is plunged into silence. She puts a blouse on a hanger, her face turned away.

"Em?" I say.

"What?" She walks over to her bed and picks up a skirt, her body angled in such a way I can't get a glimpse of her profile. Her refusal to meet my glance confirms my suspicions.

"Terry and Mic knew we were gone."

She swivels, and I see she's been crying hard. "She wouldn't do it! I know she wouldn't!!"

"Maybe she told one of her friends."

"They wouldn't do it either!"

"Em, you don't know her friends."

"Yes, I do. I met them at the party. They're nice. They were all really nice to me."

"Being nice to you"—I sweep my arm, gesturing at her torn-up bedroom—"has nothing to do with this."

Emma's cheeks and chin are a blotched red. "You think Terry did it!"

"I'm not saying that."

"Yes, you are!"

"Emma, the police asked us to remember."

"You don't like Terry. You hate her!" Emma stalks out the door.

"Come back here!"

Emma halts. "You always think bad things about her."

"I said come back here, and I *meant* it."

Reluctantly she walks back into the room, but only as far as the doorjamb. She leans against it and watches me warily.

"I don't hate Terry," I say, "but we don't know much about her."

"That doesn't mean she'd break into our house and steal things."

"And I don't think you know her very well either."

"Yes, I do! We talk all the time. She tells me things! She tells me secrets!"

"And what about Mic? Does he tell you secrets, too?"

"Mic wouldn't steal either." But her eyes have flickered sideways, and I realize I've hit a weak point.

"I just think we should tell the police about—"

"No! I don't want you to!"

"Don't you want the person who did this to get punished?"

"If you call the police, I'll *hate* you! I'll absolutely *hate* you, *hate* you, *hate you!*"

Philip arrives. "What's going on here? I can hear the two of you screaming in the basement."

"Mom thinks Mic and Terry robbed our house!"

"I didn't say that." I turn to Philip. "But they did know we were away."

"I know she wouldn't steal! I know it! She's nice. She wouldn't *do* it!"

Emma has thrown herself on the bed, crying, and Philip takes a deep breath. "All right," he says. "Let's not get carried away. This has been a very unpleasant experience. Let's not make it worse than it already is. Em, I want you to keep working on your room. Jane, could you come with me to the basement?"

In the basement Philip has been trying to put some order into our bank and tax files, which the burglar tore apart. He stands in the middle of the jumble of papers, checks, and bank statements and says, "Was that necessary?"

"Terry was watching our house."

"That doesn't mean anything."

"What about Mic? He doesn't have a job, does he?"

"That doesn't mean he's a thief."

"But he could be."

"Jane, it was a lousy move. For God's sake, the woman is her mother."

"I know who she is!"

"You should have talked to me before approaching Emma. We could have come up with some kind of strategy. But just blurting out the first thing that came into your—"

"All right! I shouldn't have said anything."

"You're driving a wedge between us and—"

"I said I was wrong. Isn't that enough for you?"

Philip inhales and exhales slowly and then looks down at the pile of paper at his feet. "All right," he says. "It's enough."

I go back to my bedroom and slam the door. "Fuck," I say to the underwear, stockings, socks, slips, and scarves that lie crumpled and strewn across the floor as if they've been part of a cheap bargain-basement sale. "Fuck, fuck, fuck."

DEAR DIARY,

My mother is a STUPID JERKY SHIT-
HOLE ASSHOLE KUNT AND BITCH!!!!

THE HOARSE CRIES AND THE THRASHING
wake Terry up, but she knows better than to
switch on the light. She's done that in the
past, and Mic's emergence from sleep was
so rough it frightened her. Now she leaves
the room in darkness and takes Mic in her arms, avoiding
the flailing hands and carefully gathering his hot, damp
body to her as if parts of him are broken. This is the fifth
night in a row he's cried and rolled around on the bed as if
someone is after him. After the second night, Terry said
idly, "Do you ever have those dreams where someone's trying to kill you?" and he said, "I told you, babe. I sleep like
a fucking baby." After the fourth night, she asked if he and
Buddy had any deals going.

Mic shook his head. "Nah, Buddy's lost his nerve. Charlene's got his balls in a nutcracker."

"Is it a car deal?"

"It's got components. It's big."

"Are you worried about it?"

"Hey, what's with the questions?"

"You're restless at night."

"Sure I'm restless. If this one goes, babe, we're out of
here."

His cries, those incoherent bursts of sound, are subsiding
into moans. He shifts fitfully but no longer fights the weight
of her arms. The first few times she was afraid to hold him
tight, but she's learned that the more secure her hold, the
calmer he grows.

*"You've had a long and illustrious career," Barbara
says. "What are you most proud of?"*

"The Oscar."

"Of course."

"And the Terry Petrie Home for Runaway Teenagers. That's very close to my heart."

"Is there something more personal—the kind of thing that wouldn't be listed in Who's Who—that has given you the most pleasure?"

Terry hesitates. How far can you go on television? How much can you reveal? How deep can you scrape into your history before the embarrassment begins? She looks into the camera eye, and it seems to her to be as dark, round, and sweet as that of a large zoo animal begging for tidbits.

"The thing I'm most proud of," she says, "is my love for Mic."

Barbara is taken aback. "What an unusual choice."

"My mother told me I was too selfish, too rotten, too much of a bitch to love anyone but myself."

"What a horrible thing to say!" The camera shifts from Terry's tear-filled eyes to Barbara's shocked face and back. It's a fine TV moment.

"But she was wrong."

"My dear, of course she was."

"Because I love him." Her life is a panorama of emotional riches spread out like a feast for the appetites of so many millions. "I truly love him!"

Terry feels Mic falling back into a deep sleep as his breathing grows deeper and his body cools. She can move now without waking him. She removes her arm, which has fallen asleep, from under his waist and pulls a Kleenex from the box on her night table. Gently she wipes along his hairline where the sweat has gathered. When she's finished, she kisses him on the temple and curls against him, pulling the blankets up around their bare shoulders and resting her forehead against the broadness of his back. She knows she won't fall asleep for several hours, but she doesn't mind. She enjoys this embrace almost more than she likes making love. It's a rare act of possession, secret and hers alone.

"It's lovely," I say. "Very nice."

"You think so?"

"I like the throw pillows on the couch."

"I thought they added an interesting touch."

"I didn't know you had a talent for interior decoration."

Des give a little laugh. "Neither did I."

The truth is, I find Des's apartment depressing. It doesn't look like him, although the look that I associate with Des— a soft, modern approach in muted shades of gray—may have been Maureen's taste all along. His new furniture tends toward hard gleaming surfaces and floppy, shapeless cushions. The color scheme is based on the dining room table, which is a black and white marble laced with streaks of yellow. The couch is black, the carpet is white, the throw pillows and a vase of dried flowers providing the yellow accent. It's too finished, too predictable. I envision Des in the furniture store, lost and bewildered in a sea of couches, tables, lamps, and chairs, malleable clay in the hands of a pretty interior designer with an eye on a large commission.

It's the evening of the day following the burglary. Philip left in the morning for his conference, and Des has invited me to dinner. Now he leads me to the table—yellow napkins, yellow plastic mats, yellow ceramic candlestick holders—and pulls out a chair for me. He switches on the stereo so that soft music is playing, turns down the illumination from the chandelier, and lights the candles. The flames dance between us to some silent melody of their own.

"You're my first guest," Des says as he pours me a glass of wine.

"I'm honored." I fan a napkin onto my lap.

"I wanted to wait until the furniture was delivered and the place decorated."

"I thought you'd split the furniture with Maureen."

"I wanted to start fresh—a new beginning."

"Let's drink to that," I say and lift my glass.

"A toast," he says.

"A toast to your new apartment. May it bring you health and happiness."

"A toast to my dinner. May it not burn in the oven."

We clink glasses and sip at our wine. Des jumps up, goes into the kitchen, and returns with two small plates. On each, he's artistically arranged slices of mango on a bed of lettuce. We both take a taste, and he frowns. "Maybe it's too sweet for an appetizer?" he asks.

"It's delicious," I say.

"You know something? I've always had this urge to cook, but Maureen ruled the kitchen."

"I'll bet you didn't try very hard."

Des gives a rueful shrug. "Not as hard as I should have."

Over the mangoes, we discuss roles within marriage: who cooks and who doesn't, who takes out the garbage, who pays the bills, who makes all the social arrangements. "And what about the unspoken roles," I ask, "like who dominates, who's passive, who sulks, who ends the fights?" We agree such roles harden over time until their rigidity becomes a burden almost too heavy to bear.

"Like armor," Des says. "You can't breathe."

I say I've usurped most of the role of parenting in my marriage, that I don't give Philip as much opportunity to be involved as I should. I'd already told Des about the burglary, but now I say, "I jumped right in and suggested Terry and her boyfriend might be behind it. It made Emma hysterical."

"God, Jane."

"I know, I know! I should have talked it over with Philip first."

Des tactfully sidesteps my guilt. "Maureen always felt she should have the last word as far as Samantha was concerned."

"Did that bother you?"

"You know how it is. She was the one who knew feeding formulas and what to do for diaper rash, and it went on from there."

"But didn't you ever want to take control?"

"I always knew who was in charge," Des says.

"Would it be different with sons?" I wonder. "Would we back off more and let the fathers in?"

Des's dinner is a chicken curry casserole with vegetables and a salad. He fusses as he puts the dishes on the table, worrying if the rice is too hard and the broccoli too soft, if the curry is too spicy and the salad dressing too bland. I'm amused and touched, particularly by his oven mitts, which are shaped like two large pale pink fish. When he finally settles down to eat, his face is flushed and damp. He pushes back the lock of hair that falls on his forehead.

"Cooking isn't as easy as it looks."

"I'll bet Maureen would just love to hear you say that."

"Maureen would probably like to hear a lot about the things I've learned since becoming single."

"Like what?"

"That I'm a workaholic. Now that I've got no one to come home to, I stay in the office until eleven every night. Maureen always accused me of having no interest other than work, and she's right. I can't think of anything else to do."

"The government won't thank you for it."

"I know." He sighs. "Serge Trottier just got the director general's job."

"But you're better qualified."

"He's a francophone. If they put me in the job, I'd spend three months in language training and wouldn't pass the test anyway."

I shake my head. "It's so unfair."

"You know what we are? WASAMs."

"What's that?"

"White Anglo-Saxon anglophone males in danger of becoming extinct. My plan is to put in my hours, take my pay, and retire at fifty-five."

"Someday this country's going to split right down language lines," I say gloomily. "Someday the politicians are going to find the costs have been way too high."

Dessert is fruit salad sprinkled with Cointreau and a homemade spice cake that hasn't risen quite enough. Des complains about the erratic temperatures in his oven and worries he didn't add enough baking powder. I say the cake's just fine and enthusiastically eat a large, damp, chewy piece. Des gives me a suspicious look that makes me laugh, and then he starts to laugh, too. The wine, which he liberally poured into my glass whenever it was empty, has now gone to my head, and I've achieved that state of inebriation in which the edges of things are paradoxically clear and yet indistinct, and I feel witty, charming, and attractive.

In the living room, we drink liqueurs in tiny green goblets, and Des puts on more soft music. I imagine someone standing in the foyer of the apartment and studying us. I'm sitting on the sofa, my shoes off, my stockinged legs crossed, both hands holding my goblet. Des is leaning back in a chair, his arms on the rests, his long legs stretched out in front of him, the lamplight reflected in the mahogany gleam of his loafers. What would that someone think? This scene is like my drunken vision, paradoxical and ambiguous. It could be merely cozy, two old friends comfortably talking, or it could be something else altogether, a prelude to seduction. I taste the word "seduction" on my tongue. It's as sweet as the Kahlúa, rich and warm. It brings me memories of those triangles I've twirled into silvery geometric patterns. Des talks department gossip while I nod and smile and study him. He's taken off his sweater and rolled up his shirtsleeves. I remember how much I like a man's forearm: the way the muscle tapers from the elbow toward the hand, etched by a line of dark hair, and the thickness of a wrist, particularly when it's enclosed in a dark leather watchband.

"Jane? More to drink?"

"Uh-uh," I say. "I won't be able to drive home."

"Are you in a rush?"

"There's Emma."

"She's probably doing homework."

"She's probably watching television, a no-no on school nights."

"You want to go home and fight with her?"

I grimace. "Uh-uh."

He comes over to pour more Kahlúa in my glass and then sits down next to me. "This will make you laugh," he says. "I've often wondered what it would be like if I'd married you instead of Maureen."

I don't laugh at all. Instead a small shiver goes through me, the trembling of the triangles before they start to spin. I conceal it by picking up my goblet, sipping the liqueur, and saying the first inanity that trips across my tongue. "It would have been different."

"The problem was that Maureen and I were too much alike. Ultimately it was boring."

"Oh, I'm not all that exciting," I say.

"Jane, you're always so—I don't know—vivacious. You liven up that mausoleum on Booth Street. You make people smile."

Surprised, I give a little laugh. "What people?"

"Well, me, for one."

"What a nice thing to say."

"It's true." He takes my hand in both of his and in an absentminded way plays with my fingers. "You've been a good friend."

He separates each finger from the others, strokes its length with his thumb, up and down, front and back. It's the most erotic sensation I've had in recent memory. The triangles turn, gather up speed, begin to whirl. "Des, I—"

"Of course, I'd like you to be more than a friend." He bestows on me the full wattage of his sexy heart-melting smile. "I'm doing this badly. Not that I was ever any good at it in the first place."

As Des looks at me and I look down at his hands on mine, I remember the girl I used to be, the heroine who rushed ahead, plunging into romance and sexuality with hardly a backward glance, a qualm, a reservation. She was impetuous and reckless, a wonderful creature so fearless and bold that the memory of her fills me with longing.

"I've wondered the same thing," I say. "If I hadn't married Philip . . . if I'd married you . . ."

Des's lips are soft, and I taste the sweetness of the liqueur on his tongue. I try to lose myself in this kiss, but I can't. Heroines, I'm thinking, don't come with husbands and children, with the pulls and tugs of other relationships. They don't have to judge the value of one good man against another or try to balance the heft of a marriage against the uncertain weight of a love affair. Sleeping with Des, I know, won't bear any resemblance to sleeping with Stuart. That was a fling, far away from home, a one-time occasion never to be repeated. Sex with Des would be complicated and difficult. I think of furtive phone calls, moments stolen from busy schedules, anxiety and fear.

I break the kiss, take a deep shaky breath, and lean back against the couch. "I don't know," I say. "I'm not sure."

But Des isn't listening. "Jane," he murmurs and kisses me again, his mouth harder and more demanding, and I remember he's been celibate for a long time. We're no longer sitting upright but angled awkwardly against the back of the couch. It's been years since I've been made love to on a couch, and my body doesn't like it. My right elbow protests at bearing my weight, my left knee is twisted, and a kink in my neck develops into a sharp pain shooting down my spine. I'm also uncomfortably aware of Des's erection; its knob butts up against my hipbone.

Sexual desire is remarkable. One moment it's full-blown, a hot-air balloon caught on a rising wind; the next moment it deflates, shriveling into nothing. I push Des away, straighten my spine, pull down my skirt.

"What's the matter?"

"I can't."

"Why?"

"I just can't."

Des's face is flushed. "Christ, Jane."

I'm flushed, too. The heat of sexual desire has ebbed, but the prickly warmth of embarrassment is quickly taking its place. "I'm sorry. I shouldn't have let—"

Des is always a gentleman. He interrupts me, trying to make a joke of it—"It's okay. I'm twenty years out of practice''—but the words hang badly, like a lopsided painting, and I rush in to take the blame.

"It's me," I say, "and Philip and Emma and the house and mortgage and the life insurance premiums and the furnace filter''—I wave my hand as if tossing this accumulation of responsibilities in the air—"the hydro bill, the grocery shopping, the—"

Des grabs my hand and squeezes it. "You're supposed to forget all that."

"I can't. I'm so . . . married."

That heroine never thought she had anything to lose in her headlong rush. She didn't see choosing Philip as limiting. She saw in him endless possibilities, an Aladdin's cave of wonderful sex, infinite nurturing, and thrilling and intimate revelations. She wasn't capable of seeing her future as all futures really are, shaped like a funnel, widest at its entrance, narrow at its end.

On the other hand—and I'm such an expert at other hands!—I don't move unhappily in that narrow area at the end of the funnel, do I? The truth is that my house, my home, my marriage, my family, are my sanctuaries, and I've fought ferociously to protect them. How can I introduce danger myself? I will not choose, consciously, to be the force that could destroy everything that matters. I'm a self-appointed goddess, a Hestia fiercely guarding the hearth and home, the husband and child, my place in the triumvirate.

I pull my hand away. "I'm so sorry, Des."

He no longer looks at me but fiddles with the cap on the Kahlúa bottle. "To be honest, I never thought you and Philip rubbed along all that well together."

"Sometimes I love Philip," I say. "Sometimes I don't."

"You know what I think? Love is a romantic myth we use to rationalize lust."

My heroine may no longer be in control, but she still clings to her beliefs. "Oh, no," I protest. "There has to be more than that."

"Tell me, then, how you can look at the person you loved, the person you told your innermost thoughts to, the person you had a child with, and suddenly realize she's a perfect stranger.'' He tries to pour some liqueur into his glass, but his hand shakes and it spills onto the table. ''Shit.''

''Here, let me.'' I reach for a napkin.

He pushes aside my hand. ''You notice she isn't even nice. There's this ugly line to her mouth you've never seen before.''

He tries to mop up the spill but fumbles with the napkin, the bottle, the goblet, and I suddenly realize his eyes have filled with tears and he can't see. ''Oh, Des.''

He turns to me, and I'm shocked to see how deep the lines in his face have become, as if a huge finger has outlined them, pressing the skin to bone. ''You know what you think when you look at this person?'' he says, and his voice begins to shake. ''You think, if I met this fucking bitch at a party, I'd turn my back on her.''

''What happens to heroines?'' I once asked Alice. ''What do they become?'' As I put my arms around Des, I find I know the answer after all. They grow like a tree, dividing and spreading and thickening, with a graceful arc here, gnarled bark there, some roots showing, others hidden, branches tangled and twisted, leaves veined and glossy, capable of capturing the sun at the top and casting shade below, the whole of it rich in fruit and flower. The heroine becomes a wife, a mother, a lover, a daughter, a daughter-in-law, a worker, a confidante, a friend, a comforter, a nurturer, a survivor, a fellow passenger. I tighten my arms around Des, feel the sobs rising within him, and discover I'm crying, too.

The telephone is ringing when I let myself into the dark house. I know it's too late at night for the caller to be anyone other than Philip. When he left for the conference, we were still unsettled by the burglary, still smarting from the stings we'd exchanged. His phone call is an indication of his wish to patch up our differences, and I rush to answer the phone, almost tripping on the step in the hallway in my eagerness.

"Hello," I say, picking up the phone.

"You sound out of breath."

"I just walked in the door," I say.

"Where were you?"

"Des invited me to dinner, remember? I was his first guest."

"How was the food?"

"He's not a bad cook, actually."

"I suppose you got all the gory details."

"He's bitter about Maureen," I say. "It all came out."

But Philip isn't really interested in Des. "I hate Detroit," he says. "You're afraid to step out of your hotel."

"How's your room?"

"Passable. I can see Canada from my window. Well, the lights of cars going over the bridge to Windsor."

"Are you in bed? Standing by the window?"

"Sitting on the edge of the bed, talking to you."

"Dressed or undressed?"

He laughs. "Is this important?"

"Just tell me."

"Well, if you must know, I'm wearing my shorts and my watch. That's it."

I can see him perfectly: every hair, line, fold, and bulge. He's sitting, hunched over slightly, right arm across the swell of his belly. His right hand supports the bent elbow of his left arm, which angles upward so that he can hold the phone to his ear. His back is patterned with hair in the shape of fern fronds that begin at his spine and curve up his shoulders. His legs, heavy at the thighs but surprisingly delicate at the ankles, are crossed, and his briefs, frayed and loose, gap in the front so that the soft tip of his penis peeks out between the folds of cotton. A gush of something tender and warm passes through me.

"I love you," I say.

"That's nice," he says.

"I plan to be very welcoming when you come home."

"Would you put that down in writing?"

"I just crossed my heart."

He laughs again. "How's Em?"

"Sleeping, I presume."

"Has she calmed down? Is she okay?"

"I think so, but we're not really talking to each other."

There's a pause while we both decide not to mention the burglary and my lack of tact. We speak simultaneously. Philip says, "How's work?" and I say, "How's the conference?"

"Work's fine," I say.

"Rubber chicken for dinner," Philip says, "and watered-down drinks at the cocktail party."

"Is Estella there?"

"Are you kidding? She never misses. We mumbled polite things to each other over shrimp canapés."

"Shrimp? That doesn't sound so bad."

"Canned shrimp, Jane. They were tasteless. I could hardly swallow one."

"You're just nervous. It'll be all over by noon tomorrow, and then you can have a good time."

He sighs. "I'll call you tomorrow and tell you how it went."

"You'll do just fine."

"I hope so."

"Break a leg."

"Right."

"Good night, honey."

"Good night. Oh, Jane?"

"Yes?"

"I love you, too."

I'm smiling as I check on Emma—a dark lump, head buried under the covers, in her messy dark cave—smiling when I go to sleep and smiling when I wake up the following morning. I hum a tune to myself as I take a shower. The tune is from a bubbly forties song whose title I've never learned and whose words I've never known. My mother hummed it for years, the same three or four bars over and over again, whenever she was feeling satisfied with herself. As her satisfactions were often at my expense—"I knew that skirt was too short" or "I knew you didn't study hard enough for that math test"—the little staccato followed by the trill of a crescendo made me seethe inside. Imagine my surprise a few years ago when I discovered my mother's tune had become part of my small humming repertoire. I've tried to excise it, but the notes leap uncalled to my lips. My mother's revenge, sly and triumphant.

I'm out of the shower and blowing my hair dry before I realize how late it's become and that Emma hasn't gotten up yet. She usually wanders sleepily into the bathroom just as I'm finishing my shower. Not surprising, I think with irritation. She probably watched television well past her bedtime. I open the bathroom door. "Emma?" No answer. "Emma!" Of course she can't hear me over the sound of her clock radio, which clicks on at seven with a blare of rock music. How she sleeps through the music I don't know, but I've often found her curled into a ball, the radio close to her head, the sound of drums and other electronic noisemakers shrieking around her.

I wrap a towel around me and stand in front of her door. The radio is extra loud, the drumbeat fast and heavy. "Emma!" I say, knocking on her door. "It's time to get up!" I knock harder and, not getting any response, push the door open. The loudness of the music hits me like a blast, and when I take a breath, the air has the stale smell of dirty laundry mixed with the cheap acidic scent of hair spray. Another burst of irritation, greater than the last, propels me inside. "Emma!" I scream over the music as I stride to her bed. But just as I get there I realize that the lump of the night before is nothing more than a heavy fold in her duvet enclosing her two pillows.

Suddenly the disorder of her room takes on another dimension. I notice her closet door is ajar and clothes have spilled onto the floor into great twisted mounds, and that the drawers of her dresser are open and half empty.

"Emma?" I say. I switch off the radio, and the silence throws her absence into stronger relief.

I step back into the hallway and call down the stairs to the first floor: "Emma!"

Halfway down the stairs: "Emma!"
In the downstairs hallway: "Emma!"
At the door to the basement: *"Em-ma!"*

The syllables of her name synchronize with the beating of my heart—*Em*-beat-*ma*-beat, *Em*-beat-*ma*-beat—in an increasingly rapid, desperate rhythm. I stand in the kitchen and stare at the counter where a dirty plate sits beside a lidless jar of peanut butter with a knife protruding from its interior. I study the refrigerator door, dotted with notes held up by magnets in the shape of fruits. Beneath a slice of watermelon is the calendar that records our days. "MY BIRTHDAY," Emma has written in big bold print at the bottom of the month. I reach for the telephone, but my hand never touches it. I can't call Philip, not with his talk first thing this morning.

"Emma," I whisper.

Em-beat-*ma*-beat.

The apartment is on the top floor of an old house in a seedy part of Centretown. The house was once a grand residence, but its generous proportions have been cut up into narrow, dark hallways and small, awkward rooms. The banister, ornate with curves and swirls, sways when I put my weight on it, and the smells caught in the peeling, faded wallpaper are those of curry and onions and root vegetables like beets and turnips. As I run up the stairs, I'm passed by people on their way to work, a black couple, an Asian woman, a Sikh in a beard, business suit, and turban. This is the other face of Ottawa, the one I rarely see, created by waves of immigration: Vietnamese boat people, Latin American refugees, the dark diaspora of Commonwealth populations. I see these people on the news at night and read about them in the papers. Canadian racism doesn't take blatant forms—we're not Americans, newspaper columnists smugly point out—but manifests itself in subtle, slippery ways. Landlords have no rooms to rent and employers no jobs. I've experienced none of this; I'm cocooned in white

English Canada, my foreign accent, slightly New York, noticed only by those with sensitive ears.

But I have no time to ponder this. I'm in a hurry, a terrible hurry, driven by a composite of emotions so awful I can hardly stand being in my own body. I'm frightened and angry, but these are the feelings easiest to bear. The others make me cringe and grimace. I caught sight of my face in the rearview mirror when I was driving here and was scared by my own features. They were twisted with guilt and self-loathing. I know why Emma's run away: I pushed her out. My mother-cruelty, honed to its sharpest edge, has sliced too deep. The accusation that Terry and Mic had broken into our house had risen to my lips so easily, so carelessly, I'd been deceived. They knew we were away, didn't they? It didn't take a genius to put two and two together. But Emma wasn't deceived. My need to hurt and attack has always been there, lying in wait like some vile creature in the dank stinking undergrowth of my jealousy. It doesn't even matter if my accusation is true or not. The burglary is no longer the point.

What kind of mother am I? To cut and gouge, to torture and punish? I'm no mother. I'm a barren woman filled with empty tubes and useless organs who has taken a child in her arms and pretended to be what she's not. Nothing can make me more than I am, not a social worker's consent, not the adoption paper with its huge gold seal of approval, not my name on school forms, not all the assumptions of neighbors and friends. For thirteen years I've been an impostor—Jane Wastenay, mother of Emma. I thought of Emma as a stranger, a nymph that could bring doom down on our house. I was wrong. I'm the stranger, the unknown bearer of danger. I've carried the seed of destruction in my heart and called it love. Exposed and debunked, I'm left with a despair that stings so painfully I was forced to run, propelled out of the house and through the streets of Ottawa in the middle of the morning rush hour, propelled so hard I ran a yellow light turning red, screeched around corners, almost hit a bus.

Now I'm racing up the stairs, purse flying out from my shoulder. "Excuse me," I murmur as four of us negotiate our way around a tiny stair landing. "Excuse me." My heart is pounding when I reach the third floor, I'm sweating and out of breath. The stairs, I think, too fast up the stairs, but I'm afraid that these symptoms have nothing to do with the stairs but are the beginning of something else. I remember the trembling that began in my fingertips and spread, fanning upward through my arms, wrists, and palms, outward into my chest, abdomen, and legs. I clench my hands into tight fists, pressing my fingers down with my thumbs.

Apartment 3D is a plain brown door. I knock on it once, twice, a third time. It's like a plain brown wrapper, mocking me with its anonymity. "Open up!" I say and slam the upper panel with my fist. It shudders and I whack it again. "Open up!" This is a building accustomed to shrieks and strange foreign behavior. No one peers out at me; the other doors clustered around the stair landing stay resolutely shut. If I weren't in such despair I would revel in my ability to scream in this un-Canadian fashion at the top of my lungs. *"Open . . . open . . . open!"* The door becomes everything I am angry about: myself, Emma for running away, Terry for existing, Philip for not being here when I need him. I drop my purse to the floor; I bang, punch, and smash the wood. *"Open this door!"*

"Jesus frigging Christ!" someone yells from behind it. "Wait a minute, will you?"

A chain rattles, a bolt clicks back, and the door is thrown open. A stocky young man stands there, unshaven, bare-chested, the fly of his jeans only partially zipped. He pushes aside a tangle of long blond hair, revealing blue eyes and a bristle of blond whiskers. He has even features and a square jaw, a type of good looks I associate with style rather than character. He stares at me, and I'm suddenly conscious of my lack of makeup, hastily combed hair, wrinkled skirt and blouse.

I lean down and pick up my purse. I take a deep shaky breath. "Mic?" I say.

"Yeah."

"I'm Emma's . . . mother."

For a second Mic looks beyond me as if he thinks there might be someone standing behind my shoulder, and my sixth sense, honed by shock and despair, picks up the faint rank scent of fear. I am suddenly convinced he's the man who broke into our house.

"Ter!" he hollers down the hall. *"Ter!"*

Her voice is faint, rusty with sleep. "What?"

"Get out here. It's for you."

Mic doesn't invite me in but swivels on his bare feet and walks down the hallway. I follow him, sidestepping a pile of empty cardboard boxes, and enter the living room. It's a small room, painted a pale blue and cluttered with old furniture—a battered coffee table, a couch with green upholstery, worn and dirty. There's no place to sit down. Every surface is littered with piles of clothes. I see into the kitchen, which I remember from the photo I found among Emma's things. From that photo and from my years of living in cheap student apartments, I've extrapolated the rest: the cracked plaster, uneven floors, stained sinks, peeling paint, rippled windows, and, permeating it all, the sad, musty smell of neglect.

"Is Emma—" I begin, but Mic sweeps up a bunch of magazines from a chair and dumps them on the floor. "Have a seat," he says and disappears down the hallway.

As I sit down, I know I haven't come to the right place. Emma isn't here. I am assailed by a sensation I haven't had since Emma was two years old and I lost her in a department store. We were in the housewares section. I was studying a frying pan; she was playing at my feet. Suddenly I realized she was gone. I was turning the frying pan over in my hands, comfortable in the knowledge she was beside me, and the next minute she was gone. With a terrified clutch at my heart, I began to search for her, finally catching sight of her after several panicky moments. She was standing by the escalator, one foot tentatively outstretched. "Where were you going?" I asked as I scooped her into my arms. She wiggled and tried to get away. "Down," she said. "I want to go down."

"Hello?"

Terry stands in the doorway to the living room. She's wearing jeans, a sweatshirt, a pair of scruffy slippers. She's just washed her face; it's still damp, and the hair at her temples is wet. When she looks at me, I'm shocked to see how much she loathes me. I realize I've hovered at the edge of her sight for thirteen years the same way she's hovered in mine. Like a translucent, shimmering bubble, I've hung in the background of her life, watching, judging, floating down now and then to rest for painful seconds on her skin.

"Where's Emma?" I say.

"Emma?"

"She's gone. She's run away."

"She isn't here."

"Then where is she?" I demand.

"I don't know. She never came here, did she, Mic?"

Mic has appeared again. He's put on a T-shirt and has a beer in his hand. "Never seen her."

"Maybe she went to that friend of hers—Felicia?" Terry asks.

"Felicia's mother would have phoned."

"Maybe Mark. Her boyfriend."

"They've broken up."

We've reached a dead end, and there's a long silence. Then Terry asks, "Why'd she run away?"

"Our house was broken into on the weekend," I say. "She was upset about it."

"Jeez, that's too bad," Mic says as he sits down on the couch and swings one leg over the arm. His foot twitches in a motion I interpret as knowing and defiant. I think of that semen-smelling towel, and for the first time I truly wish I were a man. I would hit him. I would use my fists to smash in his handsome face.

"Her room was torn apart," I say. "Her things were smashed."

"Oh, no," Terry says.

"Son of a bitch," Mic says, and my hands tingle.

"He spent hours in our house. The police think he must have known we were gone."

Mic takes a swig of beer. "No shit." His smirk has the same smug defiance as his twitching foot: *I know that you know that I know that you know.*

But I ignore Mic and watch Terry. She gives him a glance and starts to pick at the skin around her nails. My sixth sense, sensitive to every shift of emotion in that dirty room, picks up a complex amalgam of shock, anger, and fear, confirming my suspicion of Mic's guilt. Not that it matters. I have no choice but to remain silent. I can't go to the police and tell them what I know. I've already destroyed enough, and Emma won't thank me if Mic goes to jail and Terry's relationship is ruined. I want my daughter back more than I want the guilty punished. I stand up and take my car keys out of my jacket pocket. "You'll call me right away if Emma phones?"

"Yeah, for sure," Mic says, but Terry asks, "What're you going to do?"

"Go to the police."

"Good luck," Mic says.

"I could go with you," she says. "I could help you look."

Sometimes when I diapered Emma, fed her, and played with her, I imagined that other mother manifesting herself so that she and I would be looking at each other over Emma's bald little head. "She's doing very well," I would say. "That diaper rash is all cleared up." Now it occurs to me that Terry may have had such fantasies of her own. Perhaps she imagined herself handing a baby over to some woman, the weight of the child lifted from her arms, leaving them curved and empty. "She needs burping," she would say, "or else she gets these hiccups." I soften toward her and am about to agree that she come with me when Mic shakes his head.

"No way," he says.

"Just for a few hours," Terry says.

"We got packing."

Anger makes her chin as square as Emma's and colors her cheekbones a dull red. "Shit, Mic, that's not fair."

"Babe, I'm splitting by noon," he says easily and takes another swallow of beer.

"It's my fucking kid!"

"Are you coming or not?"

A struggle for supremacy is now enacted before me. They stare at each other. Mic's foot quits twitching and Terry is rigid, but their stillness is only a counterpoint to the emotions that swirl around the room, smashing against the walls and battering the windows, no less tumultuous or raucous for being completely silent. I might have found this spectacle fascinating, but the meaning of the boxes in the hallway and the piles of clothes in the living room is just sinking in.

"Where are you going?" I ask.

Mic breaks eye contact with Terry and gives me a sly grin. "South and west," he says. "L.A."

Terry abandoned Emma after she was born. She may have done this for the right reasons, but in Emma's eyes it was an abandonment all the same. It left that empty place in Emma I'd once tried to describe to Vera without success. I'd seen that empty place not as a physical thing but as an abstract idea representing a part of Emma separate and distinct from Philip and me. But this second abandonment is going to be different. This time I know the damage will be far more painful than the first ever was. That empty place will take on horrific physical dimensions, a gaping, bleeding wound that Philip and I will never be able to heal. For a moment I feel a violence toward Terry that far surpasses anything I felt for Mic. How can she hurt Emma this way? Doesn't she care? Doesn't she know what this will do? I turn to accuse her and see she's trembling and has covered her face with her hands. My fury disappears as quickly as it came. What right do I have to be so angry? I imagine us on trial like Mary Beth Whitehead and Elizabeth Stern. What would we look like in that courtroom, held in the scales of justice? Terry: a thin, awkward woman with crooked teeth who bites her fingernails and the surrounding skin until it bleeds. Jane: a tall, heavier, older woman with flyaway hair in rumpled clothes who has to clench her hands so their shaking won't betray her and whose face grows grotesque with emotion. How would a judge assess one against the other: my barren anguish against Terry's unwanted pregnancy, my years of caretaking against her sudden presence, my need for Philip against her need for Mic, my cruelty against her irresponsibility? And how would my adultery, my flirtation with Des, my disloyalty to Philip, my angers, fears, insecurities, and jealousies weigh in the balance?

I think of Mary Beth Whitehead and Elizabeth Stern standing before banks of microphones, those unwilling sisters.

Who is the rightful mother? Who is not?

Wearily I turn to leave. Mic lifts his beer bottle. "Nice meeting you," he says.

I walk down the hallway, but Terry rushes after me. Her face is blotchy, and her eyes are wet. "I was going to tell her we were leaving."

I don't say anything.

"And I'm going to write. Tell her that, will you?"

I open the door, but Terry reaches out so the raw tips of those bitten fingers graze my sleeve. "What?" I say.

"And please tell her I love her."

Terry could be Emma, with her hair loose around her face, her thin wrists and sharp elbows. She could be thirteen instead of twenty-seven. I think of Mic sitting in the living room with his beer and his ugly secrets. What happens, I wonder, to a girl like Terry who becomes a mother when she's still a child? Does she lose her own mother? Her right to nurturing and comfort?

But she's not Emma, and I'm not her mother. I don't want to care about her. My dislike of her battles with my sense of compassion, and a compromise is struck.

"I'll tell her," I say and leave.

I have an envelope containing a photograph of Emma when she was seven years old, a list of her vital statistics, and cards with her fingerprints on them. I obtained the fingerprints during a Child Find program held at a nearby shopping center. I'd gone there to pick up some dry cleaning, and Emma was impressed by the solemn police officer and enthralled by the way her fingers revealed black swirls when inked and pressed onto paper. The woman running the program carefully instructed me to keep the envelope in a safe place just in case. I didn't believe there'd ever be a just-in-case, but I obediently put the envelope in our safety deposit box and then promptly forgot it. Now, after leaving a message for Philip at his hotel—"Urgent, call home"—I go to the bank, retrieve the envelope, and pull out the photo. A gap-toothed Emma smiles at me sweetly, red hair tumbling over her forehead.

At the police department, the bureaucracy bends kindly, sympathetically, but the formalities can't be hurried. The officer of the Youth Division, Sergeant Paul Leroux, has a missing persons report to fill in, lines to be entered, boxes to be checked. I sit beside his desk, twisting the strap of my purse into tight contortions, and answer questions. Name? Date of birth? Height? Weight? Clothing worn when last seen? Jeans and a denim jacket, sneakers without socks: the teenage uniform. Sergeant Leroux sighs. Disabilities? None. Okay, ma'am, is there any history of drug or alcohol abuse? Mental problems? Has she run away before?

Should I tell him about Emma's disappearance when she was six years old and angry because I wouldn't buy her a game she wanted? Should I relate how Philip and I went from house to house asking neighbors if they'd seen her, frightened she'd run off or been abducted, only to find her hidden in our car, which was sitting in the driveway? "No," I say. "She's never done this before."

"Any reason why she'd run away from home?"

I don't like the way Sergeant Leroux's pen sits poised over the paper to record my sins, but he has soft brown eyes and the patient air of twenty years' experience. "We had an argument."

Family fight, he writes. "About . . . ?"

I can't tell him about the burglary and the connection to Mic, so I lie and say we argued about allowances, dating, boys, the usual things.

More questions about her school life, her medical and dental history, favorite hangouts, likes and dislikes, girlfriends and boyfriends, the slightest hint that she may be into drugs. "No," I insist, winding the strap of my purse around my hand.

"She have any money with her?"

"I don't know."

Sergeant Leroux sighs. "She's probably at the Rideau Centre. That's where most of them go."

The strap cuts my hand. "But what if she's not there? What if she's left town? Taken a bus somewhere."

"Any idea where she'd go?"

I pause. "Maybe my mother in South Carolina."

Sergeant Leroux says he'll have one of his men check the bus station. He also reassures me Emma's name and information will go onto all the appropriate lists so police in other towns and U.S. Immigration will be alerted.

"When will you start?"

"As soon as we can, ma'am."

But I see the report needs typing, that it must be shuttled through various levels of bureaucracy, that it will be several hours before anyone seriously begins searching. "She left last night," I say. "The trail will be cold."

"We'll do our best," he says with a comfort-the-mother sincerity that doesn't make me feel any better.

"But I could go," I say. "I could go right now."

Although his expression tells me I'll be wasting my time, he says, "If you want to make initial inquiries, Mrs. Wastenay, that's fine with us."

Armed with a more current photograph of Emma—a somber, thoughtful smile, hair pulled back in clips—I visit the bus station and, out of desperation, the airport. It's a futile, frustrating, and humiliating exercise. Not only does no one recognize Emma, but the night shifts have gone home and won't be back for several more hours. Pity fills the faces of ticket takers, cashiers, and managers, the sort of pity that turns to thank-God-it's-not-me the minute I walk away. I turn around several times and catch that expression of relief on their faces. If they see me looking, it's wiped clean, the cloth of decency scraping across their skin.

I go home to that awful silence and call Philip again, leaving another message. I call my office and tell them I won't be in. Then, as I'm standing and staring helplessly out the window, the phone rings. I grab it.

"Mrs. Wastenay?"

My heart goes into suspension. "Yes?"

"This is Hopewell School."

My heart falls back. "Oh," I say. "I forgot."

An aggravated sigh fills my ear. "We would appreciate it if you'd call about absences before school next time."

"I'm sorry."

"Will Emma be gone for the whole day?"

"Yes," I say. "She's . . . sick."

I can't stay in the house, listening to the furnace exhale, the refrigerator click and hum. The silence drives me back into my car. For a while I drive aimlessly around the neighborhood streets, peering up side roads, down alleys and driveways, as if I might surprise Emma wandering idly down one of them, plucking the leaves off bushes or running a twig along the slats of a fence. But I see only small children playing in their yards, cats sauntering across streets, young mothers wheeling babies in strollers. Everything mocks me: the cats have smug grins, flowers taunt me in their brightness, while babies, gurgling and happy, scoff at my grief. The day itself, sunny and warm, is a sign of cosmic ridicule.

Back to the house and telephone. Another call to Philip, this time: "Urgent, come home." A call to Sergeant Leroux. "Yes, ma'am, the bulletin was sent, and we have a patrol officer looking uptown. No, nothing so far." Calls to Vera, who's in a meeting; to Des, who's away on French training; to Alice, whose answering machine informs me she can't come to the phone right now but if I leave a mes-

sage at the sound of the tone, she'll get back to me as soon
as possible. I wait for the beep and then let the tape roll.
My lips form the words "Help me," but I discover I've
swallowed the silence in the house and it strangles the
sounds that want to come out. My throat aches with the
pressure of words, sounds, screams.

The Rideau Centre parking garage is full of cars so I'm
forced to go around in several circles until someone vacates
a spot. I get out of the car, lock it, and two seconds later
realize I've left the keys in the ignition. I'm not all here, I
think. I'm in a horror novel, a Stephen King extravaganza,
and parts of me are shedding or being lopped off by invisible hands. My voice is gone, my concentration fragmented,
my reason eroding. When I climb the stairs and arrive in
front of Eaton's, the horror intensifies. The first thing I see
is the escalators, those usually sedately moving stairs with
their burden of innocent shoppers. Today they are different.
As I watch, pressed fearfully against a wall, they twist and
writhe like metal snakes, and the riders leer at me, faces
turned to gargoyles. Hot sweat pricks under my arms and
crawls downward between my breasts.

"Are you all right?"

A face looms at me, its features distorted. The nose is
huge, the mouth gapes like a dark cavern, the hair crawls on
its skull, restless white grubs. *Medusa!* I open my mouth to
scream, but suddenly the face, the scene, clicks back into
perspective. The escalators stabilize, the nose and mouth
shrink, the hair turns into permed white curls. An elderly
woman is staring at me in concern. She has gold-rimmed
glasses, soft white cheeks, and heavy, pink-sweatered
breasts with a gold cross nestled between their snug curves.

"My dear, you look as if you're going to faint."

"I'm okay," I say.

But she insists I sit down on a bench and brings me a cup
of tea from the coffee shop nearby. "Hot tea always does
the trick." She sits next to me and carefully averts her eyes

from my hands, which shake so violently I can barely hold the cup. "Tea always perks me up in no time," she says.

This isn't a delicate Earl Gray but a dark over-steeped orange pekoe. The liquid slips down my throat, its heat warming me, its bitterness clearing my head. Between small sips, I take deep breaths.

"Did you have any breakfast?" She makes a scolding sound between pursed lips. "You young women nowadays: jobs, children—you have children? Of course you do, and husbands, homes to take care of. Now, my husband, he worked for General Motors. Foreman when he retired. We lived in Oshawa then. Well, he'd leave in the morning, and the children—I had four, three boys and a girl. The girl was the youngest. They're all grown up and married now. Two lovely grandchildren, born a week apart. I have a picture of them somewhere." She digs in her purse and pulls out a photo of two diapered babies precariously leaning against each other. "Aren't they cute?"

"Sweet," I say.

She puts the photo back in her purse and clucks to herself. "Where was I? Getting off track, that's where. My husband used to complain about that all the time. Not anymore of course. Died ten years ago. Heart attack. There I go again! Well, what I was trying to say was he'd go off to work and the children to school, and the rest of the day was mine. I wasn't liberated, but I could relax." She heaves a sigh. "Listen to me run off at the mouth. I'm sure you didn't need that."

"You've been very kind," I say. "Let me pay you for the tea."

The soft cheeks quiver. "Absolutely not! It's my treat." She covers my hand with hers, grips it tightly, and then stands. "Now, you get yourself something to eat. You're still as white as can be."

I haven't cried yet, but as she leaves, tears prick at the backs of my eyes. Twenty years of ridiculing Canadian reserve have made me forget how often it's paired with generosity and decency. I'm undone by the tea, that warm grasp of a hand, the torrent of words designed to give me time to recover. I take a tissue out of my bag and wipe my eyes. *Get ahold of yourself.* I blow my nose. A child of about two, standing beside its mother, sucks its thumb and stares solemnly at me with dark eyes. Slowly I bring my hands up like a shield, hiding my face. For a few seconds I hold them there and then quickly part them. *Peekaboo.* The child only blinks and sucks harder. I do it again. Blink. Suck. And again. The thumb slips from the mouth. The lips form an O. And again. The child suddenly smiles. The smile, warm and sunny, rests gently on me, the benediction of an innocent. I get up, throw the cup and tissue into a trash can, and head into Eaton's.

How does one find a missing child in three floors of a crowded shopping center? By walking. By going up escalators and down stairs. By looking into every clothing, shoe, and gift store. By weaving through the aisles of merchandise in department stores past racks of nightgowns and bathrobes, counters of purses and gloves, glittering displays of jewelery, mirrors, and lamps. I walk and walk, scanning drugstores, appliance showrooms, and fast-food outlets. I buy a tasteless muffin and eat it as I stand, like a guard, at the doorway of Emma's favorite clothing store. When I've finished, my mouth so dry I can hardly swallow, I start walking again. The muscles in my feet cramp into tight painful knots and my back aches, but I can't stop. I want to walk until I am nothing but physical sensation, until I drop from exhaustion, until I can fall into a heavy, oblivious sleep.

By late afternoon I find myself in the section of the Rideau Centre where a dozen or more fast-food booths surround a large grouping of chairs and tables. I rarely shop in the Rideau Centre, but whenever I pass by this area, it's always full of teenagers, even on school days. High school dropouts, I've always thought. Now I think: runaways. They sit huddled around the tables, their heads bent toward one another, their hair wreathed with cigarette smoke. Although the sunlight pours through the plate-glass windows, its potency isn't enough to illuminate them. A darkness surrounds them that absorbs light.

They seem to be night creatures who have crawled out of some subterranean cave beneath Ottawa's streets. Their clothes are black, their faces pale, their hair spiked and dyed into strange pastels: greens, yellows, and pinks edged with black roots. Seen from a distance, they have a peculiar silver sheen—the result, I realize, of a plethora of earrings, bracelets, studs, zippers, and sequins—but as I draw closer, the sheen evaporates. Their skin and hair are greasy. The fingers that hold the cigarettes have broken nails with grime in the cuticles. Knobby wrists protrude from worn cuffs. The girls' stockings have holes and runs, and their shoes are scuffed, the heels broken.

But I know they haven't crawled out of a cave. They've emerged from ordinary middle-class houses on quiet streets in Ottawa suburbs. Standing behind them, invisible, are parents and grandparents, brothers and sisters, teachers and friends, who have, with pain, watched these odd birds flutter out of the nest. These are the children who flap, falter, and fall, tumbling into ravines and crevices, their wings too crippled to let them soar.

One of them catches my attention, a tall boy with a shaved head and a bad complexion who stands up, flicking the butt of a cigarette onto the floor and crushing it with the tip of his black boot. He can't be more than seventeen years old. He has a growing boy's legs, thin and spidery in their tight black jeans, and only the hint of a mustache above a thick pink upper lip. He jerks his head to one side in the imperious nod of the leader of a street gang. Two other boys obediently crush their cigarettes on the floor and join him. Standing with their hands jammed into their pockets and their shoulders hunched, they confer in low tones and look now and then toward the escalator. I glance in that direction and see a frightened pale girl with red hair crouching down as close to the floor as she can get.

The girl is Emma.

Emma.

In my heart I've betrayed her.

Emma.

I've measured her against the children I couldn't have: children who would have been different, softer, easier, smarter, prettier, nicer.

Emma.

I've wondered, if she were to live or die, whether I'd cry or not. How absurd, how ridiculous. Tears flood my eyes, blurring my vision.

I wipe my eyes and see, very quickly, as if in snapshots, the three boys striding toward her, Emma flattening herself against the side of the escalator, the tall boy making an obscene gesture with his hands, Emma starting to cry.

The violence I felt toward Mic and Terry is nothing compared to what I feel now. I leap forward, and a sound begins deep in my throat and issues from between my clenched teeth. It's a snarl. A primitive snarl. The transformation from human to animal—wolf, bear, lion—is instantaneous. I don't think. I just act, running, waving my arms, the snarl rising in pitch to a scream. The animal power in me is so strong it pulses down into my hands, curling them, stiffening them, turning my fingers into claws. I will tear that boy limb from limb, gouge his eyes from their sockets, press my thumbs deep into his throat.

The scream precedes me, and startled faces turn in my direction: the boys, shoppers, a cleaning woman, the cashiers in the food booths. The tall boy stops, not sure what to do. Emma catches sight of me, stands up, and starts to run, arms outstretched, backpack flapping wildly behind her. We don't meet but collide, bodies hitting each other. She wraps her arms around my neck, pressing her face against my shoulder and sobbing into my skin: "Mom, Mom, Mom." Her arms are strong, gripping tightly around me, but they're no stronger than mine.

Mine can hold her forever.

MIC DIDN'T WANT TO TALK DURING THE two-hour drive down to the Thousand Islands Bridge, but when they clear American customs and head out on the open highway, he starts singing. Terry stares at him in amazement because she's never heard him sing, and he has a good voice. A sweet sort of tenor.

"I didn't know you could sing," she says.

"We're free now, babe. We're really going to roll. Give me a beer, will you?"

Terry opens the cooler in the back seat, pulls out a can, and opens it. Mic takes a swallow and puts the can between his legs. He steps on the gas so that the Camaro shoots forward, doing ninety miles per hour in a fifty-five-mile zone. The wind from his open window whips his blond hair into a frenzy.

"You know what we're going to do when we get to L.A.?" he shouts over the sound of the wind and the engine.

"What?"

"Call the guy John told me about." John was going to produce the demo that was never made. "He's got connections. He's going to get us in where it counts!"

Terry doesn't ask about the ranch because Mic stopped talking about it when he decided to become her manager. Lately he's focused on California houses, discussing estates with many bedrooms and bathrooms, screening rooms where they can watch Terry's videos, acres of gardens, and powerful security systems. Terry doesn't tell Mic about her dream house in Malibu, but she's determined that when they buy a place, that's where it'll be.

"And what happened when you got to L.A.?" Barbara asks.

"It was just as Mic planned. We got a demo made along with a short video, sent it to a producer, and . . . well, the rest is history."

"What about Emma," Barbara asks, "and the mother-daughter act?"

"She was too young to take along. She had to finish high school and all."

"Was Mic jealous? After all, she just came into your life . . . like that." Barbara gives a fine snap to her fingers.

Terry isn't going to tell that hungry camera anything negative about Mic. "He loved her. He adored her!" she exclaims, but gives a sideways glance so her fans will know that, of course, he's jealous. He loves her so much he can't bear to share her with anyone else.

"You have everything a woman could want—a handsome lover, a beautiful house, songs on the top of the charts. Do you ever wonder why it happened to you?"

Terry humbly shakes her head. "Lots of girls can sing. Lots of girls can act. It was a combination of hard work and being in the right place at the right time with the right song."

"Do you have any advice for all those out there who have ambitions to be a star?"

Terry has practiced sincerity in the mirror a thousand times. She looks directly into the lens, into the gaping, yearning wanting of so many. "Follow your dream," she says. "Just follow your dream."

Mic turns the radio on loud, and the music mixes with the rush of wind and the roar of the engine. He turns to her with a smile, and his sunglasses flash. "This is the life, babe!" he hollers. "This is the way I fucking dreamed it."

Terry's never seen him so happy. And she smiles back because isn't this the way she dreamed it, too? With her lousy job, her crummy apartment, and her stupid friends left behind? With Ottawa at her back and L.A. up ahead? She looks down at her hands and realizes she can forget the hundreds of codes that inhabit her fingertips and the shapes of bottles and boxes and cans. This is what Mic means about freedom. It's shrugging off the old and embracing the new. It's the road unrolling in front of the car and the horizon widening on every side. It's cutting out a bit of herself so the rest can fly in any direction she wants.

When your significant other leads, do you follow him
a. With all your heart?
b. Only partially committed?
c. Reluctantly?
d. Never?

"Mic!" she yells. She has a thousand questions: Are you a thief? Were all your deals burglaries? Did you steal in British Columbia? Is that why you had to leave? Did you break into Emma's house? Were you the one who smashed her things? Do you love me?

"What?"

"Can I drive for a while?"

"Later, babe. Later."

 I SIT NEXT TO PHILIP IN THE GYMNASIUM AT Hopewell School, waiting for the curtain to rise on *Alice in Wonderland/Alice aux pays des merveilles*. Chairs have been lined up facing the stage, but there aren't enough to seat the audience, and parents stand next to the back and side walls while younger brothers and sisters sit on the floor in the front. In addition to being crowded, the gym is hot and noisy. Talk, laughter, the scraping of chairs, and bangs from behind the curtain ricochet off the walls so that people are forced to raise their voices to be heard. Philip's taken off his jacket and loosened his tie. I've made the mistake of wearing a cotton sweater, thinking a June night would be cool, but now I pull it away from my neck in the hope that a stray breeze will enter. I ignore the trickle of sweat running down my side.

Rob and Alice are here with Sylvie, sitting several rows in front of us. Rob has gotten a good consulting job with a local engineering firm, and Alice has started another book. Life, she says, is okay, knock on wood. Vera and Des are also in the audience, several rows behind us. Since her miscarriage, Vera has come to the conclusion that having a child is not in her future. She's taking a course in Japanese flower arranging and has gotten a promotion. She tells me that she could probably move me into her department if my job disappears at the Survey, but so far rumor and gossip continue to entwine on their double helix, and I'm working harder than ever. Vera's also spending time with Emma. "If I'm going to be everyone's aunt," she told me, "I might as well make the most of it." Emma has always been impressed by Vera, and I've noted certain improvements in her appearance since Vera has taken her in hand. She now occasionally wears colors other than black and is less likely to cut holes in her clothes.

Des, to everyone's surprise, is interested in Vera. The relationship started with Des as a walking wounded and Vera as tea-and-sympathy. It's progressed further, although how much further no one knows. They're keeping company, as Vera puts it, and our speculation concerning their sex lives is lively. I think they're not, Philip thinks they are, Alice isn't sure. She agrees with me that Vera doesn't act as if she's sleeping with Des—she's too cool, too casual—but on the other hand she also agrees with Philip that Des is desperate to get laid and prove himself in the singles sweepstakes. "Otherwise, how's he going to keep his pride? Look at Maureen—she's flaunting it." Maureen has definitely not been circumspect; her lover, Vern, has moved in with her. We've all met him and agree he's a perfect jerk.

The lights dim in the gym, and there's much rustling and shushing as the curtain opens. The White Rabbit/le Lapin Blanc enters stage left, unrolls a document, and reads aloud in French. I can catch only a word now and then: *roi* and *la tête*. Then the Mad Hatter/le Chapelier Fou and March Hare/le Lièvre de Mars arrive. They talk, set up a tea party, and Alice enters. When she starts speaking, I take Philip's hand and squeeze it. Emma looks beautiful. Her hair has been pulled back and held with a black velvet band. She wears a blue dress with puffed sleeves and a white organdy apron. Unlike Alice, who had to make Felicia's tulip headgear, as mother of the star I was exempt from sewing. All I had to do was spend money: buy the dress, the headband, and the black patent-leather shoes. I know Emma won't ever wear the dress and shoes again—she thinks they're old-fashioned and ugly—but I don't regret the expense. She looks lovely up there, sweet and wholesome.

Emma was contrite and affectionate for several days after coming home. She hugged me at unexpected times, wanted to talk, helped me garden. But when life settled back into a daily routine and the meaning of Terry's departure sank in, old patterns of behavior emerged laced with a new, deeper, and harsher anger that spilled over onto Philip and me. For the first time I understood that even though Terry was no longer in Ottawa, we wouldn't be able to keep her out of our lives. She would keep returning, over and over again, entering our psyches as an unwanted guest and staying for as long as she pleased. We wouldn't know when she was coming, only that she'd appear in the future, coming at us like an echo in time.

I found a therapist, a young woman who was herself adopted. She sees Emma regularly and the three of us on occasion. She tells me I'm not to chastise myself forever, that my feelings, however awful I think they were, are understandable, that all we can do is provide Emma with love and emotional support as she works through the issues she must deal with as a teenager and as an adopted child, issues made that much more difficult by Terry's presence and then absence. In the past, I would have found it humiliating to lean on a stranger, but I find her empathy comforting and come away from each counseling session confident in my strength and resolve. By the time such feelings wear thin, eroded by tantrums, fights, upsets, and insults, it's time for another session of emotional buttressing and fortification, and the cycle begins all over again.

The Mad Hatter tea party is over and the White Rabbit reappears. He reads from his scroll and the Flowers/les Fleurs dance on stage, singing. Felicia is in the middle, the tallest and most awkward tulip. The singing is off-key and thin, but we clap loudly when the tulips bow. We're an en-

have really great clothes and jewelry and people will just love me! Then I'll move out to Holliwood and get into the movies. I'll probably marry a movie star and well have one of those big manshuns. Maybe I'll phone Mom and Dad once a month to let them know how Im doing and maybe I'll come back and visit Ottawa once a year and let everyone see how rich and famous I am. I'll come in a big car with white seats and I'll wear lots of furs and diamond rings. Thats what I'm going to do.

Bye for now.

thusiastic audience. Small children run up to the stage to wave and call to their brothers and sisters. Parents move out in the aisles to take photos, flashbulbs popping. The music teacher ignores the distractions and waves Tweedledee and Tweedledum on. We all laugh and cheer. Tweedledee and Tweedledum (no translation into French) are two small, thin boys dressed in identical blue pants, yellow shirts, and red suspenders. Their stomachs are bloated with pillows, and they wear blue beanies with small red flags. They sing and move in unison until one of them forgets his lines, stops in the middle of his song, and looks beseechingly at the music teacher, who hisses at him frantically. He recovers promptly and, with enviable aplomb, picks up the song where he left off. We applaud with vigor.

Yesterday I read Alice's manuscript, the one about the heroine who disguised herself, kidnapped her own child, and ended up marrying her former lover. It has a fast, breathless, roller-coaster plot. Along with the heroine I raced up mountains of ecstasy, fell deep into valleys of despair, whirled helplessly around curves of arousal. When I was done, I put it down and thought how much I've longed for extremes, for cliff-hangers, for dramatic moments to lift me high above my everyday life. It wasn't enough for me to adopt a husband, a mother-in-law, a country, a child. A lifelong dreamer, I was always yearning for something else, someone else.

To a loud flourish of trumpets, the King/le Roi and Queen/la Reine arrive. We know they're royalty because their heads bear crowns made of crinkly foil. The King is quite a bit shorter than the Queen and has a dashing mustache drawn over his cheeks. He waves his scepter around and makes a speech in a voice so low it doesn't reach to our row. Then Emma steps forward and starts to sing. Talent, training, and those hours practicing in front of our window have given her voice range and a rich, sweet timbre. The audience is quiet, attentive. Philip's hand and mine are clenched together. When she finishes, the final vibrato lingering on the air, the applause is tumultuous.

I clap wildly.
"Bravo!" Philip yells.
And we smile at each other.

DEAR DIARY,
Really nice weather. No zits—A MIRACLE!!!
I got my first letter from Terry today. She says she didnt tell me she was going because Mic and she decided really fast and they didn't have time. She says it was a stupid wrong thing to do and hopes I'll forgive her. She says they went to LA first and she really liked it a lot but that Mic couldn't make the right connections and like it was a real bummer so he got the name of a guy in Calgary whose big in the music business and thats where they are now. She says theyve kind of run out of money and shes got a job at a grociry store, a Safeway because they don't have Loblaws out west. She says its a good thing she had a skil to fall back on. Sometimes I wonder why she stays with Mic ecsept I gess she loves him.

Mark asked me out again but I said no way so he said I was a dumb kunt and a cock teeser. I said so what bugger off asshole. But I'm glad were going to different high schools next year because I don't need him around telling everyone that I suck. Anyway I met a guy from Glashan at the park whose real cute. His name is Peter and he liked me I could tell. Felicia's got a boy-friend from Glashan and he's real cute too but her mother wont let her date either so they talk on the phone all the time. Like her line is always busy.

I've got a science test tomorrow but I havent studied. I hate science anyway. Mom says that's shortsited whatever that means. She gave me a big lecture and then Dad started too, but I only listened to about $1/2$ of it. The rest of the time I sang to myself to droun them out. So I'll probably flunk. Who cares? I'm not going to be a scientest anyways. I'm going to be like Madonna and make millions of dollars and